WINTER PALACE

Dennis Jones

PINNACLE BOOKS
WINDSOR PUBLISHING CORP.

PINNACLE BOOKS

are published by

Windsor Publishing Corp.
475 Park Avenue South
New York, NY 10016

First Pinnacle Books printing: November 1989

Printed in the United States of America

"A HEART-STOPPING INTERNATIONAL THRILLER"
—Los Angeles Times Book Review

From the bestselling author of BARBAROSSA RED and RUBICON ONE comes a gripping and terrifying tale of suspense and intrigue—a breathtaking story of Soviet duplicity and nuclear terror . . . and of the holocaust that looms in the not-too-distant future!

WINTER PALACE
Dennis Jones

"DEFINITELY EARNS THE LABEL 'CAN'T PUT IT DOWN.' . . . THERE'S ACTION AND SUSPENSE ON EVERY PAGE. JONES HAS SCORED A 'CAN'T MISS' HIT WITH THIS PROVOCATIVE THRILLER."
—Milwaukee Journal

"SUSPENSEFUL, WELL-WRITTEN, AND ABSOLUTELY BELIEVABLE."
—James Patterson, Edgar Award-winning author of *The Thomas Berryman Number*

"HORRIFYING . . . A MULTI-LEVEL GEO-POLITICAL CHESS GAME THAT KEEPS THE READER ON THE EDGE FROM BEGINNING TO END."
—Cincinnati Post

"NONSTOP ACTION, RELENTLESS TENSION, AND (A) DETAILED LOOK AT THE INNER WORKINGS OF THE KREMLIN."
—Booklist

BLOCKBUSTER FICTION FROM PINNACLE BOOKS!

THE FINAL VOYAGE OF THE S.S.N. SKATE (17-157, $3.95)
by Stephen Cassell
The "leper" of the U.S. Pacific Fleet, SSN 578 nuclear attack sub SKATE, has one final mission to perform—an impossible act of piracy that will pit the underwater deathtrap and its inexperienced crew against the combined might of the Soviet Navy's finest!

QUEENS GATE RECKONING (17-164, $3.95)
by Lewis Purdue
Only a wounded CIA operative and a defecting Soviet ballerina stand in the way of a vast consortium of treason that speeds toward the hour of mankind's ultimate reckoning! From the bestselling author of THE LINZ TESTAMENT.

FAREWELL TO RUSSIA (17-165, $4.50)
by Richard Hugo
A KGB agent must race against time to infiltrate the confines of U.S. nuclear technology after a terrifying accident threatens to unleash unmitigated devastation!

THE NICODEMUS CODE (17-133, $3.95)
by Graham N. Smith and Donna Smith
A two-thousand-year-old parchment has been unearthed, unleashing a terrifying conspiracy unlike any the world has previously known, one that threatens the life of the Pope himself, and the ultimate destruction of Christianity!

Available wherever paperbacks are sold, or order direct from the Publisher. Send cover price plus 50¢ per copy for mailing and handling to Pinnacle Books, Dept.17-278, 475 Park Avenue South, New York, N.Y. 10016. Residents of New York, New Jersey and Pennsylvania must include sales tax. DO NOT SEND CASH.

For Sandi

PROLOGUE

Russo-Finnish Border
June 22, 1953

YATSENKO LAY motionless on the matted carpet of decaying spruce needles, staring out into the clearing. Even here, two hundred kilometers north of Leningrad, the sun was strong enough to raise a heat-dazzle from the tangled weeds and grasses of the clearing's floor. On its far side, the spruce forest beckoned, cool and dim. Perhaps two thousand meters further on, beyond the rampart of the evergreens, lay the cleared security zone and the Finnish border.

Or the border should be there. But the clearing wasn't shown on Yatsenko's map, and if he were in the right location, it ought to be. The map was a top secret one, prepared by Yatsenko's own department to show the safe corridors by which agents could slip into Finland without interference from the Soviet frontier patrols.

He folded the map and slipped it back into his leather jacket, cursing under his breath. A mosquito whined at his ear and he waved it away, not daring

7

to risk the noise of a slap. The insects had been devouring him all last night and even into the hottest part of the day; his face and ankles and the backs of his hands were puffy and swollen from their bites. When he sweated, as he did now, the itching drove him nearly mad. The things bred in the boggy places up here; in spring and early summer they swarmed through the spruce forest in clouds.

Yatsenko sat up and pulled his jacket straight. He was a swarthy man, with a Mongol slant to his eyes, protuberant ears, heavy in the gut, balding. But he could still move swiftly; there was muscle under the fat.

He made sure that the heavy black Nagan revolver was firmly tucked into the holster under his jacket, and that the safety catch was on. The gun would blow his upper leg to shreds if it fired accidentally. Then he felt in his inner pocket for the microfilm capsule. He might as well shoot himself with the Nagan and have it over with if he didn't bring that across. The Americans would likely hand him back, and he'd probably go feet first, slowly and alive, into a crematory furnace, like that poor bastard Popov. Screaming his head off all the way, even though he'd been a tough bugger up until then. Even Yatsenko, who was used to screams and had orchestrated a long symphony of them during his career in the NKVD and the MVD, had been shaken by that particular execution. He'd never thought he'd be trying to pull the same trick Popov had, defecting. But if he didn't, he'd end up with a bullet in the back of the neck, at best. Khrushchev or Malenkov or one of the other new rulers in the Kremlin would see to that.

Who would have thought Yatsenko's boss, the indestructible Lavrenti Beria, would be trapped so

8

easily? Beria, chief of the secret police, internal security, the Gulags, the whole MVD. After Stalin died back in March, everybody thought Beria was going to be the new head of the Politburo and ruler of the USSR. It must have been overconfidence on his part, going off to the Praesidium meeting like that, without any bodyguard to speak of. Hell, Yatsenko'd been talking to him not an hour before he left for the meeting and warned him. But Beria hadn't paid any attention. Yatsenko had always got along better with Beria than had the other heads of departments. He would get drunk with Beria and find girls for him, the kind the chief liked, the young green ones. Not so young or green after the encounter, though. A lot of them had jumped off Moscow bridges, and Yatsenko had hushed up that sort of thing more than a few times. That was all over now. Beria'd gone to the Kremlin, overconfident, and somebody had put a bullet through his head.

Yatsenko's friendship with the MVD chief, if that's what it had been, would be his death if Khrushchev and the rest of the new Kremlin gang caught up with him. He grimaced and got to his knees, standing up slowly. It was a good thing he'd taken out some insurance, although if Beria had found him at it, he'd have been dead before Beria. It had been a dreadful risk to take, but Yatsenko had seen the writing on the wall since last year, when Stalin kicked Beria upstairs into a Deputy Minister's post and put Beria's old enemy Kruglov into the vacated position. Stalin did that kind of thing to people he was sick of, promoted a man and then pulled the rug out after he was isolated from his supporters. And when Beria went, Yatsenko knew he would too. Kruglov had always hated both of them.

So he'd made contact with the Americans. He'd

9

been at least as wary of their ineptitude as he had been of the diligence of his own people. This new CIA of theirs didn't seem to know a lot about operational security. Nevertheless, he'd made his plans to get out, bringing his own redemption on the microfilm, he hoped. He'd been planning his break for August, but Beria, the half-wit, had gone and got himself shot, and Yatsenko had had to run early. He'd been running for four days.

He bent over and swept the brown spruce needles off his trousers. That American contact, he thought, straightening. He'd fucking well better be over there. I don't want to go wading in a Finnish swamp for a week, me and the mosquitoes. I wonder if Kruglov's figured out yet where I've gone?

He set out into the clearing. He was halfway across when he heard the plane.

Beads of sweat gathered under Alexander Markelov's helmet liner, coalesced into trickles, and then percolated through his eyebrows into the corners of his eyes. The drops stung. Ahead of him, Fedorchuk trudged along in the ancient infantryman's slog, dark green patches under his arms where the perspiration had soaked through his uniform. Markelov's own tunic felt saturated and, in spite of the heat, clammy.

The two men were following one of the patrol paths that threaded the restricted zone two kilometers east of the Finnish border. The area had been partly logged over before the war, and there were occasional clearings where the spruce forest hadn't grown back. The border zone itself was completely denuded of trees and undergrowth and heavily patrolled by security troops of the most guaranteed loy-

10

alty. Markelov and Fedorchuk didn't belong to that elite group; they were now almost as close to the frontier as they were ever allowed to go. Not that Markelov would have dared to make a break for the other side, anyway; Fedorchuk would shoot him immediately, as he would Fedorchuk if their positions were reversed. The two-man patrols were especially selected so that the members disliked each other. Markelov knew Fedorchuk didn't like him because he was a Jew. There were now only two other Jews in the security battalion; the rest had been weeded out over the last few months. Markelov thought he'd probably be reassigned to a construction brigade before the summer was out. He didn't relish the prospect but he only had a year of military service left. Then he could go back to Moscow and start in at the university, assuming his father's cronies could exert enough influence to get a Jew in. The authorities had been steadily reducing the quotas for the past couple of years. Markelov wanted to study Russian literature. Maybe some day he'd be able to teach it.

He summoned his wandering thoughts back to the path and the business at hand. He'd better be alert; they'd been briefed to watch out for a fugitive who was heading for the border. If found inside the two-kilometer zone, the man was to be warned once and then shot if it looked as though he were about to get away. In addition, the patrols had been ordered not to search the man (or his body); anyone found to have done so would be severely punished. There were even planes looking for the poor devil. Markelov had heard them three times since noon, and one pilot had come down low to inspect him and Fedorchuk, waggling his wings and climbing away

11

after they had waved and he had identified their uniforms.

Fedorchuk stopped suddenly in the center of the path. Markelov almost ran into him.

"Listen!"

Markelov listened. From above the spruce canopy, ahead of them, he could hear the sound of an aircraft engine. Its buzz rose and fell angrily, like that of a wasp imprisoned in a jar.

"There's somebody up ahead," Fedorchuk said. "Come on, *Zhid.*"

As always, the word made Markelov's stomach turn over with a mixture of fear and anger. He'd never be a Russian, he'd always be a *Zhid,* a Jew. All the other nationalities in the Soviet Union were described in their internal passports as Lithuanians, Uzbeks, or whatever. But not Jews. If you were Jewish, it didn't matter where you had been born or brought up. Your passport said you were a *Zhid.*

Fedorchuk broke into a run, unslinging his rifle, snapping a round into the chamber. He wanted to be the one to catch the fugitive, there'd likely be some kind of a reward or other, maybe even a couple of days' leave. He'd make sure Markelov didn't share any of the credit. Not that they'd give a Jew any, no matter what happened out here.

The gloom under the spruce canopy was lightening, the trees thinning out as the men approached an open space in the forest. They broke out into the clearing, which ran in a gentle slope down to a level area dotted with pools of standing water, lush with bright green marsh grasses and white flowers like small stars. There would be sucking mud under the vegetation and at the bottom of the still, dark pools. On the far side of the bog the spruce forest resumed

12

again, a solid rampart of dark trunks and feathery branches.

Markelov couldn't see the plane; it was too low, but it was there, off to the right, buzzing furiously. Suddenly, a plume of orange vapor boiled into view above the treeline. The pilot had dropped a smoke marker.

"He's over there," Fedorchuk said excitedly, gesturing with the muzzle of his gun. "Don't screw up, we'll be in the shit if he gets away."

Go fuck yourself, Markelov thought. You're no better at this than I am.

They started running toward the treeline, choosing their direction to skirt the eastern edge of the bog. Markelov's boots thudded in the long warm grass. His canteen, which was still full, bounced heavily at his side, throwing him off balance. Fedorchuk, who had longer legs, pulled steadily ahead.

Idiot, Markelov thought. Suppose he's sitting behind a treetrunk, waiting for us? You're a perfect target.

With a deafening roar of the search plane hurtled overhead, just over the crowns of the spruces. Involuntarily, Markelov glanced up. The plane was climbing, the red stars on its wingtips standing out against the olive camouflage paint.

We've got him now, Markelov thought. The other patrols will be heading this way by now. He'll never make the border. Who is he? A spy?

Fedorchuk was well ahead now. Markelov slowed down. Despite his rigorous training, he was slightly out of breath.

It happened so quickly that, despite all the warning he'd had, Markelov was startled. A figure pounded out of the trees, running flat out, a hundred meters to Fedorchuk's left. Fedorchuk changed

13

direction with a jerk, shouting unintelligibly. Markelov swung to cut the running man off. He was stocky, much older than Markelov. As he pelted through the weeds, he fumbled under his jacket for something.

"Halt!" screamed Fedorchuk. He stopped, raising his rifle to his shoulder. "I'll shoot!"

The fugitive spun in his tracks, dropping to one knee, his hand no longer under his coat, arm up and straightening, a huge black revolver in his fist.

Fedorchuk fired. At that distance, with a rifle, he could hardly miss. But he did.

The revolver boomed twice. Both bullets hit Fedorchuk, the first one in the middle of the chest, the second in the exact center of his upper lip. His face exploded in a splash of tooth fragments, blood, tissue, and scraps of bone. He fell over backwards, the rifle muzzle aiming momentarily and pointlessly at the sky as he collapsed.

The revolver muzzle swung toward Markelov. He couldn't risk a shot from the hip, not against a marksman as good as this. He threw himself flat into the weeds as the revolver fired again. The heavy bullet passed his right ear with a whiplash crack.

He had nearly winded himself. He kept his head down, bringing the rifle butt to his shoulder, up on his elbows now, risky but necessary, peering through the weeds, waiting for the next shot, the blow against his forehead, the big bullet slamming through his helmet—

The man was running again, maybe he thought his last round had hit. He ran right into the bog, arms flailing as the mud gulped at his boots, staggering, recovering quickly.

Markelov got the sights on target, between the shoulder blades, and squeezed the trigger. The rifle

14

bucked. The fugitive threw his arms out wide and collapsed forward into the muck. Markelov couldn't tell where the revolver had gone.

Shaking with reaction, he got to his feet. He'd never shot a man before. His training took over and he moved toward the edge of the bog.

The man wasn't dead. He was half-submerged in a slurry of mud and water, twisted to one side, pawing feebly inside his jacket. Blood pumped out of the wound in his back, drenching the white marsh flowers. Flies and mosquitoes whined.

Markelov stopped at the edge of the bog, three meters from the struggling figure. He couldn't see the revolver but kept his rifle aimed at the man anyway. He didn't know what to do next. Fish the man out, try to patch him up with a field dressing? Wait until an officer came? The plane was gone, but it'd be back soon, with help.

The fugitive was in shock, muttering unintelligibly, seemingly unaware of Markelov. His right hand was still inside the mud-caked jacket, but sliding out, sudden and astonishingly quick, something bright—

Markelov fired. The man jerked under the impact of the bullet in his side. Blood jetted out of his mouth. His left arm continued its throwing arc for an instant, and then folded bonelessly into the mud. The bright object tumbled clear of the dead fingers, bobbing in a small pool of dark water almost at Markelov's feet. The fugitive had tried to throw it away, Markelov thought.

Markelov's knees were trembling; he felt light-headed and sick, detached from his body. Almost involuntarily, he bent over and plucked the object out of the water. It was a small metal can with a screw top. His hands seemed to take on a will of their own. He cradled the rifle in the crook of his

15

arm and began twisting at the cap. It had been sealed with wax and turned stiffly at first, then spun loose. He removed it and peered inside. Something dark. He shook the contents into his palm. A film. A camera film. Markelov unrolled part of it. It was already developed. He could make out pages of infinitesimal, unreadable text.

Off in the distance the plane buzzed, returning.

Markelov stared at the film between his fingers, appalled at what he had just done. Nothing the fugitive carried was to be touched, those had been the orders. They'd know he'd open the can, the broken wax seal would tell them, even if he recapped it and replaced it in the dead man's pocket. The penalties for disobeying orders out on the frontier were savage. He'd get twenty years in the punishment battalions, if they didn't shoot him.

He had to get rid of the thing.

Curiosity awoke, though. What was recorded on those tiny pages that was so important? It might be useful to find out, someday, somehow. He didn't know why it might be useful, but this was his instinct.

He decided. He ran to the edge of the spruce forest, scrabbled away under a tree root, excavating a small cavity. The plane was nearer. Into the hole with the container, dirt back over it, a dusting of spruce needles. When he stood up there was no sign that anything was buried there. No one knew, no one would find it.

Except Markelov, if he dared.

Dusk was falling, late as it did in these latitudes at this time of year. Desmond Lacey waited by the abandoned railway spur line, swatting at the mos-

16

quitoes. He'd just about given up hope; he'd heard the planes over there on the Russian side of the border during the afternoon, and then about 3:00 P.M. the engine noises had stopped, as though the border patrols had found whomever or whatever they were looking for.

And Yatsenko should have been across by now, if he were going to make it at all. Lacey had decided some time ago that he probably wasn't going to. What a waste. All the preparations, the risks in Moscow and here in Finland.

And for what? Lacey wondered. Something called Winter Palace. Something big, the Russian had said. A propaganda victory to end all propaganda victories, one to show the Communists up for what they really were. But that was all he'd tell, until he got out. Now he wasn't going to get out.

Winter Palace, Lacey thought, slapping at another mosquito. I wonder what it is? Was? Might have been? I don't suppose we'll ever know, now.

Or, he corrected himself, perhaps we won't know until it's too late.

17

Maryland, USA
October 17, 1990

THE MASERATI'S engine howled as Cole downshifted into second gear. Ten meters ahead of him, Price was setting up his blue Lamborghini for the hairpin turn at the end of the backstretch, a puff of smoke from the tailpipes as he also geared down, a little late, the Lamborghini's stern fishtailing slightly; that was Price slamming the power back on. The Maserati's red hood shook as Cole gave the car as much throttle as the pavement conditions would allow, the rear beginning to drift a little, the tachometer needle steadying, engine revolutions right in the center of the maximum power range, closing in on the Lamborghini now, the Maserati *was* faster in the turns, dammit, no matter what Price thought, tricky though in its balance because of the engine's position in the center of the car behind the driver. And dangerous, too, it'd crush you through the instrument panel if you ever hit anything. But if you knew how to handle its four hundred eighty horsepower—

Cole risked a fraction of a second's glance in the side mirror. Bell's Porsche was on top of the hairpin now, followed some way back by Pulham in the yellow Lancia. Pulham was the slowest driver in the club, but he kept trying.

Out on the backstretch now, up into third, engine wailing, slam into fourth, he'd be hitting a hundred seventy by the time he reached braking position for the left-hand sweep into the last lap, the Maserati always ran better in this cool dense autumn air. Last lap of the last race of their private season. The club only had ten members, all men who for one reason or another enjoyed risking their lives one Wednesday afternoon a week and didn't need to worry about the rental fees for the use of the Davis Glen Raceway, nor about hiring expert mechanics to keep their vehicles in racing condition. Professional drivers would look down their noses at the club, though. The cars were a heterogeneous collection of makes and models and some were faster or handled better than others; a few of the members even drove their machines to and from the Wednesday meets. It was all very unprofessional, and a great deal of fun, except perhaps for the wives and girlfriends. Nobody had been killed yet.

Cole was trying to get into Price's slipstream when he realized that the Lamborghini was in trouble. Its speed was plummeting and a cloud of blue-gray oil smoke boiled suddenly from the right exhaust pipe. Cole flicked the steering wheel and the Maserati shot past Price's machine. The track ahead was clear, a gray ribbon with the last turn just before the finish line. Beyond the turn lay rolling hills, vivid with the smoky reds and yellows and oranges of the autumn woodlands. The air was so clear that Cole felt that he could almost make out individual leaves.

He was on top of the last bend, downshifting into third, when the image came to him, unbidden as always. *Berdeyev*.

19

Berdeyev was hurrying out of the Sokolniki subway station into the late Moscow winter afternoon, his button nose already pink with the cold but the rest of his face dead white, fishbelly white, and he was moving too fast. There was no reason for it, he was in plenty of time for the emergency rendezvous. Cole knew without a second's thought that there was something wrong, even though Berdeyev was displaying the all-clear signal, a copy of *Pravda* under his left arm. Cole had taken the usual precautions but knew he was clean, had been ever since he'd left his apartment. He was displaying his own all-clear, his coat collar turned up at the back. He waited at the bus stop to follow Berdeyev to the rendezvous point.

But Berdeyev was walking toward him and still no sign of shifting the copy of *Pravda* to indicate danger. Maybe his watch was wrong. Maybe he thought he was late, not enough time to get into Sokolniki Park and the rendezvous. Why had Berdeyev called the emergency meeting anyway? Did he want to get out, defect? They'd probably take him; he'd been furnishing information from the Science Ministry for nearly a year. Snowflake had suggested him to Cole eighteen months before as a likely prospect for recruitment. Snowflake was good at spotting weaknesses and dissatisfaction among people he knew. He'd furnished several leads, a number of them fruitful, like Berdeyev.

Berdeyev was thirty meters away now, still hurrying, eyes not meeting Cole's. And then Cole spotted them leaving the subway entrance, big men in the usual dark overcoats, not even subtle. The vise clamped around Cole's stomach. *Jesus, they've turned him around, doubled him.* He's going to walk right over to me, he'll be carrying something they gave him to

20

set me up with and it'll put me away for months, years unless there's an exchange—

The Russian had seen Cole. The strain on Berdeyev's face cleared, as though he'd made a decision. He looked over his shoulder at the pair of KGB men, and ran. Ran right out into the traffic on the Rusakovskaya, all four lanes of it.

Christ.

The Maserati was already into the corner, far, far too fast, still in third, the wrong gear; he'd lost his concentration at a hundred twenty miles an hour and it was going to kill him. The shriek of the Maserati's tires sounding like those of the truck that hit Berdeyev, the car skidding sideways, straw bales coming up, golden stalks flying as the bale disintegrated, but the car bouncing back on the track from the impact. Still too fast but a little more under control now, risk dropping a gear to straighten her, didn't work well. Try the wheel, try to go through the barrier backward because of that damned engine behind the seat. Blur of faraway gold and crimson hills somehow intermingled with the KGB men running after Berdeyev. He'd given Cole the only exit he could, kill or disable himself so he couldn't make the contact.

The Maserati's rear bumper hit the barrier of straw bales, the car jolting and slamming on the rough ground beyond the track shoulder. Nothing to do now but ride it out like Berdeyev had had to, because the truck hadn't killed him. He was just banged up and they grabbed him and threw him into a black Chaika, probably the one they'd been going to put Cole in. The Maserati was slowing down. If she didn't turn sideways and flip on the ridged ground, he might make it—

The world suddenly became stationary. Cole could

21

hear engines approaching, Price and the others, but he couldn't see them because of a swath of loose straw draped over the windshield. No sign of fire. Get out anyway; the emergency truck and ambulance'd be along in a minute or two, don't want to worry anybody unnecessarily. Megan. Would she have seen it from the pit area?

The seat harness was digging into his shoulders. Christ, Cole thought, I'm going to be sore tomorrow.

Not as sore as Berdeyev was.

He'd never seen the Russian again, nor any of the other three people he'd recruited through Snowflake. Two days after the aborted meeting, Gorbachev had fallen from power and the KGB started their roundups. A week after that, Cole had received a package in the embassy mail. He opened it. Inside was a garnet signet ring, one he'd seen on Berdeyev's middle finger. It had been crushed flat and there were rusty stains around the stone's setting. There was nothing else, but the message was clear: *We know who you are. Go home.*

Cole sat, looking stupidly at the instrument panel. After a moment he switched off the ignition. He thought: They crushed that ring while it was still on him. They'd have had to cut his finger off to remove it, after that. I hope he didn't take a long time dying. But he did, don't fool yourself. And my other two, Abramov and Grishin. Picked up the same day, never heard of again. What tipped the KGB? Something I did? Something I didn't do?

He unbuckled the harness. Some of the straw blew off the windshield. The ambulance was only a hundred feet away, coming up the track, lights flashing. I've got to do something about this, Cole thought.

22

It's haunting me. Today it damned near killed me. What will it do next time?

They tried to make him lie down in the ambulance on the way to the pits. He told them to go to hell and sat up on one of the stretchers. When they arrived at the service area he could see Megan waiting by her van; she'd driven over that morning from Washington to watch the race. It was becoming windier, and her heavy auburn hair tossed in the gusts. She was tall and slim, with an oval face and hazel eyes. She had on an old duffel coat and jeans; Cole's sheepskin jacket was draped over her arm.

He got stiffly out of the rear doors of the ambulance; reaction was setting in and he felt a little shaky. Megan was beside the vehicle now, her face very still and pale.

"Sam. Are you all right?" Her Welsh accent was pronounced, as it always was when she was upset or angry.

"I'm okay." He gave her a brief hug to prove it. "I messed up at the end of the backstretch."

"What happened?"

Price and the others were coming up. "Don't know." He didn't want to talk about it. "Pushing too hard, I suppose."

Price was hovering behind Megan; he was a tall reedy man with sparse blond hair and a dry sense of humor Cole found appealing. There was no sign of amusement in his eyes at the moment, though.

"Jesus Christ, Sam. I couldn't believe it when you didn't slow down. I saw you go into the bales." A trace of the wit crept back. "All I could see was straw. It looked like you'd traded the beast in for a combine harvester."

"I may have to trade the beast in anyway," Cole said. His chest hurt. "God knows what I did to it."

23

"They'll be bringing it in in a few minutes," Price said. "I checked."

"You need a drink?" asked Pulham. "We've got that champagne we bought for the winner's party."

"Who won, anyway?" Cole asked. "I wasn't in a position to see." He wanted to sit down.

"We figure you did," said Price. "You had it all wrapped up. Anyway, you beat the grim reaper. That's good for the winning circle in my book."

"I think I'll pass on the champagne," Cole said. He shivered.

Megan took charge. She handed him the sheepskin. "Put your coat on, Sam. Then you're going to get into the van and warm up for a while. Till they bring the car in, anyway."

"Let the poor bastard have a drink, at least, Meg," said Bell from behind Pulham. Harvey Bell was the roughest of the men in the club; he'd made a fortune in heavy construction in the Middle East. Megan couldn't bear him, and Cole's reaction to him was just short of active dislike.

"There's whiskey in the van," she said brusquely. "Come on, Sam."

He got in, Megan following, and he closed the sliding door behind her. Just as the door thudded shut he heard Bell's voice:

"—quick roll in the hay—"

Harvey, you bastard, Cole thought. You ignorant shit. All money and no manners.

"What's the matter?" asked Megan. She hadn't heard.

"Nothing," Cole said. "Nothing a Jack Daniels wouldn't cure."

"Right you are." She opened the bar, which was set into a cabinet behind the driver's seat. The van's interior was like a small lounge, with wood paneling

24

on the walls, and seats, covered in blue crushed velvet, for five. Cole sat down in one of the seats and stretched his legs out in front of him. The toes of his shoes almost touched the opposite wall; he was a tall thin man, but his slenderness was that of wiry strength, not fragility. His face was lean, with a noticeably triangular chin. He had brown hair with reddish lights in it, going somewhat gray at the temples, a gray close to the color of his eyes. He was thirty-eight, two years older than Megan.

"Cheers, Sam." She handed him the glass of whiskey and curled up in the seat to his right, tucking her legs under her. The late October sun was keeping the interior of the van warm despite the wind, and she unfastened the duffel coat while he looked at her. He was abruptly and physically aware of her femininity.

Death, he thought. You get that close and survive and the physical reaction translates into sex. The ancient animal at the base of the brain. He saw that she had noticed his look, and he knew that she knew what had caused it; she was good at sensing feelings.

Reaching over and putting her hand on his forearm, she said, "Are you sure you're all right? You didn't hit your head, I hope? If you did, you shouldn't have the whiskey."

"I didn't knock it against anything," he told her. "There's nothing in it to damage, anyway."

"Rubbish," she said flatly. "Sam, what happened out there? You've never gone off the track like that before. Was it the car?"

He knew she didn't like the racing, no matter how relatively sedate and slow it was by professional standards. "It wasn't the car," he said. "I lost concentration for a moment." He paused. "It's happened

25

a few times in the last year. Not in those circumstances, though."

"You mean those times when you seem to go off somewhere else for a few seconds or so?"

"That's right."

"I know a little about it," she said.

He looked at her, the tumbler of spirit halfway to his lips. "Oh?" he said.

"You dream, Sam. You talk about Moscow. Someone named Berdev, or something like that. And a ring. I've had to wake you up three times in the last two months. In the morning, you don't remember it."

"Oh, shit," he said, closing his eyes. "I didn't know, Meg. Really?"

"Really. You don't cry out, though. You just thrash around in the bed and mutter. Look, I know you were in the CIA. You still teach for them on contract. I also know you were in the Middle East and Moscow. But that's all I know, and I know you're not allowed to tell me anything else. But something happened in Russia, didn't it? Something that's gnawing at you." She turned to look out the van window; sunlight glinted at the corners of her eyes and he realized that she was blinking back tears. "I was *afraid* today would come. Sam, if you keep racing, if you don't get rid of whatever's troubling you, you're going to die out there. Or out on the Atlantic, in *Whiskeyjack*. Alone, either way. I know it."

The whiskey was relaxing him. "Look," he said. "I know I've been having a few bad moments. But it won't last. I was perfectly okay when I got back from Russia. I will be again. Soon, likely. Anyway, we shouldn't exaggerate it, we're both shaken up

26

from the accident, that's making it seem worse than it is."

She got up abruptly and opened the sliding door. Cole looked at her, startled. She climbed down onto the ground without a word and then turned to look in at him. "Sam," she said, and the Welsh lilt was back, stronger than ever, "for somebody so smart, how can you be so *bloody* stupid? Come and let's look at your bloody car."

She stalked off into the service area where the mechanics were poking around the racing cars. After a moment he put his drink down and followed her.

She had, at least outwardly, lost most of her annoyance by the time they had turned into the lane that wound down to the river. Megan was driving the van; the Maserati's bodywork had been severely dented in the accident and Cole had sent it into Washington with one of the mechanics for repairs. They had decided not to stay for the post-race party.

Cole's house was at the end of the lane, nestled among maples and beeches in the curve of an oxbow in the river. A mile downstream lay Chesapeake Bay, into which the river flowed. The house was a good century old, a rambling white frame building with long verandas on the river and landward sides, and a cedar-shingled roof. A curved gravel drive swept past the veranda on the land side, ending at a detached three-car garage to the left of the house. Two cars were drawn up in front of the garage. One belonged to Mrs. March, Cole's housekeeper. He didn't recognize the other, a blue Ford.

"Were you expecting visitors?" Megan asked as she braked the van to a halt by the flagged walk that led to the veranda.

27

"No," Cole said. "I wasn't. I told Ruth we wouldn't be back until after nine."

They got out of the van. It was cooler down here by the bay, the sunlight almost level. On the other side of the little river a line of willows cast long shadows across the stubble of the harvested cornfields.

"Three more days' holiday," she said. "Then I have to go back to work. I love my job, but this, sometimes . . ."

Cole nodded, almost absentmindedly. It was a beautiful place. It had been his father and mother's; they had kept it as a summer home to which they could retreat with their only child for a few weeks in June, July and August. They had spent Thanksgivings there, and several Christmases. Cole had inherited it, with the rest of the estate, in the last year of his doctorate at Harvard. His parents had been killed in an airplane disaster while returning from a holiday in France. Cole's father had had old New England money, and had been an economic adviser to three Presidents; his mother had been the daughter of a wealthy New York art dealer. Their estate was a large one, even after all the bequests had been settled and the lawyers paid. Cole might have relaxed and devoted himself to the study of languages and to the art and history of the Middle East, and never done what most people would call a day's work in his life. But there was a restlessness in him, a need to make a difference to the world in some concrete and obvious way. Moreover, his father had left him with a strong sense of social responsibility and the knowledge of a tradition of service to the United States that dated from the First World War. Given his insatiable curiosity, his deftness with languages, and his passionate interest in the Middle East, it was hardly surprising that when he was approached by

28

the Central Intelligence Agency, he accepted. He spent several years working out of Ankara, the Turkish capital, and then was posted to Russia.

He had become disillusioned by that time, oppressed by a growing sense of futility that, in the long run, whatever he did would count for nothing against the impossibly convoluted loyalties and ancient feuds of the Middle East. There a massacre of a thousand years ago could rouse passions as violent as if the slaughter had happened yesterday, as if it were happening even now. There, the past infused itself into the present, as vivid as a hallucination. Moscow had almost been a relief. But not for long.

When he was recalled, after the presumed death of Berdeyev and the others, he spent seven months working in the analysis section of the Middle East Desk at CIA headquarters at Langley, Virginia. One day he resigned, without thinking about it; it just happened. That had been three years ago, around the time he first met Megan.

As they climbed the veranda steps, Cole heard barking inside; Megan's dog, Griffin. The inside door opened suddenly and Ruth March stood behind the screen. She wore a blue apron and her hands were floury; she was dusting them with a dishtowel. "Mr. Cole? Griff and I heard the car drive up. I didn't expect you back so early."

"We should have called." He looked toward the garage. "Who's here?"

She opened the screen door and held it for Megan. Griffin bounced up and down around their knees. He looked like a small English sheepdog, shaggy gray and white, of indeterminate breed.

"A man," Mrs. March said. "He came about ten minutes ago. Griff wouldn't let him in. A big man. He said he'd wait. He's down by the dock, looking

29

at *Whiskeyjack*. I've been nervous as a cat ever since he got here. He said he knew you, and he was friendly enough, but I've had the door locked anyway, what with John not being here today—"

John March looked after the grounds of the house, painting, cleaning, things of that order. His wife managed him as well as she did Cole's establishment, but she never let her husband know it. Cole let the screen door close behind him and asked, "Did he give his name?"

"Rich-something. I didn't catch all of it. He said he'd wait outside, down by the boathouse. Griffin here wanted to bite his foot off."

They were in the wainscoted hall leading to the rear of the house and the kitchen. Griffin bounced ahead, tail flying, nails clicking on the waxed maple floor.

A big man. Rich-something. "I know who it is," Cole said. "It's okay."

"Who?" Megan asked over her shoulder.

"Somebody I used to work with."

"Oh, oh," she said, "trouble?" She didn't seem to be expecting an answer. Cole didn't provide one.

They entered the kitchen, a long airy room in the southeast corner of the house, with windows on two sides. Megan shrugged out of her duffel coat and hung it on the rack by the side door leading to the summer kitchen. "Are you going to fetch him?"

"I'll see what he wants, first," Cole said.

"If Mrs. March will put up with me in her kitchen, I'll start some coffee. It'll be ready shortly."

Cole nodded to her and went out into the summer kitchen with its old gas stove and pump-fed sink and the hoard of canning utensils Mrs. March used for making jams and relishes. The back door of the summer kitchen opened onto a flagged path that led

30

down to the dock and the boathouse, which now sheltered only an old cedar canoe slung from the rafters. *Whiskeyjack* was moored at the floating dock: a Northern Cross thirty-five-footer, cutter rigged, with a canoe stern and buff upperworks on a white hull.

Richland was standing on the dock, looking at the boat. He heard Cole's footsteps on the gravel and turned as Cole came up to him.

"Hello, Sam."

"Hello, Rich."

Cole studied Richland, looking for signs of wear. He hadn't seen the head of the Middle East Desk for more than two years. Richland's Christian name, which was a relic of his southern ancestry and which he loathed, was Decatur. But no one who knew him well, as Cole had back in Ankara when Richland was head of the CIA station there, ever dared call him anything but Rich. He gave the impression of being roughly the size of a transport truck, with blue eyes set wide apart (like headlights, Cole had always thought) in a broad red face which suggested, incorrectly, high blood pressure. Richland was one of the most imperturbable men Cole had ever met. During the seven months between his flight from Moscow and his resignation, Cole had been one of Richland's chief analysts.

"It's been a while," he said.

"Yeah." Richland turned and pondered *Whiskeyjack*. "Nice boat. All I know is that the sharp end's the front. You use her a lot?"

"Most weekends, spring through fall. I take her outside the bay a few times a year. Single handling."

"You mean alone?"

31

"It isn't dangerous. Not if you know what you're doing. I've been sailing since I was ten."

"Nice work if you can get it," Richland said.

It stung slightly. "I get by," Cole said. "How did you know I was going to be back here, just now?"

"I made a good guess. You had an accident. Your Maserati's going to need some bodywork."

Cole leaned over and checked the tension on one of *Whiskeyjack*'s mooring lines. Straightening up, he said, "What're you watching me for, Rich? I teach two afternoons a week for the Company. It keeps me in touch. But after this long away from the desk, I'm hardly a security risk."

"We were just worried about you. Like this afternoon. You might kill yourself by accident. Fast cars. Sailing on the Atlantic alone. It would be a hell of a waste."

"How long has this been going on? Watching me?"

"Not long."

"Why?" He already knew the answer.

"You want to come back in, Sam?"

Whiskeyjack's forestay needed tuning, there was a bit too much slack in it. He'd get out and do it in the morning, before breakfast.

"No. I've done all I want to."

"Because of Moscow?"

"Yes."

"We're not asking you to go back to Moscow."

"You don't understand," Cole said. "I'm not interested. I've got other things on my plate now."

"Can we talk inside?" Richland asked. "It's a little too open, out here."

"If you like."

The walked up the gravel path to the summer

32

kitchen. Cole let Richland in ahead of him. The main kitchen was empty; a coffee maker hissed gently on the counter.

"I'll get us some coffee," Cole said, "when it's ready."

"Not for me," Richland said. "Thanks. I've had too much today already. Where's that dog?"

"With Megan somewhere. We'll talk downstairs."

They went into the hallway and Cole opened an oak door to reveal a paneled stairwell leading down. At the bottom was a vestibule with a gray metal door set into the wall; next to the door was a pad of numbered buttons. Cole pressed an apparently random sequence. The door locks clicked.

"You've gotten paranoid, Sam? Or is this a fallout shelter?"

"Neither," Cole said. "Come on in."

They passed through the door. Cole heard Richland's intake of breath as the subdued lights turned themselves on.

The long wide room was a curious blend of library, office and museum. At its far end stood a rosewood desk, and to the side of the desk a lounge area with four deep leather chairs and a low round table inlaid with what looked like Byzantine mosaics. Bookshelves stood behind the desk, and more of them ran halfway along the left wall of the room. On the remainder of that wall, the one opposite, and in cases and on pedestals throughout the room, was a collection of sculpture, jewelry and metalwork that could have been the life's goal of a curator of the Metropolitan Museum of Art.

"Jesus Christ," Richland said.

Cole waited, while Richland absorbed it.

After perhaps fifteen seconds, Richland added, "I

33

knew you were a collector, but I never suspected anything like this. Where in God's name did it come from?'' He moved slowly to one of the cases, which was lit by a dim spotlight from above. The long swordblade under the glass shimmered.

"My father brought some of it over here," Cole said. "I added the rest. That's one of my father's items." He indicated the sword.

"What's it made of?" Richland asked, still looking into the case.

"It's bronze. Forged about three thousand years ago. You can see how the blade's outline repeats that of an axe. I think the hook behind the slashing end was for catching the enemy's spear shafts. It's a brilliant piece of engineering, even apart from the metallurgy."

Richland stood up from his inspection of the sword. "You've brought some of this in yourself, you said."

"Commissions from museums, sometimes. I've a few contacts in North Africa and the Levant and Turkey. It's sort of an import business."

"I know," said Richland. "We had a look into it. You got to know a lot of people while you were over there, didn't you?"

"That was my job."

"It gave you something to build on, anyway." Richland, in spite of himself, was bending over another of the cases. "What's this? It looks like a totem pole."

"It came from what's now Iraq," Cole said. "It's a cosmetic container, bronze, shaped like a woman. The part with the demon head on it is the upper end of the applicator stick. You can see the same thing on any cosmetic counter nowadays, in principle, anyway."

"I don't imagine the Iraqis would be too keen on losing something like this," Richland said.

"They don't know it ever existed," Cole said. "They still don't. This is kind of a gray area, ethically. Do you leave these things lying around to be pillaged or blown up in some pointless war or hidden away in the basement of a government building in Damascus or Baghdad, or wherever?"

"They're in kind of a vault here," Richland pointed out.

"Not for good. And it's safe. Some of it I give away, to the Kirschner Museum, for example. Megan's a collections curator there."

"Yeah," Richland said. "Megan Thomas, isn't it? What does she think of this import-export business of yours?"

He knows exactly where she works, Cole thought, and what her last name is. And what she does at the gallery. Of course they'd check. They've been watching me ever since I resigned. I know a lot of people over there, as Rich so pointedly pointed out. Langley would want to know what I talk to them about. I must have come up clean. Not surprising. I am clean, by their standards anyway.

"It varies," he said. "She'd like the pieces to belong to the countries whose history they represent. Often that's not possible, given the state of that part of the world. It's like holding bits of the past in trust, against the day when they can be given back."

He realized, as he spoke the words, that they sounded pompous, and an excuse for acquisitiveness. He loved having these things, and the histories that lay in them. But he meant what he had said.

"Can we sit down?" Richland asked. "I've been on my feet all day."

Cole nodded and led the way to the grouping of

35

chairs near the desk. The lamps in their stained-glass shades threw a warm radiance over the wood and supple leather. Cole was feeling uncomfortable. He had liked Richland, and was annoyed that the other was putting him in the position of having to refuse what was, after all, a favor. "Drink?" he asked.

"Please. Bourbon?"

"I've got some authentic white lightning."

"That'd be fine."

Cole made the drinks at the bar. When he had finished he asked, "Music okay?"

"Sure."

Cole pressed a button on the stereo system. A harpsichord chimed in the room, accompanied by the darker line of a viol. Richland closed his eyes, listening. Cole sat down across from the older man.

Richland opened his eyes. "What's that?"

"William Byrd. Elizabethan composer." He passed Richland the glass. "What's on your mind, Rich?"

"We want to know if you'd be interested in coming back in."

"To operations?"

"You're wasted teaching people who are still cutting their teeth."

"I like teaching."

"Yeah. You're a goddamned good teacher, too. And nobody I've ever seen can soak up languages like you do. How many do you speak now, anyway?"

"Same as before. Arabic, Turkish, Russian, French and German. Why?"

"No particular reason. But we need other things more than language experts, at the moment."

"What for?"

"Turkey, to start with. Your old stomping ground. You read the papers, there's a leftist government there now, and it's making noises like it wants out of NATO. If we lose Turkey, even if it goes neutral, we've lost the southern hinge of our defenses against the Russians. And that bunch of Stalinists in Moscow, Kulagin's outfit, they're promising the moon to Ankara. Aid, weapons, machinery, dams, generators, you name it. All Ankara has to do is pull out of the alliance with the West. And let me tell you, they're thinking about it."

Cole thought. Washington had placed new arms export restrictions on Ankara last year, after the Turks crossed the U.N. partition lines in Cyprus and taken the rest of the island from the Greeks. There had very nearly been war between Greece and Turkey over that, and when Washington came down on the side of Athens, the centrist government in Ankara had fallen and been replaced by a leftist-socialist coalition. The Turkish military, normally leaning away from the Left, had been angry enough at the American arms embargo to throw in its lot with the new government. The Turks were still allied with the United States through NATO, but the alliance was hanging by a thread. A neutral position, or even one friendly to the Kremlin, might be attractive in Ankara. India had had a relationship like that with the USSR for years.

"I don't see what I can do about it," Cole said unhelpfully.

"There'd be a good deal. You've got the knowledge, the background, the experience. We could use you, Sam."

"No," Cole said. "I've got my life in order. I want to keep it that way."

37

Richland looked at him speculatively. "We wouldn't ask you to go back to Moscow."

"That doesn't make any difference."

Richland drank half his glass of whiskey. "It's not just Turkey."

"What else?"

"Israel."

"That's supposed to be a surprise?"

Richland sighed and contemplated the dimly lit room, the serene and ancient busts and figurines and mosaics. "Okay, I'll give you a little more. Jerusalem's sure the present Syrian government's going to fall within months. It's almost certain to be replaced by a fundamentalist Islamic regime. That would be extremely dangerous for Israel."

"The Muslim Brotherhood," said Cole. "They've been working against Assad for years. So they're finally read to revolt."

"Mossad thinks so. But we need more information. You know people in Syria, art dealers, businessmen. Working out of Turkey, you'd be in an ideal position to dig around."

"When I wasn't trying to pull the rug out from under the leftist government in Ankara."

"Something like that."

"Will a Brotherhood government in Syria go for the Israelis' throats?"

"Quite probably. They'd have to get the country in order first. But sooner or later."

"This is all pretty thin to start the alarm bells ringing. Or to tempt me to come back."

"You know I can't tell you any more if you stay on the outside."

"Rich," Cole said, "the answer is still no. I'm sorry."

"Okay," said Richland. "I said I'd try. I've

tried.'' He finished the whiskey in a gulp and set the glass down. "Thanks for the drink."

"Drop in again anytime."

They stood up. At the doorway leading to the upstairs, Richland stopped, looking around at the display cases. "These things you've got here. They're fragments, scraps of civilizations, all that's left of a lot of human endeavor. It can happen so easily, Sam. If someone isn't on guard. Think about it for a couple of months, just think about it. You might change your mind."

"I'm afraid not, Rich."

Richland nodded and started up the stairs.

"You're awfully moody," she said. She was sitting at the dressing table in front of the mirror, brushing out her hair. A low fire burned in the grate of the bedroom fireplace, casting a golden light over the book-lined shelves along one wall. Cole lay on the bed in his dressing gown, a book propped on his stomach: *The Military Life of Frederick the Great*. He wasn't really reading it.

"Is it Richland?" she asked.

"Yes."

"What did he say to you?"

"They want me to come back in."

"Not back to *Russia?* It's Russia that's been troubling you so."

"No. Middle East."

"What does that mean? Are things even worse there than the papers say?"

"Rich says so."

She put the hairbrush down and turned to face him. "How much worse?"

"They don't know. They're just worried."

39

"Because there's something to be worried *about*."

"Apparently."

"You sound incredibly cool about it all."

"There's nothing I can do at the moment," he said.

She picked up the hairbrush and began to smooth its bristles with her palm, as though it were some small animal. He noticed once again how fine-boned her hands were. Megan had grown up in Wales, and studied Celtic art at the university in Aberystwyth. She was a brilliant art historian; the Kirschner had hired her soon after she received her degree, and she had been curator of their Celtic collection for the past eight years. Cole had met her when he was negotiating a sale to the museum, and the initial attraction had been edging toward a permanent bond ever since.

"Another war out there?" she asked.

"Possibly. It's always possible, that."

The fire was beginning to fade, the log's white ash veined with orange. "They're all mad, out there," she said. She put the hairbrush down. "Now I'm turning morose. I'm sorry. This is supposed to be a holiday, after all. Did you want to go on reading, Sam?"

"No." He rolled over onto his stomach, putting the book aside to let her curl up on the bed beside him. She smelled of soap and the flower-scented shampoo that she used. He went up on one elbow, to look down at her. Her knee brushed his, stayed. "Can't concentrate."

Her face on the pillow was framed by her heavy bronze hair. "I can't imagine why not."

He leaned over and kissed her mouth. After a minute she broke away and murmured, "You're causing me a problem, Sam Cole."

40

"What might that be?" His fingertips traced small arabesques over the silk of her nightgown, over her breasts.

"I seem to be becoming rather slippery."

"Really?" His hand drifted downwards, stroking delicately. Her breath caught for a moment. "See?"

"Yes. I see. Your passionate Celtic nature again."

"Don't tell me you don't approve of my passionate Celtic nature." There was a shiver in her voice. Her hand moved against him, searching. "You seem to have something of a problem yourself."

"That's *your* fault."

Her grasp was gentle, cool. She knew all his nerve endings. "If it's my fault, I should do something to correct it, shouldn't I?"

He started to answer but she did something to the tip of his penis that took his breath away. When he got it back he said, "That only seems just."

"You've got too many clothes on."

She undressed him, took off her nightgown, and pushed him onto his back, leaning over him, lips nibbling down over his chest, his stomach, the shaft of his penis, the tip, tongue flickering, small wet sounds.

"You'd better stop that," he said, "or I'm going to have an accident."

She came back up and kissed him. "Oh? Do you often have accidents like that?"

"Only when you do what you've been doing."

"Would you consider it an accident if it happened inside me?" Kneading him.

"No."

"Hmn. Stay. Don't move."

She straddled him, her breasts pressing against his chest, opening herself. Sliding into her, locked in

41

her, deep. Her spasms started almost at once, drawing him on, out of control finally, the soft primeval explosion emptying him into her, warm and liquid, impregnating, mated, complete.

National Photographic Interpretation Center Washington Navy Yard November 21

THE COMPUTER-ENHANCED images flickered across the big screen mounted on the wall of the dimly lit processing room: snow-covered landscapes viewed from above, with the cross-hatching of cities, towns, villages, threads of railway lines, roads.

"That one," said the man with the pipe. The technician at the processing console touched a key and the image froze in place.

"What's got you worried?" the woman asked. She was in her mid-fifties, without makeup, sloppy, black hair going to gray. She swiveled in the chair to look up at the man, who had remained standing and was tamping tobacco into the bowl of his pipe with a nicotine-stained thumb. He and the woman were senior analysts at the NPIC, which was responsible for extracting the last morsel of information sent down from the surveillance satellites orbiting the earth.

"I'm not *worried,* exactly," he said. He finished

compressing the tobacco and with a slow deliberate movement inserted the pipestem into his mouth. "Not *worried,*" he repeated around it. "It's just odd. Plain construction, probably not intended to last, and with no *obvious* purpose. My team's been watching this stuff going up since late last spring. I wanted a second opinion from someone who hadn't seen the material before."

"Get your pipe lit, then," she said, "and let's start looking. I've got a budget meeting in half an hour."

The man nodded and applied the flame of a plastic lighter to the tobacco. Smoke spurted, heavily aromatic. The woman winced.

"Okay," he said. "Have a look in the lower right quadrant. What is it?"

She studied the image. "A military base. Look at the grid. It's normal, at least from this height."

"Zoom, please," the man said to the technician. The image expanded, as though it were seen through a window and the room were falling towards it.

"Stop." The image froze.

"Now look."

"Barracks," she said. "An administration area." The man was watching her face. It took on an aura of puzzlement. "Wait a minute. Where's the vehicle park?"

"It's there," said the man. "Eastern side, near the admin complex. What's wrong with it?"

The woman pursed her lips. "From the number of barracks, that place should hold an infantry division. But the vehicle park's not nearly big enough."

"That's right."

"Maybe they're not finished building it?"

"It was finished three weeks back. They cleaned

44

it up, and then left it. It's been like that ever since. It's not the only one, either."

"No information from the ground?"

"None's been given to us."

"The admin block's in the wrong place, too," she said. "Can you get closer?"

"Zoom," said the man. The image expanded again.

"It's off to the side," she said. "And there's wire around it, separating it from the main part of the camp."

"That's right," said the man. His pipe had started to go out and he relit it. "Anything else?"

"Let me see the perimeters."

The technician zoomed out a little.

"There's a railway siding up there," she said. "Where does it come from?"

"The main line down from the northeast."

"Any traffic?"

"Not yet. It's new. It went in the same time they started to build the complex."

She frowned. "There's a compound of some kind at the end of the spur line. Is that wire around it?"

"Yes."

"Why would they put a spur line into an army base? They don't normally do that. How many other places like this are there?"

"Forty-two. They're spread in an arc all the way down through European Russia. The ones in the south were finished first."

"But not used?"

"Not yet."

She pondered. The man with the pipe puffed. The technician waited.

"I've seen something like this before," she said. "Where is this installation?"

"Near Dolinskaya, down in the Ukraine."

"But the ones I studied weren't in the south," she said. "They were in the Arctic."

"Tell me what it is, though."

"There's no doubt about it," she said. "It's a prison camp."

Moscow, USSR
December 15

THE SMALL COURTROOM was packed, but in it there was not one friend of the accused, Valeri Markelov. Valeri was very tired; in the month since his arrest he had not had one hour of unbroken sleep. They had been very careful not to let him know, either, whether it was actually day or night outside the walls of Lefortovo Prison. It was part of the disorientation technique, to wear you down, to make you say and even believe what they wanted you to. But despite his exhaustion, Valeri felt a muted sense of achievement; he hadn't broken. Yet. They could always take him back, put him through the process again—they called it the "conveyor"—until there was nothing of him left.

He didn't think they would, though; otherwise they wouldn't have brought him to trial. He sat in the prisoner's box, paying little attention to the special prosecutor's summing up of the case; they wouldn't let him go, and it was only a matter of how many years they'd give him. And where. The one possibility that still had the power to frighten him was that of being put in one of the psychiatric hospitals. He might go in as Valeri Markelov, but he wouldn't come out that way. He'd known another writer who'd had the full course of drug treatment; when they released him the man hadn't even been able to read any more. Valeri was twenty-eight, and there'd be plenty of time for them to do whatever they wanted.

". . . vicious and obscene slander of the Soviet state that he pretended was poetry, coupled with refusal to reconsider what he had already done, despite repeated requests to do so . . . given every chance but still preferring to vomit his poison abroad . . ."

The special prosecutor's voice was rising. Valeri ignored it and looked at the green courtroom walls, the bare floors and the benches filled with KGB-hired hooligans who had applauded every point made by the special prosecutor and hissed at the feeble efforts of Valeri's defense counsel. Portraits of General Secretary Kulagin, flanked by those of Lenin and Stalin, hung on the wall behind the judge's dais. Stalin the old butcher, Valeri thought. How proud they are of him again, how glad they are to have him to love once more, how they've yearned to kiss the whip again. My crimes really are only two: I wrote the truth, and I'm a Jew. Stalin hadn't finished with the Jews when he died. I'll be one of the first. My parents, especially my father, will say it's my own fault. He'll keep saying it until they come for him in the night. He thinks being a bigwig at the university will save him, renowned scholar, the fool. A troublemaker for a son, that's all that worries him. Afraid he'll lose his precious position because of me.

Valeri had in fact been causing the authorities— and his father—no end of trouble for the last three years. He had insisted on circulating his poetry, which was steeped in an almost mystical Judaism, in the underground *samizdat* press, as well as importunately sending it off to the editors of various Soviet literary magazines. A collection had been smuggled out of the country and published in translation in Israel and the United States. The work had brought Valeri an international reputation: here was a poet of major stature.

It brought him recognition of another kind in Russia, especially after Gorbachev's gestures towards liberalization had been eclipsed along with Gorbachev. Valeri had been picked up by the authorities a dozen times for questioning before his actual arrest; the last time, after two days of interrogation and one savage beating, they had offered him a deal. They said they would let him out of the country if he stopped writing and publicly condemned his own work. Valeri had refused. The KGB then let him go for a couple of months, to give him enough rope to hang himself, which he obligingly did by writing more poetry, this time on the subject of Stalin, although he didn't actually name the old butcher.

Finally the KGB arrested him on charges of anti-Soviet slander and subversion, and tossed him into jail. His three-day trial, of which this was the sentencing day, was the result. He'd been told that three of his close friends had also been tried and convicted on similar charges, although he hadn't been allowed to know what their sentences were. At least the KGB hadn't taken his brother Sasha, four years younger, the baby of the family. Sasha had always worshipped Valeri and had helped to distribute the *samizdat* poems on Stalin.

He was snatched out of his reverie by the special

prosecutor's voice, which was getting progressively louder. The woman had worked herself into a frenzy.

". . . too good for this obscenity, this wrecker, this saboteur of the revolution and our Motherland. He is a sickness, a plague, he infects all he comes near. He can no longer be allowed to spread his poison among us, to defame our freedoms and justice abroad, to feed Zionist conspiracies against the workers' and peasants' state. I ask, I demand, in the name of Soviet man, that he receive the maximum penalty allowed under the law."

She sat down. The courtroom exploded into applause. Valeri looked at her in a kind of dazed wonder. Zionist conspiracy? Was that so close to the surface of her hatred? And to that of how many others? Even his KGB interrogators hadn't accused him of such a thing.

The courtroom was quietening. The judge, flanked by two people's representatives, looked at Valeri. His face was empty and cold.

"There is no need for deliberation in this case. The defendant Markelov is clearly guilty." He looked to each side of him, at the people's representatives who were supposed to serve as a jury. "Is there any disagreement from the people's representatives or the council for the defense?"

Silence.

"I will now pass sentence. Defendant Valeri Alexandreyevich Markelov, you are immediately to be incarcerated in a strict-regime correctional labor camp for a period of thirty years."

Thirty years, Valeri thought under the storm of applause. Two years ago they could only have given me seven. They changed the laws for people like me. How they hate and fear us.

Sasha, oh Sasha my brother, I'll never see you

50

again. Where are you, Sasha. Oh, keep yourself well.

Outside, it was mid-afternoon and bitterly cold. A large crowd of Russian Jews was milling around the steps of the courthouse and spreading out of the small square in front of it into the road. Beyond the road lay a maze of railroad tracks; the courthouse was a district one, on the outskirts of the city. On the far side of the road and across the front of the courthouse, stood some forty or fifty uniformed MVD militiamen. Here and there among them were men in plainclothes, KGB. Several of the KGB men were wielding cameras and clicked away steadily at the crowd.

Sasha Markelov kept his head down, trying to avoid the cameras. He was intensely aware of three things: his brother's unseen presence in the courthouse, the sullen anger of the crowd, and the hovering menace of the KGB men and the MVD militia. There was a fourth thing that floated in the back of his mind, but he intentionally kept it there, not thinking about it in case his face betrayed him: the gun.

His head was thronging with images, many drawn from his older brother's poetry. It was through reading Valeri's intricate verse that he had at last come to be aware of his Jewishness, and that he would never, could never, be a Russian. He was a Jew, and his people had been ground down too long. He had sworn to himself the oath that had come out of the Holocaust: *never again.*

The trial would be over soon. If they let Valeri go, all would be well. If not, he would strike. Whatever happened to him, the Jews of Moscow would remember that one of them had had courage to act.

He had already picked out his target, a big flat-

51

faced KGB man in a fur coat and sable hat. By his manner to the others, and the way he was dressed, Sasha was sure that he was a senior officer. He had been edging his way closer to the man without being obvious about it; he had to be close, because he had never dared fire the gun and he was not sure of his marksmanship. The gun was a small flat pistol, the kind that army officers used for a sidearm. He had succeeded in buying it, by great and painstaking effort, on the black market, from a Georgian.

Suddenly, the mutter of the crowd diminished. Several men were coming out of the double doors of the courthouse, laughing and yelling—some of the thugs and toughs the KGB had used to pack the courtroom. Sasha strained to hear what they were saying. In the hush, the shout of one of them carried distinctly in the freezing air.

"Thirty years! The little Jew shit only got thirty years in the camps! They should shoot all the *Zhid* wreckers!"

Suddenly Sasha heard engines starting up, somewhere in the streets to the south. The militia and the KGB men stiffened. They began to unsling their weapons.

Sasha took off his mittens and felt in his pocket for the pistol. He knew enough to release the safety catch and pull the trigger, but that was about all. He yanked the gun out, pointed it one-handed at the KGB officer and squeezed. The gun cracked and bucked, muzzle jerking upwards. He had forgotten to allow for the recoil. The militiamen were turning, looking for the source of the shots. Sasha, remembering something he had seen in a movie in which a Russian secret agent was holding off a mob of CIA killers, dropped to one knee, emptied the pistol at the KGB officer, threw it away, and began rolling sideways among the legs of the crowd, trying for the front of the square. If he reached the street, he might get away. As he went, he glimpsed the KGB man toppling backwards, his face masked in sudden red.

Automatic weapon fire ripped through the square; the militiamen had begun to shoot. Sasha kept going, hearing the screams, behind them a rumble and roar of heavy engines. There must have been army trucks hidden down the side streets; the heavy vehicles were thundering along the road, soldiers leaping out of them, Mongol troops not Slavs, fanning out, wading into the crowd, rifle butts flying. The screaming split the eardrums. Some of the Jews were trying to fight back, only to be smashed to the ground with broken faces and ripped flesh. More shots. Sasha felt something strike his left thigh with a shattering blow. He tried to turn back, away from the Mongols, but he couldn't get up. The sun seemed to have gone behind a cloud; he couldn't see properly. He found that he had rolled onto his back and was staring at the snowy sky.

A bullet fired at random by one of the militiamen struck him in the throat. It made a dreadful crunching noise inside Sasha's head, like the sound of swallowing under water. It changed course as it sliced through his carotid artery, severed his spinal cord and smashed out through the back of his neck. He died without being able to make a sound.

53

The Kremlin, Moscow
January 15, 1991

FRESH SNOW had fallen in the night. Two KGB soldiers were busy with shovels around the bases of the columns supporting the portico on the west side of the old Tsarist Senate building, where the wind had piled the snow into long tapering drifts. At dawn the wind and snow had ended, and now the men's breaths hung white and almost motionless in the bitter air. Across from the Senate's yellow facade, the upper story of the Arsenal glowed in the morning sun; it was still very early.

Four more guardsmen, led by a major, marched out of the passage leading into the Senate's interior courtyard. The two soldiers with the shovels redoubled their efforts, slinging showers of powdery snow at the mountain they had already raised. The major halted the security squad and said, "You'd better hurry it up. They'll be here any minute."

"Nearly done, Comrade Major Ivashenko," said the taller of the two shovelers, tossing a last spray of white crystals onto the heap to the side of the portico. As the thrown snow fell it caught a reflection off the windows of the Arsenal opposite, glittered for an instant, and then was extinguished. "Done, Comrade Major," said the soldier. He stuck the shovel into the heap; the blade clanged on the pavement underneath, the sound sharp and metallic in the icy air. He and the other shoveler snapped to attention.

The major eyed the pavement critically. It ought to be swept, but there was no time. These lazy slugs had been messing about for half an hour, they'd have to be disciplined. In the meantime he'd keep his fingers crossed that Comrade General Secretary Kulagin didn't slip and break an ankle, or worse, on the fine powder remaining on the pavement.

"Throw sand on it," he said. "And be quick."

They ran to get the buckets. The four other guardsmen stood rigidly at attention, as though they had frozen to death on the spot.

"Stand easy," the major said. Despite the temperature of minus thirty degrees centigrade, he was sweating under his heavy winter uniform. He always did when he was in charge of the security detail for one of these special meetings, the ones the Party bigwigs didn't like to hold in the Central Committee building down in Staraya Square. He hadn't been so edgy when Gorbachev was running things. Gorbachev had had some humor, although they said he had steel teeth inside that smile. Kulagin was different, never a tooth showing, but you knew they were there, never a smile like Gorbachev's. Those black eyes that seemed to be looking at you even when you were sure they were looking at somebody else. He was a real *vozhd*, a boss who wouldn't put up with any crap from the whiners, the intelligentsia and the *Zhids*. The intelligentsia were all infected by the Jews, anyway, none of them wanted to work. Look at what *Pravda* had been reporting lately about

55

economic sabotage out in the provinces. There was a Jew behind every case. The country'd be better off without them, always sniveling about emigration. Get rid of the lot of them, that was the answer. Then there could be some discipline, the country'd get back on the rails.

The major wondered for a moment what had become of Gorbachev. Resigned for reasons of health, *Pravda* had said. But the rumors afterward were that he'd been half-poisoned from a treatment by a Jewish doctor, turned into a vegetable. Gorbachev, up there on the podium on Lenin's tomb one day, gone the next, just like that. Jews.

The major shivered momentarily; he'd been standing still too long, and the perspiration on the back of his neck was turning to ice.

The two slugs had got the sand on, and none too soon. A black Zil limousine and a pair of Chaikas were entering the Kremlin from the entrance under the Nikolsky Tower and moving slowly toward the Senate. The Zil might have Secretary Kulagin in it; because of the security it was never possible to tell. The major disposed his men, personally ensuring that their AKMS rifles were loaded but that the safety catches were on. He always did this very carefully; men of the Ninth Directorate, the Guardsmen, were the only soldiers in the Union allowed to carry loaded weapons in the presence of the senior members of the Party, and no sloppiness could be permitted with that trust. Not even the minister of defense (perhaps especially not him, nor other members of the armed forces) possessed such a privilege.

The Zil and the Chaikas drew up at the portico. The major barked his men to attention. The Zil's driver left the car, quick and disciplined, and opened its rear door. General Secretary of the Communist

56

Party of the Soviet Union, Valentin Vasileyevich Kulagin, bulky in his thick sable coat, got out of the Zil. He was wearing a fur hat with earflaps pulled well down against the cold, so that his narrow dark eyebrows formed two horizontal parentheses beneath the hat's rim. The eyes flickered across the major and the guards, as though Kulagin searched for assassination, conspiracy, betrayal. The major fixed his gaze on a window in the exact center of the Arsenal's second story, and thought carefully of nothing.

Apparently satisfied, Kulagin said, in his thin, dry voice, "Has anyone else arrived?"

"No, Comrade Secretary," the major said. "You are the first today."

Kulagin nodded and went on into the Senate, followed by the KGB men from the Chaikas. The major permitted himself a tiny sigh of relief. Not for the first time, he thought: We have someone different here. Kulagin is not like Comrade Gorbachev was. Not at all.

They were using the old pre-Brezhnev Politburo office on the top floor of the Senate, in the building's southwest corner. The curtains had been drawn over the windows of the long room, closing off the view of the Arsenal and the Trinity Tower rising over the red-brown Kremlin walls.

Kulagin sat at the head of the polished mahogany table, under the portraits of Lenin and Stalin. The lighted chandeliers above the table reflected themselves in the wood's sheen; on the table were not the usual pads of writing paper, pens and pencils, but bottles of Georgian brandy and white and red wines, vodka in chilled silver carafes, wineglasses on linen

57

napkins and trays of *zakuski,* appetizers: cured sturgeon, various kinds of patés, sliced cucumbers and tomatoes, plates mounded with black granular caviar, *blinis* to spread the caviar on, pastries filled with jam for those with a sweet tooth. This was not so much a meeting as a celebration.

When they arrived, the other ten Politburo members arranged themselves, in no particular order of precedence, along the table's two longer sides. Kulagin looked up and down the table. Today his expression was almost amiable, as though he were contemplating some major achievement for which he was alone responsible. "To Winter Palace and success," he said, picking up the vodka carafe from the table in front of him. He poured the clear spirit into a small wineglass and picked it up. "Let's drink. This is a day for rejoicing."

The other members of the Politburo obeyed. Viktor Frolov, head of the Committee for State Security, the KGB, covertly studied the general secretary over the rim of his glass. Kulagin was draining his vodka, reaching for a slice of cucumber, sprinkling it with salt, popping the white and green disk into his mouth. He was never still, except during the rare public appearances he made on top of the Lenin Mausoleum; he was always toying with something during meetings, his pen, his cigarette lighter, underlining or crossing out items on the agenda. He was of slight stature, but because his legs were too short for his body he seemed ungainly rather than deft. He had the pale "Kremlin complexion," from so many years spent sitting in offices. He had been party secretary for Leningrad for a long time before reaching the supreme post of general secretary, and had ruled that city and its district with a harshness reminiscent of Stalin's day. It was this reputation for ironhanded rule that had brought him to the forefront of the opposition to Gorbachev when it became clear to the Central Committee, the Politburo and the KGB that Gorbachev's loosening of political controls was going to lead the country into chaos. Russia needed a good dose of discipline, had needed it since Stalin died. Kulagin was an appropriate choice; he had always been Stalinist in his leanings, and had no patience with reinterpretation of Marxist-Leninist doctrine. Another advantage was that he did not have a large power base in the Central Committee and the security organs; the men who had voted for his secretaryship had been confident that he would remain under control, since his power depended on KGB and CC support. They didn't want any more loose cannons like Gorbachev crashing about the decks, threatening to sink them all.

But, Frolov thought as he set his own glass down and refilled it, we *may* have made a mistake. Dear Valentin Vasileyevich Kulagin has been playing the game very well. He's a lot more secure than he was, maneuvering his Leningrad compatriots into the Central Committee, and lately he's been doing the same with my own outfit. And he's so good at it, he's very difficult to stop without the appearance of disloyalty to the Party. Even I can't afford that. He'd like to get rid of me so he could put one of his own lot in. Then what?

Even the aromatic warmth of the Stolichnaya sliding down his throat didn't dispel the cold finger that seemed to caress the back of his neck. That was the way Stalin had begun, slipping his own people into obscure but important posts. For several years after he took power following Lenin's death, the Old Bolsheviks and the main ranks of the Party hadn't been

59

molested. But then, in the thirties, Stalin attacked, in the purge known as the Great Terror. Millions had been executed or sent to die in the camps.

What particularly exercised Frolov's imagination these days was that every one of the men who had served as chief of the security organs while Stalin lived—Menzhinsky, Yagoda, Yezhov—had been arrested and executed when their usefulness ended. Beria had probably been next on Stalin's list, but the Boss died, and his successors had disposed of Beria. If Kulagin were really taking Stalin as his model, and he certainly seemed to be—

He cut the thought off. Kulagin was looking at him, a full glass raised in a toast. "To our industrious and ingenious head of the security organs," he said. "Viktor Mikhailovich Frolov. Without him we would not be in a position to celebrate the beginning of this great historical process. To Comrade Frolov and Winter Palace."

The others also raised their glasses and drank. Frolov shot a look at Truschenko, the foreign minister. He was going to have a difficult job, interpreting Winter Palace to the West in the best possible light, even with the widespread disinformation campaign the KGB had devised to support it. Never mind. In a year or so it would be over, or so the West would believe, and the capitalists could go back to sleep. Until it was too late.

It was Yuri Andropov, just before he died, who had had the idea of resurrecting the old plan. He'd even decided to keep the name Winter Palace, as there was no evidence that the project had ever been compromised. The time for it was even more auspicious than it had been back in 1952, when Beria had devised it for Stalin. Andropov had been convinced—perhaps it was depression brought on by his illness or the knowledge of his impending death—that the Soviet Union was going to lose the ideological and economic war with the West, unless drastic action was taken. Since a military solution was too risky, only massive subversion of western political will and confidence remained. If the West could be convinced that it had lost its struggle with the world revolution, the fact would soon follow the conviction. Frolov remembered the conversation very clearly; it had taken place in Andropov's hospital suite out at the Kuntsevo clinic.

"But," Frolov had objected, when Andropov had described the dilemma, "we'd have to move a tremendous number of well-trained people into the West over a short period of time. Training the numbers is no problem, we can handle that. It's the insertion that's the difficulty. Western security checks everyone who leaves here, and they do it very carefully. We'd have to swamp them, so most of our people could slip past." The dimensions of the old man's proposal struck him. "If we could manage it, though, it would be like implanting malignant cancer cells into a healthy body. In ten years, or twenty, we'd have a lot of our people in positions of influence. Imagine! We could achieve control of, for example, the Zionist lobby in Washington. We could wreck relations between Israel and the United States. We might even insert operatives into the White House staff. And they could all recruit others—"

"You are showing the imagination I expected of you," Andropov said. "There's a way to do it, Viktor Mikhailovich. Why did you mention the Zionists just now?"

"Well," Frolov said. "If some Jews were among the people we sent over there, we could include some of our own—"

61

Andropov held up a hand to stop him. "Why just *some* Jews?" he asked. "Why not *all* Jews?"

There had been a short silence. The old man's breath rasped in the silence of the room.

"Yuri Vladimirovich," Frolov said, "that's brilliant." He meant it.

"Yes." Andropov's voice was dry. "We permit all Soviet Jews to emigrate, since that's what they want so much, what the Zionists in Jerusalem say they want so much, what the Americans say we should do. All two million of them. How do you think the Western governments will react to two million *Zhids* landing on their doorsteps?"

Frolov thought about London, Washington, Paris, Bonn. "They won't like it."

"Of course they won't. Except for Israel, they don't want Jews, especially Russian Jews. *But they'll have to take them.* Because of Hitler, no Western government can now politically afford to refuse Jewish immigration. Their bourgeois-liberal papers would raise a hue and cry, naturally enough, since they're all controlled by Zionists. We gain a number of advantages. First, the major one. At the moment we have only three and a half thousand deep-cover agents in the Western target countries. That's not nearly enough. But with what I am planning, we can move fifty thousand abroad, into Israel, North America, France, England, anywhere we like. In a decade or two we will have an intelligence and espionage net in Europe and the Western hemisphere that has never been equaled in history. It will enable us to destroy, safely and from within, the will of the capitalists to resist or attack us. Second, we inflict a serious economic burden on the countries that accept the emigrants, especially Israel. Her economy's already bad. If she takes in two or three hundred

62

thousand Jews, it'll be on the point of collapse. And if Jerusalem *refuses* to take them, the political clashes over the decision will wreck the Israeli government. We win either way.''

"And not least," Frolov said, warming even more to the vision, "we get rid of our *Zhids.* "

"Yes. I've thought about doing that, off and on, for some years. But there's never been any point in letting them out in driblets, like Brezhnev was doing. That's just frittering away their political usefulness."

Andropov coughed deeply, raggedly, caught his breath, and went on. "Viktor, I think there are hard times coming. We are not going to be able to feed ourselves for some years. We need two things. We need iron discipline, and we need targets for the anger of Russians who do not have enough to eat, or we ourselves will be the targets. The *discipline* I leave to my successor and to the KGB in general." He coughed again. "I have been saving the Jews to be the targets. Most of them deserve to be, anyway—you know what *Zhids* are like. You personally must see to the Jews, and to carrying out what we've been discussing. Otherwise I fear for the Russian future."

"I will begin immediately," Frolov said.

Andropov gave that closed, frostbitten smile of his. "I have a surprise for you," he said. "The plans already exist. They have existed for years. They are code-named Winter Palace. Only the heads of the KGB have ever had access to them. They are very complete; you'll find that only the transport schedules and some of the camp locations need to be changed. The organizational structures are all there."

Frolov nodded. "One thing more," Andropov went on. "The handling suggested is strict-regime.

Keep to that, for two reasons. One, harsh treatment will put enormous pressure on Western regimes to take our Jews as fast as possible, to save them from illness and imminent death. Second, Western intelligence services are going to know that we're hiding agents among the Jews, so no KGB people can be conspicuously better treated than they are. You'd better make arrangements, though, so that your people can protect themselves in an emergency. As for the others, expect a death rate of about two percent. We're not going to pamper these people any more. I'll tell you where to find the documents. Then get to work.''

Andropov had died two days later, without seeing Frolov again. Frolov had been somewhat startled, in reading through the Winter Palace plans, to find that the executive order had been drafted and signed by Beria, although Stalin himself had never signed it. It had been a little like a voice from the grave.

And now, Winter Palace was ready, nearly a decade after Frolov had taken the operational documents from the safe where Andropov had hidden them. Characteristically, and despite the toast to Frolov, Kulagin had taken the credit for himself. For the moment, Frolov didn't care.

He raised his own glass and toasted back. ''To you, Valentin Vasileyevich. You are a brilliant example to all of us who love the socialist Motherland. We applaud your willingness to accept the great burden of your office.''

More toasts around the table. Serious drinking was about to begin; Frolov knew the signs from other meetings, some of them out at Kulagin's *dacha* near Uspenskoye. Kulagin never got drunk, though; despite his less than average size he was extremely hardheaded. Frolov, luckily, also tolerated alcohol

64

well. That was partly because he was a big man; he knew that his colleagues referred to him, because of his shambling walk, as "the Bear." The only outward sign when he drank was that his face, which he normally kept expressionless as though his features had been poured from concrete, grew slightly pink. Too much alcohol, though, caused him hemorrhoids. To reduce the rate of absorption he spread caviar on a *blini* and ate it. Across the table, Foreign Minister Truschenko was already getting plastered, a sight no Western diplomat would ever see. So was Lesiovsky, the minister of defense. Somebody down the table was telling a dirty joke; Kulagin was lighting one of the British Dunhill cigarettes he always smoked. There'd be another round of toasts in a minute. Frolov wanted to get back to his office. With Winter Palace so close to execution, he wanted to start fine-combing the directives for mistakes. There was no getting away at the moment, though. Paragraphs from the directives began drifting through his mind.

. . . internal administration of WINTER PALACE falls under three operational divisions:

A. Collection of subjects and shipment to transit camps.

B. Transit camp procedures.

C. Control measures.

Part A. Collection:

Subjects designated in each geographical division of the country will be collected by the KGB special squads as scheduled in the detail orders provided on an individual basis. Collection will be by truck, and is to be carried out between 0100 and 0500 hours on the selected dates. Holding areas near rail yards will be cleared by 0800 each day, using the rail transport provided. . . .

"Viktor Mikhailovich, you're not drinking!" Kulagin called from the end of the table. "Come on, fill your glass! Where would we be without the KGB? You can't desert us now!"

Dmitri Lesiovsky, the defense minister, was looking at Frolov, his eyes slightly narrowed. Agents in the KGB Third Directorate, the security organ that monitored the loyalty of the armed forces, had reported to Frolov that Lesiovsky was not entirely content with the disregard Kulagin generally showed him. Frolov had not passed that information on to the general secretary. He had, very discreetly and carefully, let Lesiovsky know that he hadn't.

"I was thinking about work," Frolov confessed with a wry smile. He poured vodka and helped himself to a slice of sturgeon. "There's a great deal to be done."

"There's always a great deal for the security organs to do," said Kulagin. "But relax this once, Viktor. Today is for celebration. You can get back to your desk later. A toast to the cleansing of the Motherland!"

Frolov drank. Despite the lining he had given his stomach, he was beginning to feel the rosy glow of the spirit working through his bloodstream, his muscles, his brains. Kulagin could be disposed of if necessary, it wouldn't be that much trouble. Not, really, any more trouble than a couple of million *Zhids*. That really was something to be proud of, the directives were well thought out, precise. Andropov would have been pleased at the efficiency of the operation.

* * *

66

. . . Intake. After unloading from the transport cars, subjects will be processed into the camps. Men and women will be separated at the initial processing barriers. Children under six will be permitted to remain with their mothers. . . . Delousing procedures will be carried out immediately.

' . . . Nutrition will be held at minimum survival levels. Only extreme medical conditions will be treated. Dispensation of drugs and pharmaceuticals will be strictly controlled. . . . Mothers unable to nurse will receive rations of dried milk, as available. . . .

. . . Control Measures and Discipline:

Officers assigned to control and disciplinary measures must maintain constant vigilance. The subjects have a long history of subversion, and are adept at conspiracy. Any signs of resistance to control must be dealt with immediately and summarily. Military courts are not required, as the subjects have removed themselves from the protection of Soviet law by their desire to emigrate.

Because of the subjects' propensity for unlawful organization, the principle of collective responsibility will apply. If officers in charge of disciplinary detachments see fit, punishments may be extended to an individual's family, or to as many other transportees as deemed necessary. Punishments may range from deprivation of water and food to the extreme penalty.

Mutiny, either physical or verbal, will be punished by summary application of the extreme penalty. This is to be carried out by shooting. Mutiny will be defined at the discretion of the commander of the disciplinary detachment. Individuals under twelve will be exempted, but a member of their fam-

67

ily over that age must be substituted. Applications of the punishment should be carried out in full view of the transportees. Disposal of the remains . . .

But, damn it, Frolov thought, there *is* a problem, no matter how I try to convince myself otherwise. A lot of *Zhids* are going to die, many times more than Andropov estimated. And Kulagin has pushed so fast on Winter Palace that we haven't been able to make complete preparations for hiding the deaths. We're going to be called butchers.

Correction. Viktor Frolov, head of the KGB, is going to be called a butcher. Not Secretary Kulagin. Butcher, as they called Beria and the others before him. And Kulagin will—

He was suddenly aware that the table had gone quiet. He yanked himself out of his reverie.

"Well, Comrade Frolov?" Kulagin said. "What's on your mind this time?"

It wasn't always easy to tell when Kulagin was working himself into a rage. Sometimes, when he was on the edge of fury, he stopped fidgeting. He wasn't fidgeting now.

"I was considering what I have to do when I get back to the office," Frolov said. He realized instantly that despite all the years of honing his wits and watching his tongue, he had made a mistake. Perhaps it had been the vodka, but he had sounded as though he were accusing Kulagin of sloughing off responsibility when there was work to be done.

"Always there is work for Comrade Frolov," Kulagin said. He was smiling, but the smile did not quite reach the eyes. "Perhaps you work too hard, Viktor Mikhailovich. You shouldn't, none of us would want to see your health suffer."

68

I don't have to put up with this shit, Frolov thought. If it weren't for me and the security organs, you wouldn't be sitting at the head of this table.

Still, he guarded his words. "I'm gratified by your concern for my health, Valentin Vasileyevich. But you needn't worry, I'm indestructible."

It was not quite a challenge. Kulagin studied the KGB chairman for a moment, and then nodded. "That's always been plain to all of us. Viktor Frolov, you're a credit to your service. I toast you again."

The moment had passed. The conversation and clinking of glasses around the long polished table resumed. Frolov thought: He judges it is too early to strike directly against me. But he is considering it. I must not let my guard down for a moment.

Winter Palace. There may be more uses for it than I realized at the beginning.

Dulles International Airport
February 28

COLE FOUND LAUSCH exactly where he said he would be, in the Boiler Room Lounge on the main concourse. The customs broker's nose was buried in some tomato juice concoction that had a stalk of celery protruding from it.

"Bit early, isn't it, Moe?" Cole said as he slipped into the chair beside Lausch. The clock over the bar showed ten minutes short of noon.

"You'd better have something too," Lausch growled. "There's some kind of hassle over this shipment."

"What kind? There's never been any with consignments from Aksay."

"There is this time." Lausch drank half of his cocktail. "You sure you know what you're doing with that Turk?"

Cole considered. Kemal Aksay was an art dealer in Istanbul and Cole's principal antiquities scout in Turkey; Cole had got to know him during his CIA days in the country. Aksay was an expert fixer, and probably could have exported the Suleiman Mosque, piece by piece, to anywhere its buyer specified. He was careful, though, and usually only dealt in antiquities that could be proven to have originated outside Turkey. Normally the objects came from Syria or Iraq or Iran.

"There shouldn't be any trouble, Moe," Cole said. Dammit, he thought, this is what I pay you for, to clear things through. What did you drag me up here for?

"I hope you're right."

"Who do we see? Fraser?" Fraser was the customs officer Cole and Lausch usually dealt with.

"Nope." Lausch finished his drink. "Somebody new. I don't think he's with Customs, either. I think he's a cop."

"You're kidding." Oh, shit, Cole thought. What the hell did Aksay put in that shipment? I specified the three terra-cottas and the bronze. He said they were Iraqi. Why would the police get involved over that?

"Let's go and find out what the hell's going on." Cole waved the hovering waiter away; he'd have a drink after this was settled.

Lausch shot his wrist out of his shirtsleeve and looked at his watch. "Sorry, but I can't. I've got another shipment to clear before half past."

"Moe. What's bugging you?"

Lausch turned to look at Cole. "Look, Sam, I've been working for you for two years. But cops I don't need. I make my living at this, I can't afford to be mixed up in any fast-track stuff. I don't think you're up to anything, but I don't trust Aksay. You sort it out with whoever's interested, then get me at the office and I'll clear up the paperwork. That all right with you?"

Cole studied the broker for a moment. "Okay. When'll you be back?"

71

"By three."

"Where do I see whoever-it-is?"

Lausch told him and left hurriedly. Cole thought: He's scared. What of? He's had arguments with Customs before.

Except that this doesn't seem to be Customs. Let's find out what it is.

He left the lounge, and with some difficulty found the office Lausch had directed him to. It had a frosted glass door with a number on it, and that was all. He knocked and went in.

There was a desk and two chairs inside the office. Gilbert Jackman was sitting behind the desk. Maurice Lambert was sitting on it.

"Hello, Sam," Jackman said. "Long time no see."

I might have known, Cole thought. Rich couldn't persuade me, so they've sent these two. That was pretty goddamned stupid. "Well. Tweedledum and Tweedledee. You guys got a promotion to Customs? Congratulations."

Jackman flushed. He was a very short man, with a round baby face and thinning silver hair, executive assistant to Carl Procunier, the head of the CIA Soviet Desk. Cole was fairly sure that Jackman had been behind his transfer out of the Soviet section back to the Middle East Desk, after the Berdeyev disaster in Moscow. It had been a reprimand and a demotion of sorts. Jackman had always disliked Cole, a dislike he extended impartially to people with money or talent. He was not untalented himself, but he resented men who possessed equal or greater competence.

Lambert was another out of the same mold, although a few years younger, taller, and not quite so

72

chubby. He bore the same relation to Jackman that Jackman did to Procunier.

"Don't give us a hard time, Sam," Lambert said. "Mr. Jackman and I came down here especially to talk to you. You don't need to get insulting."

"Was it you who scared the wits out of my customs broker?" Cole asked. "Gil here's too short to upset him."

"I spoke to him, yes," Lambert said. "We wanted to get to you as inconspicuously as possible."

"So you come on like a KGB goon," Cole said. "That was really bright. He's going to forget that in a hurry, I'm sure."

Jackman's flush was disappearing. "That's enough. We haven't time to bicker, Sam. We want to offer you a job."

Cole stared at him. *You* want to offer *me* a job? Had you noticed that I don't really need the money? Or that Rich asked me the same thing last fall? The answer's still the same. No."

"I don't think you quite understand," Jackman said. "The situation's changed since Richland was talking to you. This is bigger than the Middle East. We think it's a lot bigger."

"Oh?"

"Snowflake's active again."

Cole stared at Jackman. Snowflake had been a talent scout, furnishing leads to potential recruits— Berdeyev, Abramov and Grishin among them. All of them dead, now. Snowflake had never passed information himself; his usefulness lay in the breadth of his social circle and his ability—before Kulagin took power—to have foreign contacts without official disapproval. His identity was among the most closely

73

guarded secrets of the Moscow CIA station, and Cole had been his handler. "What?"

"You heard me. After Berdeyev and the others were taken and you left, he cut off. He pretty well had to, after Kulagin started to get tough with Russians who knew foreigners. But he's come out of the woodwork."

"Why?" He'd expected, for months after leaving Moscow, to hear that Snowflake had been picked up. But he hadn't been; his continued safety had been one small success to make up for the other disasters.

"He's got something for us. He's desperate to get it out of the country. A document with the code name 'Winter Palace.' But he won't tell us what's in it."

Despite himself, Cole was becoming interested. "Any ideas?"

"There's one strong possibility. Kulagin's been cracking down on the Jews over there. There was Valeri Markelov's trial in December. You know the connection."

"I know it. They gave him thirty years, but he'll be dead long before that. There was some kind of a riot outside the courthouse."

"Four people were shot dead by the militia," Lambert said. "They opened fire after somebody in the crowd drilled a KGB man and killed him. The Soviet press has been hanging a conspiracy theory on the whole event. Jewish spies, saboteurs, assassins. I'm telling you, Sam, it's starting to look really ugly over there."

"I don't see," Cole said, "why you dragged me all the way up here to tell me this. What the hell am I supposed to do about it?"

"We want you to go back to Moscow. Just for a

couple of days. To make contact with Snowflake and get the document out.''

"I seem to recall," Cole said, "a rumor that the CIA has a station in Moscow. Maybe you could check that out. There might be somebody over there who could help you. But it won't be me.''

"It has to be you, Sam. Snowflake won't talk to anybody else. He wants you, and only you.''

Cole stared at Jackman. Only me, he thought. It's not so surprising. Agents are always frightened of working with somebody they aren't familiar with; it's hard to trust. Snowflake still trusts me. Even after the disaster. "What's so important about Winter Palace?''

Jackman looked up at the ceiling, as though searching for microphones, and then down at Cole. "That's just the problem. We don't know. But we *do* know that whatever it is, it's been running a long time.''

"How long?''

"When Snowflake surfaced with the code name, we went back through the archives. We found it in 1953. A Russian was trying to defect, one of Beria's department chiefs. His bona fides were documents about this Winter Palace. It was important, very important. But the Russian never made it, and the records were filed and forgotten. Okay, that was fine. Lots of leads burn out. But now it turns up again, out of the blue. That's bad. Something that's been running this long, Sam, we have to know what it is.''

"I can't go," Cole said. "The KGB knew damn well I was running Berdeyev. You don't think they've forgotten, do you?''

"You won't be going in as yourself. You'll be a substitute for somebody who's supposed to be as-

75

signed to Moscow as a trade attache. KGB surveillance on new people doesn't pick up for a couple of days. That'll be all the time you need. Then you'll develop a case of something virulent and have to be taken back to the States for medical treatment. The documents will go out in the diplomatic bag.''

"KGB files have enough photographs of me to fill a book.''

Jackman looked Cole up and down. "You've changed. You've lost weight and your face is a lot thinner than it was then. We'll change your eye and hair color. It'll hold for two days.''

And if it doesn't, Cole thought, I'll end up like Berdeyev. They'll take me to a cellar somewhere, or to an operating room where they can monitor my heart and brain and the rest of my body, and they'll take me apart until I tell them anything they want me to. There won't be any exchanges, not these days.

But if he went back, just for that long, if he managed to get out at the end of it, he might lose the racking sense of failure that had dogged him ever since the disaster in Moscow. Was it something he had done, some subtle error that he still could not recognize, that had committed Berdeyev and the others to filthy and tormented deaths? While Cole departed Moscow in the clean bright cabin of an airliner?

It was unlikely that he would ever know. The best he would be able to do would be to go back, succeed and come home again. Then he might be able to put Moscow, and the rest of it, behind him. And Berdeyev's terrified face wouldn't rise up between him and the Maserati's windshield, one day next spring, out on the hairpin turn at a hundred sixty miles an hour.

76

Crap, Cole thought. Going back to Moscow isn't going to get rid of Berdeyev's ghost. Time will, or I'll have to get used to it.

"You'd better start digging around for another look-alike," he said to Jackman. "Because my answer's still no."

Lambert said, "Sam, we've been doing a lot of work on this. We've been depending on you. We need you."

"That's pretty goddamned presumptuous," Cole said. "You've got no business planning anything that involves me without my permission. I'm not in the business any more."

"Oh?" Jackman said. "You kept up a contact with the Company, though. Teaching languages. Almost as though you really weren't finished with us."

The bastard's been talking to the psychologists out at Langley, Cole thought. That's what they'd say. But why *didn't* I break off every connection? Megan asked me that once. I didn't have a good answer.

"I'm finished now," Cole said. "After this semester, the instruction directorate's going to have to find somebody else."

He realized that it sounded petulant and that they were putting him on the defensive. They're a slippery pair, he reminded himself. I'd better get out of here as soon as I can. As soon as they do whatever it takes to release that shipment. Poor Moe. He didn't realize what he was up against.

Jackman sighed. "Sam, okay, I'm sorry. But you have to do this."

"I have to *what?*"

"You gotta go," Lambert said.

"Shut up," Cole said. "I wasn't talking to you. What do you mean by *have to*, Gil?"

77

Jackman leaned back in the chair. "Tell him."

"Well, Sam," Lambert said, "it's like this. You know that shipment your broker was trying to clear today?"

"Don't be an asshole. What the hell do you think I'm doing here?"

"Well, apparently your Turkish dealer shouldn't have exported it. There's an item, a gold circlet, that came from a museum in Ankara. Stolen goods. Your name's on the waybill, as consignee. That's pretty solid grounds for suspicion. You shouldn't have gotten into contraband art, Sam."

"I'm not into contraband art," Cole snarled. "There wasn't any gold in the letters of agreement."

"Well, there is in the package. We X-rayed it. It's there, all right."

"You bastards. You set this up."

"You owe us something, Sam," Jackman said coldly. "Somebody screwed up in Moscow. It might have been you. We lost a lot."

"There was nothing about anybody screwing up in the damage assessment report. That's horseshit. The KGB were doing what they're supposed to."

"Suit yourself," Jackman said.

This is pointless, Cole thought. They're determined. "Okay," he said. "I'll get in touch with my attorney this afternoon."

"You go ahead and contact your attorney," Jackman said. "But let one word of this conversation out, and you're going to find that treasure trove you have down in your basement belongs to just about everybody else in the world. It'd do credit to a museum, I hear."

"You son of a bitch," Cole said. "Did you get that from Rich?"

78

"Nope. We didn't need to. We've known about it for some time. It's pretty legal, I guess. But it could be argued."

"On the subject of the gold circlet in the shipment today," Lambert put in. "I suppose you know we've got an extradition treaty with Turkey over that sort of thing. You know what a Turkish jail's like, Sam. Remember *Midnight Express?*"

Cole looked at the pair of them. After a moment he said, "You two must have been taking management courses on how to increase corporate loyalty. You just got it a little off center."

Jackman looked at his watch. "You were always prone to dramatics, Sam. Maybe that was the problem in Moscow. We'll give you some time to think about it—a couple of weeks. In the meantime you can have the shipment. Except for the gold circlet and the waybill. That'll keep everybody honest."

"I haven't said yes."

"Oh, but you have. You know how it works, Sam. You did it to Berdeyev. Just remember, it's you Snowflake wants. We'll be in touch, tell you what's next. You going to call your attorney?"

They were right, about the acceptance. He knew already that he was going to go. Somewhere inside him there was a small blossoming sense of relief.

"No," he said. "I'll wait till later."

Moscow University
March 19

ACADEMICIAN ALEXANDER MARKELOV walked up the steps of the great glass and steel humanities building and with some difficulty opened one of the heavy doors of the main entrance; his hands were badly arthritic again. He smiled and held the door for a young woman student who was on her way out. She didn't return the smile; in fact, she looked a little frightened.

I wonder if she knows, Markelov thought. I don't remember ever seeing her before, but she might know who I am. That would account for the expression. Perhaps she doesn't know. Ah, well, my memory for faces isn't what it was.

He turned along the concrete corridor, heading for the elevators. It was late afternoon and there weren't many students about. He was thankful for that; some of the young men reminded him of Sasha. Sasha, cold now under the frozen earth, somewhere. They wouldn't even let the body go; parents couldn't bury a child who was a murderer and assassin. It was killing Esfir as surely as the bullets had killed her son outside the courthouse. Why had Sasha gone? There was nothing he could have done to help Valeri. Where on earth could he have laid his hands on that gun? And Valeri, my firstborn, either still in Lefortovo or already on his way to the camps. Thirty years. I'll never see him again.

He stopped outside the elevator bank and pressed the button. The grief for his two lost sons rose hot in his throat and threatened to strangle him. He thrust it down. Esfir wept all the time. He couldn't be like that; he couldn't collapse now. The KGB had been at both of them for weeks. Where did Sasha get the gun, was it your other criminal son who got it for him? Or was it your daughter Irina? Who does Irina's husband see? What are their names? How did you, a respected scholar, raise such trash? Did you teach your sons to hate their Motherland? Why?

—I haven't seen Valeri for two years. We quarrelled.

—How do we know that?

—You must know I disowned him. He hates me.

—You're a subversive, if you raised subversives. What are you teaching your granddaughter? The same filth?

It was the same every time, the same questions, but asked as though they weren't really interested in the answers. As though they were going through some kind of ritual whose end was already preordained.

The elevator doors slid open. The cubicle was empty; Markelov entered. How he had wanted to tell Valeri the truth. But if he had, he'd likely be in prison himself by now—Valeri would have been tortured into telling them. His son's scorn had eaten at him like an acid. He remembered the accusations the day Valeri walked out to live from hand to mouth with those friends of his.

81

—You're a fool, you're a scared old man. You won't speak up, you're afraid for your precious position. You're sterile, you pretend you love literature, but to you it's just a meal ticket, you don't really know anything about it, you root around in other people's work because you're too scared to do any of your own—

What could he have said? That he was a spy, that he found people who would work for the Americans? That he had a code name, Snowflake? That his years of conformity, his submission, no, call it by its real name, his groveling, were all self-protection so that he could go on working against the regime, against the gray men who told him what he could or could not read and think and write? That it all had been doubly hard, that he had had to be doubly compliant, because he was a Jew? That what he had done grew out of the same beliefs that Valeri held?

He didn't think Valeri would have believed him. And now it was too late; he would never be able to explain. He would go to his grave with the knowledge that his son hated him, no, worse, despised him.

The elevator stopped. Markelov looked up at the indicator; he was only at the fourth floor. The doors hummed open. Outside stood Ivan Kiselev, a senior in Markelov's Pushkin class, and one of his best students.

"Good afternoon, Ivan. Are you going up?"

Instead of answering, the young man stepped away from the door, his expression compounded of one part dismay and two parts fear. He started punching the elevator call button distractedly.

"Ivan," Markelov said from inside the elevator, "you won't get another one until this one's gone."

The clacking of the button stopped. Ivan stepped

82

out of sight of the open door. The elevator closed and resumed its upward journey. Markelov leaned against the wall, a rush of humiliation and anger washing through him. He was familiar now with this kind of attitude among his students, but it had never been as overt as this. They didn't ask questions in class any more or come up to him after the lecture was over to find out his opinion on obscure points of literary style. Ivan was still willing to attend classes, where he was protected from Markelov's baleful influence by the presence of others, but he wouldn't ride in the same elevator. The contagion would be too direct.

Ninth floor. At least Humanities Director Rostovsky was still on his side. Markelov had known Vladimir for twenty years. They were friends; every Tuesday afternoon like this one they met in Rostovsky's office to drink Armenian brandy and talk and smoke the rough *papirosi* cigarettes that Rostovsky loved, although he certainly could have afforded better. It had never seemed to matter that Markelov was Jewish. Even after Valeri's arrest, when other faculty had begun to avoid Markelov, Rostovsky had kept up the Tuesday tradition.

He left the elevator and walked along the hall to the main humanities office. Rostovsky's private office was tucked away at its rear, behind an oak door with maroon leather panels. Ordinarily Markelov nodded at the secretaries and went right in, but this time Vera, the senior woman in the office, held up a hand to stop him.

"The director's on the phone, Academician. You'll have to wait." She pointed. "There's a chair for you."

She was usually friendly; ingratiating would be a better word. Today her voice was extremely cool.

83

As he sat down, Markelov caught a glimpse of two of the other women leaning over their desks, glancing at him, whispering. Three months ago they would not have dared act that way.

"How long?" he asked.

"I don't know." It was just short of rudeness.

The office was overheated, as usual, and he unbuttoned his coat and rested his hat on his knee. Anger was building in him, mixed with the grief.

And the fear. Markelov had always had a very simple self-protective device: unless he was actually involved in subversive actions, he made himself believe that he was exactly what everyone except a very few Americans thought he was—a senior member of the Russian Literature Department at Moscow University, a prominent Pushkin scholar, with a great many friends and acquaintances in the upper circles of Moscow's cultural elite, and with numerous social and professional contacts among the foreign population of the capital. But that had all ended suddenly when he'd heard that at least three of the men he'd set up for the Americans had been arrested. For months after, he'd lived with an anxiety he could scarcely conceal, until it really did appear that the security organs hadn't made the connection between Berdeyev and the others and himself. At the same time, Markelov had severed all connections with the Americans and every other Western nationality. In this, he appeared to be following the new Party line, since Kulagin's new regime had quickly made all unauthorized contacts with foreigners into a gamble with the good nature of the KGB.

That had been his life until Valeri's arrest and the calamities that had followed it. But he had been growing uneasy for several months previous to that. At first it wasn't anything he could put his finger on, but little by little he began to see the shape and then the outlines of it, as though he were in a darkroom watching a photograph develop. It probably became clearer to him more quickly than to anyone other than those men who were planning it, because he had seen it before. When Valeri was arrested he retrieved from their hiding place the prints he had made long ago from the microfilm he'd found near the man he killed in the spruce forest north of Leningrad.

Winter Palace.

He'd read the grainy blurred prints again, late one night just after Valeri's arrest, under the dim glow of the bedside lamp in his *dacha* near Peredelkino; he hadn't dared bring them home. The rumors, the newspaper articles and editorials, the sporadic arrests of Jews, the trial of one of his sons and the murder of the other, took on a terrible consistency and coherence in the light of the text of the old microfilm.

Winter Palace. After nearly four decades, they had brought the nightmare back to life. Stalin risen from the grave. He realized, as he pushed the sheets of photographic paper back into the tarnished aluminum box, that he hadn't really believed they'd do it, that at the very least someone of his reputation and stature wouldn't be touched. But it was clear from the documents that he and his kind would receive particular attention. The Jewish intelligentsia were to be as vulnerable as those farther down the social ladder. Even Party membership would be no protection.

He'd known for years what the documents said, but he'd refused to believe them, pushed it all into the back of his mind with the label: *They couldn't do that, not now. It's nearly forty years old, anyway, nothing*

85

but a footnote in history. For the same reason, he had never told the Americans what he knew. Until now.

Pogrom, he thought. The dreadful, hateful word, fraught with hundreds of years of anguish and despair. When the Tsars had enraged their people beyond all forbearance, it was always there to turn the wrath away. *Pogrom:* it is the fault of the Jews. Cossacks in village streets, hoofbeats, lances, blood, the smell of burning.

He looked up at the office clock. Ten minutes had passed. Vera glanced over at him, nervously. She was obviously hoping he'd give up and go away. No. He'd not admit defeat like that.

After hiding the aluminum box again in the grounds of his *dacha,* he had decided to go back to the Americans. There was an emergency contact procedure that he had never used, that he had hoped he would never need to use. He wasn't even sure if it was still in effect, or whether it had been compromised if it was. He had to risk the contact.

Quite to his surprise, it worked: the call made from a telephone booth to the American embassy, asking for a person who didn't work there. The brush contact in the crowd at the Lenin subway station, the exchange of newspapers. On the sheet from the onetime pad he had been given years ago for emergency purposes, Markelov had simply encoded:

There is something I have to give you. It is called Winter Palace. Send Cardinal. No one else.

Then he had begun to wait. He was still waiting. Perhaps Cole wouldn't come and they were trying to find a way to make him accept someone else. They wouldn't. Cole would come. Markelov still trusted him; he and the American had worked together fruitfully for two years, and he was the best handler Markelov had ever had. He had become quite de-

86

pendent on Samuel Cole for encouragement and sympathy, and had been desolate when the American vanished so abruptly. The relationship of an agent and his handler, to Markelov's occasional faint amusement, had some of the characteristics of a marriage.

The intercom on Vera's desk buzzed. She picked up the receiver, listened, and responded, "Yes. He's still here." After a brief pause she replaced the receiver and said coldly to Markelov, "You can go in."

Bitch, Markelov thought as he rounded the end of the counter on his way to Rostovsky's office door. It opened and his old friend stood in the doorway.

"Alexander, come in, take off your coat, I'm sorry I kept you, but . . ." Rostovsky's voice trailed away. His manner seemed normal, but there was an undercurrent. Markelov entered the office, hearing the door thud softly closed behind him.

Nothing in the office seemed out of place or unusual for a late Tuesday afternoon: the decanters on the little table between the two armchairs next to Rostovsky's ornate desk, the glasses, the air already heavy with the harsh sweet smell of *papirosi* tobacco, one of the cigarettes sending up a blue plume of smoke from a heavy ceramic ashtray. Rostovsky fussed over the decanters, pouring a glass for Markelov, one for himself. Markelov sat down in one of the armchairs. But Rostovsky didn't take the other seat; Markelov watched as he took his drink and went to sit behind the desk.

"Well. How are you, Volodya?"

Rostovsky avoided Markelov's eyes. "There's somebody who wants to see you. He should have been here by now."

"Oh?"

87

"Alexander, you're in deep trouble. I've been trying to keep it away from you, but now—"

"The organs?" Who else would it be? Markelov thought.

Rostovsky was spared answering by the sound of the door opening. Markelov half-turned in his chair to look behind him. A tall man with a smoothly shaven pink face was already in the room. He closed the door. Rostovsky, who customarily would have been outraged by an unannounced entry, didn't say anything.

"Academician Rostovsky," the man said, crossing the office and sitting down in the chair that Rostovsky usually occupied. "This is Citizen Markelov? If I can *use* the word citizen?"

"I am," Markelov said. What have I got to lose now? he thought. "Who are you?"

"That's none of your business. I've been investigating your professional behavior. Tell him, Academician Rostovsky." He took one of the glasses from the small table and poured a liberal dollop of brandy into it.

The humanities director picked up a brass letter opener and began fiddling with it, keeping his eyes on the desk. Markelov took a sip of his brandy. He felt distanced from all this, as though he were watching a poor production of a badly written play. I ought to be feeling sorry for poor Volodya, he thought. But I don't. He's going to knuckle under. What else can he do?

"Academician Markelov," Rostovsky said, still without raising his eyes, "my department has come to the conclusion that your services are no longer required. Your position here at the university is terminated as of tomorrow morning."

"On what grounds?" Markelov asked evenly. I

88

may be an old man, he thought, but I'm not going to let them walk over me.

"Grounds?" snapped the KGB man. "You wonder about grounds? Do you think we'll let someone who raises his children to be murderers and Western provocateurs go on teaching decent Soviet youth? Infecting them with the same diseased ideas you spread in your own family? Zionism? Anti-Leninist slander and bourgeois Jewish nationalism? You should never even have gotten into a university, let alone wormed your way as far in this one as you have. We're going to find out who helped you do it." He looked over at Rostovsky, who turned a shade paler. "There are diseased elements all through this place, and they're going to be rooted out."

"In short," Markelov said to Rostovsky, "they want all the Jews kicked out of the university and you're not going to lift a finger to stop them."

"Please believe me," Rostovsky said with an air of desperation, finally looking up at Markelov. There was torment in the man's eyes. "It's for the good of the faculty. You can't stay on. Maybe it's not your fault what you made of your sons, but we can't have you here any more."

"For the good of the faculty," Markelov repeated. "Are you going to console yourself with that, Volodya, when they come for you in the middle of the night?"

"That's more anti-Soviet slander," said the KGB man. "Don't think it'll be forgotten. Get rid of him, Academician Rostovsky. Right now."

Rostovsky seemed to collapse inwardly. "Go and clean out your desk," he said. "We'll need your office in the morning."

"But all my books and papers," said Markelov,

89

the full impact only now beginning to hit him. "I can't get them all out by tomorrow—"

"You're not taking *anything* with you," said the KGB man. "You're not entitled to any of it, the way you've behaved. Stay away from your office. Any personal things, we'll send them to you. Perhaps. Just leave."

"Volodya," Markelov said. The nearly completed manuscript of his book on Pushkin was in the bottom drawer of his desk. He had been working on it for six years.

"There's nothing I can do," said Rostovsky. "You'd better go."

Markelov got up, taking his coat from the rack and pulling it slowly over his shoulders. "What they've made you do to yourself, Volodya. What they've made you do."

"Shut your filthy mouth," the KGB man said, "and get out."

He left without closing the door behind him. As he passed through the outer office he saw Vera looking sideways at him, wearing a smug grin she wasn't even trying to hide. He wanted to strike her.

Out in the corridor, he stopped, paralyzed, for a moment unable to take another step. Longing for his two lost sons flooded through him. Sasha he could never see again, not even visit his grave. Valeri was a ghost somewhere in that spectral limbo that was the nation of the labor camps.

My son, my son, Markelov thought, *Valeri my son, where are you now?*

90

East of Moscow
March 20

THE INTERIOR of the KGB van smelled of metal and disinfectant. Valeri Markelov sat on the steel bench on the right side of the prisoner compartment, listening to the hum of the tires on pavement. A dim bulb glowed behind a heavy steel mesh in the van's roof. Its light struck dull reflections from the metal shackles around Valeri's wrists.

Across from Valeri, Lev shifted his feet. His leg irons clinked. Beside Lev, Yuri was sitting with his head tilted against the metal side of the van, his eyes closed. Nina, the fourth person in the compartment, was on the right-hand bench with Valeri. They were all Valeri's friends, the inner circle that had helped distribute his writing despite the persecution by the authorities, and they were all Jews. They had been sentenced just before he had, and had been in solitary confinement in Lefortovo Prison ever since. He hadn't known anything more than the fact of their arrests and convictions—thirty years each—until a couple of hours ago, about 5:00 A.M. as nearly as he could judge, when the guards had taken him down to the prison courtyard and put him into the van.

91

The other three had already been in it. They'd talked for the first hour on the road, but all of them were too weak and dispirited to converse much longer than that. Lev and Yuri had been heavily interrogated even after their convictions and their faces were bruised and puffed. Nina hadn't been touched, physically, but she was very withdrawn.

Valeri felt numb; the fatigue and the cold were taking their toll. The van's compartment was unheated and the four prisoners wore only the rough prison clothes. Valeri's feet and hands felt like slabs of ice; his manacles and leg irons were so cold they burned.

They hadn't been told where they were being taken, but the van must be well away from Moscow by now. Valeri knew that there was a labor camp a hundred kilometers or so to the city's east, but it was for common criminals, not political detainees. He hoped that wasn't where they were going. Politicals had a very hard time in a criminal camp. Sometimes the authorities put them there on purpose.

He stopped thinking about it and began to compose a poem in his head. He had already decided how he was going to spend his years in the camps: he would compose at least one volume of poetry in his head, and memorize it. Then, when they let him out—if they ever did, if he even could survive thirty years—he could start right in again.

The van swayed; it was turning. It went on along for five minutes or so at a lower speed, the road surface much rougher now, and then slowed still more. The four in the compartment stirred; wherever they were going, they had almost arrived.

The van stopped. After a brief pause, Valeri heard the rattle of the door being unlocked. It opened, ad-

92

mitting a gust of clean icy air that smelled of pine needles. Behind the van was a black Chaika. Two men were getting out of it.

"Outside," said the guard who had unlocked the door. Valeri followed the others out into the road; they all moved clumsily because of the leg irons. There was fresh snow on the road—it was more of a track, really—and the flakes sifted into his prison clogs. The road lay between a stand of pines and a grove of leafless birches. The sun would be up shortly; the eastern horizon was banded orange-red. Where the light reached it between the trees, the snow was tinged with pink.

There was no sign of a camp gateway.

Valeri felt his knees weaken for a moment. There wasn't going to be a camp. What was about to be done, would be done here. He looked at Nina. She had realized. Even in the dim early light he could see that her eyes were wide with fear. Yuri and Lev were turned away from him; he couldn't see their faces.

There were the two guards from the van and the two men in plainclothes from the Chaika. One of the latter walked up to Valeri. It was the KGB colonel who had conducted Valeri's interrogation in the weeks before the trial.

"I hope you're satisfied," said the colonel. "You just wouldn't shut up, would you? Now your friends are going to pay for your stupidity. What do you think of that? Eh?"

Valeri didn't say anything. He was watching the way the dawnlight illuminated the trunks of the birch trees. It would be difficult to get that effect properly into words.

"Line them up," said the colonel.

The KGB guards from the van used their pistols

to prod Nina, Yuri and Lev to the edge of the road, facing the woods. Then they and the second man from the Chaika stood behind the prisoners.

Lev said, "This is illegal. We were sentenced to prison." His voice shook.

"Be quiet," the colonel said. "We can't waste space on the likes of you, *Zhid.*" He turned to Valeri. "You. Watch. See what you've done."

Valeri felt as though he were somewhere else, not here.

"Get rid of them," said the colonel.

The KGB men placed the muzzles of their pistols at the base of the prisoners' skulls. There were three dry, flat snaps. Nina and Yuri and Lev pitched forward into the snow, as though all their joints had suddenly dissolved.

The man who had shot Nina hadn't aimed properly; she was moving her arms about and making sounds like a cat's mew. He turned her over with the tip of his boot, leaned, and shot her between the eyes. The movements and the sounds ended.

Valeri felt a small hard pressure on the back of his neck. The colonel was behind him.

"It's good enough for you, too," the colonel said, and the world stopped.

Damascus, Syria
March 21

IT WAS EVENING, just after the sunset prayer. The street in front of the Suq al-Hamadieh was almost deserted, the torrent of battered Mercedes taxis and three-wheeled Isuzu delivery trucks evaporated. The entrance to the ancient bazaar was empty of its crowds of gesticulating touts and money changers and their customers, all gone to ground until the fighting ended.

And it will end soon, thought the old man wearing the fawn *galabiyeh,* as he waited in the shadows a dozen meters from the gates of the bazaar. Now that most of the army was in revolt against President Assad, the victory of the Muslim Brotherhood was certain. Within days there would be an Islamic religious government in Syria, one that would assume the banner of Islam's revival from war-exhausted Iran.

He watched the *suq* entrance for another moment, drawing the folds of his robe closer, head cocked, listening to the intermittent rattle of gunfire to the northeast, where the Syrian Officers' Club and the Armed Forces General Headquarters lay. Finally, satisfied with what he heard, he adjusted the checked

95

headband of his *kaffiyeh*, pulling it down to his eyebrows, almost to the top of his long straight nose. It was a perfectly characteristic Arabic nose, for which he had been grudgingly grateful the last four decades. On another continent, it could perhaps have been set between a pair of cold blue Aryan eyes. His eyes, however, were not blue. They were a deep brown, as brown as his now thin gray hair had been nearly half a century ago, before his time in the furnaces of the Russian Front.

The government troops hadn't got around to sealing the entrance to the *suq*. Sloppy, sloppy, the old man thought. In Russia we always secured the public areas first. They never learn. Fortunately.

He was now in the *suq*'s main covered way, its rusted iron roof black above the ancient worn stones of the paving. Normally the *suq* was thick with buyers and the sellers, the booths and goods rammed together in indescribable confusion: feather boas, Tabriz carpets, silver tea trays, Bedouin and Turkish embroidery, cheap plastic bowls nested together, electronic calculators, old tables inlaid with mother-of-pearl, lacquered stools, blond wigs on white plastic heads like ancient trophies decapitated in a forgotten war, chessboards in ebony and ivory, attar of roses or jasmine in bottles that, judging from their film of dust, were shaped in the last days of the Ottoman Empire. Not now, though; only a few hardier or more optimistic merchants were still in place, waiting for fortune to drop a little trade into their laps. One of them, the owner of a display of cheap glassware and a meagre collection of pottery jugs, had established himself a couple of meters from the alley of the woodworkers. He was smoking a *nargileh*, the water in the pipe's belly bubbling softly.

"Greetings," said the old man, in Arabic. He had long ago ceased thinking in German.

The merchant took the *nargileh*'s silver mouthpiece from his lips. "Two greetings to you," he returned. "Why have you come, in such troubled days?"

"There is no trouble when one goes in the sight of God," replied the old man.

"God is great," the merchant said. "Pass, and peace be with you."

"And with you, peace," said the old man. He went on, to the alley entrance; the merchant guarding the entranceway returned to his *nargileh*.

Inside the alley there was even less light, and the old man twice stumbled on broken paving. The narrow carpenters' shops lining the alley appeared deserted, but the old man thought they were likely not; not, at least, if the lessons he had taught for years had been learned.

The end of the alley was sealed by a heavy wooden door bound with iron. He knocked three times, then three more. After a moment the ancient lock grated and the door swung open. He passed by the guard into the courtyard, where desiccated vines drooped from the walls and the crumbling balconies. At the far end of the court was another doorway, this one arched and carved with half-obliterated arabesques. The door under the arch was open; beyond it the old man could see the glimmer of a kerosene lantern.

Inside the room was a splintered wooden table, which held the lamp; in one corner, next to the door leading deeper into the house, stood an unlit charcoal stove. Four decaying cane chairs were arranged around the table. The old man ignored the chairs and squatted on the paving next to the courtyard entrance. Outside, the light was fading rapidly. He could still hear gunfire from the northeast, but here

97

it was muted. He was feeling better now; for the moment the pain in his belly had gone. The doctor had said it would get worse and more frequent before the end, but the end was six months away. Time enough.

He waited for perhaps five minutes. Then the interior door swung open and Khalil Dirouzi came through it. The head of the Muslim Brotherhood's Inner Council was about sixty, with a seamed face and a short gray beard. The gray *galabiyeh* he wore hung from his shoulders like a shroud.

The old man stood up and bowed slightly.

Dirouzi said, "Good evening, Selim Youssef."

The old man had carried that name for nearly half a century, but even now the resentment coiled and uncoiled deep within him, the cold small voice so familiar he was hardly conscious of it any longer, the one that spoke in German: *Ich heisse Hans Gerhard Foerster, Standartenfuehrer, Waffen-SS, Division Totenkopf.*

"Good evening," he said. Despite his long association with the Brotherhood, he had to be careful with Dirouzi. He had to admit that the Syrian was fearsomely competent, and equally ruthless. Foerster had been on much better terms with Dirouzi's predecessor Nazem Saleh, who had recognized the young German's planning ability back in 1949, shortly after Foerster arrived in Damascus with nothing but the clothes he stood in and a money belt containing gold coins and six flawless diamonds. The coins and jewels had been provided by the SS escape organization Odessa, together with a list of pro-German contacts in the Syrian capital.

Saleh had been the first contact on the list. At that time, the Syrian Brotherhood and the Muslim world in general were trying to comprehend the catastrophe of their defeat in the first Arab-Israeli war, and

98

anyone who had fought against the Jews and Zionists—particularly an ex-SS officer—was a valuable resource. For Foerster, the Brotherhood was the means by which he could continue his pursuit of the Jews. He and Saleh had formed an alliance that had lasted more than forty years, ending only with Saleh's death two years earlier. Under Saleh's tutorship Foerster had converted to Islam, and the conversion and his ability had in their turn admitted him into the Inner Council of the Brotherhood, of which Saleh had long been the head. Over the years, Foerster and Saleh had conceived and then elaborated the plan that Foerster had dubbed, in German, in the old military nomenclature of the Third Reich, *Fall Zion*.

Even Saleh had eventually begun to use the German code name as had others of the Brotherhood, all of them fascinated by the concept in its audacity and grim patience. *Fall Zion*'s essence had been expressed in three directives Saleh and Foerster had written as early as 1954. Even now, if he closed his eyes and remembered carefully, Foerster could see the words tapping themselves across the page in the ancient typewriter, under the shadeless flyspecked light bulb in the cellar room. They were still young then, and Foerster had tried to make the pages look as official as he could:

FALL ZION

1) The Muslim Brotherhood will take whatever measures are necessary to establish a godly Islamic government in Syria.
2) As soon as this is accomplished, the full strength of the Brotherhood will turn against the Zionist entity in Palestine, and obliterate it.
3) Upon the destruction of the Zionist entity, the

99

Brotherhood will draw under the rule of Islamic law, by peaceful means or by *jihad* as necessary, all Muslim peoples, thereby reuniting and reestablishing the House of Islam under God.

The executing of *Fall Zion* was far more difficult than stating it, as both Foerster and Saleh had realized from the beginning. It was not until many years later that Foerster conceived the last and most audacious development of the plan.

He and Saleh had often discussed the possibility of using nuclear weapons against the Zionists. When the Iraqis had begun to construct their Osirak reactor, it appeared that at last an Islamic bomb was a possibility. Then Israeli warplanes had destroyed the complex, and it was obvious (at least to Foerster) that the Jews would never permit the construction of such a device. That left the one ultimate solution to the problem: the Brotherhood would have to steal nuclear weapons.

Having decided that much, and with the approval of Saleh and the Inner Council, Foerster set to work. After considerable thought and reading, he decided that the minimum number of devices required was two: one for Tel Aviv and one for Haifa. That would destroy most of the Israelis' industrial and service infrastructure, with a good half-million dead Jews thrown in for good measure.

The next problem was to determine what sort of weapon was best tailored to these targets. Foerster submerged himself for several months in reference books and declassified American military documents, and eventually identified what he needed. The most likely warhead for his purpose was the Type W33, an early-model weapon that would be easier to arm and fuse than the later, more sophisticated devices. Each one had a maximum yield of twelve kilotons, a little less than that of the Hiroshima bomb.

Having chosen his weapon, Foerster began looking about for a supply of them disposed in a vulnerable location. To his incredulous delight, there was such a supply almost on his doorstep.

The overconfident Americans had stationed W33 warheads in Turkey, in the form of loads for 203mm artillery shells. If Turkish military men could be recruited over time into the Brotherhood and placed in the right positions, the destruction of Israel would be within reach of Foerster and the Brotherhood. The major technical problem had been to find someone who could bypass the safety devices that prevented unauthorized arming of the bombs, so that they could be detonated; but Foerster had found a solution even to that difficulty. Saleh had been delighted with the German over that.

But Foerster privately had no particular interest in Islamic fundamentalist aspirations except as they served his purpose against the Jews. Saleh had been a convenient tool to hand; with the Syrian's help and with the Odessa gold and diamonds, Foerster had established himself in Damascus as a fairly prosperous import-export agent. President Assad's *Muchabarat,* Syrian Intelligence, had known him from early on to be German (and a former SS officer), but they had never shown any inclination to hand him over to the West, perhaps on the principle that their enemy's enemy was their brother. This attitude Foerster had judiciously reinforced by putting his agency at the *Muchabarat*'s disposal for the overseas equipping of anti-Zionist terrorist teams, providing pipelines for arms, explosives, documents and useful equipment. This afforded him a certain wry

101

amusement, since his contacts with the *Muchabarat* had from time to time given him information which could be used by the Syrian Brotherhood against the Assad regime.

Foerster did wish, however, that Saleh had picked a more opportune time to die. With his death, people suddenly remembered that Selim Youssef was a German, a Westerner and, whatever his appearance or his words, a convert not born in the faith.

But I still have time, Foerster thought, studying Dirouzi's face in the clear yellow lamplight, although I am ill. A few months perhaps, and the Jewish scab will be peeled from the face of the earth.

"You wished to see me?" Foerster asked. He was, despite his elation at the Brotherhood victory and what it meant for Israel, somewhat uneasy over Dirouzi's summons. At this critical time the Brotherhood leader ought to be at the secret operations headquarters deep in the labyrinth of the *suq*.

"I did. You know that we are going to win."

"Yes."

"You have been with the Brotherhood for many years. When we were poor and untrained in war you helped us. Saleh chose wisely in you."

"I was unworthy of his consideration," Foerster said. "He was as a father to me."

"And to all of us," Dirouzi said. "But as times change, so must we all change. God permits change, insofar as the prescripts of the Holy *Qu'ran* are not transgressed."

"God is great," Foerster said shortly. "All is as God wills, although we do not always see the design." Dogs, he thought. Swine. I know what you are going to say. Arabs. How I've labored for years to use them, suffering their incompetence, their in-

102

decision, their miserable whining Islam. And now this, the weapon breaks in my hands.

"Yes," said Dirouzi. "You have learned our faith well. It is for this reason that I am sure you will understand the decision of the Inner Council. We believe that the Zionists are better defeated by blood and courage, rather than by the devil-inspired weapons of the Christians."

Foerster kept his face quite still. "I understand. The Council has elected not to carry out the second directive of *Fall Zion*." He was seething inwardly, thinking: So much preparation, so much planning, and now Dirouzi and the Council are drawing back from the brink. Why can they never carry out anything to its end? As we would have done, could have done forty years ago with the Jews, if only we'd had a little more time. I am perhaps the last of the real SS, all the others dead now or surrendered. I am the only one still fighting to rid the world of the Jewish vermin. Only I have not given up.

"You understand?"

"Yes," Foerster said. "Might I ask why?"

"It risks the destruction of the Syrian Brotherhood and the revolution. If we were to use such weapons against the Zionists, they would use their own against us. God says that we must wait until it is correct to drink, although the cup may take a thousand years to fill. We would be denying the will of God if we were to carry out what you have planned."

"I see," Foerster said. Without warning, the pain in his abdomen slashed at him again. Accompanying it, as though his mind echoed his body's paroxysm, came the hatred and with it the killing urge, the craving that he had been able to satisfy only a little in the Dachau camp, driving the Jews into the gas

103

chambers, seeing them afterward twisted and blue from the cyanide. As he would like to see Dirouzi now, as he would like to see everyone—into the ovens, the clean fire. Fire. Burn the world, he thought through the pain. I am the last of the Reich that you thought you had destroyed. But not quite destroyed. I will burn you all. I will.

He took a short breath and said, "It is as God wills."

"Yes," Dirouzi said. "The Council also feels that your long services deserve the reward of a restful age. For this reason, we are releasing you from further responsibilities to the Council. It will not be necessary for you to serve as adviser to further meetings."

"The Council is merciful in its regard for a tired servant," Foerster said. "I will use the time to study the blessed *Qu'ran* and prepare my mind for God."

"God is great," Dirouzi said, standing up. "I must go. The protection of God be upon you."

"And upon you," Foerster responded. "In the sight of God, nothing is forgotten."

Dirouzi nodded and left the room. Foerster stood, looking into the incandescent heart of the lamp-flame.

No, he thought. It is not over yet.

Maryland
April 2

MEGAN STARED through the venetian blinds of Cole's kitchen window, down across the sweep of lawn to the river and the empty quay. A shingle had loosened on the boathouse roof and the wind slapped it up and down, up and down; the wind had been growing steadily worse for the past hour. The day had been sunny until late afternoon, when she'd left work to drive down to the bay with Griffin, but by the time she had reached the lane to the house the sky had filled with low hurrying clouds out of the northeast: outriders of a violent spring storm.

She remembered the kettle she was holding, turned from the window, and plugged it in to boil. While the water heated, she picked up Sam's note from the table and read it for at least the eighth time.

Six A.M.—Dearest Megan, a beautiful morning. I tried to get you at home but no answer. Going out in *Whiskeyjack* for the day, back about four this afternoon. I left cold meat and cheese

105

in the fridge. Will fix us something better when
I get back,

> Love,
> S.

She must have been in the shower when he called;
she was an early riser. She looked at the clock on
the stove. Ten to six. Twelve hours later than his
call. Too early to get worried, although she always
did when he went out alone.

She looked out the kitchen window again. Griffin,
curled underneath the table, thumped his tail half-
heartedly on the floor; he didn't like storms and
hadn't eaten much of his supper. "It's all right, old
friend," she told him. "I won't let it get you."

The wind was really savage now, piling even the
sheltered river into waves that snapped at the boat
quay in curtains of spray. She remembered Aberystwyth on the Welsh coast where she had gone to
university: the great storm rollers would pound in
from Saint George's Channel and Cardigan Bay,
hammering at the land as though they would devour
it whole. Megan knew enough of the sea to know it
was no one's friend; it had swallowed whole fleets,
harbors, cities, great liners, warships and fishing
schooners. It could erase you in minutes, without
passion or intention.

But Sam was a careful sailor. He would have
checked the marine weather forecasts before he left;
he wouldn't get caught in a nor'easter if he could
help it, especially on a lee shore.

Which was where he'd be, in this weather, if he
were still out on the Atlantic, outside the bay.

The water bubbled in the kettle. Megan made coffee, and then sipped at it at the kitchen window,
peering around the window frame to look down-

106

river. The wind was beginning to carry rain. For a moment she thought she could see *Whiskeyjack*'s slender hull at the river's bend, but when she blinked the illusion was gone. Wishful thinking.

There was no denying it, she was worried about him. Not only because he was alone in a small boat out on an ocean ripped by a northeast gale, but also because of the way he'd been acting in the last few weeks. He'd been having mood swings she'd never seen in him before: sometimes euphoria, as though he had been relieved of some tremendous emotional stress, and then long spells of silence, as though he were contemplating . . . she didn't know what. Occasionally she suspected he was frightened about something, although never having seen him frightened of anything before, she could not use past experience to judge. If he *was* frightened, he didn't talk about it, and her efforts to get him to do so had been fruitless.

Damn the man anyway, she thought. Damn men in general. They persuade you to worry about them, and then they go off and do whatever it is they want to do, even if it's stupid and dangerous. And then they expect you to wait for them and meet them with a happy contented smile and fall right into their arms when they finally do come back. Self-absorbed, men. Completely self-absorbed.

The clock in the hall chimed six. She went into the living room with her coffee and turned on the big multiband radio. Griffin trailed disconsolately behind her, nails tick-tacking on the polished hall floor. The wind was rattling the windowpanes now. Sam had a barograph on a table in the corner next to the fireplace, with a windspeed and direction indicator next to it. The barograph trace showed the

107

pressure still dropping and the wind up to fifty knots in the gusts, dead out of the northeast.

She knelt in front of the fireplace and laid a fire while she waited for the marine forecast to come on the radio. When it did come, it was worse than she had expected, even with the evidence of Sam's instruments: small boat warning, force eight winds. *Whiskeyjack* was a good sea boat, she knew, capable of surviving a full storm. But an accident that would be no more than a nuisance in good weather could be fatal under storm conditions. A snapped backstay and the mast overboard, a weakened lifeline or rudder pintle, a split hatch cover; any number of other catastrophes.

The marine forecast ended. She lit the fire, flames licking up around the kindling and split maple logs' orange light flickering through the long room, gleaming on the brass barrel of the little starter's cannon that had belonged to Sam's father.

The daylight was almost gone. Megan closed the drapes over the veranda and side windows, considered for a moment, and then opened the sideboard. She poured herself a Hennessey and returned to the fireplace, where she stretched out in one of the chairs and swung her legs onto the ottoman. The dog curled up on the floor beside her and she absent-mindedly reached over the arm of the chair to scratch his ears. "Where's that Sam Cole then, Griffin?" she asked him. She sipped the brandy. "What do you think we should do, eh?"

Call the coast guard and ask for a search? No, not when he was only two hours overdue. They wouldn't say as much, but they'd think she was a panicky female. They might be right. She thought about the generations of women on the coasts of both sides of the Atlantic who had watched their men go off to

108

sea in the whalers and brigantines and the great clipper ships, knowing they'd be gone for three or four or five years, or maybe more, or maybe forever. And she was worrying about a couple of hours.

Still . . .

She reached out to the radio and found an FM station broadcasting music. The fire warmed her calves and feet nicely; the cognac was doing the same for her insides.

Sam, she thought, what am I going to do about you? About us? A few months ago I thought this was going to be permanent. Now I'm not sure. I don't know if I can stay with you, the way you're becoming. It all looks so good from the outside. . . . You're intelligent, charming, you seem to be able to do anything you decide to put your hand to. You're a wonderful lover, gentle, passionate. But just now you're not *there,* not the way you used to be. You've gone away somewhere. Is it because you're tired of me, and you don't want to hurt me by saying it? Don't you understand how that thought makes me draw back, which makes you draw back more. . . .

Sam, where in the name of God *are* you? How am I going to get through the night? I love you, damn it, is that going to be the worse for me? What will I do if I lose you?

Perhaps I'll call the coast guard anyway, let them think I'm a stupid panicky woman. But Sam's careful. He could ride out a storm in *Whiskeyjack,* if he had enough sea room. What did he tell me, once? There are old sailors, and bold sailors, but there are very few old, bold sailors. He'll be back tomorrow.

She realized she had finished the cognac. She put the glass on the table next to the radio. It was playing something by Telemann.

In a moment, she thought, I'll get up and make

109

some soup and a sandwich. I haven't eaten since noon.

Her eyes closed.

They opened again, suddenly, some indefinite time later. Music still played on the radio but the fire had burned down to dull streaks of orange, and the far end of the living room was in shadow. She could make out the circle of the brass ship's chronometer mounted there, but not the time its hands displayed. The wind was howling now, and the rain on the windows sounded like machine-gun fire. She looked at her watch.

Midnight. Griffin was asleep on the hearth rug.

Could he have come home and gone straight upstairs to bed? No, he'd have smelled the fire and at least checked to see whether she was in the living room.

"Griffin?" she said. "Where's Sam? Where is he?" The dog looked at her, ears pricked up. "He's not here, is he?"

She climbed stiffly out of the chair and went out to the kitchen. Rain pounded at the windows in great slats. The switch for the dock floodlights was by the back door; she pressed it and went to the kitchen window. The boathouse and the dock were barely visible in the driving rain, but she could see enough to be certain that *Whiskeyjack* and Cole hadn't returned.

He's still out there somewhere. Sam, what have you done? She shivered.

The telephone was on the wall by the kitchen table. Posted next to it was a list of numbers, including the local coast guard station's. She stabbed at the buttons, fingers clumsy with anxiety.

110

"Coast guard. Lieutenant Harrison speaking."

"My name is Megan Thomas. A friend of mine and his boat are overdue. He's in a thirty-six-foot cutter and I'm afraid he may be in trouble outside the bay. He was supposed to be back late this afternoon."

"What's the name and registration, Ms. Thomas?"

She told him. A short silence.

"We've logged no distress calls on Mr. Cole's registration. Could he have put in somewhere else?"

"He would have called me."

"We'll post him as overdue and alert our patrol cutters. Was Mr. Cole alone in the boat?"

"Yes."

"Is he an experienced sailor?"

"Yes. Very. He's single-handed to the Caribbean several times."

"Okay. I'll get this on the radio immediately."

"What's the weather like out there?"

"It's not good, Ms. Thomas. But if he's experienced and has enough sea room, he'll likely be okay. Give me the number where you're staying and I'll call you as soon as we have something."

She did, listening to the wind beat at the eaves. "Thank you."

"You're welcome, Ms. Thomas. If he's still overdue by first light, we'll start a search. Try not to worry."

"All right. Thank you."

She rang off and looked around the kitchen, not really seeing it. I have to live one minute at a time until I hear something, she thought. Behave normally. But I'm so tired. Oh, God, where is he?

I should go to bed properly.

She moved slowly out of the kitchen, Griffin awake

111

now and following. But instead of going directly upstairs, she wandered through the ground floor of the house for perhaps ten minutes, aimlessly touching knickknacks, stroking things that Sam had touched. Eventually she found herself back in the living room. The radio was hardly audible over the beat of the rain. She sat down again, staring into space for some time before she realized that, despite her anxiety, she was hungry.

In the kitchen she heated soup and nibbled at crackers and cheddar cheese. Griffin sat up for a piece of cheese, looking at her wistfully, but still showing little interest in the food in his bowl.

The telephone remained silent. When she had finished eating she washed her dishes, dried them, put them away, and went back to the living room. Perhaps she should try to read.

She hunted through the bookcase for a few minutes and then decided to put the books in alphabetical order by author. It was a large bookcase, and the task took her nearly an hour. The book she had given to Sam, the one she had written on pre-Roman Celtic art, was among the volumes. She took it back to her chair and began to leaf through it, surprised again that she'd been able to put so many, and such authoritative, words on paper. It was as though someone else had written it.

Eventually she dozed off, the book open on her lap. Griffin stretched full length on his belly on the hearth rug, head between front paws, brown eyes open in the half-light. His ears flicked at each gust of wind.

The telephone woke her. Gray light was filtering through the curtains; the brass chronometer showed

112

ten past eight. She couldn't tell whether she had slept or not, although she must have, for the dawn to have come without her being aware of it. She scrambled groggily out of the chair and reached the hall telephone on the fourth ring.

"Hello?"

"Ms. Megan Thomas?"

"Speaking."

"This is Lieutenant Harrison, coast guard. You called me last night."

"Yes." They haven't found him, she thought. I don't know how I know it, but I know.

"I'm afraid I have some bad news, although it may be less serious than it appears. One of our patrol vessels picked up some wreckage at first light. A life ring and a smashed hatch cover, some cabin seat cushions. The name on the life ring is *Whiskeyjack*. I'm sorry to have to tell you this."

"That's . . . all right." She felt utterly numbed, anesthetized. How this will hurt later, she thought.

"Did *Whiskeyjack* carry a life raft?"

"Yes. Yellow, inflatable, with a shelter."

"Our cutter didn't find it. Mr. Cole may be aboard it, and quite safe. We'll get search planes up as soon as possible. But the visibility out there is very poor."

"Thank you."

"Would it be possible for you to come down to the station and identify the items we've picked up, when the cutter brings them in?"

"Yes. Let me know when."

"Don't give up hope. We find most people."

"Yes." She hung up. Griffin sat at her feet, sensing her mood, and gave her a baleful look. Sam, Sam, she thought. Why did you do this? Why couldn't you have thought, just a little, about me?

113

She knelt to pat Griffin, taking comfort in the dog's presence. Then, suddenly and without warning, she began to cry; not weeping, but great agonizing sobs that wrenched at her chest and abdomen. "Oh, Griff. What are we going to do if he's gone? What are we going to do without Sam?"

Aleppo, Syria
April 4

IT WAS ALREADY very late afternoon, the tiny court-yard's western wall long fallen into shadow with the sun's passage. In the center of the courtyard stood a fountain, its dry basin scattered with small almond-shaped leaves from the vine that grew along an over-head trellis. Near the fountain, under the trellis, was a low stone bench, on which Dalia Stein had been seated for the past hour, waiting.

She pulled back the sleeve of her black *galabiyeh* to look at her watch again. Mustafa should have ar-rived long before now. For the last hour she had been worrying that the Brotherhood Revolutionary Government might suddenly impose another cur-few. One had been proclaimed just after the Islamic Revolution against the Assad regime succeeded, but it had been lifted the day before. If there were a curfew she'd have to delay moving Gabriel out for another twenty-four hours. That could be disas-trous; the pickup zone wouldn't remain secure in-definitely, and she hated the thought of having to use the overland route.

Mustafa, she thought, *where are you?*

115

The rapping at the heavy wooden door separating the courtyard from the alleyway made her start. She listened. The code was the correct one, the staccato Morse S-S-S. Dalia picked up the light Scorpion submachine gun from the bench beside her and went to unfasten the barred door. As soon as it was free she stepped back against the wall, on the hinge side. The door swung open, then closed with a deep *thud*. The man she knew as Mustafa turned around very slowly to face her. She lowered the muzzle of the Scorpion.

"I wish you wouldn't do that," he said in Arabic. His native language was Hebrew, but he spoke Arabic flawlessly. As part of the Mossad network in northern Syria, he had lived in Aleppo for nearly twenty years. He was one of the few originals left.

She pushed the veil away from her face. "I'm still alive," she pointed out, in the same tongue. "What's happened?"

Mustafa studied her for a moment; it was the first time he'd had a chance to get a good look at her. If he had not known she was Israeli, he would probably have taken her to be an unusually attractive Syrian woman: the almond-shaped dark eyes and full mouth and high cheekbones framed by waves of heavy black hair. He thought she was about thirty-four or -five.

He rammed the heavy bar back across the door. "They were delayed. There were Revolutionary Guard checkpoints on the road near Hamah. Ibrahim had to go around another way. He's bringing Gabriel here now, in the Toyota."

"We've no time to spare," she said. "I may not be able to extract him tonight if we're not at the wadi by two. And I have to get him to Ankara as quickly as possible."

116

"I know," he said. "Let me find my kit and we're gone."

He headed quickly into the safe house. Dalia pulled the *galabiyeh* up to her waist, clipped the Scorpion onto its sling, and dropped the hem back around her ankles. As she knelt to adjust a sandal strap, her hands quivered a little. She knew that once they were moving she would be calm, but at the moment she was frightened again. She forced the fear down into the place in her mind she had made for it, where it coiled like a cold worm along with the nightmare. The nightmare hadn't come for months, until the night before she crossed into Syria. She had known it would.

Mustafa came out, carrying a squarish leather knapsack. "We'll leave by the alley," he said.

She picked up the canvas bag containing her identity papers and four extra clips for the Scorpion and slung it over her left shoulder. Mustafa unbarred the gate. "Wait," he said. "I'll go first."

A moment passed. "Now," he said, and she slipped under the lintel into the narrow passage between the limestone walls of the houses. Mustafa eased the door carefully into its heavy stone recess. "Down to the end," he said.

There, in a narrow side street, a dusty tan Toyota Land Cruiser was drawn up to the curb. Two spare tires were lashed to a rack on the roof and a hand winch was bolted to the front bumper. Brackets on the tailgate held jerry cans of fuel and water. Mustafa opened the passenger door and said to someone inside, "We have to go immediately."

A narrow, triangular face peered past Mustafa's shoulder. Ibrahim, she supposed, the one who had driven Gabriel up from Damascus. In the rear seat,

117

a man was rubbing a palm across his face, as though awakened from a deep sleep: Gabriel.

"Wait for me in the house," Mustafa said to Ibrahim. "The bar is off the gate."

Ibrahim got out of the Toyota and came around the hood. "I found enough petrol to fill the tank," he said. "I put a couple of cans in the racks too. And water. The blankets are still inside."

Mustafa turned to Dalia, who was still standing in the alleyway. "Come quickly. We have to go."

She crossed the narrow street and got into the Land Cruiser. As Mustafa started the engine, Dalia turned in her seat to look at the man from Damascus.

He was far from impressive at this moment, or perhaps at any other: a long, thin, hooked nose, receding chin, and large eyes set a little too close together under a narrow forehead.

"Gabriel?" she said.

"Yes." The voice did not seem to belong to the face: deep and round, resonant.

"I'm Dalia Stein. I'm getting you out tonight," she said. The Toyota started moving, jerking over the cobbles on its stiff springs. "Do you think anyone's looking for you?"

Gabriel rubbed his nose. "I don't believe so, not yet. The Revolutionary Government in Damascus is still getting organized. A lot of the old regime's people have gotten away." He produced a small wry smile, which accentuated his pointed features even more. "Including me."

He's calm enough, Dalia thought. Not surprising, if you're an Israeli mole in the Syrian defense ministry you get used to stress.

"Are you armed?" she asked.

He looked apologetic. "Not very well. A Beretta.

118

No stopping power.'' He patted the pocket of his suit jacket. ''I didn't have an opportunity to get anything heavier.''

It could have been worse. Mustafa was carrying a 9mm Browning pistol in a holster under his arm, and she had the Scorpion. ''Did Ibrahim give you the new identification?''

He nodded, touching his jacket over his heart. ''Right here. I burned the ministry papers.''

''Good.'' She grabbed at the dashboard handle for support as Mustafa pulled the Toyota around a corner. The Scorpion's ammunition clip prodded her in the stomach. Carrying the weapon under the *galabiyeh* was uncomfortable, but doing so kept it both out of sight and near to hand. She had only to draw her arms in through the robe's sleeves to be able to use the gun; she had cut a slit in the cloth about ten centimeters long just above waist level, so that the muzzle would clear the robe's fabric.

''How far to the pickup point?'' Gabriel asked.

''About a hundred kilometers,'' Dalia said, watching the narrow street in front. There was just enough pedestrian traffic to slow their progress; fortunately, no other vehicles disputed the right of way. ''The last leg is off the road. We have to do that after nightfall.''

''We ought to just make it,'' Mustafa said. ''If I can leave you by two, I'll be back on the road by dawn.''

Dalia nodded. Mustafa had been waiting for her when she'd arrived from crossing the Turkish-Syrian border the night before; it had taken a good three hours to negotiate the jagged terrain from the pickup point to the Aleppo road.

''How are we getting out?'' Gabriel asked. ''My

119

shoes won't stand much more. If we have to go across country. . . ."

"I'll tell you later," she said.

"Very well." He didn't sound insulted by her reticence.

Thirty minutes passed before Mustafa was able to get them onto the main road out of the city. After that they drove northeast for about a quarter of an hour. On either side of the highway the north Syrian steppe, not quite desert, dissolved away into the horizon. Low ridges of desiccated stone, slashed by the shadowy blue lines of wadis, materialized and faded beyond the telegraph poles that flickered into existence ahead of the Toyota and disappeared just as endlessly behind.

Dalia looked at her watch. "How are we?" Mustafa said.

"It's just after six-thirty."

He speeded up a little. "We need to make up some time. We'll have to slow down when we're going around El Bab, and Membij after that. Once we get off the road it'll be even slower. But we should make it. If we don't go through both spare tires. Or break an axle."

She turned to see what Gabriel was doing. He had fallen asleep, slumped sideways across the seat. "What?" Mustafa asked.

"He's sleeping."

"Let him. He'll have to be alert later on."

They drove across the plain without speaking. The yellow-brown landscape was turning ochre, the sun riding low on the horizon. There was very little traffic: some cars and a few light trucks, occasional military vehicles. Out here in the country, the Syrian Islamic Revolution might never have been.

Three kilometers short of the outskirts of El Bab,

120

Mustafa turned off the highway onto a dirt road and then took a series of rough tracks around the town. It was now quite dark. When they regained the main road he stopped to top up the fuel tank. When he had finished, he put his knapsack and a canteen on the front seat. Gabriel was still asleep.

"There's food in there," he said as he pulled back onto the road.

They ate disks of unleavened bread, hard goat cheese and olives as the Toyota's lights bored into the dark. Out on the horizon the moon was rising.

"I'll have to turn our lights off when we leave the main road," Mustafa said. "It's a good thing we'll have some moonlight."

A couple of kilometers passed; Dalia found she could get no more of the food down. She always found it hard to eat on an operation.

"I've had enough, too," Mustafa said.

She sensed him regarding her out of the corner of his eye. "How did you get into this business, anyway?" he asked.

"I worked for Mossad before I went into operations," she replied. "I speak a lot of languages. They thought I had potential. They needed women for this, as well as men. I accepted."

"What does your husband think of that? Of this?"

Always the assumptions, she thought. "My husband was in the army. But he died before I joined Mossad."

"Oh." A pause. "I'm sorry." Another pause. "You didn't remarry?"

"No."

"No children?"

"No."

But there *had* been a child, and suddenly the nightmare was back, images as vivid as the moonlit

121

landscape outside the windshield, as clear as they had been in reality eleven years ago in the wildlife sanctuary by the sea—hardly a sanctuary.

They had been on a picnic, she and Yaron (on leave from his unit) and eighteen-month-old Aviva, not very far from the shoreline. It was early evening, they were packing up to leave. Dalia had taken the picnic basket up to the car, which was parked on the access road in a grove of cedars. In another five minutes they would have been gone. (For years afterwards she had replayed the afternoon in her mind, imagining all the things she could have done, or not done, to gain those five minutes, those three hundred seconds beyond price). She had put the basket into the car, and started back down the wooded slope toward her husband and daughter. Perhaps a hundred meters away from the picnic site she heard Yaron's voice, raised angrily, and Aviva's wail, then silence.

She broke into a run, toward the voices. But in the clearing where they had eaten there was no one, only the picnic blanket in a heap and the carryall that held Aviva's bottles and diapers on its side spilling its contents onto the grass, the white folded cloths vivid in the fading light.

They've gone down to the beach, she thought. She had an agonizing stitch in her side but she ran on, not thinking of what she would do if she caught up with them.

The wooded area ended at the lip of a rocky slope that dropped steeply to a narrow beach of mixed shingle and sand. On the beach below Dalia, Yaron was kneeling, hands clasped over the back of his neck. A black-haired man in dirty camouflage clothing stood over him, a rifle pointed at his head. Another man was dragging a rubber raft toward the

122

low waves. A third held a struggling Aviva, palm clamped over the child's mouth. The surf was not high and the men's voices carried clearly.

"Put the whelp down," the man with the raft was snarling, in Arabic. "We haven't much time, *they're coming,* in the name of Allah!"

Palestinian guerillas, she thought, O my God, what am I to do? They'll take them away, away, away.

She was partly hidden by a tree trunk and they hadn't seen her. Frantically she looked for a weapon, a stone, a dead branch, anything. But there was nothing. *Soldiers,* she thought, *where are our soldiers?*

The man with the raft was having trouble, its bulging sides catching clumsily on the stones. The Palestinian guarding Yaron was looking north, up the beach. Suddenly he stiffened. "They've come!" he shouted hysterically. *"Hurry!"*

Dalia looked up the long curve of shingle. Five men, bent low, were racing toward the Palestinians, about three hundred meters away, combat boots pounding the sand, weapons ready.

O God, thank you, Dalia thought, O Lord of Israel, thank you.

The Palestinian with the raft dropped it, unslung his rifle, and fired a burst at the Israelis. Two soldiers threw themselves flat on the beach, the others kept coming, jinking back and forth. From the ground one of the Israelis fired a short burst. The raft hissed and began to collapse.

Then it happened, unbelievable, incomprehensible:

—The Palestinian behind Yaron centering the muzzle of his gun on Yaron's clasped hands.

123

—The Palestinian holding Aviva half-dropping her, but intentionally, to grasp her small ankles and feet in his dirty fists.

—The gun at Yaron's neck recoiling, again and again.

—Aviva swinging up, screaming, in a wide arc, above the Palestinian's head.

—Yaron thrown forward onto the small stones of the shingle, with his ruined head.

—Aviva's body curving down, down, gathering speed, the Palestinian swinging her with all his strength. The small dark head meeting the flat rock, the crack clearly audible over the surf's mutter, like the breaking of the world. The aching silence after the child's voice ended.

—And then the rip of the Israelis' weapons, too late, too late, the Palestinians cut down, rag-like, tumbling in heaps across Yaron and Aviva and the bloody stones.

She never was quite sure what happened immediately afterward, or of what passed during the following two months. When she regained herself to a degree, she still could not fathom the randomness of the attack. If either of them had been important people, it would have been different, there would have been a reason for them to be selected for murder. But the murders had been purposeless, reasonless. She and her family had simply been in the wrong place at the wrong time. Six months later, she had been recruited by Mossad, because of her language skills. She had later accepted operations work, not exactly for revenge, but on the principle that if the Palestinians came for her too one day, she'd at least have given them a reason for doing it.

124

"What's the matter?" Mustafa said. He was looking at her directly, eyes off the road.

She realized that she had been silent for a long time. "I'm fine," she said. "You'd better watch where we're going."

He looked at her doubtfully for an instant, then returned his attention to the road.

Gabriel woke up as they were approaching Membij. Dalia handed him the knapsack and canteen and he ate and drank without speaking. "How far?" he asked when he had finished.

"We're going to go around the town in front of us," Mustafa said. "Membij. We're heading for the hill country northeast of the town, across the river." He paused to look at the dashboard clock. "We should be there around eleven. *Insh'Allah.*"

The highway was now totally deserted. Mustafa took a set of almost invisible tracks past Membij, but instead of regaining the highway north of the town turned farther east. Half an hour later they reached a secondary road of pitted macadam, not much wider than the Toyota. The vehicle had ground along it for only a few minutes when Mustafa said, "Lights out," and flicked the switch.

Dalia was abruptly disoriented, especially since the Toyota was tilting steeply as Mustafa maneuvered it off the road into a dip.

"Can you see?" she asked.

"Well enough," Mustafa said. "The moon helps a little, but I've been up here before. Doing the same thing. We were moving people across this border twenty years ago. It's always leaked. Not even the Brotherhood's revolutionary government's going to stop that."

"Gabriel?" Dalia said, half-turning in her seat.

125

"You were on the inside, in Damascus. Will the Islamic government last?"

"I think so. The Brotherhood prepared the rebellion very well. Do you know what I was in, in the Syrian defense ministry?"

"No."

"Domestic counterintelligence. Just before Hafez Assad died I found out some things. The Brotherhood's had an adviser for a long time, a German, an old Nazi. We—I mean Syrian counterintelligence—thought he'd provided the Brotherhood with the organizational strength to do what they've just done."

"He must be dead and gone by now," said Dalia. Ahead of the Toyota a low ridge of pale stone glimmered in the moonlight.

"Apparently not," Gabriel said. "Apparently he's still alive. But Syrian security didn't have time to find him. They wanted him, badly, and in a hurry, though."

"Why?"

Instead of answering, Gabriel said urgently, "What's that?"

Dalia snapped around to look out the windshield. "Where?"

"Ahead, a little to the right. Beside that rockfall."

It was a blocky object, darker than the jumble of stone behind it, its details broken up and difficult to see in the wan moonlight. Mustafa let his foot off the accelerator and downshifted into lowest gear. "It's a truck," he said.

"What's a truck doing out here?" she asked. She felt her stomach muscles tighten and a soft flutter begin under her breastbone.

Mustafa said, "Somebody trying to get across the border, Assad's soldiers running from the Revolu-

126

tion, who knows? Whoever they are, we don't want to meet them."

The Toyota ground forward across a drift of loose shingle, the tires digging deep, the engine laboring. The black bulk of the truck drew nearer.

"I'm going to accelerate hard as soon as we're out of the gravel," Mustafa said. "Be ready."

Dalia clamped her left hand around the grab handle of the Toyota's dash. Behind her, she sensed Gabriel bracing himself.

"Look out!"

She was too late. The shadowy figures that had leaped from behind the truck must have been in position for several minutes; only one of them fired but his aim was good and he kept it to a four-round burst, aiming high to miss the Toyota's engine and radiator. The bullets smashed through the center of the windshield, spraying pebbles of smashed safety glass through the cab. The muzzle flashes were blinding.

She heard Mustafa curse in Arabic, then the engine kicking to a stop as the Toyota stalled. It took her several seconds to regain her night sight, and by that time her door had been wrenched open.

"Out! Out!"

A hand seized her upper arm and dragged her out of the cab. She stumbled and fell to one knee, skinning it even through the thick cloth of the *galabiyeh*. The Scorpion's muzzle jabbed cruelly into her breast. She stayed down for perhaps three seconds, just long enough to rearrange the weapon, and then slowly rose.

The man who had yanked her out of the Toyota was standing two meters away, the dim moonlight falling upon him. He was wearing Syrian army uniform and held a Russian AK-47, its muzzle pointing at her stomach. "Up," he said. "Your hands on your head."

She obeyed. On the other side of the Toyota she could hear scuffling sounds, and then two thuds in rapid succession, followed by a groan. "Out in front," the Syrian told her. His voice was brittle, with fear or anger or fatigue, or all three.

She walked obediently around the front fender of the Toyota. Mustafa was there, crouched, arms clenched across his stomach. Another Syrian was standing over him, his assault rifle loosely cradled, holding a black object in his left hand.

"He had a gun," the second man said. "He tried to get it out."

"Walid!" called the man who had dragged her out of the Toyota. From his tone she judged he was the leader.

A third soldier materialized from the fall of rocks ahead of the Syrians' truck. "Captain. Here."

They don't know about Gabriel, she thought. They didn't check the back seat. He's in there, waiting.

"What are they?" said the man standing over Mustafa.

"It doesn't matter," the Syrian captain said. "We need their machine."

"Captain," said the man from the rocks, "What if they're Brotherhood? One of them had a gun, maybe they were sent to look for us."

The captain was studying Dalia. In the robe, in the moonlight, she could have been old or young, male or female. Three of them, she thought. As it was, then, on the beach.

"Wait," he said. "You. Take off your *kaffiyeh.*"

Mustafa was still hunched on the stony earth. Without the gun he would be of little use, in any

128

case. Gabriel still had not moved. She thought: He's waiting until they're closer together. With the Beretta he can't do anything else.

She pulled back the headdress, exposing her dark hair.

"A woman," said the man from the rocks.

"A Brotherhood woman," said the man next to Mustafa. "Why else would they be out here, in the back country?"

Mustafa said, from his crouch, "Beloved Lords, believe me when I say we are like you. I am fleeing the Brotherhood. I am a vegetable merchant from Aleppo, and this is my wife. We are trying to reach the border before the Brotherhood madmen take us."

His intervention was startling, and the three Syrian soldiers switched their attention to Mustafa. Dalia drew her arms back into her sleeves. The Scorpion's ammunition clip had tangled in one of the folds of the heavy cloth; by the time she had cleared it the moment had passed.

"They're Brotherhood," said the man over Mustafa. *"Aren't you?"* He drew his boot back and slammed it into Mustafa's side.

"I think you're Brotherhood," the captain said to Dalia. "We'll find out." He turned to the soldier from the rocks. "How much time do we have?"

"Enough."

"Find some wire. Is the truck battery still good?"

"I think so."

"We'll make her remember who she is. If she won't tell us, maybe he will, when he hears her yelp."

The men were still too far apart, and still nothing from Gabriel. Mustafa was coiled, fetus-like, on the gravel. The three men moved toward her, bunched

129

at last, the captain holding his gun carefully. She had the Scorpion in a firm grasp but didn't dare bring the muzzle up; they'd see it in the moonlight and be too fast for her.

Without warning, Mustafa screamed, "In the name of God the merciful and the compassionate, we are none of the Brotherhood."

The shout distracted them for the necessary instant. Dalia fired through the slit in her robe, the whole clip, the bullets' impact lifting the men and then folding them over like blown newspapers. Hot cartridge casings cascaded out of the gun, burning her legs and feet. She hadn't thrust the muzzle quite far enough beyond the slit in the robe and when the clip was gone the muzzle flash had almost ignited the cloth. She damped the smoldering threads with her palm, not feeling the pain, and stood there for a moment, watching the Syrians for movement.

I killed them, she thought. At last. Three of them, like the ones on the beach who killed my husband and my child. But this time I did the killing. At last.

Why is it so empty? It was like crushing insects. What did I want?

Reaction began to set in, nausea, trembling, as the adrenalin in her muscles began to break down. With an effort of will she stopped the shaking. The nausea receded a little.

A stir in the moonlight. Mustafa struggling to sit up. She detached the Scorpion from its sling and pulled it out, yanking off the empty clip as she did so.

"How bad?" she asked, kneeling beside him.

There was blood around his nose and smeared over his chin. "Ribs," he said. "Kicked me just before I yelled at them."

"That saved us," she said. "It gave me the time."

"Yes. Gabriel?"

"Wait." She looked at his mouth, searching for fresh blood, but it was impossible to distinguish colors in the moonlight. She was thinking: I can drive us up to the zone if I have to, but if he can't get back we'll have to leave him. What then?

"Are your lungs punctured?" she asked.

He was in a full sitting position now. "I don't think so." He paused, took a deep breath, wincing at the end of it. "It's not too bad. Cracked a rib, maybe. Tape me up. There's an aid kit in back with the blankets. Where's Gabriel?"

"Wait," she said, and ran over to the Toyota. Inside it Gabriel lay crumpled, half on the seat, half on the floor. The truck was full of the sweet rusty iron smell of blood.

"Mustafa," she called. Anger and despair flooded through her. "He's been hit."

They got him out of the back seat, Mustafa breathing heavily with the wrench of his damaged ribs, and laid him on the rough shingle with a folded blanket under his head.

"How did they hit him?" Mustafa said. "They fired up, through the windshield."

She had Gabriel's shirt off now. "Lamp," she said.

"It's dangerous."

"I have to know how bad he is."

Mustafa brought a battery lantern and switched it on, shielding its hard white beam with his palm. The diffused light lay across the Israeli's white, almost hairless chest, and the dark jagged clot of blood just above the breastbone and to the left of the heart. Mustafa studied the wound.

131

"A bullet bounced off the roof," he said after a moment. "That's the only thing that could have done it. Look how ragged the edges are." He lifted Gabriel delicately a few centimeters and felt under his back. "No exit wound. It's still in him somewhere."

"Gabriel," she said. "Can you hear me?"

The Israeli's head turned a little. "Yes."

"Can you breathe well?"

"Not as well as I did." Weakly. "It feels warm, down there."

It was a sucking wound. Dalia found plastic sheets and tape in the first-aid kit and sealed the entry hole, so that Gabriel's lungs could go on working. After that she wrapped tape around Mustafa's rib cage and helped him get his shirt and coat back on. Then came the painful process of getting Gabriel back into the Toyota; they made a kind of bed for him by lowering the rear seat and spreading the blankets on the resulting flat surface. Mustafa closed the tailgate and Dalia said, "Can you drive?"

"Yes."

She looked at him. He was haggard. "You'll need your strength to get back. Let me take us up to the zone," she said.

"We'd need more time. You don't know the track."

"We've got until two."

He considered. "Yes. Drive. I'll navigate."

She went back for the Scorpion, reloaded it, and got behind the wheel. The engine started easily, and she put the vehicle into low gear. Mustafa breathed heavily in the passenger seat.

An indefinite period of time passed. She felt it growing late. At last Mustafa said, "It's here. Slow down."

132

She backed off the gas until the Toyota was barely moving. Seen from the opposite direction, the landscape was unfamiliar. Then details began to slip into place: the wadi banks, the notched ridge above it.

And at the far end of the packed sand bed of the wadi, a smooth hummock of stone.

"He's still here," she said. "They didn't find him." She had been afraid that she would return to the wadi and find a heap of charred wreckage. And with that, the burden of the long trek over the ridges to the border, with a wounded—perhaps dying—man.

She stopped the vehicle. "Give me the Scorpion," she said. "I want it in case they're waiting. When I'm gone one minute, give the code."

She hurried away from the vehicle toward the side of the wadi, keeping low. Behind her, the sidelights of the Toyota blinked in Morse: T-S-T. She watched the stone hummocks at the wadi's throat. There was an answering light, very dim: V-S-V.

He's here, she thought. He's still here.

She moved up the wadi. Behind she heard Mustafa start the Toyota, following. "Avi?" she called, nearing the rounded stones.

"Yes." He appeared from her right, Uzi submachine gun in one hand, lantern in the other. "You did it."

She came up to him in a flurry of robes. "You're safe."

"Yes. But we have to get out of here. Where's your passenger?"

She gestured at the Toyota. "He's in there. But he's been hit, badly, in the chest. The bullet's still in him."

133

"Shit." Avi Maoz shifted the Uzi and scrubbed a square hand through his thicket of short dark hair. He was a small man, thin as steel wire, and as strong, the youngest male operative in the Mossad's External Projects section in Ankara. "Can he take the ride?"

"I don't know," Dalia said.

Mustafa came up then, walking stiffly. "What happened?" Avi said.

"We ran into some Syrian troops trying to get across the border," Mustafa told him. "I wasn't quick enough."

"Where are they?"

"They're dead," Dalia said briefly. "There were only the three."

"Good," said Avi. "Let's go and get the netting off. There's no time to waste."

When they reached the hummocks at the far end of the wadi, Avi knelt and started pulling wooden pegs out of the ground. Dalia helped while Mustafa stood guard. When they had finished, Avi said, "Good. Up now."

She stooped and felt under the sand for the edge of the camouflage screen. "Got it."

"Now."

They tugged upwards. The face of the hillocks stirred, shivering off small runnels of sand that had been deposited there by the wind. The fabric lifted easily; it was not much thicker than tissue paper, even lighter, but very strong.

"Careful over the wingtips," Avi said.

They finished in less than five minutes, the camouflage sheeting curled in a dusty wreath on the ground around the two ultralight aircraft. In the moonlight they resembled enormous moths: square-tipped gray wings, delicate angular tail fins and rear

134

stabilizers, all connected by a thin skeleton of alloy tubing which supported seats and controls and, at the rear, air-cooled engines and two-bladed propellers. The engines were shrouded in elaborate silencers.

"They're in good shape," Avi said. "There's no wind, and we've got a slight downhill run for takeoff. We should be able to lift in fifty meters."

Dalia walked around her machine, drumming the support wires to check the tension. Hers was a two-seater, Avi's a single. The planes cruised at seventy kilometers an hour, so they would be over the Turkish border in just over twenty minutes from takeoff. Another thirty minutes would take them to the pickup zone in the uplands north of Demirci. There, in the last two hours before dawn, the ultralights would be dismantled, packed into crates, and loaded into the truck that would take them all back to Ankara. The little flying machines were ideal for clandestine work: they were impossible to detect on radar, flew very low so that the pilot could navigate by the ground, and, if properly silenced, could pass unseen at night unless an observer was almost underneath them.

Gabriel's breathing was no better. Avi listened for a moment. "He's bad," he said to Dalia.

Gabriel had heard him. In the moonlight Dalia saw him open his eyes. They were glazed.

"Gabriel?" she said. "How are you?"

"I'm not," he said, in almost a whisper, "going to make it, am I?"

"Yes, you are," she said, and took his hand.

His grip was surprisingly—frighteningly—strong. "Don't leave me," he said.

"I won't leave you," she said. "I promise. I'll get you out."

135

From the darkness behind her she could hear Avi's breathing, quick and soft. "Dalia," he said quietly, "we have to go."

"Wait," Gabriel said, gathering his strength. "What I was going to tell you earlier. About the German."

After a moment she said, knowing he would know what it meant, "You'd better tell me now."

"There is something else in the wind. I saw a dossier I shouldn't have. It was just after Hafez Assad died, when the Brotherhood rose." He stopped, his fingers about hers weakening. Then he went on, "The dossier said the Brotherhood was planning a full-scale attack to destroy Israel, as soon as the Assad regime was overthrown."

"But that would be part of their plan anyway," Avi said.

"*No.*" The word bubbled out of Gabriel's throat. "Without waiting. Immediately." The bubbling again, liquid and thick. "The German planned it."

"But *how?*" she asked.

"The dossier didn't say. Nobody knew. Knows. Except the Brotherhood."

"But soon."

"Yes."

"What else?"

Gabriel's breath made a soft blurred sound in his throat. "That's all. Warn them. In Jerusalem, in Tel Aviv." He was failing rapidly, the grip on her fingers slack.

"I will," Dalia said. "I will." Her eyes stung.

"We have to get him out of here," Avi said. "Now."

"Yes," she said. "Get the suit for him."

They had some difficulty getting him into the ex-

136

posure suit; it was necessary even at low altitude because of the windchill, and the temperature on the ground was already edging below the freezing mark. Gabriel helped as well as he could, but he was very weak.

"Sorry," he said faintly, as she at last strapped him into the plane's rear seat.

"We'll be out soon," she told him. "There'll be help at the other end."

She and Avi got into the pilots' seats. Mustafa stood behind her, holding the starting handle. "Go," she said.

He pulled hard. The engine popped, kicked, and fired. It was very quiet; the Mossad technicians had designed the silencing carefully.

While the engine warmed, Mustafa got Avi's going. In front of Dalia, the moonlight illuminated the sand that stretched away towards the wadi's mouth. Mustafa came up to her.

"I'm moving the Toyota now," he told her. "I'll wait until you're safely off."

"Good luck," she said. "Are you sure you can get back?"

"I'm sure. Go. *Shalom.*"

"*Shalom.*"

He walked away down the sand and got into the Toyota. When it was out of sight beyond the wadi mouth, Dalia raised her arm, brought it down, and took her feet off the brakes. The ultralight began to move, swiftly picking up speed. Suddenly, it was airborne, scudding out of the wadi into the moonlit air above the plain.

As she swung the craft north, she glimpsed the Toyota falling away beneath her, a shadow beside it that might have been Mustafa waving. She glanced back at Avi's machine rising out of the wadi behind her, almost invisible, like a great moth flying toward the moon.

Somewhere over the ancient hills, although Dalia never knew exactly when, Gabriel died.

Moscow
April 4

PINE FOREST on the land below the plane's window, fields still heavy with snow, dark bands of roads and highways. The Aeroflot-Ilyushin-76 banked, slipping into its landing approach. A warning bell chimed, and Cole instinctively tested his seat belt again. As he did so, he caught a glimpse of his face reflected in the glass of the port and felt the small involuntary start again: it was the face of a stranger. The CIA artists were good, there was no doubt about that: they'd darkened his hair, given him a virtually irremovable moustache, and provided perfectly fitted contact lenses to alter the color of his eyes from gray to brown.

He refocused his eyes to look through the glass of the port. The Ilyushin was down in its final approach now, well below the cloud cover, roads whipping by underneath, the snow looking dull and gray in the late afternoon light. Puddles of water stood here and there on the roads; Moscow must be having a thaw. Winter would release its hold in a few weeks. The cherry tree near the boathouse back

139

home would be in bloom before long; barring disaster he'd be back in plenty of time to see it.

Home was a long way away. The CIA launch had picked him up from *Whiskeyjack* about noon, two days ago, and none too soon either. He'd been worrying about the deteriorating weather for an hour before it hove into sight, more or less on schedule; he'd already had to take in a reef in the mainsail. Then the crew had tried to take *Whiskeyjack* under tow and it had happened. It still enraged him, when he thought about it.

There was, perhaps, some excuse. The sea was very rough, and there'd been one of those rogue waves, twice the height of normal rollers, that came out of nowhere. *Whiskeyjack* had shot almost under the launch's stern, the towline sagging in the sudden heave of the rogue. The launch had spun out of control, sliding down the wave face, Cole watching from the bridge, the corner of the big square transom slamming into *Whiskeyjack*'s bilge curve as she rolled, the fiberglass shattering, a huge hole smashed in the white hull, the sea pouring in. There'd been nothing anyone could do; the crewman at the towline had only just managed to cast off before *Whiskeyjack* rolled onto her beam ends and sank like a rock, bits of wreckage, seat cushions, a life ring floating above her like a funeral wreath.

The worst of it was that Cole thought Jackman had been pleased. He'd originally agreed to have the sailboat concealed until Cole returned, whereupon they'd take her back out to sea, make her appear disabled, and tow her back in with Cole aboard. That would cover his three-day disappearance. But from Jackman's point of view, losing the boat would make everything simpler and even more convincing, at least until it was time to resurrect Cole. The en-

140

tire situation infuriated Cole, but there was nothing he could do about it.

The Ilyushin's landing gear thumped onto the runway. Outside the glass Cole could see the hangars of Vnukovo airport, with other Ilyushins and Antonov transports spotted here and there. The light private planes that would have been thick on the ground at an American airport were conspicuously absent.

Meg. How was she taking it? When he allowed himself to think about what he had had to do, remorse washed over him in cold waves. But Jackman had been adamant: Cole was to give absolutely no one any idea that he might disappear unexpectedly, no matter what the personal cost. There was no choice in the matter; he *had* to meet Snowflake, he had to go to Moscow. And with his previous record in the Soviet capital, there was no possibility of entering the country under his own identity. It was always possible that KGB people in the United States checked on him occasionally, and given the extreme dangers attending any meeting with the Russian, Cole could take no avoidable risks at all, not even to give Megan a hint that might reassure her. And he could not simply drop out of sight; any surveillance would spot that immediately and the alarm bells would go off, first in the Soviet embassy in Washington, and then in KGB headquarters in Moscow. He had to appear, at least temporarily, dead.

But he felt like a bastard about Meg, just the same. He had a sudden image of her on the beach at Cape Cod last summer, laughing in the sunlight, her copper hair flying in the wind. Strong and fragile both. His Welsh witch, he'd called her more than once.

The Ilyushin had rolled to a stop. Thumps from forward, where the exit gangway was being mated to the fuselage. He could spare no more resources to worry about Megan right now; he had to be totally focused on the job at hand for the next forty-eight hours, or he'd jeopardize his chances of survival even further.

The passengers around him were standing, stretching, assembling their cabin baggage. Cole extracted his own bag from under the seat in front, unbuckled the safety belt, and got up stiffly.

Inside the terminal there was the usual swamp of uniforms that Cole remembered among the civilian travelers: security, customs, aircrew and cabin attendants, a few army officers in walking-out dress. Customs were the first test. If, somehow, they'd found out that he was a substitute for somebody else, they'd pick him up here when they found the Martin Bryce papers. Or perhaps not; they might let him run, to see what he'd do or who he'd meet.

He joined what appeared to be the shortest line in the diplomatic entry area, and waited. The inspections of baggage and papers were much more rigorous than he remembered. That was Kulagin's KGB: foreigners were at best a necessary, corrupting evil. The Bryce papers were perfect, though. They ought to be: they were genuine. Martin Bryce had been a new assignee to the Moscow CIA station, as an assistant trade attache; he was single and resembled Cole sufficiently. What Bryce thought of the substitution, Cole had no idea; he was likely quite annoyed. If Cole fouled up, Bryce would never get a Moscow posting, ever. At the very least, he was going to have to cool his heels in the States for a few weeks, until the "illness" that would require Cole-

142

Bryce's hurried return to the United States had been cured.

The man in front of Cole got his stamped papers back from the customs official and hurried off with a distinct expression of relief. Cole mentally turned himself into Bryce.

"Passport and visa."

Cole handed them over. Bryce spoke Russian, but not as fluently as Cole. He'd do what talking was necessary in English.

"Martin Bryce. American citizen." Thumbing through the passport.

"Yes."

"You have never before been in the Soviet Union?"

"No."

"Where were you stationed before?"

"Holland."

Now the diplomatic visa. "At the American embassy, what will you be doing?"

"Trade attache. Assistant."

No comment, only a brief look from the flat blue policeman's eyes under the peaked cap. "This is a one-year visa. You are aware?"

"Yes."

"Where were you born?"

"Fall River, Vermont, U.S.A."

"Date?"

"July 9, 1956."

"Open your bag, please."

Cole did so. The man riffled through it, shook the aerosol can of shaving cream. "You have very little baggage for a one-year stay. Where is the rest of it?"

"It's coming along in two days. I'll manage with the embassy stores until then."

"I see. Wait here."

143

He took Cole's papers, walked to the far wall of the area, and disappeared through a frosted glass door.

Christ, not already, Cole thought. He forced his breathing to steady. There was no point in having a lot of adrenaline in his bloodstream if he could neither run nor fight.

The official came back, alone. "A Mr. Andrews from your embassy was to meet you?"

Breathing a little easier. "Yes."

"There is a message for you from him. He has been delayed. He will meet you at the main information kiosk twenty minutes from now."

"Thank you." The man began stamping the visa and passport.

Jesus, Cole thought, I nearly missed it. "Where is the information kiosk?"

The official looked up, expressionless. "Ah. I forgot you have not been here before. Upstairs, near the center of the terminal. There are signs. Here are your papers. Enjoy your stay in Moscow."

Peredelkino—Moscow
April 4

THE TWIGS of the birch trees rattled in the darkness over Markelov's head, tossing in the raw cold wind and scattering drops of freezing rain over the back of his neck. At his feet the hole he was digging was a dimly visible dark smear against the snow. He stood, resting, and not for the first time thanked God there had been a thaw. If the ground had been thoroughly frozen he'd have been at work for hours with a pickax, as he'd been in February when he buried the box.

Painfully, because of the arthritis, he renewed his grip on the handle of the spade and continued digging. The shovel's blade scraped on pebbles, a tree root, then on something hard. The box. Markelov stopped for a moment to catch his breath and then dug around its sides, working with difficulty in the dark. When he judged it was free enough of the grip of the half-frozen earth, he rammed the spade into the pile of dirt and knelt. The ground was sodden and muddy from the freezing rain, and his fingers inside his gloves were numb and stiff. He levered the box out of the hole, placed it carefully on a clean

145

patch of snow, and took off his gloves. The oilcloth seemed intact. He unwrapped its folds and ran his fingers over the seams of the box. The wax he'd resealed it with was still there, although brittle with the cold. Markelov peeled it away and opened the lid, shielding the box from the rain with his body. Only then did he venture to switch on the flashlight, which he had carefully shrouded with a perforated disk of cardboard over the lens.

The positives from the microfilm were still there, exactly as he had left them in February. There was still no mold or mildew. In one corner of the box lay the microfilm capsule, its dull metal as untarnished as it had been that day in the spruce wood north of Leningrad. He still wondered, sometimes, who the man carrying it had been, the man he'd killed. He didn't suppose he would ever know.

He decided not to leave the capsule in the box; it was too precious. He removed it and thrust it deep into his trousers pocket, switching off the flashlight as he did so. Then he closed the aluminum container and put it to one side while he filled the hole. By morning the rain would have removed most of the traces of digging, and the weather was so bad anyway that no one was likely to venture into the birch wood. After a moment's thought he took the cardboard off the flashlight lens and threw it away into some underbrush.

Cole is on his way, he thought. Tomorrow night I'll get the film to him and he'll take it away and I'll have done what I could. Perhaps someday Valeri will know, not think so badly of me. I wonder how long I have, before they come for me as well? If only they will leave my wife and daughter and grandchildren alone. But we're all Jews. They won't stop with me.

146

He started through the woods back to the *dacha*, the box under one arm, the shovel in his other hand. His coat, an old one he kept at the *dacha* for gardening in, was heavy with rain and gave him no warmth. He was a little worried. At his age, and with the strain he'd been under, pneumonia was quite possible. He'd have to warm up in the house first, before leaving to go back to Moscow. Since he'd become so abruptly unemployed he had come out to Peredelkino and the country home three or four times, alone, just to see if he were being followed. He had been on the first two occasions, which had terrified him. He had to retrieve the documents and the microfilm before Cole arrived, and he couldn't do that if the KGB was breathing down his neck. But it had all fallen out right, as though something *wanted* him to succeed. He'd had a smooth brush contact the week before on the subway; the note the woman had passed him had given him the location of the dead drop that contained the rendez-vous instructions. Today the KGB had left him alone to go out to Peredelkino, and the ground had thawed enough to let him dig up the box without too much difficulty. It was all working out, as though God were taking a hand in it.

When he got back to the *dacha*, he'd burn the prints of the microfilm in the fireplace. Then he'd change into his city clothes, make tea and warm up, and go back to the capital. With luck he'd be there by ten, to get Esfir settled down. She wouldn't go to bed, much less sleep, if he weren't there.

The *dacha* was just ahead, a dark bulk against the snow and the slender white trunks of the birches. For safety's sake he hadn't turned on the lights when he arrived. Outside the back door he carefully cleaned the shovel blade with snow, leaned the shovel

147

against the wall of the house, and then went in. The kitchen smelled unused and damp. He pressed the wall switch and the light over the table came on. Outside, the wind was rising in strength; it hissed among the birches and drummed around the eaves of the house. Markelov stood for a moment, considering, and then lit the stove for his tea. The kettle could boil while he changed his clothes.

He took the aluminum box upstairs to the rear bedroom. He was beginning to shake with cold and fatigue. You're nearly sixty, he reminded himself. You're too old for this. Get warmed up, right away, or you'll get really sick, and then who'll take care of Esfir?

He put the box on the floor and, almost as an afterthought, pushed it under the bed; he'd have to get the fire going in the fireplace before he could burn the documents, anyway. It took him several minutes to peel himself out of his wet things and put on the clothes he'd worn down from Moscow. He transferred the microfilm capsule to his dry trousers and put the damp garments in his wardrobe. They'd dry well enough in there, if he left the wardrobe door open.

Tea. Markelov went back down to the kitchen and spooned the loose black leaves from the canister into the teapot. The water was just on the boil, bubbling nicely. He poured it into the pot. There was a mirror on the opposite wall and he caught his reflection in it. For a moment he saw himself with a frightening clarity, as though he were being given a brief glimpse of a stranger: elderly, gray, heavy in the jowls, thinning hair disarranged, fleshy prominent nose.

I must be about as old as that man in the forest was when I killed him, Markelov thought, looking back at his reflection. But I had to. He would have killed me. Who was he, to be carrying such a thing?

I have to light the fire and burn the papers and get out of here. Enough dreaming.

He went into the parlor, made sure the curtains were closed, and turned on a single lamp. The wind soughed and buzzed around the window frames. There were logs in the woodbox but not much kindling. Anything outside would be too wet to burn, he'd have to make do with what there was. At least he'd remembered to bring several copies of *Pravda* to start the blaze.

He had the wood laid and was about to strike a match when he heard a sound. A thud. Wind blowing the back door? A loose shingle? He stood up, his knees creaking.

More thuds, this time from the front porch, and a voice:

"There's a car, somebody's here. Be careful." Hammering at the door. "You inside there! Open up!"

Markelov stood immobile with shock. The wind, he thought. I couldn't hear their car because of the wind. He knew he should run for the stairs, for the box, but his legs wouldn't move.

"Open up!"

He wrenched himself out of his paralysis and started for the stairway, but it was too late. The front door burst open with a crash of splintering wood, its latch shattered. The beam of a powerful hand lantern flicked across the walls, the floor, settled on Markelov.

"You. Put your hands up. *Now!* Remain still."

Half-blind from the light, he obeyed. The overhead chandelier snapped on and the man in the doorway turned off the lantern. He was big, bigger

149

than Markelov, with a fleshy pallid face, wearing a brown leather coat. Spots of rain glistened on its surface. Two other men loomed behind him in the shadows beyond the door. The man with the lantern was pointing a gun at Markelov.

"Who are you?" Markelov asked. His voice cracked, throat dry with adrenaline. He was angry with himself for being so frightened.

"KGB, Special Investigations. This house is being sealed pending search for illegally acquired property. Where are your papers?"

"In my coat. In the parlor."

"Get them."

He followed Markelov into the living room. Over his shoulder he said to the others, "Seal the back door and the windows. We'll start digging through the place after I've dealt with the *Zhid*."

Markelov picked up his coat and fumbled clumsily through the pockets for his internal passport. Rain lashed at the windowpanes. His hands didn't want to work properly.

"This is my *dacha*," he said, finding the document at last. "You have no right—"

"Shut up and give me your papers."

He did so. One of the other men was moving around upstairs, in the front bedroom.

The box, Markelov thought. Dear God, if I can get out of here before they find it and look in it, I may get away. If I can get back to Moscow, call Esfir, warn her about this, then hide, just for a day, if I can stay free until tomorrow night, just long enough for Cole to come—

"You're Alexander Ilyich Markelov?"

"Yes."

"The academician?"

"Yes." The KGB man knew perfectly well who

he was, he wouldn't have been sent out here without a briefing. Taunts.

"It says here you're been sacked."

"That's right. For no reason."

"It also says here you're a *Zhid*. You think maybe that had something to do with it?"

"It had everything to do with it." He had to get this stopped, somehow, soon, get away, unless they were going to arrest him on the spot. He could feel the pressure of the microfilm against his thigh. The man upstairs was thumping around in the hall now. The other one slammed a cupboard door in the kitchen.

"You don't like that? You think maybe trash like you ought to have nice soft jobs at the university?"

Markelov gave a helpless gesture. Shut up, he thought, in the name of God just shut up and let me go. "It's not a crime to be Jewish."

"Not yet. Why haven't you got a job?"

"I've been looking."

"You know it's illegal to be unemployed? Parasites are unemployed. You turning into a parasite? That's a five-year term at correctional labor nowadays."

"Yes."

The KGB man made a disgusted noise in the back of his throat and tossed the passport onto the chair beside Markelov's coat. "I'm glad you're somebody else's problem and not mine. All right. Get out."

Careful now. Not too eager to leave.

"You mean—"

"Didn't you hear me? *Get out.* This place isn't yours any more. It's reverted to the Central Committee for reallocation."

"But it was allocated to *me*—"

"You ought to keep track of things more, *Zhid.*

151

Jews aren't allowed more than one residence any more."

Markelov gaped at him. "That can't be true."

"Oh, it is. A *ukasi* from the Praesidium of the Supreme Soviet, issued this afternoon. You're not going to be the only Jew to lose his cosy little nest. Good Russians'll get them. Is that your Zhiguli out there in the driveway?"

"Yes," Markelov whispered.

"Get in it and leave. You're lucky to be able to do that, if I had my way you'd be walking back to Moscow." His voice rose to a yell. *"How long do I have to breathe the same air as you?* Get the hell out of here!"

Markelov grabbed his papers, threw his coat around his shoulders, and fled the room, down the hall, out the front door into the dark and the bitter rain. Ice had sheeted on the car's windshield. He smashed it off with his fist, almost panicking. Surely the one upstairs was looking under the bed by now, finding the box, opening it, dragging the prints out onto the floor, eyes widening as he read, racing now downstairs to find the man with the gun—

Stop the Jew.

He hadn't really heard it; the house was still silent. Enough of the windshield was clear that he could drive. Keys in the wrong coat pocket, *for God's sake find them,* there they are. Into the ignition now. Still nothing from the house. The starter motor grated. If only I could have found a new battery before tonight. *Start, damn you.* The engine firing at last. Headlights, wipers on, don't dare go off the road. Swinging away from the house into the laneway now, the white trunks of the birches along it bright and slender in the lights. He glanced in the

152

rearview mirror but the rear window was pebbled with ice.

Not until he was five kilometers down the main road did he start to believe he might get away. They'd be looking for him soon, but once he was in Moscow, if he could get that far, he'd abandon the car and hide somewhere until tomorrow night. He would have to do it alone. Anyone he knew would be watched; he wouldn't even be able to risk buying food. He had a fair amount of money with him, but he wouldn't be able to use it except for public transit and any telephone calls he couldn't avoid making.

Money, he thought. What's Esfir going to do for money? Bad enough I lost my job. When they arrest me they'll likely take the apartment back as well, confiscate what money I've still got in the savings account.

A voice in the back of his head said: But they're going to do all that anyway. You don't think they're going to stop at Jews' *dachas,* do you?

I have to let the Americans know, he told the voice. They'll help.

They didn't last time, the voice countered. With the Germans. They won't now.

Shut up. I have to concentrate.

He began to think about his immediate problem. As soon as they found out what was in the box there would be roadblocks on the direct routes into the city. He'd better go in by a roundabout way, dump the car at the most outlying metro station he could, and get into the city by subway. They'd know, as soon as they found the car, where he'd gone underground, but given half an hour he'd be far away.

The wipers scraped and bumped over the ice on the windshield. The road was turning slippery and he began to worry about skidding off it. Fortunately

153

most people with cars were staying home tonight because of the weather; there was very little traffic on the highway. After a few minutes the windshield started to defrost and the driving became easier; the rain even slacked off a bit.

By the time he reached the intersection of the ring motorway and the M5, without seeing any militia at all, he was beginning to feel almost optimistic. There'd have been a block at the ring and the M5 if there was going to be one anywhere. That probably meant he had a little time to spare before going down into the metro; he could risk calling Esfir. She'd be worrying about him by now, because of the freezing rain.

A block south of the Kashirskoye subway station he passed a phone kiosk. Twenty meters on there was a side street; he swung the Zhiguli into it and pulled over to the curb a little way from the intersection. The rain, which had grown heavier again, started to freeze on the windshield as soon as he stopped the wipers. He turned off the engine and sat very still, listening to the beat of the heavy cold drops on the car's roof. For a moment he pondered going to the American embassy and trying to bluff his way past the militiamen guarding it, but gave the idea up as impossible. They'd never allow him to pass, even if they hadn't been alerted to watch for him. He didn't even dare use the emergency telephone number he'd been given to memorize; if it were being monitored, the KGB might realize that there was an operation under way, and that would make it even harder for Cole to make the rendezvous.

He sighed and climbed out of the car. Now that the adrenaline was out of his bloodstream he realized how cold and desperately tired he'd become. Curling up in a back alley doorway out of the rain seemed like a good idea suddenly, and he actually considered doing it.

No, he thought, seeing as he looked at a streetlight back on the corner that the rain was beginning to turn to snow. I might never wake up. It's getting colder. I have to keep moving.

He pulled his gloves on and walked slowly along the side street back to Kashirskoye Boulevard. At the corner he stopped and looked both ways. There were no pedestrians, but a few cars hissed over the pavement, gleaming with wet yellow highlights under the sodium-vapor streetlamps, slush peeling up from their tires in sprays of dirty amber.

He could see the telephone booth; there was no one in it. Feeling agonizingly conspicuous, he walked along the pavement, overshoes crunching on patches of half-frozen slush. The temperature was dropping rapidly, there would likely be a lot of snow before morning.

He entered the telephone kiosk. For a moment he almost panicked when he couldn't find a two-kopeck coin to put into the slot. Eventually he discovered one in his back trousers pocket. He deposited it, dialed, and waited. The line whirred.

"Yes?"

He was startled. It was his daughter Irina's voice. She was supposed to be with her husband Yakov; they had been going to go out somewhere.

"It's your father," he said quickly. "Is your mother all right?"

A muffled choke in the receiver, it might have been a sob. He suddenly felt as though the wind had gotten right under his overcoat and was blowing onto the small of his back. "Yes. Mother's all right. As well as she can be."

"Irina. What's the matter?"

155

"Daddy, you have to come home right away. They've arrested Yakov."

"What?" Yakov was a junior editor for *Trud,* stolidly Party, unimaginative. He was one of the last people Markelov would have imagined being at risk. Except that he had *Zhid* stamped in his passport. "When?"

"This afternoon. They took him right from work."

"Why?"

"I don't know. Daddy, what are they trying to *do* to us?"

"I don't know," Markelov said. *But I do. Winter Palace.* "Have you got Tania there?" After losing two of his three children, he didn't think he could bear losing his granddaughter as well.

"Yes. She's safe. Daddy, you've got to help us get him out. They've taken him to Dzerzhinsky Square. To the Lubianka."

The old KGB headquarters and prison. Thousands of Stalin's victims, Jews and Gentiles alike, had died wretchedly in its cellars. "I can't, kitten. I'm in trouble myself. Let me speak to your mother. I haven't much time."

"In trouble? Have they got you, too? Where are you calling from?"

She must be distraught, or she wouldn't have asked him such a question. "I can't tell you, they may be listening. Let me—"

"Daddy, Oleg Lezin's here. He wants to talk to you."

"Oleg, there?" Lezin was a full professor in the history faculty, a friend of Markelov's in an occasional way. He was also Jewish but had been able to hang onto his job, as far as Markelov knew. But

156

he hadn't called, not once, since Markelov had been fired. "Irina—"

But she was gone. He heard the bump and rattle of the receiver being handed over. "Alexander?"

"Yes." No time for anger or recrimination. "Oleg, what's the matter?"

"Alexander, they fired me today. They did it to six others yesterday afternoon. All Jews. They—"

"Are you surprised?" He tried to keep the bitterness out of his voice, but could not.

"That's not it. Alexander, they're arresting us, all the Jews in the university faculty. Kovalev, Petrosian, Retzov, Machekhin, Veber, Vopelovsky. Those are just the ones I know about. The vans came for them this morning, before it was light, I found out because Kovalev's wife called me and I started checking. They've all been taken away, I don't know where, but it might have been the Lubianka. Veber's and Petrosian's families were taken too, even the children. There are rumors that they're not just picking up the intelligentsia. Retzov has relatives in Smolensk, he told me yesterday that the organs were arresting Jews there too."

"You're still out," Markelov said.

"I haven't gone home since I heard. I wanted to warn you." A pause. "I felt bad that I didn't speak up when you were fired. If I'd known—" Another pause. "If you can't find me tomorrow, you'll know what's happened. Try to save yourself."

"Oleg, please leave the apartment. They may know you're there now. If they come for you my family may get hurt."

"I'm going, don't worry. Good luck."

"Good luck. Please put my wife on."

"Yes."

157

A silence, then: "Alexander. Alexander, I've been so worried."

"I'm safe." *For the moment,* he added silently. He had been in the kiosk far too long. Up the street the red neon M of the subway station beckoned tormentingly. But Oleg's news . . . Winter Palace. If he had had any doubts, they were resolved now.

They are coming for Jewish children in the night again.

Where had he once heard that?

"Alexander? Are you there?"

"Yes, beloved." He had always called her that, in their most intimate moments, ever since they were married. Until the death and imprisonment of their sons there had been a strength in her that he never thought could be broken. But she had been broken. There was so little of her left.

They'll pay for what they've done to us, he thought. I'll make them pay. "I'm here," he went on gently. "But I can't come home tonight. I'm doing something important."

"Alexander, I need you. Please come. They won't hurt you."

Her voice was reproachful, querulous, an old woman's. He hated them for what they had done to her. It was as though they had murdered her spirit and then, derisively, given him back her body.

"I can't. Beloved, I have to go. Go to bed and get some sleep. I'll see you soon. Irina will take care of you."

"Alexander—"

He felt himself weakening. He should be there with her, with his daughter and granddaughter, with his decimated family, try to protect them, at least *be* there; he was their husband and father, he was responsible. . . .

"Alexander." The whimper again.

158

No.

"Sleep," he said, and hung up. The rain really had turned into snow now, heavy and wet, clinging to the glass of the kiosk. The amber sodium lights edged the flakes with gold.

He turned his collar up, feeling the microfilm's light pressure against his outer thigh, and left the kiosk. Ahead of him, the red M over the subway entrance blurred in the whirling snow.

2 Dzerzhinsky Square, Moscow
2:40 A.M., April 5

KGB CHAIRMAN VIKTOR FROLOV was reading at his desk in the straw-colored glow of a single desk lamp. The rest of the office was sunk in obscurity, the high wood-paneled walls and heavy curtains barely visible. On the desk in front of him lay the daily intelligence digest, the thick wad of material prepared for him every twenty-four hours by the analysts of the First Chief Directorate.

He turned a page and frowned. For some reason the analysts had seen fit to include the full translated text of a *Washington Post* lead article dated two days previously. It had been written by a pair of Russian émigrés who had once worked for the Novosti Press Agency in Moscow. Frolov remembered them; they had been good at finding skeletons in closets that senior Party members and government officials would have preferred to keep closed. They'd got out of Russia just before Kulagin kicked Gorbachev out, and lucky for them—their activities would nowadays earn them thirty years in a strict-regime camp, rather than a pair of exit visas.

Still, he had to admit they were astute observers.

The article took Kulagin's regime to task for its "reversion," as the authors called it, to the rigid controls of the Stalin years; control of everything from economic planning to the ideological faithfulness of individuals. Frolov skimmed down the text.

. . . we are seeing now a centralization of power in the Kremlin, and an intolerance of legitimate and constructive dissent, unequaled since the 1930s. Mikhail Gorbachev's attempts at liberalization, cosmetic though many of them were, so frightened the conservative component of the Soviet ruling class that their only reaction could be to depose him. We see the return to Stalinism, as well, in the renewed attempts by the Kremlin to direct the affairs of the Eastern European nations, especially those of Poland and Hungary. . . .

That was all true enough, Frolov thought, although it would be worth your life to say it to Kulagin. Poor Gorbachev. He had been swimming against the tide from the start.

He went further down the text. What he had read so far was nothing new. Why were the analysts wasting his time with this?

Then he came to it, and his eyebrows lifted.

. . . repressive measures against non-Russian minorities have increased. Most disturbing is the campaign of the last three months in the Soviet press against what the authorities call "Zionism." This campaign is, in fact, a revival of the historic Russian tendency to anti-Semitism. It is also a fact, however, that this campaign reflects not only popular feeling among many Russians; this campaign has the backing and the authority of the Kremlin, and, implied by that, of General Secretary Kulagin. If the diatribes in the Soviet press were all that was going on, it would be bad enough. But, apparently, there have been overt sanctions applied to Jews in several areas of Soviet life, particularly in the arts and the teaching professions. Because of the increased closure of Soviet society since the present regime came to power, it is more difficult than before to tell exactly what is happening in areas where Westerners are not allowed to go. But there have been rumors, in Moscow and elsewhere, that large numbers of Russian Jews are being detained in specially built camps. It is too early to tell whether this is true, or if it is what it means, but it is uncomfortably reminiscent of the Nazi Germany of 1933 and later. . . .

Raising that old apparition again, Frolov thought. But we're not going to *kill* them. Oh, no. We're letting them emigrate, exactly as everyone has always wanted us to do. Tomorrow, Truschenko announces in the United Nations the release of all Soviet Jews. If some are too weak to bear the necessary rigors of travel. . . .

On the other hand . . . at the Politburo meeting the previous Thursday, Akseyev, Frolov's deputy in charge of camp construction, had presented some inconvenient and annoying facts. He had ended his report, closed the file folder, and said, "We are behind schedule, for the unavoidable reasons I have stated. We are planning to move nearly two million Jews. The camps at present have a capacity of only six hundred thousand."

162

And Kulagin, sitting at the head of the table, had contemplated the smoke rising from the Dunhill cigarette he had just lit. "So much the better. Are we finished?"

No one had said anything, although Kulagin had just issued what amounted to a death warrant for an indefinite number, perhaps hundreds of thousands, of Soviet Jews. Overcrowding, malnutrition, disease: they'd die like flies. Except for the KGB-trained people, of course; they'd be safe enough.

Frolov closed the digest, staring into the gloom at the opposite wall. He was worried, although not about the fate of the *Zhids*. Frolov's mother, father and sister had starved to death in Leningrad during the Nazi siege of that city in 1942, and the sight of a well-fed Jew still annoyed him. What disturbed Frolov, and had been disturbing him ever since the supposed celebration in the Kremlin when he first confronted his reservations about Winter Palace, was the dismissive attitude to Western reactions Kulagin had revealed. Andropov had suggested a casualty rate of a couple of percent. Kulagin was willing to accept eight or nine times that, which would work out to at least three hundred thousand deaths, and he was adamantly refusing to allocate to the KGB more resources for camp construction. Much as the general secretary might like to believe it, this wasn't Stalin's day; you couldn't let that many people die without the West finding out about it.

And then he, Viktor Mikhailovich Frolov, head of the KGB, would be blamed. The man who hadn't provided enough shelter or food or medicines for the Jews, the man who had caused a propaganda disaster for the Soviet Union. He could see the indictments now. For committing serious errors of judgement and for violating the rights of Soviet cit-

163

izens, V. M. Frolov has been relieved of his post. V. M. Frolov has been arrested and is awaiting trial. For crimes against the Soviet people and the socialist collective of workers and peasants, the criminal Frolov has been convicted and sentenced to death.

The criminal V. M. Frolov has been shot.

It was a useful technique. Stalin had used it against the men who ran the great purges of the 1930s for him. He would have used it against his last secret police chief, Beria, as well, if his own death hadn't intervened.

Or had Beria really killed the old man, as the rumors still had it? Even Frolov, with all his resources, hadn't been able to get to the bottom of that. But it could have happened.

If it had happened once, why couldn't it happen again?

Beria had made one fatal mistake, though, after Stalin's death. He'd been on his way to ultimate power, but had been overconfident, had misjudged Khrushchev and the others. Frolov wouldn't make that mistake.

General Secretary of the Communist Party of the Soviet Union, Viktor Mikhailovich Frolov. It wasn't the first time that phrase had passed through Frolov's mind.

He would have to prepare carefully. Turn Winter Palace against Kulagin, somehow, before Kulagin could turn it against him. If Kulagin could be lured into a disaster in foreign affairs, that would likely be the end of him. He'd lose the support of the Central Committee, the Secretariat, and the rest of the Politburo. That had happened to Khrushchev, come to think of it. Screwed up domestically, with his crazy agricultural projects and goulash communism, and

164

then internationally with that insane idea of putting nuclear missiles into Cuba, back in 1962.

Kulagin had to go. It was just a matter of how and when. But it couldn't be too long from now; Frolov's instincts of self-preservation were strong, and he knew that his own days were numbered.

He went on through the digest. One item caught his eye and gave him a faint satisfaction. It was from the KGB *rezidentura* in Washington, which kept an eye on known CIA officers, active or (supposedly) retired, in the United States. Samuel Gregory Cole, the one who'd been running that net in Moscow a few years ago, had been drowned at sea off the east coast of the U.S. Good riddance. That was one they wouldn't have to worry about again.

The green internal telephone whirred. In spite of himself, Frolov jumped. At least it wasn't the Kremlin line, with Kulagin at the other end. That would have been truly unnerving. Sometimes it seemed that the man could read minds.

He picked up the receiver. "Frolov."

"This is Lyko, Chairman."

Lyko was head of the Jewish Department of the KGB Fifth Directorate. He was responsible for the operational aspect of Winter Palace—the identification, collection and shipment of the emigrants.

"Yes. Is something the matter with the pickups?"

A short silence. "We'll have another thirty thousand on the trains by dawn. The main concentrations are from here and Smolensk and Kiev. It's according to plan."

"How many have we got on the way to the camps so far?"

"One hundred and ten thousand. Those are mostly in the southern camps. The first wave of shipping's at Odessa."

165

"Good. The Foreign Office will begin finding countries to ship them to after the U.N. announcement tomorrow. Is something bothering you?"

"Chairman, I should come and see you."

Something he won't say even over an internal line? "Very well. Come."

Lyko's office was only three doors away. Not thirty seconds passed before his knock.

"Come in."

Lyko was looking even paler than usual. In his hands he carried a tarnished metal box, not very big. He sat down in the chair facing Frolov's desk.

"What?" the KGB head asked.

Instead of answering, Lyko set the box on the desk in front of Frolov and drew up the lid. Inside was a sheaf of what appeared to be photostats, curled and yellow at the edges, old.

"This is important?" Frolov asked. He had a lot of work to do before he could get to bed. He removed the first half dozen sheets from the box and spread them on the desk. Lyko didn't say anything.

Frolov read the first two paragraphs. Then, without raising his eyes, he removed the rest of the papers from the box and leafed through them. The signature was there, on the last page. It was as though a ghost were suddenly standing beside Frolov, looking over his shoulder.

Lavrenti Pavlovich Beria. Minister of State Security.

"Where did you get this?" Frolov asked.

Lyko told him.

New York—Washington
April 5

THE RUMORS had been flying for two days: the Soviet Union's foreign minister was coming to the United Nations to deliver a major policy statement about the USSR's position on human rights. That, at least, was the most believable of the rumors, rather more likely than the one that had Moscow and Peking announcing the formation of a new alliance against the West. Foreign Minister Konstantin Truschenko's speech was being awaited with considerable anticipation; General Secretary Kulagin's regime hadn't been noted so far for its displays of humanitarianism, and there were said to be more political prisoners in the Gulags now than there had been since Stalin's day.

Lee Palzer, the American ambassador to the United Nations, took a sip from his water glass, wished it were bourbon, and looked up at the great olive-wreathed map of the world above the speaker's dais at the front of the Hall of the General Assembly. Truschenko was going to be up there on the dais in a couple of minutes. Palzer would have liked to have had more information about what the Russian was going to say, but despite the flood of gossip, no one appeared to have any concrete information. Not even the CIA's spooks, apparently.

He leaned back in his chair, half-turning to speak to one of the aides behind him. "Anything from Washington?"

"No, sir. I just called State. They haven't anything at all on what Truschenko's going to say."

"Okay. We'll have to ride it out."

He looked around. The General Assembly hall was full, fuller than he'd seen it for some time. The spectator galleries were jammed with press; the air hummed with voices. Palzer took another sip of water and settled down to wait.

The noise in the hall suddenly diminished; Truschenko was coming. Palzer studied him carefully as he walked down the aisle and took his seat with the Soviet delegation. The Russian moved methodically and calmly, his silver hair perfectly arranged, his Western suit impeccable in its cut. A self-possessed man, hard as armor plate, but then he needed to be to survive in Kulagin's government.

The U.N. general secretary introduced him, and Truschenko took the dais. Palzer plugged in his earphone for the simultaneous translation.

"Members of the General Assembly," Truschenko began. "I bring you greetings from the government of the people of the Union of Soviet Socialist Republics, and in the name of the Communist Party of the Soviet Union, from General Secretary Valentin Vasileyevich Kulagin." He paused, looked around briefly, and then resumed.

"It has always been the deepest desire of the peoples of the Soviet Union to promote freedom, peace, and the right of every human being to the essentials of life."

More of the usual, Palzer thought. He gave the Russian half an ear, making a few notes on his writing pad as the man went on and on. Moscow had probably been feeling tender about its plummeting reputation in the area of human rights, particularly in the way it seemed to be treating its Jews, and had sent Truschenko trotting over here to obscure reality with rhetoric.

Bullshit baffles brains, Palzer thought, drawing a series of concentric circles on the pad. Still, even when the Russians don't say anything, they're still saying something. Even if it's just to tell the world to leave them alone while they beat the brains out of some defenseless Jews or Uzbeks, or whomever.

Another hour of this, likely, before he could begin to hope for a cup of coffee. It didn't appear that there was going to be much in the speech to interest Washington; it would be significant, if at all, in what Truschenko didn't say.

The Russian had paused again. He seemed to like doing that, placing small weighty silences in his prepared text. Palzer started to yawn, but stifled it. It would be undiplomatic, to say the least, to be seen to yawn during an address to the United Nations General Assembly by the Soviet foreign minister.

Truschenko swept his glance across the ranked delegates, his eyes resting for a brief moment on the Israeli ambassador.

"The Soviet Union has always upheld the right of all peoples to self-determination," he said. "We are open and unafraid in this regard. But, for many years, we have been unjustly accused of barring emigration of some elements of our population. These groundless accusations, I am sad to say, have been used by the United States and Israel to malign us to the world. Even sadder is the success which these

169

two nations have had in this slander; we have finally had to admit that our goodwill and love of peace are no defense against maliciousness and spite. The imperialist nations have defiled the reputation of the Soviet Union by representing it as some vast prison, whereas, as all men and women of goodwill and clear vision know, the USSR is the greatest hope of justice for all humankind. But the slander has become too painful for the Soviet people to accept any longer. My government has instructed me to tell you that we are about to refute these accusations in the most immediate and direct way that we can."

He stopped again. Palzer stopped doodling; he sat bolt upright, his eyes fixed on Truschenko.

"It is for this reason," Truschenko said slowly and carefully, "that the government of the Union of Soviet Socialist Republics, under the guidance of the Communist Party of the Soviet Union, has decided to permit the immediate departure, from within its boundaries, of all Soviet citizens of Jewish nationality."

Pandemonium erupted in the hall. Truschenko tried to go on, but couldn't. Palzer looked at the representative of Israel. The woman's face was alight with joy.

The American ambassador had been in his profession too long to share her feeling. There are nearly two million Soviet Jews, he thought. Wait until she's had time to think. Wait until everybody's had time to think. The only people smiling then will be the Russians.

James Parnell, president of the United States, sat behind his desk in the Oval Office. Even at the desk he appeared tall; standing, he was six foot three and lanky, with long stone-gray hair that fell sideways across his forehead, almost to the left eyebrow. There were strain lines around his mouth that made him look older than his age, which was fifty-six. The lines were even deeper than usual at the moment; he was reading the last page of an intelligence briefing. With him in the office were the members of what could have been called his inner cabinet: Secretary of State Kimberly Cornelissen, wearing thick-lensed glasses and a baggy tweed suit; Secretary of Defense John Lusby, jowly with close-cropped red hair; Director of Central Intelligence Cooper Tarkington, the apparently never-lit pipe jammed into one corner of his mouth, and Secretary of the Interior Richard Cox, whose only distinguishing mark was an extremely narrow black moustache, which gave him a faintly sinister air. He shaved it off before major press conferences and then grew it back again.

The tall clock in the corner of the office chimed ten as Parnell finished the last page. "You know," he said, looking up and tapping the intelligence brief with a long index finger, "we should have expected something extreme like this, especially knowing what we know about Kulagin. The way the Russians have been behaving recently toward their Jews pointed to it. They were building up to something. Did any of our estimates include massed and forced emigration, though? Kip?"

Kimberly Cornelissen stirred in his chair and pressed his glasses back onto his nose. "No, I'm afraid not. I have to admit we've been caught with one foot in the air, over at State. But the Soviets've always been adamant about restricting emigration of all kinds; the problem with Jewish emigration's simply been the most obvious because of the connection with Israel. We never expected this."

"Coop," said Parnell, "this intelligence brief of yours says that Moscow's not behaving this way because it's suddenly discovered a deep love of Jews in Marx or Lenin."

Cooper Tarkington looked out the window and then back at Parnell. Taking the unlit pipe out of his mouth, he said, "Mr. President, if you look at the contents of the CIA brief in conjunction with the requests delivered by the Soviet ambassador this afternoon, it's possible to see a pattern emerging. It's blurry at the moment, but we think there's a lot more here than meets the eye.

"To begin with, and I think Kip will agree with me in this, the Russians have gained a big, although I believe temporary, propaganda victory. We've been telling them for years to open the gates and let the Jews out, and anybody else who wants to go, and now they've told us, in effect, to put our money where our mouth is. Nobody expected them to let all two million go at once. Think about that for a moment. What countries are going to be willing to take in a share of two million Russian Jews? The Israelis might like to, but they simply don't have the resources to do it, and if they could, the country would suddenly be nearly half Russian. I don't think even Jerusalem could handle that prospect. Then," he put his pipe back in his mouth and removed it again, "you can be sure as God made little green apples that they're not all going to be plain and simple Russian Jews. If I were running the KGB, this would be the chance of a lifetime."

"To infiltrate agents, you mean," Parnell said.

"Exactly. How many operatives could you hide in two million people? A thousand? Ten thousand? Remember, we don't know how long the Russians have been preparing this surprise. They could have

172

had time to train as many as *fifty* thousand, or even more. Suppose we or the Israelis or the French or the British, or whoever, managed to identify half of them. What would we do? Spend the next three or four decades watching twenty thousand or so suspected agents? Bring them all to trial and jail them? On what grounds? We could never do it. In the meantime, the other twenty thousand or so are going cheerfully about their business. The KGB's business. It could be a disaster.''

"Christ," said Cox.

"What do you think, Richard?" Parnell asked the secretary of the interior. "How many could we take?"

Cox was tight-lipped. "A few Soviet Jews is one thing, especially if they're perceived by the general population as being refugees. But ten thousand? Or half a million, maybe? You know as well as I do that there's one hell of a lot of anti-Semitism in this country, under the surface, and always has been. We took a few thousand boat people from Vietnam, and you know the troubles that caused. We have to face facts. This country may be all in favor of Israel and detest the Arabs, but it doesn't want more Jews." He looked at the others. *"No* country wants more Jews. Remember what somebody said, before the last war? 'None is too many.' That may have gone underground, but it's still there."

"Going back a little, Coop," said Parnell. "You said this might be only a temporary propaganda victory for the Kremlin. How so?"

"Because these people, many of them, aren't going to be willing emigrants. It's a misconception in the West that everybody in the Soviet Union wants to leave. They don't."

"Surely the Russians aren't going to load them

on trains and ships and simply throw them out?'' said Cox.

"That is exactly what we think they are going to do.''

Everybody looked at Tarkington with varying expressions of disbelief.

"Coop,'' said Cornelissen, "you didn't tell me this.''

"I know,'' said Tarkington. "It isn't in the brief I brought you either, Mr. President. It's too sensitive. I prefer to report it verbally.''

"What?'' asked Parnell.

"The Russians have been building concentration camps. A lot of them. We thought at first Kulagin might have been planning a straightforward purge of his political enemies, like Stalin did in the thirties, but with the U.N. announcement today . . . it has to be for the Jews.''

"But they can't get away with that!''

"But they can, for a while. They'll call them transit camps, or temporary relocation centers, or some innocuous term like that. But I wouldn't care to be in one. We've estimated the maximum number of people those camps can hold, even with overcrowding. Five to six hundred thousand. If you jam twice that number in, there are going to be a lot of dead Jews before they're all out. The experts out at Langley say maybe half a million. That's not including the ones the regime simply decides to get rid of in other ways. For example, we *think* there are two million Jews in Russia. What's to prevent the Kremlin from saying we were wrong, there were only a million and a half? If there *had* been two million, who would ever know what happened to the others?''

"Another Holocaust,'' breathed Cornelissen.

"Not as big as the last. But big. That's why I said

174

a temporary victory. But by the time the truth's out, so will be a few tens of thousands of KGB agents."

"Is there anything," Parnell asked Cornelissen, "we can do about it?"

The secretary of state was looking rather shaken. "At the moment? I don't know. I can tell you one thing, though. The Russians are just waiting for us to drag our heels on this. If we appear reluctant to take a lot of the emigrants, or if we accuse the Russians of tactics like the Nazis used, they'll be absolutely delighted. They'll say we're looking for excuses to keep the Jews out, that we were never serious about wanting free emigration from the Soviet Union, that we were only using the Russian-Jewish question for our own ends. A lot of other people will see it that way, too. We could *really* look bad."

"God damn it," Parnell said. "How did we get *put* in this position?"

"We never thought the Russians would do it," Cornelissen said. "It never even occurred to us."

"It should have."

"Yes, Mr. President. I know."

"Okay. We won't pursue that any further. What're we going to do about finding somewhere for these people to stay after the Russians start shipping them out, until we and the British and Europe and Israel can sort out how many we're each going to accept as refugees?"

"The Austrians have said they'll arrange facilities for as many as they can. The real problem is that the Russians are going to let a lot of Jews out by ship, through the Black Sea and the Dardanelles. Some can go directly to Israel, but we're going to have to find somewhere for the bulk of them so that we can at least make a start on security checks and

175

provide proper entry visas and documentation. The best place, for a temporary camp, seems to be Turkey, near Istanbul.''

''Will the Turks agree? We haven't been on good terms with them since they took Cyprus from the Greeks.''

''I think, Mr. President,'' Cornelissen replied, ''that if we agreed to at least a partial lifting of the arms embargo against Turkey, President Celebi would accept responsibility for such an arrangement. He took pains to remind me that the Turks gave the Sephardic Jews a home five hundred years ago, when the Spanish expelled them from Spain.''

''You've checked this out?''

''Yes. Informally.''

Parnell sighed. ''Okay. We have to do something, and fast, or the Russians will start saying we don't want these people.''

''Mr. President,'' said Richard Cox. ''Do we? I suspect we don't. I don't think many other countries do, either.''

''Are you suggesting,'' Parnell asked ''that we do *nothing?*''

A short silence, which Tarkington broke. ''There is to be considered,'' he said, ''the extreme danger represented by the KGB plants among the bona fide refugees. We can't discount that. I *must* advise against wholesale acceptance of the Russian Jews.''

''I know,'' Parnell said tiredly. ''That's your job. To advise me. You've advised me. But I have to decide. We can't sit by, for even the best reasons, and let these people die.''

176

Moscow
April 5

SNOW WAS BEGINNING to sift down from the night sky when Cole left the embassy, although the temperature was still just above freezing. He walked south along Tchaikovsky Street toward the intersection with Prospekt Kalinin, listening to the familiar boom of Moscow traffic. Off to his right, he could see the tall lighted towers of the SEV building, near the river.

He'd picked up surveillance as soon as he left the embassy, as he'd expected. He and Aldine, the CIA station chief, had debated using a scatter operation when Cole set out on his run, but Cole had finally decided against it. The Russians used it all the time in Washington, dispatching a dozen or so known KGB people into rush hour traffic to cover the one who was on the KGB's real business. Here, though, the technique was of less use, since the Russians didn't stint their resources when it came to surveillance. And since it was used less, it would draw more attention than Cole wanted.

He had two hours to clean himself off, anyway; it was unlikely that Dzerzhinsky Square would be so interested in his arrival that they'd put in a full team, which took at least twelve people and really would be hard to shake. As far as he could tell at the moment, there were just three men, two walking behind him and one in a green Chaika sedan rolling slowly along the curb. It would be normal operating procedure against any new arrival, just to let him or her know that in General Secretary Kulagin's Russia foreigners were not welcome.

He waited through a green light at Prospekt Kalinin, just to be sure. The Chaika waited obediently, and the man behind him developed a sudden interest in a store window. Good enough. He'd get rid of the car driver by taking the metro, and unless the other two were exceptionally deft or determined, he could easily shake them off in the next two hours. Then Markelov, the package, whatever it was, and home. There was a Mayday book prepared for the operation, if Cole couldn't get out via the embassy, but with reasonable luck he wouldn't need the emergency plans. The KGB surveillance team would know he'd shaken them on purpose, but that wouldn't necessarily make them think he was on a mission; CIA staffers at the embassy regularly eluded followers, not only for the fun of it and to keep their hands in, but also to keep the groundwork laid for operations like this one.

The lighted M of the Smolenskaya metro station was just ahead. A faint nostalgia pricked at Cole. Ever since returning to the Russian capital he'd been feeling little twinges of it, a sense of familiarity. In some ways he had been rather fond of the grim gray city on the Moskva River, although it was a fondness touched by an undercurrent of fear.

Down the escalator under the big chandeliers. Still crowded down here, although it was past seven

178

o'clock: the inevitable hunched *babushkas* with their string bags, women in headscarves and shapeless cloth coats, the men wearing hats with earflaps, ordinary Russians. Most looked tired and pasty, strained. Cole had taken care to wear clothes similar to Russian ones; even his boots were nondescript and worn at the heels. He was carrying the Bryce papers. They'd considered sending him in with a flash-alias as a Russian, but discarded the idea. If he were picked up carrying whatever Markelov gave him, he'd have a better chance of bluffing his way out if he were diplomatic staff.

Onto the platform, now. He could hear the rush of a train in the distance, growing louder. In his mind he'd named the two KGB men Igor and Boris; they were still with him, arranging themselves to flank him on each side, maybe ten meters away.

The train. It burst into the station in a rush of wind and noise, wheels screeching on the tracks. Cole watched it slow down, estimating. If he could get an end door, either Igor or Boris would end up in another car, unless they were willing to be obvious about it and hurry toward Cole's.

The train stopped, obligingly placing an end door precisely in front of Cole. It slid open, releasing the thick smell of a Russian crowd: old perspiration, damp cloth, garlic, cabbage, wet leather. Cole wriggled into the car. Igor had lost out; he was in the car behind Cole's. Boris was in the center of this one, hanging onto a strap.

The train started to move. Cole gave it one stop, and then, just outside Kalinin Station, began moving for the door. Boris obediently shifted. Cole glanced at the end of his coach, getting the window of the connecting doors in his line of vision. Boris was there, watching him without appearing to do so.

179

Into the station, Cole waiting by the door, his nose almost touching the glass. Stopped in a hiss of brakes. Door opening. Step out onto the platform. Igor too. Stop. Igor stops. Time to play poker. Turn suddenly, remember this isn't my stop, start for the doors as they begin to hiss closed. Igor panicking, whipping himself back inside. Wait a minute, this *is* my stop, what a relief. Pull back with the doors nipping at a coat sleeve.

Igor was still inside. Cole avoided looking at him as the train began to roll.

Dammit. Boris was a little quicker off the mark. There he was, four meters down the platform, adjusting the flaps of his hat, tugging at his gloves. Well, he wouldn't be able to call for help, or he'd lose Cole.

Off to the escalator, now; let's see what the outside has to offer. Cole began to realize he was enjoying himself. There was no real danger involved in this. They wouldn't pick him up for playing tag, and he could clean Boris off without difficulty well before he had to head for the rendezvous with Markelov.

As it turned out, Boris was a good deal better than Igor. It took Cole three buses, another subway ride, and a visit to the GUM department store to get rid of him. Cole wasn't really certain he was gone until he walked across Staraya Square without a sign of the man; by then it was nearly time to go. As he went down into the subway, Cole thought, I may have been a little too cocky. Another fifteen minutes of that and I'd have been getting worried.

He left the metro at Danilovsky station and went up the escalator to the street. The snow was a bit heavier now, and was beginning to lie on the pavement. He didn't take the main street, but kept to the back ways as he headed southwest. He reached Sabolovka Street just south of the Donskoy Monastery and turned left. Three blocks along was the entrance to the Danilovsky Cemetery. Cole looked at his watch in the glimmer of a streetlight. Exactly on time.

He went in through the cemetery gates. Inside, the narrow paths among the graves were dimly lit by the reflection of the city's lights. Birches and firs cast irregular blots and stripes of shadow across the snow. Cole made his way to the back wall of the graveyard, to a point about a hundred meters from the Intercession Gate. A stone plinth bore a large model of a JS-III Stalin tank, a memorial to the commander of an armored division of the Second World War. The man hadn't been forgotten yet; a sprig of greenery an a single white flower lay between the treads.

A shadow detached itself from the plinth. Cole stopped. "It's late," he said, "to be here, remembering."

"It's never too late to remember," a voice said. "Samuel?"

"Yes," Cole said. "They sent me."

The shadow stood up. Cole couldn't see Markelov's face well in the gloom, but there was exhaustion in the Russian's voice. "I wasn't sure it would be you. Thank God. Are you well?"

"Yes. You've put yourself in great danger."

A wry chuckle. "I am already in great danger. Did you know that a few weeks ago I was fired from my job? All Jews at Moscow University have been dismissed. Last night I learned that several of my colleagues have been arrested. And their families with them."

"It's true, then," Cole said. "We've been hearing rumors. They haven't come for you yet?"

"They may have," said Markelov. "But I haven't gone home since last night. I've been hiding, until I could meet you."

"Then you haven't heard?" Cole asked.

"Heard what?"

"It was this morning. Truschenko announced in the U.N. that all Jews are going to be allowed to emigrate from Russia."

Again the wry laugh. "I knew what they were going to do in February. That's why I risked contacting you. Your people shouldn't have taken so long to send you."

"I'm here now," Cole said. "What did you need to give us?"

Markelov took something out of his coat and pressed it into Cole's glove. "This. It's a microfilm of the orders for a plan called Winter Palace. It's a very old plan, Samuel. I took it from the body of a man I killed near the Finnish border, almost forty years ago. I've had it ever since. But I never believed they would do it. They have. What you've heard, the rumors, the U.N. announcement, are all part of it. Winter Palace."

Cole squeezed the microfilm container hard in his palm, then slipped it into his coat pocket. "Does anyone else know you had it? Your wife?"

"No one knew until last night. That's why I'm running, Samuel. They almost caught me with it. There were prints I made from the microfilm years ago, and I didn't have time to burn them. They'll have found them by now. I've been hiding since last night, in the streets. When I go back to my apartment, they'll be waiting. They won't question me immediately, and I'll keep silent as long as I can. Will that give you enough time to get away?''

"I'll be back at the embassy within an hour. But I might be able to get you out," Cole said. He was thinking furiously. It would be tremendously difficult. He couldn't do it. He would have to abandon Markelov, again.

"I don't think you can risk it," Markelov said. "What I've given you is what needs to get out. Tell the world what they're really going to do. They're going to kill us, Samuel. They don't care whether we live or die, as long as they get some use out of us. It will be the children and the old, at first. But the longer the outside world delays helping us, the more deaths there will be. Tell them.''

"I will," Cole said.

"Did you ever wonder," Markelov asked, "why I offered your people my services?''

"Yes," said Cole. He thought: I have to get out of here, it's too dangerous to stay. But Alexander's as good as dead. I'll never see him again. "I wondered. You had everything.''

"When I was fifteen," Markelov said, "my family lived in Moscow. It was in 1948, at Rosh Hashanah. Israel had just been established, and Golda Meir was the Israeli foreign minister in Moscow. That day she and all the Israeli legation went to the Great Synagogue for the services. It had been rumored among the Jews of Moscow that that would happen, and my father took me to see them, the Israelis. When we got there the street was overflowing, there must have been fifty thousand of us. All Jews. I remember people were calling out to Golda Meir, stretching out their hands, calling *Shalom, shalom.* ' My father was crying. We were only a meter from her, I remember she looked at me, I couldn't believe it, a

183

Jew from Israel right there in front of me. I reached out and touched her sleeve; she was crying too. Then the crowd separated us, and I was left with my father while she went into the synagogue for the service. We waited until she came out, but there were too many people, I couldn't get near her. But I'd touched her.''

Markelov fell silent. Cole didn't speak.

"I never forgot," Markelov said. "I knew then that I was Jewish. That I always would be. And that the Russians hate us. Do you understand now, why I worked for you?''

"Yes," Cole said.

"You must go. I've kept you too long. I'll wait for five minutes before I leave. *Shalom*, Samuel.''

"Good-bye," Cole said, and then: "Alexander, I know I'm leaving you. There's nothing else I can do.'' As I left Berdeyev and the others, he thought. Would they have accepted that excuse, that reason? "Don't think too badly of me.''

"Don't worry about me, Samuel," Markelov said. "I've done with my life what I was supposed to. Not many men can say that.'' He touched Cole's coat sleeve. "Now you have to go. Quickly.''

Cole turned away from the old man, past the monuments through the dim light. Once he thought he heard Markelov call after him, but the call wasn't repeated. He reached the cemetery entrance and risked a brief look outside. There was no one.

He transferred the microfilm container from his coat to his trousers pocket and set off toward the metro station, again using the back streets. Visibility was much poorer now, the snow thickening steadily. The sidewalks were extremely slippery, snow over freezing slush. Cole walked carefully in his worn boots.

As he turned a corner into an even darker side street, his right foot slid out from under him. He staggered, trying to regain his balance, arms flailing, half conscious of a pair of shadowy figures approaching a few meters away. No good. He lost his balance completely, and fell flat on his back. The fur of his hat prevented the back of his head from hitting the pavement too hard, but even so he was slightly stunned. He half sat up. The two figures were standing above him. Peaked caps, overcoats, slung weapons. Militiamen.

"Another drunk," one of them said. "They're all over, tonight." He had a bushy handlebar moustache. Reaching down, he grabbed Cole's arm and started pulling him to his feet. Cole twisted out of his grip. "I'm not drunk," he said in Russian. "I slipped on the ice."

"We'll see," the militiaman said. "Get up and show me your papers."

Cole stood up carefully, brushing slop off his coat sleeves. "It's all right," he said. "I'm just on my way home."

"Papers," said the other militiaman. He was clean-shaven. They were both quite young, not out of their twenties.

The microfilm capsule pressed into Cole's thigh. "I'm an American diplomat," he said. "There'll be trouble if you molest me."

"Let me see your papers," the one with the moustache said, stolidly.

Cole took out his passport and residence visa. The one with the moustache took out a flashlight and shone it on the pages, then at Cole's face to compare him with the photograph. The other one said, "What are you doing down here at this time of the night?"

"I needed a walk."

"Search him," said moustache. "Undo your coat."

Their guns were slung, no danger. Cole moved as though to undo his overcoat. The militiamen waited, watching him.

Cole's hand slammed upwards, catching moustache under the chin, snapping his head back. The man flew backward and Cole heard a sharp crack as his head struck the masonry of the wall behind him. He pivoted and kicked the other man in the belly, just under the solar plexus. The man folded over and Cole chopped him across the back of the neck. The militiaman collapsed onto the pavement.

Jesus Christ, Cole thought. Now I've got trouble. Move, quickly.

He snatched up his papers and ran. He might be able to get back to the embassy before they woke up and sounded the alarm. That would still leave him in deep trouble; the Russians didn't take kindly to foreigners assaulting their police officers. But the microfilm would go out in the diplomatic bag, that was the important thing.

He risked a glance over his shoulder as he ran.

Oh, Christ.

One of the militiamen was sitting up, silhouetted in the glow from the far end of the street.

I should have hit him harder, Cole thought. It's going to be the Mayday book, after all.

186

Moscow
April 5

WITH GREAT EFFORT, Frolov kept his voice even and free of rage. "And what did he do after he disposed of the two militiamen?"

Pavel Osipov wore an expression of suppressed fury, which was unusual; he was usually as stone-faced as his superior. He was head of Frolov's personal executive group, which the KGB chairman used for investigations or operations too delicate to be entrusted to the regular organs. Osipov and his men owed allegiance to Frolov alone; if the KGB chairman lost his post, they'd follow him. And if they made a serious mistake, such as this one, there would be no one to protect them from Frolov's rage. It was a mark of Osipov's confidence in his usefulness to the chairman that he looked just as infuriated; most men in his position would have worn quite another expression.

"He went on the run. He's very good, there's no doubt about it. Normally, with a full team, there's no chance for the subject to get away. He managed it, damn him. But before we lost him, he stopped at

187

the public washrooms outside Taganskaya metro station. It was likely an emergency dead drop.''

''He didn't leave whatever it was he picked up from the Jew?''

''No. We checked the washrooms. They were clean.''

Frolov permitted himself a small internal sigh of relief. The last thing he wanted was a roll of microfilm delivered triumphantly to his desk, by Osipov or anyone else. Osipov didn't know, yet, what was on the microfilm, only that whoever had it was to be located and tracked. If this surprised him, he showed no sign of it. He was accustomed, like most KGB operatives, to obeying orders without question.

''You don't think he'll try to get back to his embassy?''

''He'd be a fool if he did, and he's not a fool. We've been watching Tchaikovsky Street, but he hasn't come near it. The militia's all over the place there too, waiting for him. They're really pissed.''

''What filthy luck,'' Frolov said. ''The damned MVD *would* have to stumble on him. Timoshek over at Homicide will be turning the city inside out, if his boss lets him.''

''The American shouldn't have hit that militiaman so hard,'' Osipov said. ''Assault's one thing, but murder's different. Especially murdering a cop. You're right about Timoshek.''

''Are you *sure* Bryce didn't spot the real surveillance team after he left the embassy?'' After finding out what had been under Alexander Markelov's bed, Frolov had moved quickly and discreetly. He had told Lyko to forget he'd ever seen the documents; he, Frolov, would handle this personally because of its sensitivity. No special action was to be taken in

188

the case of the Jew; he was to be picked up as he would have been in the normal course of the collections. As soon as he'd dismissed Lyko, he called in Osipov and put him to work. Osipov felt it likely that the Jew still had the negatives of the documents with him when he'd left the *dacha,* and the fact that he'd retrieved them probably meant that a courier was on the way to pick them up. An American junior diplomat entering the country within the last couple of days would be a good bet; lo and behold, there was Bryce. They'd found Markelov too, about fourteen hours after he would have got back to Moscow from Peredelkino. He was riding the metro, clearly putting in time until an appointment. When the two surveillance teams spotted the pair moving toward each other, Frolov knew that Osipov had guessed right. It made up to some degree for having lost the American afterward.

"He didn't pick us up between the embassy and the cemetery, I'm certain of that," Osipov said. "After the dead drop, possibly. He did everything in the book to lose us."

"And succeeded," Frolov pointed out sharply. It wouldn't do to let Osipov forget that. "Let me tell you one thing, Osipov. There's a lot more riding on this than you can imagine. If you let the MVD grab this American, you'll be for the high jump. Depend on it."

"Yes, Chairman," Osipov said flatly. "We'll locate him."

"Do that," Frolov said. "Now get going."

When the head of the special team had left, Frolov leaned back in his chair, stretching his arms out on the desk to get the kinks out of them. He was very tense, and no wonder. He was playing an extremely dangerous game; if Osipov began to suspect that

189

Frolov *wanted* the American to get out of the country with the Winter Palace microfilm, he might start thinking too hard.

Devil take the MVD, anyway. It would have been so simple if Bryce had gotten to the embassy, got the film out. You could bet that in a few days, a week or two at the most, the Americans would start broadcasting what was in it to the four corners of the world. Kulagin had been careful, in the Politburo and the Central Committee and the Secretariat, to take credit for the idea and the operation. Very well, he could take the blame for it, too. Frolov had very carefully sounded out the minister of defense two days before, to find out what he thought about the general secretary's prize project. Lesiovsky had been guardedly critical; he, too, seemed to be worried about Kulagin's direction. Stalin had purged the military's officer corps during the 1930s, and ninety percent of all senior officers had ended in the camps or against a wall in the Lubianka. Lesiovsky wouldn't have forgotten that.

If Frolov had the military on his side, and if there were enough men in the Politburo and the Secretariat who were as worried as Lesiovsky . . . Kulagin could be removed. Legally, by a vote.

Or the other way.

Anastas Timoshek, Chief of the Homicide Division (Moscow) of the MVD, studied the wall map of the city. Somewhere, among the eight million people that map represented, was the man who had killed a policeman. Timoshek wanted him, badly.

"The surviving militiaman's report states that the murderer said he was American?" he asked Detective Belchenko, who had had the misfortune to be chosen as Timoshek's assistant for this particular case. The two men were sitting in Timoshek's office, down the corridor from the Militia Operations Room. They could hear, faintly, the clatter of teletypes, since the door to the hall was open. Timoshek usually stayed away from Operations, with its computer terminals and printers and illuminated wall maps, preferring to work with his own smudged map, a battery of telephones and a collection of dog-eared file folders. The office walls hadn't been painted in years and the once-cream paint was scabbed and peeling. Timoshek's desk wasn't much better, the varnished wood tea-stained and riddled with cracks. The two wooden chairs in the office were supremely uncomfortable.

"That's right," said Belchenko, shifting painfully on his chair. He'd brought the statement up from Interviewing as soon as it had been taken. "But the survivor didn't actually see the identification. The murderer could have been lying. He spoke Russian with no accent."

"There's a description, I see, though. Moustache. No eye color given—hardly surprising in the dark. Not particularly well-dressed, so maybe *not* a foreigner. We should be able to do something with that. Has it been put out to the precincts yet?"

"It's being sent out right now. If he *was* foreign, though, it's a matter for State Security. Are you going to call them?"

Timoshek looked at his assistant with annoyance. "There's no reason at this time to believe it was a foreigner. If I find out differently, I'll tell the KGB."

"Yes, sir. It was only a suggestion."

"Keep those kinds of suggestions to yourself."

Belchenko looked at his superior. He hated work-

191

ing with Timoshek; everybody did. To start with, the man was physically repellent, with suety jowls and two prominent moles, one on the right cheekbone and the other in the middle of the left cheek of his heavily lined face. His eyes were sunk in a mass of puffy wrinkles and he didn't bathe or shave very often. Monday mornings, if he hadn't been on duty the day before, he usually carried the sweetish-sickly scent of unmetabolized vodka. Rumor had it that he was really hard on his wife, his second and a lot younger than he. Belchenko had met her once; she was a real stunner. He couldn't imagine how she'd gotten hooked up with a pig like Timoshek.

He was a good cop, though, there was no doubt about that. Any criminal who got Timoshek on his tail was as good as behind bars. And he never gave up. He'd been in Homicide for a long time, and he had friends in other police departments all over western Russia, which gave him a lot of freedom of movement; it was said he could even get plane tickets on half an hour's notice. He'd once pursued a rapist-murderer all the way to Gorki, using his contacts, and had arrested the man personally and brought him back to Moscow. Even the militia commissioner was careful of him and let him do pretty much as he pleased. He'd also stood up to State Security on a couple of occasions and gotten away with it.

"I'm going to handle this one myself," Timoshek said. "You're detailed for the case for the duration. If you haven't got bulletins out to the train stations and airports, do it. I won't have cop killers on my patch, do you understand?"

"Yes, sir."

"I'll follow this bastard all the way to Vladivostok, if I have to. Grab one of the footsloggers and get him over to start looking for witnesses. I want a report on my desk from you in three hours. Forget about going home to bed.''

Moscow
April 5

ALEXANDER MARKELOV was almost home.

He stopped at the entrance to Ryleev Street, to gaze along it for what was almost certainly the last time. Snow was falling again, heavily, turning the streetlights to vague luminous circles and blurring the outlines of the apartment buildings. They weren't the ugly concrete towers most people had to put up with, that began to fall down almost as soon as they were finished; these were made of precisely laid honey-colored bricks. A few years ago Markelov had managed, by judicious cultivation of a number of influential friends and the use of his considerable academic reputation, to get a four-room apartment in one of the blocks.

Those friends would flee from him now, disown him for their own safety. It didn't matter. He had told the Americans about Winter Palace, and perhaps they would believe him. Perhaps they would even be able to stop it. How they might achieve that, Markelov couldn't imagine. But he himself had done what he could.

He began walking through the snow toward his

194

building. It was only about half past ten and many of the windows were still yellow with lamplight. He thought the KGB would likely be waiting for him; they'd know he'd turn up sooner or later. He didn't have the resources to run far, and he was cold and hungry. Perhaps they'd let him warm himself and eat something before they took him away.

He peered through the wind-driven snow, but there didn't seem to be a security vehicle pulled up in front of the building. A white Volga that belonged to the industrial ministry official on the sixth floor was standing by the curb, but that was all. That was curious. Maybe they'd put their car in the parking lot on the building's other side. *Nichevo,* it didn't matter. He'd be seeing the inside of it soon enough, anyway.

Snow lay thickly on the front steps of the building. Markelov unlocked the main door and let himself in. The lobby walls were finished in blue and white tiles and there was a tiled checkerboard pattern on the floor. The tiles were from Finland. Esfir had always liked them a great deal.

He half-expected them to be waiting for him in the lobby, but it was empty. He crossed to the elevator bank and pressed the call button. The door opened with a faint hum. Inside, he pressed number three. He'd have one more ride in it, downward, and that would be that.

Esfir. Would they take her as well? They might; they'd assume she knew *something.* His daughter Irina's husband had already been arrested. Surely, though, they wouldn't take Irina herself or little Tania; the child was too small to be left without her mother.

But Lezin had said on the phone last night that

195

they were taking away whole families. Jewish families.

Is that why I'm so free of anguish at what I'm inflicting on my family? he wondered as the elevator doors opened. I expected to feel torment at having brought this on them, on my daughter and wife and grandchild. But if they are taking us all anyway. . . .

He stood for a moment in front of his apartment door, breathing deeply, gathering himself. They were in there, waiting. For a moment he almost lost his nerve, almost turned away to go down the fire stairs and out into the snow-covered streets again.

He put his key into the lock and turned it. The door swung open.

The living room was in semi-darkness, lit only by one lamp. On the couch lay Esfir, wrapped in a blanket. Irina was in the chair next to the window, her head drooping to one side. Her eyes were closed. There was no one else in the room.

"Esfir?" he said, disbelieving. Were they waiting for him in the bedroom?

Irina sat up with a jerk. *"Father?"*

Markelov closed the door behind him. His legs were trembling so that he almost fell. "Yes. I'm home."

Esfir was stirring, sitting up. "My dear God, Alexander." Her voice was thick with sleep. "What's happened to you? Where have you been?"

"I'll tell you in a minute," Markelov said. "I need to sit down."

Irina leaped out of the chair. "Sit here. I'll make tea."

"Yes. First give me a glass of vodka."

"I will," Esfir said. She seemed to have regained some of the old spark; although her face was hag-

196

gard and gray, there was a strength in her voice he hadn't heard since Sasha died.

"I need to eat," Markelov said. "We all should. Where is Tania?"

"In the bedroom, sleeping," Irina called from the kitchen. Markelov could hear water running, the clink of china. Esfir returned from the kitchen with a glass of Stolichnaya; Markelov took it from her and tossed it straight back. The bottle had been in the refrigerator and the spirit was at first icy, then burning and aromatic in his throat. He put the glass on the table beside the chair and closed his eyes, feeling the liquor scald in his stomach.

I probably shouldn't have done that, he thought. I'll get tipsy. That's no condition to be arrested in.

Where are they?

He opened his eyes. Esfir was kneeling at his feet. She put her arms around his calves and laid her head on his knees. Her shoulders shook. Markelov put his hand on her hair, stroking. "Don't cry, beloved. I'm here."

"I thought I had lost you, too," she said in a choked voice. "I couldn't have borne that with everything else." She lifted her head to look at him; in the low light, tears gleamed on her cheeks. "Alexander, what have you done?"

He stared down at her, wondering how much to say. She had been his wife for nearly forty years; her looks were gone and she was pudgy and her breasts and belly had the stretch marks of bearing three children, but he loved her as he had never loved anyone. Even when they fought, and there had been much of that when they were starting out, when there was never enough money and they were living with three other families in a four-room apartment with a communal kitchen, they had known that they

197

belonged together. Neither of them had ever contemplated giving the other up.

Now he had brought this on her. If they were taking whole families, as Lezin had said, they would take her, too. How long would she survive in a prison, at her age?

Irina came back from the kitchen with a teapot and silver-mounted antique tea glasses on a wooden tray. She put it on the table next to Markelov's glass. "I'll bring bread and sausage."

"No. Wait," Markelov said. He reached out and touched her arm. "Please sit down."

"Let me pour the tea, papa."

She did, Markelov watching her. He wasn't quite certain how he had managed to sire such a beautiful young woman; the high wide cheekbones, enormous eyes, generous mouth. She did not look in the least Jewish. But that didn't matter. It was stamped in her passport.

He sipped at the tea as she sat down on the floor next to her mother. "I would like to see Tania in a minute. Has she been asleep long?"

"For a couple of hours. I'll wake her."

"Have you heard anything from Yakov?"

"No," Irina said. "I tried all day to get some information, but no one at Dzerzhinsky Square would tell me anything."

"You went *there?*" Markelov said, aghast.

"Yes. Why shouldn't I? Yakov is my husband." There was anger in her voice. "They had no right to arrest him. He'd done nothing. But I couldn't find out anything, so I came back to see if you had come home. Mother kept Tania here; she didn't go to school."

"Alexander," said Esfir. "What's happened with you?"

198

"I am almost certainly going to be arrested. Probably tonight. I think, from what Lezin said yesterday, that they will take us all. As soon as we've eaten, we must put some things together to bring with us, things we'll need."

"But Alexander, *why?*"

"Because we are Jews. They've planned this for a very long time."

"Father, how do you know that?" Irina asked. "It may not just be Jews. They—"

"Kitten, it is the Jews. I know."

"Oh." She looked at him hard. "Is that why you were gone since yesterday? Something to do with that?"

"Yes."

"But you can't have done anything wrong," Esfir said. "Surely they'll know that. You're a literature professor, we have—we had—friends who might help us. . . ."

The door to the bedroom opened. Tania stood in the opening, her nightgown rumpled, her brown stuffed bear clutched under one arm. Markelov had brought it from East Germany when she was a baby, six years before. It was worn now and battered, but the child loved it dearly. With a constriction in his throat, Markelov thought again of how much she looked like her mother.

"Grandpa. You're back. I heard you talking and I woke up." Markelov expected her to run across the room and throw herself into his arms, but she didn't. She walked slowly toward him, eyes wide. "Why did you say we were going to have to go away?"

"We may not have to," Esfir said. "It's a mistake—"

The child stopped half a meter away from her

199

grandfather. Markelov reached out and drew her to him. She nestled her head in the cove of his shoulder and neck; her skin was warm from sleeping. "They said that to me the other day at school," she murmured.

"They said what? Who?"

"Ekaterina Sokolov. And Nadia Kaminsky. They don't like me. And I don't like them. They said everybody like us was going to be taken away and put in jail, because we're Jews."

"You didn't tell me this," Irina said. "Muffin, you should have. Did the teacher hear?"

"Yes."

"What did she do?"

"Nothing. Except she smiled. I didn't say anything because I knew you'd get angry. Why is it bad to be a Jew?"

"It isn't," Markelov said, holding down the fury. "They—"

Noises in the hall, heavy footsteps, stopping in front of the door. Three heavy knocks.

Oh, God, Markelov thought, they're here.

"Open up in there," a rough voice called. More pounding on the door. "Now!"

Markelov got wearily to his feet, but he was too late. There was a heavy *thud* of a boot striking wood and the door flew open. Dim light filtered in from the hallway. It was, as at the *dacha*, three of them, except that this time they wore uniforms and carried rifles.

"Residence of the Jew Alexander Markelov and wife?" said the leader. His voice was flat and merciless.

"It is."

The man peered around him. "Who are these other two?"

200

"My daughter and granddaughter."

"Jews?"

"Yes."

"You have fifteen minutes to pack one bag each containing clothes. Do not bring any food. It will be supplied. Leave any currency in your residence. It will be sealed and personal property will be held for you."

"Wait," Markelov said, trying one last time. "I'm the one you want. Don't you have orders for my arrest?"

The KGB lieutenant eyed him as though he were some kind of animal that had miraculously learned how to speak. "Don't fool with me, old Jew. I've got no orders except to remove anyone found in this apartment from it, in the next fifteen minutes. Get moving. Or do you want me to turn my men loose? They like searching Jews' apartments." He eyed Irina. "And Jews."

Markelov thought, incredulously. They didn't find the box? They must have. They'd know I had it. They should be taking me straight in for interrogation. Did I give the information to anyone else? Where did I get it? They'd be wild to know. But they're not. There is something odd about this.

"Where are we going?" Irina asked. Her voice trembled.

"You're in luck, *Zhid*. All Jews are being expelled from Russia. Every last one. We want you all out of here."

Esfir gasped. "Emigrate? But we don't want—"

"We're wasting time," Markelov said. "We have to pack. Esfir, Irina, find clothes. Tania, go and get dressed."

Tania said, "But I want to go back to bed." There was fear in her voice.

201

"I'm afraid you can't, kitten," Markelov said as gently as he could.

The child burst into tears. Markelov looked furiously at the KGB officer.

"You've got ten minutes," the man said. "Get moving."

Moscow—Odessa
April 6—8

COLE WAS PERPLEXED, and frightened.

He stood next to one of the waiting room pillars, looking up at the arrivals and departures board of Leningrad Station. The Leningrad express would be pulling out in twenty minutes, and he still hadn't been able to shake his followers.

He'd spotted them ten minutes after leaving the dead drop in the public washroom: two cars, probably a third somewhere to back them up. That meant there would be four or so on foot; there were still enough pedestrians about to mask them. Altogether, probably a full team of six to eight. He had no idea how long the surveillance had had him snared. It was possible they hadn't detected his meeting with Markelov, since there had been no sign of anyone in the cemetery. He thought he'd brushed them off half an hour after first seeing them, but by the time he reached Leningrad Station they'd picked him up again. Cole realized now, too late, that Igor and Boris had been feints. He'd been rusty and overconfident: a deadly combination. He'd let himself be distracted by the two obvious watchers, and the mistake was probably going to kill him.

But if they'd seen his attack on the militiamen, why hadn't they moved in?

Answer: they were waiting for him to do something. But what? Perhaps they thought his excursion into the Danilovsky Cemetery was meant to throw off any followers, and that he was still on the way to a rendezvous. But then, if they'd seen Markelov come out. . . .

It was too confusing, and he didn't have time to work it out now; he didn't have enough information. The long and the short of it was that he had to lose them. He had a chance, if the documents he'd picked up in the dead drop held. Cole could feel their sharp corners nestled in the small of his back, in the concealed pocket of the overcoat. There was a time limit, though, to how long they'd be good for: less than a day and a half. After that, he'd be on his own, which was as good as to say captured.

It was a quarter past eleven, but the Leningrad Station waiting room was still crowded, as Russian stations always were, even under Kulagin's strict regime: women in headscarves and topcoats of rough dark cloth, men sprawled on the scarred benches eating black bread and lumps of sausage, children asleep or glassy-eyed and too tired to cry.

Much as he wanted to curl up on a bench like one of the innocents around him and sleep, he had to go on. The MVD was already putting a watch on the stations; he'd seen four militiamen enter this one as he was approaching it. They weren't in the waiting room, though; they and others would be checking identification at the platform entrances.

He wrinkled his upper lip, which still smarted from the solvent he'd used to remove the false moustache. It had been thoughtful of Aldine to leave that in the dead drop, since the moustache adhesive could have taken a layer of skin with it. After getting rid of the moustache and checking the descriptions in the false papers, he'd removed the contact lenses and flushed them down the toilet. Before he left the public washroom the Bryce papers also went down the toilet, shredded.

He left his pillar and went up to the second floor and the ticket booths. There was a militiaman at each booth, gun slung loosely, minutely scrutinizing each purchaser. Cole joined the shortest line. He had no idea how good a description they had of him; the street had been dark, and he didn't think the one who took his papers had had time to get a good look at them. Cole winced at the memory. He hadn't meant to hit the man that hard; that crack as his head struck the masonry had sounded deadly.

I may be wanted for murder, he thought. Maybe the KGB and the MVD will interrogate me on alternate days.

He was at the head of the line. "Leningrad express," he said, sliding his internal passport and *putyovka* into the wicket. The *putyovka* was a trade union pass, allowing him somewhat preferential treatment in hotels and railway stations, and implying permission to travel more or less where he wished to. He was purportedly Sergei Balitsky, a mining union official and a native of Moscow.

The line had been slow, and he now saw why. The ticket clerk was noting the Balitsky identity on a pad of paper. When he finished he tore the sheet off and placed it on a stack of others. The militiaman stared fixedly at Cole while the clerk prepared the ticket. Any description circulated by now, though,

205

would surely include the moustache. Cole thanked God for Aldine's solvent.

The ticket was pushed toward him. He paid, from the wad of rubles that had been in the dead drop. While the clerk counted the notes, an arm came into view behind the wicket, picked up the sheaf of identifications, and vanished.

They're checking already, Cole thought. *Is* there a Sergei Balitsky? And if there isn't, how long will it take them to find out? How long have I got?

He left the wicket with the feeling that the militiaman's eyes were boring into the small of his back, seeing the hidden documents.

The train was pulling out in six minutes. Cole hurried through the waiting room, joining a stream of other passengers heading for the platform. The MVD was checking identification at the barriers.

"Name?"

"Sergei Ilyich Balitsky."

"Papers."

Cole handed them over. Flip, flip. "Moscow resident?"

"Yes."

"How long are you going to be in Leningrad?"

"Two days."

"Go on."

Out on the platform, now, the cars of the passenger train muddy green under the lights. A strong wind was blowing out of the night. The running gear of the coaches was caked with dirty icicles and ridged cornices of snow; plumes of steam poured from the pipes under the couplings, obscuring the platform and Cole in turbulent luminous clouds. The momentary feeling of security was a comfort, although Cole knew it was illusory.

He reached the hard-class section of the train, just

206

behind the Czech-built CHS2 locomotive, and clambered up the steps past the stewardess, who looked like a female reincarnation of Khrushchev. Inside the carriage there was a strong smell of coal from the stove at the far end, moist heat, cabbage, the remnants of cooking. A man stepped on Cole's heel and mumbled something, not an apology. Cole slipped into an unoccupied seat as near the rear of the car as he could.

He was going to have to lay his hands on some luggage. On a trip to Leningrad the lack wouldn't be conspicuous, but where he was going. . . .

Were they on the train yet? He couldn't have shaken them in the train station and hadn't tried. He thought he'd identified one of the foot surveillance in the waiting room, a large man with pockmarks and a fur hat, but he couldn't be sure. There would be more of them than that, of course.

Why had they let him get this far?

There. Pockmarks, passing by, finding a seat some six meters on. Maybe not him, though. Cole put his head against the hard greasy wood of the seat back and closed his eyes, then opened them. He was going to have to stay awake for a long time.

Clanks and jerks. The train lurched forward. Cole looked out the window. He didn't have a lot of time before the train got up speed. He also couldn't wait until the railway line left the station district and ran along Murmanski Boulevard; too exposed out there.

Three minutes passed. Twenty kilometers an hour.

Now. He had to move.

He got quietly out of the seat, bracing himself against the sway of the train. Pockmark didn't stir. Now it was his turn to be overconfident; he probably didn't think Cole would have spotted a full surveillance. There'd be one other, at least, in the carriage, though; they'd want to bracket him.

He went into the lavatory, which reeked, and tried the window on an off chance. No good, locked or painted shut. The other way, then.

He stuffed his fur hat into his pocket, waited an appropriate length of time, and opened the bathroom door. Clink of glass from farther up the carriage, punctuated by quiet drunken laughter. Thirty-five kilometers an hour now, almost too fast.

He opened the end door of the carriage and stepped through it. Snow was already crusting the end of the next car, wind-driven. The metal hump over the couplings was slick with ice and ledges of slush. A slip and he'd be down under the wheels; fear trickled through him.

Grab the outside edge of the car, just enough purchase on the bolt heads. Start the swing. Feet leaving the walkway. God I didn't get enough start, it's going to be the wheels, the corner of the next carriage striking me in the ribs, spinning me outward. . . . Okay now, maybe, start running in the air now before you hit, get ready—

Please don't let there be a switch handle in the way, or a railroad tie, anything with sharp edges, Christ suppose the film slips out of my pocket, I'll never find it out here—

His boots hit the ground. He managed to stay upright for three strides before the gravel caught him and he fell. When he rolled to a stop, he was lying flat on his back. Above him the Moscow smog glowed yellow-orange. Snowflakes melted on his cheeks. His shoulders hurt; it felt as though he'd skinned the right one. Fearfully, he put his hand down and felt for the film canister. It was still there.

The world wasn't spinning so much now. He got unsteadily to his feet, took the film out of his trou-

208

sers, and slipped it into the coat pocket with the forged documents. He put his hat back on. Up the line, the train's red taillights were disappearing in the falling snow. The snow would cut visibility, which was all to the good.

I have to get moving, he thought. I've got less than an hour to get to Kiev station. The Odessa express. I likely won't make it. The Kiev fast train, then. God damn, I'll have to change at Kiev. If only they haven't screwed around with the timetables.

He set off into the falling snow, heading along the train line toward the northwest. Just short of the Suscovski road overpass he got off the rail right-of-way, into a district of small streets east of Prospekt Mira. The snow was slackening a little. As he walked, he wondered what had happened to Markelov. The Russian would have been home by now. Who had been waiting for him?

Not surprisingly, there was no one watching him as he approached the Prospekt Mira metro station. Pockmark might have discovered his absence by now, but Pockmark was on his way to Leningrad, unless he stopped the train, which was quite possible. Cole paused near a lamppost to take stock of his appearance. He looked scruffy, but he'd do.

It was warm and humid in the metro. Five past midnight. The Kiev train, number 43, left at one. It was going to be tight, but then he didn't want to wait any longer in the railway station than he had to. He was a lot safer when he was in motion.

He went down to the subway platform and was lucky; a west-bound train pulled in just as he reached it. He got into the car and slumped into a seat. He was already exhausted, and he had a very long way to go. There were only four other people on the car, and he felt very conspicuous, but they didn't give

209

him so much as a glance. After a few minutes he relaxed a little.

The stations passed; there weren't many on this section of the line and he had time to rehearse what he'd do when he reached the Kiev railway station. It wasn't much of a plan, but he didn't have much to work with. He had to be in Odessa in twenty-nine hours, at the very most.

The train hissed, slowed, pulled into the Kievskaya metro station. Cole got wearily out of his seat and left the carriage. The metro was going to be shutting down in twenty minutes; he'd just made it. Or made it this far. The railway station, and another step on the way home, was almost over his head.

"We've got him again," Osipov said at the other end of the telephone line. He was calling from the special Executive Operations Room down in the subcellar. It was off-limits to everyone except the executive team.

"Where?" said Frolov. He'd been taking a half-nap on the office couch and his mouth was dry.

"We picked him up about twenty minutes after we lost him the first time. He's taken the train to Leningrad."

"Probably making for the Finnish border. Does he know he's being tracked?"

"I don't know. His movements might only be precautionary. But he's definitely on the train."

"Did you get the photograph processed?" They'd photographed him with a low-light camera just outside Leningrad Station.

"Yes."

"How many have you got with him?"

210

"Six. They'll use the train radio to keep in touch." Frolov heard a bell ding in the background. "Message coming in. Please wait."

Frolov heard a static-laden voice at the other end, impossible to understand, and then Osipov saying, "Shit."

"What's the matter?" Frolov asked as he came back on the line.

"He's slipped us again, devil take him. He must have jumped off the train somewhere outside the station."

Frolov was gripping the receiver very tightly. "Find him. He's going somewhere else. What are the MVD doing?"

"Checking all rail travelers at the stations. He's got rid of his moustache, by the way. He hasn't had any trouble since he got away from them the first time. But he will, if Timoshek really gets after him."

"Remember what I told you," Frolov said, and replaced the receiver. He was sweating. Osipov could call on a considerable number of watchers and trackers, but his resources weren't unlimited. This Bryce was stretching them thin already.

Unless I call in help from the Surveillance Directorate, he thought.

No. I can't risk it. It's going to be dangerous enough to let Osipov know what I'm doing, and I'm going to have to, later, or he'll make a mistake at the very end. It's a good thing he knows Kulagin would cut his throat soon after mine.

At the precinct headquarters they were still checking the railway station identifications. Belchenko's eyes felt sand-laden. "Nothing on him yet," he told

211

Timoshek. "All railway travelers clear so far. But we've got hundreds to verify residences for."

Timoshek said, "No positive checks on the street pickups?"

"No. We've got about twenty possibilities, but we're still working them over."

"Hurry it up," said Timoshek.

Cole was sitting on one of the wooden benches in the corner of the waiting room, hand in one pocket fingering the ticket to Kiev. His overcoat was the worse for wear, but no shabbier than those on the backs of several other men in Kiev Station. They probably didn't have badly bruised shoulders and ribs, though.

It had been just as easy and just as nerve-racking this time, the same performance at the ticket booth, the same feeling of eyes boring into him. He'd wanted to get the Odessa express, but as he'd expected, it had already left. That was good in a way, though; it meant they hadn't changed the timetables. He'd used the second set of identity papers and the other *putyovka* this time. His name was now Gennadi Agayan. If the MVD did expose the Balitsky flash-alias, they'd be looking for him in Leningrad—he hoped. The KGB would likely know by now that he wasn't going there at all, but there were good odds that he'd shaken them off, for a while at least. There was no sign of Pockmark, and he hadn't been able to identify any other followers.

That was no proof of anything, of course. The Surveillance Directorate could call on hundreds of men and women, and you might never be watched twice by the same person. There was nothing he

212

could do about it at the moment, though; he had to keep moving.

He looked up at the waiting room clock. Ten to one. Almost time to go.

The luggage, now. He'd picked the most likely possibility, a small fiberboard suitcase at the end of a bench ten meters away, on the route to the platform. Its owner was sprawled asleep on the seat, breathing though his mouth, clearly the worse for vodka. He hadn't stirred for a good ten minutes.

Cole stood up and walked steadily toward the exit from the waiting room. Others were moving in the same direction. As he passed the sleeping man he bobbed a shoulder, picked up the suitcase in one fluid motion, and kept on going.

No shouts of alarm. Now for the identity check at the platform.

The new identification got him through again. A few minutes after two in the morning the train pulled out for Kiev, with Cole drifting into a troubled half-sleep in the second car from the engine. The microfilm capsule pressed against him. A document, Markelov had said. The destruction of Soviet Jewry, was that what it contained? What else? Images floated through the twilight in his mind: Markelov's face in the dim orange light in the cemetery, light like the glow of a furnace, an oven; men wearing uniforms; freight trains whose freight was men and women and children; all somehow contained in the tiny aluminum capsule that rode with him through the Russian night, southward to Kiev.

Osipov was making progress, but it wasn't the kind he'd expected. They still hadn't found out where the target had gone, but while he was waiting

213

for news Osipov had run the target's photograph through Records, on maximum priority, for a match with known American CIA people who had worked in Moscow. The match had come up positive. Bryce had never been in Russia. The man they were following was Samuel Gregory Cole. He called Frolov immediately and told him.

"Cole is supposed to be dead," Frolov said. "He was drowned last week. Or so the Washington *rezidentura* said."

"It's a positive match," Osipov said stubbornly.

"All right." There was no particular surprise in Frolov's voice. The KGB had used the technique plenty of times itself. "That means the Americans are attaching extreme importance to whatever he's doing. Keep looking for him, and keep tabs on the MVD search. They may point us to him, if you can't find him yourself. Get to work."

The day, as it now was, being eight in the morning, was turning from bad to worse for Belchenko. He looked blearily around Timoshek's office; most of the HQ staff tried to humanize their areas with a little something or other, a poster or a personal tea glass or something like that, but Timoshek's was barren. Belchenko found it profoundly depressing.

They'd finally isolated a likely suspect, one Sergei Balitsky; there was no such person living at the address he'd given and never had been. Timoshek had had the Leningrad train stopped and searched at Bologoye, but Balitsky hadn't been on it. Possibly he'd never even gotten onto the train at all, or had jumped. But if he wanted to go anywhere far away, he had to have jumped in Moscow. What was curious was that the train had been stopped once before, for no obvious reason, half an hour outside Moscow. Timoshek might not be the only person after Balitsky, or whoever he was. The others would have to be the security organs. He had refrained from mentioning this to Timoshek.

He had not, of course, been able to hide the fact that the fugitive wasn't on the Leningrad train. Timoshek had lost his temper when Belchenko told him, bellowing so that he could be heard all the way down the corridor to the Operations Room. It all had to be done over again, with the net cast even wider. The best that could be said was that the ticket clerk at Leningrad Station remembered something about Balitsky; he hadn't had a moustache, his hair was brown. When this was added to what the surviving militiaman had told them there was a little more to go on. Belchenko started the amended description circulating, hoping that Timoshek would give himself apoplexy and collapse of heart failure.

It wasn't until twelve-forty that afternoon that they got another lead. When one of the night ticket staff at Kiev Station was questioned, he remembered someone who vaguely resembled the fugitive's new description. He specifically remembered a dark brown coat, which might have been Russian but looked . . . different. Unfortunately, the identity slips had already been distributed for checking, and he couldn't match a name to the half-remembered face. Belchenko ordered each identification division to look for a second slip with Balitsky's name on it. There wasn't one. The best thing they could do now was to get the existing description to the Kiev MVD and have them check the train passengers as they got off.

Timoshek started calling in favors. He grabbed

215

the long-distance phone and began to dial. After two or three minutes he got through.

"Vasily. Anastas Timoshek here." Vasily Suchkov, Belchenko knew, was the Kiev head of Homicide. "No, I'm in Moscow. Listen, remember a year ago when that black market—yes, that's the one. I'm in a position where you could help me out. Yes. Yes. There's somebody we want pulled off the Moscow-Kiev train. He killed one of my militiamen here last night. Yes, really. No, we haven't got a name. Here's what to look for." He read off the amended description. "Can you? Good. What? Oh, fuck, *fuck* it all. Well, try to do what you can. I *want* this one. Good. Let me know."

"Fuck," he said again, and put the receiver down. Belchenko regarded him expressionlessly.

"The train from Moscow got in twenty minutes ago," Timoshek said. His voice rose and kept on rising. "That bastard could be going to Odessa, Poltava, Kharkov, Donetsk, Zhmerinka, *or God knows where else!*"

Belchenko really did think Timoshek was going to have a heart attack this time, but he didn't.

Cole finally slept for a few hours on the run down from Moscow, but around dawn he woke up and couldn't get back to sleep again. He stared dully out the window until the train pulled into Kiev. When he got off the train there were no special checks; obviously the authorities were concentrating their search in Moscow. He bought a ticket for the Odessa train and then found the washrooms. The stolen suitcase had been a lucky choice; as well as half a loaf of black bread, which Cole had already eaten, it contained underwear, a shirt, socks, trousers, and

216

a light topcoat, all dirty. His overcoat, which had been fine for Moscow weather, would be a liability down here where the weather was a lot warmer, and would be even more so in Odessa. As well, a close inspection of his clothes would reveal that they weren't Russian. He took them off in one of the cubicles and put on the stolen ones, stuffing the old garments, except for the overcoat, behind the toilet tank. He put the microfilm and the third set of papers inside the lining of the topcoat, sliding the Agayan passport and *putyovka* into the breast pocket.

Out of the washrooms, into the waiting room. Ten minutes until the connecting train for Odessa. Then another eleven hours and he'd be there.

Now to get rid of the coat. Cole perched on the corner of a bench and slipped the folded coat underneath it, next to a pile of someone else's belongings. After a couple of minutes he got up and wandered haphazardly in the direction of the platform exit. No one seemed to notice that he'd left the coat behind, or if they had, they obviously weren't about to remind him of it. Cole joined the stream of Odessa-bound passengers.

He was aboard the train, and looking out the window, when it happened. A man sauntered out of the station building, with Cole's overcoat draped across his shoulders. Behind him trotted a pair of militiamen, followed by another pair.

Oh, Christ, Cole thought. How did they catch up with me so fast?

He tensed, ready to try to make it out the other side of the carriage if the police did come on board. They might have a physical description of him by now—

One of the militiamen shouted and pointed at the man wearing Cole's coat. The man whirled around,

217

shock on his face, his plastic valise swinging. The first militiaman reached him and smashed the bag out of his hand with his rifle butt, then hit him in the pit of the stomach with it. The man folded over and collapsed.

The train began to move. The last Cole saw of the unfortunate victim of the coat, he was being dragged away by the arms, head dangling.

Timoshek had been angry for so long that it felt natural. "Kiev MVD *said* they had him. Now Such-kov calls back and says they *don't*. And it took three and a half hours for those idiots in Interrogation down there to find out that the man they had was from Bryansk and had been in Kiev for two days. He was wearing Balitsky's coat and they took it for granted they had him." He slammed a file folder down on the desk and swore until even Belchenko raised his eyebrows. "The coat wasn't Russian, either. Balitsky's a foreigner."

"Yes, sir," Belchenko said, because anything else would have been too dangerous. He'd napped for thirty minutes before the call from Kiev MVD came in, but it hadn't helped. "Where did he get the coat?"

"He said he stole it in the waiting room."

"Did he see Balitsky?"

"He didn't see him, he says. An opportunist," Timoshek snarled. "And a stupid one. All right. Get me Kiev MVD. I'll talk to Suchkov again. I'll get him to start checking the ticket receipts. Maybe we can get something that way."

Timoshek watched as his subordinate dialed. This was no ordinary criminal, that was clear. He might even be a spy. Timoshek felt a surge of excitement.

218

If he could catch a real foreign agent, one the KGB didn't even know about . . . he was going to pull in every favor anybody owed him and stop every train that was on its way out of Kiev.

It was about eight in the evening, more than half-way to Odessa. Cole was sitting near the end of one of the hard-class carriages, trying to sleep; he had a long night ahead of him. He could feel the film can nestling against his left side in the jacket lining, faintly comforting and terribly dangerous. The car was quiet for the moment, except for loud snores emitted from one of the seats farther ahead. In the seat facing Cole was a woman of about twenty-five, with high Slavic cheekbones and tawny hair caught back under a blue headscarf. She had got on the train at Vinnitsa, with two children: a baby of about eighteen months and a girl around three. The girl looked very much like her mother. Cole had been afraid at first that she was going to strike up a conversation, but she hadn't; she looked as morose and tired as he felt. The children had been good, though, if listless; the baby had slept on his mother's lap for the last two hours, and the girl had alternately dozed and looked out the window, sparing the occasional curious glance at Cole. She looked rather wan.

The train was slowing down. Cole tilted his head to look out the window. There was smoke outside, drifting along the rail line. He heard sudden mutters and gasps of astonishment from farther up the carriage.

"On fire—"

He saw it then in the fading pink light, as the passenger train pulled farther around the curve, traveling now at no more than a swift walk. A freight

219

was drawn onto a spur track leading away from the main line. Billows of smoke poured from the far end of it, near the engine. It looked as though the locomotive had caught fire and was igniting the rest of the train. Flames spurted orange, garish in the gathering dusk. Men were running up and down the line of the freight. They wore uniforms.

Soldiers? A military train?

The soldiers didn't seem to be doing anything organized. Cole looked at the boxcars more closely. Each had a small barred window, high up at one end.

Hands were protruding from the windows, waving frantically.

Jesus, Cole thought. *It's a prison train.* And then: *The Jews.*

The soldiers had seen the Kiev train and became even more agitated. Several of them climbed up onto the rear boxcars and began to smash with rifle butts at the reaching hands, trying to force them back inside. The hands didn't draw back, but clutched at the gun butts, supplicating.

In the name of God, Cole thought, *let them out.* His car was abreast of the prison train's locomotive now; the engine was about half a kilometer away and burning fiercely. Three of the boxcars behind it had already been engulfed in fire. Cole thought he could see hands still at the barred windows. The young woman across from him was staring at the freight, her face drawn in horror. Someone in the carriage shouted, "Stop the train! We've got to help them!"

The burning locomotive's fuel tanks exploded; inside the passenger car it sounded like a dull *boom*. Farther up the car a woman shrieked and began sobbing. A ball of flame rose fifty meters into the air and then seemed to fall back, spreading like liquid.

220

It flooded over the unignited cars, right to the train's rear. The guards fled. The passenger car was full of shouts and moans of horror; across from Cole the young woman was weeping silently, clutching her children as though she would never let them go. The girl burst into tears.

The Kiev train jerked violently and gained speed. The tracks swung away from the burning freight, until Cole could no longer see it, although light still played on the telegraph poles along the railway line. An angry male voice shouted, "Why wouldn't they stop? We could have helped—"

"I pulled the cord," another answered. "They kept right on going. The bastards—"

The young woman was still crying, looking at Cole through her tears, horrified. "Why wouldn't they stop?" she said. "Why wouldn't they *stop?*"

Winter Palace, thought Cole. That's why they wouldn't stop. "I don't know," he said. He was feeling sick and full of horror himself. "We could have done something." He felt like crying himself, thinking of what it must have been like inside those boxcars.

She started to weep again, deep racking sobs that she couldn't seem to stop. Cole reached out and took her hand, held it tightly. The baby stared at him with wide terrified eyes. The little girl was still sobbing.

"I'm sorry," the woman said, when she had got herself under control. "Hush, Tamara, I'm all right, stop crying, it's all right now." Cole let go of her hand. She undid her scarf and used it to wipe her eyes and her daughter's. "It was horrible. Why didn't they stop?"

"I don't know," Cole said again. "The soldiers should have done something."

221

"My husband was burned to death," she said. "He was driving a fuel tanker, and it turned over on the Minsk highway. There wasn't any of him left." She almost began to cry again, but stopped herself. Tamara's face was buried in her mother's shoulder. "What's your name?"

"Gennadi Agayan. And you?" Somehow it seemed important to achieve a normal conversation.

"Ekaterina Chernayeva."

"You're going to Odessa?"

"Yes." She sniffed and dabbed at her eyes. "This is Nikolai, my son. And Tamara. We're going to stay with my mother there, I couldn't make ends meet by myself, after Andrei was killed."

"I'm sorry."

"It was seven months ago. I'm starting to get over it. But that train—"

"Yes," Cole said. "I understand." He didn't want her to start crying again. The rest of the passengers had become silent, as though contemplating their own frailty in what they had just seen. "Would your children like something to eat? I can try the restaurant car."

"I have some things with me. But they've both had stomach flu. I would have waited until they got better, but I had to leave the apartment today."

That explained the children's peaked looks. "Just a few hours to Odessa," he said. "I'll get them a drink, if you—"

The train, which had regained its normal speed, jerked and began to decelerate hard. Outside the window the outskirts of a small town slid into view: ramshackle board houses with corrugated iron roofs, streets with broken pavement, washing hung out to dry, unpainted wooden fences. The sun was almost down.

"We're stopping," she said. "We're not supposed to stop here, are we?"

"No," said Cole. He was wishing he had a gun. The station slipped into view: Bordulino, it said on the sign. The train was almost stopped. Spread out on the platform were at least twenty militiamen. Cole looked through the other window. There were as many more on the other side.

They're searching the trains, Cole thought. Christ. Will the Agayan papers hold? Do they know what I look like?"

The train stopped with a jolt and a long squeal and hiss of brakes. Militiamen ran for the doors. Cole heard thumps and rough voices as they boarded, a conductress's voice raised in querulous irritation.

"—murderer aboard—"

They were starting at both ends of the car. He had perhaps a minute before the couple in the seat behind showed their identification to the militiaman who'd entered at this end.

Ekaterina said, "Could you please take Nikolai? I've got to find my papers."

"Yes, of course." Maybe they'd think he was part of a family, it might throw them off. He took the small boy onto his lap; Nikolai stiffened and then went relaxed. The child was too hot, Cole noticed with a corner of his mind; he really was ill. Ekaterina had her passport out now; Tamara, her face tear-streaked, regarded her mother with apprehension.

The militiaman was standing above them. He had a receding chin and didn't look very bright; a provincial cop, more used to egg thefts than murderers on the run. He also smelt of secondhand vodka and looked queasy; a two-day hangover queasiness.

223

"Papers," he said irritably.

Ekaterina handed hers over. He leafed through them and gave them back. "Yours."

Cole gave him the Agayan passport and *putyovka*. The militiaman glanced at the front cover of the passport and then at Cole.

At that moment Nikolai leaned over and threw up, all over the militiaman's breeches and boots. He'd eaten something aromatic and sulfurous, maybe an egg.

"Christ damn it," yelled the militiaman. He jumped back, almost falling into the seat behind him. "Can't you keep your brat under control?"

The smell hit him. He went, literally, pale green. Cole wondered if he were about to throw up on Nikolai in retaliation. He didn't. He threw Cole's papers at him, turned, and scuttled toward the carriage doorway; Cole heard sounds of retching. He quickly stuffed the papers back into his jacket. Nikolai, fortunately, had missed his trousers.

The child had burst into tears. Ekaterina, stricken with embarrassment, dragged him onto her lap, found a cloth diaper in one of her bags, and started mopping Nikolai, the floor, the arm of the seat. The militiaman didn't come back. The other one, who had started at the far end of the car, worked his way steadily toward them but when he reached Cole and Ekaterina he didn't ask for their papers. Instead, he made a disgusted face and hurried on into the next carriage.

Fifteen minutes later the train started to move again. Ekaterina apologized to Cole and the passengers around them for the next half hour. Cole spent most of it wanting to laugh hysterically.

* * *

Ten after midnight, the train reports were all in, and the six suspects Kiev regional MVD had picked up had all been cleared. It didn't fit. Timoshek kicked his filing cabinet and swore.

"Maybe he didn't get on a train," Belchenko said unhelpfully.

"He got on a train," growled Timoshek. The conviction he'd had for the last hour hardened into certainty. "He was on a train as far as Kiev, he's not stopping now."

I know it, he thought. I've had this feeling before, and it's never been wrong.

"He's going to Odessa," he said. "That's the only way he can get out. He's a spy. The overcoat proves it."

Belchenko was looking at him doubtfully. Timoshek wanted to yell at him, but there wasn't time. He picked up the long-distance phone. Time to call in some more debts.

"Odessa?" Belchenko asked.

"Yes." Dialing. Clicks and hums from the receiver. "Odessa Central Militia Operations."

"This is Moscow MVD, Timoshek. Get me Valeri Pashukov."

"The chief's not on duty."

"Call him at home. Get him to phone me right away. Moscow, 222-1911. Anastas Timoshek. He'll know who it is."

"Yes. Immediately." Mention Moscow, and they shook in their boots down there. Timoshek hung up.

He wanted this man, Balitsky, or whoever he was, he wanted him as he sometimes craved alcohol. Balitsky wasn't Russian, he was a spy as well as a murderer. If Timoshek caught him, he'd be next in line, maybe, for militia commissioner, not to mention giving State Security one in the eye.

225

He wanted to be there when Balitsky was captured. And if he wasn't there to keep the pressure on Pashukov, the bastard might get away again. There was only one way he could get to Odessa fast.

"Belchenko," he said. "Get out. And close the door behind you."

Belchenko left with barely concealed relief, not quite slamming the door. Timoshek glared after him. He was about to pick up the Moscow switchboard line, when the long-distance phone jangled. It couldn't be Pashukov, not yet. "Timoshek."

"Suchkov here, Anastas. We've got a possible name for you from the ticket receipts."

Timoshek gabbed up a pen. "Go ahead."

"Gennadi Agayan. He fits the description you gave us."

"But he wasn't on any of the trains you stopped."

"No."

"I think he was."

"The regional precincts say he wasn't."

"He's headed for Odessa."

"Suit yourself. Glad to be of help."

"Thanks," Timoshek said with an effort. "Call me if you need anything."

"I will."

Timoshek got off the line, hoping Pashukov hadn't been trying to get through. Now for the tricky one. But it was the only way to get to Odessa.

He dialed a Moscow number. After five rings a man's voice, heavy with sleep, answered. "Hello?"

"This is Anastas Timoshek. Good morning, Alexei Alexeyevich."

"Comrade Timoshek." The voice was alert instantly, with a tremble of apprehension. Good, Timoshek thought. He hasn't gotten cocky. He'd better not. I can nail his balls to the wall any time I

226

want, if I'm willing to put up with the consequences. "I need a plane. That Ilyushin-310 of yours. And a pilot. I need to go to Odessa."

A silence. "You know I can't do that."

"Oh yes you can. You've done it before. You know why you have to do it, you bugger. Remember?"

Alexei Vyatkin would do it, too. Three years previously, Timoshek had investigated the rape and strangling deaths of two sixteen-year-old girls. The bodies had been dumped outside Moscow, but the circumstantial evidence led straight back to Vyatkin, who was known in police circles to arrange orgiastic weekends for a circle of friends at high ministry levels. The two girls had likely been killed at a gathering that had gotten out of hand, but Timoshek hadn't been able to obtain conclusive proof. What he did know, though, was enough to ruin Vyatkin, even though the man had friends in the Central Committee. If Timoshek struck at Vyatkin, he would risk unofficial retribution, but Vyatkin would lose more, and knew it. As long as Timoshek's requests weren't totally unreasonable, Vyatkin reluctantly complied with them. He was head of the Aeroflot division that provided special flights and private jets to senior members of the Party and the government and was in a position to provide similar services to his friends, or in Timoshek's case, his enemies.

"You're walking close to the line, Timoshek."

"I need the plane at Domodedovo in half an hour. Don't fuck around with me or I'll hang you up by your thumbs."

A silence. "Very well. I'll make the call. But you can't do this indefinitely."

"As long as I need to," Timoshek said, and hung up.

227

The long-distance line rang. Timoshek picked it up, looking at the clock. Twenty-six past twelve. "Moscow Homicide, Timoshek."

"Anastas. This is Pashukov. What's up?"

"Sorry to get you out of bed. I need a bit of assistance." Pashukov was a cop like himself, grimly determined, not like that lightweight Suchkov in Kiev. Timoshek and Pashukov had helped each other out on more than one occasion.

"What?"

"There's a Gennadi Agayan on the Kiev-Odessa train. He killed one of my people up here last night."

"The son of a bitch. Description?"

Timoshek gave it to him, and said, "Look, he's slippery. Try to get him before he gets out of the Odessa station, otherwise he's going to be hard to find. And he's dangerous."

A short silence at the other end. "The Kiev train gets in at midnight. He's long gone."

"Maybe not. I had it stopped for a search on the way down. It's delayed. That might give you another few minutes."

"I'll try. You want me to ship him back to you?"

"No. Hold him. I'm coming down to get the bastard myself." And, he thought, to keep things moving if you lose him. "I'll be there in three hours, maybe a little more."

"You're joking."

"Have somebody meet me at the airport. I'm in an Ilyushin-310."

Pashukov said, with faint amusement, "You're coming up in the world, Anastas."

"Just get me that shithead off the train," Timoshek said. "Maybe I'll give you an airplane ride."

* * *

228

"He's in Odessa for sure," Osipov said. He was pleased with himself. There were KGB people planted in every major and minor MVD headquarters, and using them to track Timoshek's hunt for Cole had worked beautifully. It also served to keep Frolov's and Osipov's hands out of sight.

"Good," Frolov said. His voice on the internal telephone sounded pensive.

Osipov asked, "Now what?"

"Pavel," Frolov said, "you'd better come up here."

Twenty minutes later the colonel in charge of Odessa port security received a telephone call from Moscow on the priority line. He stiffened when the caller identified himself. "Yes, Comrade Chairman."

"Have you been alerted by Odessa MVD regarding a fugitive?"

"Yes, Comrade Chairman."

"There has been no sign of him in the port zone?"

"No, sir."

"If," the voice said carefully, "he penetrates the zone and the militia requests you to search for him or hand him over, you are to agree fully with their request and offer them every assistance. Then you are to do absolutely nothing at all, until you have contacted me. Do you understand?"

"Yes, Comrade Chairman. Nothing at all."

"See to it."

The line clicked and went dead.

He had to get out of the park.

He'd gone to earth there after leaving the Odessa

railway station, hoping to avoid the MVD until it was time to make the run down to the dock area and the sea terminal where the Turkish Maritimes ferries from Istanbul came in. He had a Turkish passport, a travel visa for the Soviet Union, and documents that proved him to be a Turkish agricultural specialist on his way home from studying Soviet methods of dry-land farming. It was another flash-alias, and wouldn't stand up to any but the lightest investigation, but it would have been an effective way of getting him out of the Soviet Union if he hadn't had the MVD hot on his heels.

It hadn't been until two years ago that the Russians had begun to allow Turkish vessels to travel between Istanbul and Odessa, as part of Kulagin's efforts to draw Turkey into deeper economic dependency on the Soviet Union. Cole had wondered, when he'd first seen the ticket in the washroom in Moscow, if any other CIA people had used this particular escape hatch. Probably not. They'd reserve something like this for an extreme emergency.

The *Antalya* sailed for Istanbul at 5:00 A.M., but he didn't think he was going to be aboard her. He'd done everything he could think of, even stolen another suitcase in the train station to give him cover when he went through Customs at the sea terminal. But they were out after him in force.

He could see the lights of the patrol moving among the trees to the northeast, on the side of Shevchenko Park toward the dock area. They had cut him off from the sea and his escape. There was nothing to do but start running again. It was nearly two in the morning; he had a little more than three hours to go. He was running on nerves and instinct now, almost too exhausted to think.

230

I'm turning into an escape machine, he reflected. Maybe that's better. Don't worry, only act.

He left the bushes and jogged toward the west entrance of the park, keeping to the shadows. The stolen suitcase bumped against his leg. He wasn't sure what he was going to do when he reached the street; he couldn't seem to think that far ahead.

Out on Dzerzhinskogo Boulevard he stopped running and headed north. The street was deserted except for a couple of staggering figures up ahead, likely drunken sailors from the port. They crossed the street, to Cole's relief, and disappeared; Odessa, like most port cities, was a dangerous place. Keep going, he told himself. Almost to the intersection with Belinskogo Street now, conspicuous on the empty sidewalk. Now what? Keep walking?

What?

Stopped at the intersection, motor humming quietly, was a streetcar.

Cole, still walking, stared at it in disbelief. They don't run past one o'clock, he thought. Do they? Maybe the hours have changed. Maybe.

The ghost of an idea flitted through his numbed brain. The streetcar was just ahead. It looked empty. Better and better.

He climbed up the steps into the yellow half-light of the car interior. The driver looked up incuriously as Cole paid his fare. He was an older man, with thick lips and a faintly Mongolian cast to his eyelids. Bushy gray hair protruded from beneath the brim of his uniform cap. Cole put his case on a seat on the opposite side of the car and sat down. The car, except for the driver, was indeed empty.

"You just caught me," the driver said. The doors thumped closed. "Lucky. This is my last run."

231

Shit, Cole thought. I had to get a talkative one. "Good," he said.

The car motors hummed and the vehicle began to roll. Cole had no idea where it was going; he hadn't looked at the outside signboards. It didn't matter at the moment.

The driver half-turned and glanced at the suitcase. "You're from out of town."

"Minsk," Cole said.

"No hotel, eh?"

"I had one," Cole said, "but when I got there it was *defitsit.*" Which was another way of saying that the room had been taken by someone with more pull; it was a common hazard for Russian travelers. He watched the driver's hands and feet on the controls.

"Hard to get another one this time of night," the driver said. He pulled up at an empty stop, opened and closed the doors, and drove on. Cole noted that the brakes locked on as long as the doors were open. "Where are you headed?" the driver asked.

"It doesn't matter," Cole said. "Somewhere in the central district."

"I'll be passing through there in about half an hour. Then it's back to the barn. You'll have to get off."

"Yes," Cole said. "I'll find something tomorrow. I thought you only ran till one."

"Oh, they extended the schedules two weeks ago. Half past two, now. It's because of the extra dock shifts they've put on. Just the streetcars, though. No buses."

"I always wondered," Cole said, "what would happen if a driver got sick suddenly and lost control of one of these things."

"Ah," said the driver. "That's not dangerous.

232

Not dangerous at all. You see, there's another pedal over here to the left of the brake. If I let up on it, the brakes come on by themselves. It's called a dead-man switch. That's the power pedal there, on the right of the brake."

"That's interesting," Cole said. "It must be relaxing, not having to steer." Maybe it wasn't such a bad thing his driver was talkative.

"Well, you might think so. But these things are real brutes. They weigh in about forty tons, and that's empty. And they'll hit seventy kilometers an hour, if there's enough voltage in the lines. The problem is, they can be buggers to stop. It's steel wheels on steel rails you see, and I've slid a hundred meters with the brakes full on. The sanders, too."

"Sanders?" Cole asked.

"Boxes of sand, over the wheels. I just flip this switch here and the sand drops out onto the rails so she'll stop faster. But if you've got a nice shiny new Zhiguli, you remember to keep away from street-cars. They'll make porridge out of anything on the road, a bus even, and not show a dent."

"So," Cole said, "you just go round and round on the same route all the time, being on rails."

"Well, not quite. You see that bar there," gesturing at a meter-long steel bar clipped to the panel beside the stairwell. It had a looped handle at one end and a flattened chisel point at the other. "I use that to push switches over, change routes if the inspector tells me to. Not that I'll see any inspectors out this time of the morning. They don't like these late shifts, they're all off getting pissed on vodka somewhere. Same with the dispatchers back at Transport Central. They all hate these extended hours. I don't mind it, though. Sometimes I make up a lot of time and if the car's empty I pull off

233

on a spur, there's one up ahead for example, and have a smoke. Nobody bothers you."

"That's good," Cole said. What appeared to be a route map was taped to the control panel next to the door toggle.

The streetcar was passing through a narrow street, dark, part of the old section of the city that hadn't been flattened by German artillery during the war. Cole got out of his seat. The driver half-turned. "Did you want out here?" he asked in surprise. "We're nowhere near—"

The edge of Cole's hand came down on the back of his neck, not fatally, but hard enough. The car jolted and the brakes squealed as the driver's foot came off the deadman switch and he slumped out of his seat. Cole laid him out on the floor, dragged off the uniform jacket, and tied him up with his own suspenders and shoelaces. Part of a shirt from the stolen suitcase provided a gag.

Get rid of him, quick.

He opened the front doors and looked out. No one. An alley mouth gaped beyond the sidewalk. He dragged the man down the steps and then several meters up the alley. A pile of trash, old boards, wooden boxes, put the poor old bastard behind them. There. Run for the car, pull on the tunic, where's the goddamned hat, there, jam it on. Close doors, into the seat, deadman switch, power pedal. Moving, jerkily, but moving, thank God. Harder target, harder to stop, harder to catch. Less than three hours to go, have to hide somewhere, plan the escape route to the harbor, wait until the last minute to make a run for it. A spur line, the driver had said, not far on.

He almost missed it, where it swung off the main line into a narrow side street. He was somewhere

234

near Pushkin Boulevard, he thought; he didn't know Odessa nearly as well as he knew Moscow.

He got out of the car, carrying the switch bar, and after three tries in the bad light to locate the pivot point he got the rails moved over. Back aboard, he moved along into the side street. There was a patch of shadow between two lamps up ahead, the buildings on either side anonymous and dark. He took his feet off the controls and the streetcar rumbled to a halt, only the hum of the motors remaining. After some inspection of the bank of controls on his left he located a toggle marked MAIN POWER. He snapped it over and the motors wound down into silence. The lights were still on. He studied the route map on the dashboard. The spur line didn't go anywhere, he'd have to back out. Okay. Then up to Karl Marx Street, go right, move the switch over if necessary, then a straight run to the corner of Lastochkina, and he'd be almost on top of the Potemkin Steps and the sea terminal. Then he'd have to trust to the Turkish documents. And luck.

He found the light switches and turned off the interior and the headlights. Darkness invaded the streetcar. Cole folded his arms on the control panel and leaned on them. He was aching to put his head down but he knew if he did, he'd fall asleep. His stomach was so empty it hurt. Maybe the driver had a midnight snack under his seat. He searched for it, without luck.

He sat up straighter, and began to wait.

At 3:00 A.M. the switchyard reported to Transit Central that the Number 23 run hadn't come in. The dispatcher was about to go off shift and was badly hung over from a late afternoon of hard drink-

235

ing. He decided to leave a message for the morning dispatcher, who would come on at five when the system started up again. The driver was likely sleeping it off on a siding somewhere, they sometimes did that after a late run and brought the car back in the morning, just before five. They caught the devil for it, but they did it anyway. To hell with Number 23, whoever he was.

Nearly two hours, somehow, had passed. Suddenly, lights in the side mirror, a patrol. Cole snapped awake and scrambled down the length of the car to the rear. He crouched behind the last row of seats; it was the best he could do. The doors were closed, at least.

He waited. The sound of boots on pavement, half-intelligible conversation, becoming clearer as the patrol approached.

"—drunk or else the car's broken down—"

"Bang on the door, wake him up if he's in there. Maybe he's seen something."

They hadn't found the driver, then. Odessa was a big city.

Thumps on the front door. "How do you open these things?"

"Don't know."

"To hell with it. We'll report it when we go off shift. The motor's not even running."

"Broken down, I told you. They're always doing that."

The sound of boots again, receding into the night. Cole turned his watch to reflect the weak radiance of the streetlights. Four fifteen. Time to go.

He returned to the driver's seat, crouching all the way, and then peered over the bottom edge of the

236

windshield. The patrol's lights were gone. Give them another couple of minutes, then the last run, the last try. He slumped against the steel panel. He had nearly reached the end of his resources.

It was time.

He got into the driver's seat and flipped on the main power but left the lights off; he'd be a harder target that way. The car hummed into life. Find the reverse lever. There. Start backing, slow now, rear end out onto the main line, nothing coming, move past the switch point. Get out and change the switch over. Still dark, some time until dawn yet. Back aboard, almost now as much a machine as the streetcar.

Karl Marx Street was the second main intersection to the north. He could see it ahead as he crossed Lenin Street, the lights green for him, probably far too early for public transit. Only one car and a truck rumbling up from the dock area, the city hardly beginning to come awake.

He reached Karl Marx without incident. What direction was the switch going? He unclipped the switch bar from the stairwell, got out, and went to look. Wrong way. Insert the bar's tip, pull, ache in the muscles, not much strength left. There, it was over.

He got back in and laid the bar on the floor beside the seat. The car grated around the corner, swaying as though it were about to derail itself in protest at the change in route. A straight run to the Potemkin Steps, now. The signs on the car wouldn't be right. No help for it.

Get up to a good clip. What was it the driver had said? These things would go as fast as the power would allow. Not too fast, though. Don't want to

237

draw attention. Going to make it. I'm definitely going to make it. Only a few blocks to go.

The unmarked patrol car was pulled over to the curb, facing away from the harbor, motor idling. The militia lieutenant behind the wheel was listening to the search report on the radio. There'd been no trace at all of the man they were after. He might, the lieutenant thought, have gotten into the port zone by now, and they'd have to wait on the KGB border people. Too bad.

"What in hell?" exclaimed the sergeant in the passenger seat.

"Hmn?" said the lieutenant.

"That streetcar. What's it doing out this time of the morning? Without lights. It isn't even dawn yet."

The lieutenant looked down the street. A streetcar was moving rapidly toward them, no more than half a block away. "Shit," he said. "It could be him. We'd better stop it." He slammed the Volga into gear and gunned the engine. The sergeant reached for the radio microphone, but it slipped out of his grasp as the car swung violently out into the street.

Cole saw the Volga's headlights as it left the curb, swerving across the line, pulling up right on the tracks. *The stupid bastards,* he thought, *don't they know how hard these things are to stop?*

He couldn't bluff his way through, not this time, he had to ride it out. The Volga was thirty meters away. He rammed the power pedal down and the streetcar surged forward. Fifty-five kilometers an hour. Sixty.

They didn't realize he wasn't going to stop until the last seconds, when they were getting out of the

238

car. The front bumper of the streetcar slammed into the Volga's passenger door, crushing one of the MVD men against the frame, the other caught by the rolling patrol car and ground into the pavement underneath it. Then the full mass of the streetcar tossed the wrecked vehicle aside, the gasoline tank rupturing against a lamppost, sparks showering, the tank exploding in a garish hemisphere of flame. Cole kept the power pedal down all the way and the streetcar hurtled past the burning Volga. Three blocks to go now, have to get out, have to throw them off.

He slammed the brakes on, the car sliding, sliding, would it never stop, damn the thing. He remembered the sand switch, threw it; a grinding sound from underneath, finally slowing, slowing, stopped. He opened the doors to set the brakes and then jammed the deadman switch down with the switch bar. He needed something for the accelerator; the fire extinguisher was heavy enough. He used the driver's jacket to keep it from rolling. He almost forgot the suitcase as he left the car. Outside, he went around to the open driver's window, reached up for the door toggle and snapped it over. The doors closed and the car jumped forward under full throttle. Light from the burning Volga flared down the street. That would keep them busy for a while.

Cole turned and ran for the covering darkness of an alley. The streetcar was a hundred meters ahead now, still accelerating toward Lastochkina Street.

Christ.

A fuel tanker was pulling out of a side street. Its driver saw the runaway streetcar too late and tried to brake, but his heavy rig slid on into the intersection. The car rammed the tank trailer squarely in the center, ripping it open. The trailer reared up and a jagged spear of metal sliced into the overhead electrical lines. There was a great blue flash, and the tanker blew up. Cole shot into the alley's mouth, pursued by a blast of heat.

Too fucking late again, Timoshek thought. Always too fucking late. The fatigue and the flight from Moscow were rapidly catching up with him. He was sitting with Pashukov in the latter's office in the Odessa militia headquarters. The two men were drinking vodka. It was ten past five in the morning. Phones out in the operations center were jangling steadily; there'd been some kind of an accident downtown that had caused a big fire.

"Nothing I could do about the train from Kiev," Pashukov was saying. "It must have been pulling in while I was on the phone to headquarters. But we should have him by noon, if he's still in Odessa. We've got three million people here, but he won't be able to hide out indefinitely."

"You're sure we can't seal off the harbor?" Timoshek already knew the answer to that one.

"No, sorry. That's KGB Border Directorate territory. We're off limits there. I called them to ask for a special watch, but you know what they're like."

"Shit," Timoshek said. He was still furious with Pashukov for having brought the organs in, although he'd been careful to conceal it.

"I know," Pashukov said, although he didn't. He poured them both more vodka.

The telephone rang. Timoshek sat up, and Pashukov reached for the phone.

"Pashukov," he said. "Oh. A *what?* How do you know?"

Twenty seconds' pause, while Pashukov listened.

"Damnation. Keep looking. What about the patrol? Oh. You can't be serious. *Fuck! Get onto it!*" he shouted. He hung up. "I don't believe it." He looked as furious as Timoshek felt.

"What?" Timoshek's stomach turned over.

"They just found the driver of the streetcar that hit that fuel tanker. He says somebody stole the streetcar. The thief also rammed one of our mobile patrols with it. The patrol didn't have time to report what they were doing and the car burned so nobody knew it was one of ours until now. *Fuck.*"

"It was him," Timoshek said.

Pashukov was regaining control of his temper. "You may be right." He looked at Timoshek. "You really picked a dandy this time, didn't you, Anastas?"

"I'll catch the bastard yet," Timoshek said. But somewhere, in the back of his head, the instinct that had brought him to Odessa told him he would not.

Istanbul
April 8

THE EVENING was drawing down, the low sun blinding behind the minarets on the Stamboul shore of the Golden Horn, and long shadows were gathering in over the ferry landing south of the Galata Bridge. An intercoastal steamer was unloading over the quay near the customs house, iron gangways rattling, peasant families uprooted from somewhere in Anatolia moving, bag and baggage, out of the ship, like termites dragging pupae from a smashed nest. The white flanks of the steamer glowed in the slanting light, the streaks of rust along the seams of her iron plates standing out like old blood.

Foerster, leaving the ferry just north of the quay, watched for a moment as the swarms of displaced Turks left the ship. They reminded him, for a moment, of Russia and Poland, and Dachau: the trains arriving in the evening, as they always did, so that the dispositions could be made after dark.

The memory gave him the old nostaglic ache. Sometimes he wondered whether he returned to Europe only to imagine how it might have been had they won: the Reich from one end of the earth to the other, as they had believed in the early days, before Stalingrad and Kursk, before the Russians bled Germany to death.

Not to be, now, he thought. But something can yet be done, so that they will know we were not defeated, that we can still strike back, out of the tomb they thought they left us in.

He found a *dolmus,* one of the taxis that ran regular routes between the ferry landing and the hotel district. It took him, with many stops and starts to collect and deposit other passengers, to the front steps of the Pera Palas Hotel. He dragged his overnight case from under the calves of the others in the taxi, being careful not to be rough; he didn't want anyone to remember him. His cane gave him a little trouble, since it was a good meter long, but one of the women in the *dolmus* untangled its end from among her baggage and passed it carefully out to him, glancing only for a moment at its silver tip.

He thanked her politely, in Turkish. The cane had been with him for a long time; it had been given to him in 1945, when Berlin was falling, by Himmler himself. In retrospect, Foerster would have been more willing to receive the token from someone who had fought to the end, like Sepp Dietrich, or one of the really good SS generals, such as Walter Model. Himmler (Foerster realized now) had been putting on a show, even then trying to negotiate with the Allies.

Still, he treasured the cane. It was one of the last of his mementos; the SS dagger had gone before he came to Syria, as had the belt buckle carved with the SS oath. Apart from the cane, he had nothing to remember his former self by, barring a cracked black-and-white photograph of himself in a knee-length Wehrmacht overcoat, with the Iron Cross

243

First Class just pinned onto the collar by one of Himmler's aides just a few seconds after the SS-Reichsfuehrer had presented him with the cane. The loss of the dagger still troubled him, at times. He had been presented with it, as had all SS recruits, at the torchlight swearing-in ceremony that made him a full member of the *Schutzstaffel,* before the war. His mother had been extravagantly proud of him, she who'd never seemed proud of him before; she'd always compared him unfavorably to his father, who'd been killed fighting the Russians in 1917, just before Hans was born. She herself had died in 1945, incinerated in the firebombing of Dresden. If it hadn't been for Roosevelt, who had got the United States to attack Germany, she might have lived to see victory.

He shook the memories off, thinking of himself as the Syrian merchant his passport proclaimed him to be.

Inside the hotel he registered and lugged his overnight case up the stairs and down a long dim corridor to his room. The Pera Palas had been built before the First World War, in the time of the great European hotels, and maintained still the atmosphere of the period: dark mahogany everywhere, high ceilings, tall windows with heavy drapes, cavernous wardrobes, bathrooms in white tile.

Foerster sat on the bed and took off his shoes. As he leaned over, the pain slashed at him again, clawing deep in his belly. It was one of the worst attacks he had had so far. He straightened up, gasping, fumbling at the zipper of the overnight case. The vial with the pills was right down at the bottom. He gulped two of them, swallowing dry, then stumbled into the bathroom to wash them down with a glass of water.

The fool of a doctor said eight months, he thought, six before I am incapacitated. Long enough, if I don't delay, if Nadim Haddad will answer my needs. If any of these useless Arabs ever can.

He went back into the bedroom, loosening his tie, unbuttoning his collar. He took off his jacket, tie and shirt, and then the underarm holster with the Makarov pistol in it. When he went to see Haddad he would carry the weapon in his pocket; the holster was too uncomfortable. He put his shirt and jacket back on, looking at his watch: almost time to go.

The painkillers started to take effect. He checked the action of the Makarov, picked up the cane, threw his light raincoat over his arm—he felt chill weather more than he had in past years—and threaded the dim vacant corridors and stairways down to the deserted lobby. Satisfied that there was no surveillance, he walked rapidly along Mesrutiyet Street, avoiding the taxi rank, and took the underground funicular railway down the hill to its terminus near the eastern end of the Galata Bridge. Near the bridge he found a cab and settled back against the worn upholstery, the cane upright between his knees. The taxi, an ancient American DeSoto, gasped its way along the approaches to the bridge, among the fish sellers with their braziers on wheels, the melon and fruit pedlars on their way home pulling almost empty shallow carts, the late commuters heading for the ferry quays bound for Usqudar or the northern river suburbs. On the bridge itself the traffic was lighter, the twinkling lights of the Stamboul side drawing steadily closer, the yellow smog haze above the ancient city of Constantine softening the curves of the great domes and the spears of the upthrusting minarets.

At the Stamboul end of the bridge, the taxi driver

left the shore boulevard and started up the hill. Even with the poor street lighting, the advanced state of dilapidation of the buildings was apparent: ancient walls crumbling into masonry-choked side alleys, windows barred with grills whose iron bars looked as though they would crumble into flakes of rust at the lightest blow, peeling, decaying shutters, dry fountains carved with dust-filled inscriptions unread for five hundred years.

Finally the cab stopped. "I can go no farther," the driver said. "The streets are too narrow from here." He was looking at Foerster oddly. Foerster realized that he had been humming a tune, a German one. He couldn't remember precisely, but he thought it had been the *Horst Wessel* song.

"I know the way," he said irritably. He paid the man and got out, pulling the raincoat over his shoulders. The alley he wanted ran off to the right. After a few meters, it crossed a slightly wider one. Foerster turned left. A blank two-story wall ran along the alley on his right, disappearing into the murk ahead of him. A few meters along the wall, a heavy wooden double gate stood partially open. Foerster slipped through the gap, his hand in his pocket on the butt of the Makarov.

Inside the gate was a courtyard, overlooked on three sides by ranks of windows representing half a dozen styles of the Ottoman Empire. Most were barred and grilled: the court and the surrounding building had once been a *han*, a compound built in Imperial times for traveling merchants, their pack animals, and their wares. The ground level had once been arcades containing shops and smithies and stables, but they had long been hidden by the mass of ramshackle workshops thrown up haphazardly by cobblers, tinsmiths, copper founders and other arti-

246

sans of the ancient city's laboring class. Lights glowed in three of the second-floor windows, but their dim radiance barely penetrated to the court-yard floor.

Foerster waited in the gloom, cane in left hand, the Makarov cradled in his pocket by his right. Perhaps two minutes passed.

A scraping noise from the far corner of the court, perhaps the scuttle of a rat. After a few seconds the sound repeated itself, more recognizably: boot-heels on stone. An indeterminate form emerged from the darkness.

"Selim Youssef." It was a statement, not a question.

"Yes." Foerster stood without moving. He knew, as he had known from the beginning of his journey, that he was in considerable danger.

"Follow."

There were none of the usual honorific Arab greetings. A bad sign. But if Nadim Haddad, leader of the *Jund Allah*, the Soldiers of God, would give him a chance to speak before acting. . . . Foerster was trusting to the underground leader's curiosity to preserve his life, at least until he had had time enough to speak.

A door creaked, revealing a trapezoid of dim lamplight. "In," said the man.

Foerster entered. The workshop, if that was what it was, seemed dedicated to bicycles and small machinery: in the half-light he could see an oily workbench mounted with a heavy iron vise, bent wheel rims sprouting twisted spokes like maddened sea urchins, sprockets hanging on the walls like iron spiderwebs.

At the far end of the workshop was a cane chair. Nadim Haddad was sitting in it; behind him, to his right, stood another man, his face obscured in the shadows. He was cradling an American M16, whose muzzle was pointed exactly at Foerster.

"Selim Youssef," said Haddad. "The German whose real name I do not know."

"Yes," Foerster said. His legs were aching and he looked about for somewhere to sit. A meter away from him, on the dirt-caked stone floor, was a small wooden keg. He took a step toward it. The man with the M16 gestured violently, silently. Foerster stopped.

"I want to sit down," he said. "I am an old man."

"See if he is armed," said Haddad.

The man with the M16 came forward, put the gun's muzzle against Foerster's belly, and ran his left hand over the German. He found the Makarov, retrieved it, and then returned to his original position.

"It was for my own protection," Foerster said. "May I sit?"

"Sit," Haddad said. After a pause he added, "Why did you ask to meet me here?"

Foerster shrugged. "It was appropriate from the point of view of security." He laid the cane across his knees.

Haddad's eyes narrowed to slits. His face was very thin, cheeks sunken, eyes indented into pits beneath thin black eyebrows. In the lamplight he looked like a gargoyle fallen from some ruined Gothic cathedral.

"I know of you," he said. "You worked for the Brotherhood, before the revolution. My *Jund Allah* has no quarrel with the Brotherhood. Assad's regime let us have our camps and training grounds in Syria. We expect that the Brotherhood will continue

248

this. We are all Muslims. Our war is against the Jews and Zionists. What do you want?"

"I am no longer of the Brotherhood," Foerster said calmly. He was taking a considerable risk in stating it. There had been a veiled threat in the terrorist leader's words: if the Brotherhood government in Damascus didn't continue to support the Soldiers of God, Haddad might very well turn his men against the revolution. There were many of them, and they were well armed. Haddad himself was an experienced assassin, and was known to have had people tortured and shot on the merest suspicion of treachery. Being a member of the Brotherhood would have given Foerster some protection from such a fate, but Haddad needed to be aware right from the beginning that the Brotherhood had no part in Foerster's plans. Damascus would move heaven and earth to stop him, if they were to find out.

Haddad was eyeing him in silence. Then he said, "I thought as much. Otherwise there would have been no need for us to meet here in Istanbul. Damascus would have done as well." The eyes narrowed again. "Who are you working for?"

"I am working for no one."

"Everyone is working for someone. I think perhaps you are in fact working for the Brotherhood. But you deny it. It is very dangerous to do that. With me."

"I am working for no one."

"You therefore have no protection. If I kill you, no one will come for me. Why should I believe you?"

Foerster shrugged. "I am an old man, with few years to lose. But if you kill me, you will discard an opportunity for a great blow against Israel."

"You speak in circles." Haddad turned and said

to the man behind him, "I want to know who sent him. Impress upon him the necessity of telling us."

The man nodded and stepped forward, into the light, reversing the M16 to strike with its butt.

Foerster twisted the head of the cane. Out of the cane's tip shot thirty centimeters of bright steel. The blade's point was pressing into the man's solar plexus before he could bring the gun butt down.

"Be quite still," Foerster said. "You cannot turn away more quickly than I can strike."

They remained so, poised in the lamplight, for perhaps four seconds. Then Haddad spoke:

"I could shoot you, old man."

"Yes. Listen first. Then decide."

"Adnan. Leave him be."

The man backed away, very slowly, from the gleaming point, lowering the gun equally slowly. Foerster allowed the sword's tip to drop, then pushed the blade back into the cane against the side of his heel. "Thank you," he said.

"Tell me what you have to offer," Haddad said. "You may yet leave here with your life."

"First remove your man. This is for you alone."

Haddad considered for a moment, and said, "Adnan. Wait outside."

"But, lord—"

"Outside."

Adnan left sullenly. When the door had creaked shut, Foerster set the tip of the cane on the floor between his feet and clasped his hands over its butt. "Were you aware of the plan I made for the Brotherhood, regarding the fate of Israel?"

"No."

"Good. The Council did not intend you to be, nor anyone else. The plan encompasses the final solution to the problem of Israel."

A flicker of interest in the black deep-set eyes. "Ah."

"But it may never be carried out."

"Why not?"

"Because of Khalil Dirouzi. He has drawn back from executing it fully."

"I see," said Haddad. "So you wish to make use of my Soldiers of God."

"That is correct. Your organization has the strength and the contacts to do what can be done. Under my guidance. I also have money."

"You may have the money. But by what right do you claim guidance?"

"Because," said Foerster, "I know how to obtain nuclear bombs. And where to find someone who knows how to make them explode."

A long silence. "This is the truth?"

"Under God."

"Tell me," said Haddad.

Ankara, Turkey
April 11

THERE WERE THREE of them in the secure room in the American embassy in the Turkish capital: Cole, Richland and Davis Webster, the CIA chief of station for Turkey. They were waiting for the Israelis and mulling over Cole's debriefing again. He'd been out of Russia for seventy-two hours now, but his ribs were still sore and he was very tired. Richland and Jackman had flown out from the States as soon as they had heard he was safe in Istanbul, and Jackman had started in on the debriefing as soon as Cole reached Ankara.

Cole was surprised to see Richland, since the operation had been under the control of the Soviet Desk, but the situation in the Middle East was growing tense enough to warrant the presence of both officers. Jackman didn't like it, of course. And Cole, remembering the blackmail Jackman had used to get him to go on the run, barely kept his temper through the debriefing. At the end, Jackman told him, "that little import matter has been cleared up." Cole thought: not for me, it hasn't. I'm going to remember that very clearly.

Jackman left for the States after draining Cole dry, but Richland stayed on. Cole called Megan right after the debriefing ended. The memory of the conversation was agonizing.

"Megan? It's Sam. I'm safe."

A long silence, then a muffled sound. "Sam? You?"

"Yes. Meg, let me explain."

"Sam Cole. Is this some sort of joke?"

"It's me, Meg. I'm safe. I'm out of the country at the moment. I'll be back soon."

"You weren't on the boat? Who was on the boat?"

"I was, but—"

"*Sam*. It was on *purpose*? You went—back, and you didn't *tell* me?"

"I couldn't. I can't explain everything on the phone, but—"

"You *bastard*. You—how could you *do* that?" The Welsh was strong in her voice. "I've thought for days you were dead. I was out at the house, looking at your things. Poor Mrs. March was in a terrible state. Good God, Sam, how could you *do* such a thing? How could you do that to me? Couldn't you imagine how I'd feel? Didn't you *care?*"

"Yes. I cared, of course I cared, but I didn't have any choice. I had to do it. I'll explain when I get home. Meg—"

"Shut up, Sam. Just shut up, now. I don't know what to do about you. You're dead, and then you're not. It still seems like some horrible joke. How can you say you love a person, and then do what you've done?"

"I love you. Give me a chance to explain."

253

"I don't think you can explain this. Not even going back—there. Especially going back there."

He'd known it was going to be bad, but the reality was far worse than he could have imagined. "Meg. Wait till I get back."

"And how long might that be?"

"A few days. Meg, give me a chance."

"I don't think you deserve one. I'd been thinking about us, even before you left. It was starting to go wrong. Wasn't it?"

"It was because of . . . this. I'd known about it for some time."

"But you didn't tell me."

"I couldn't."

"And what other things are you not going to tell me, if it should happen again?"

"It won't happen again."

"How can I believe that? I trusted you, Sam. With all of me. I don't know if I can again."

"Just wait for a little bit. Give me a chance."

"I'll see, Sam. But I don't want to talk to you any more right now. I have to think."

Silence.

"Meg?"

"I'm still here."

"I love you."

"I don't know if that's good enough. Good-bye, Sam."

"Megan—"

The line clicked, and then hummed.

I've lost her, Cole thought. She's gone.

"You okay, Sam?" Richland asked.

"I'm fine," Cole said. "Just tired."

254

"The Israelis will be here in a few minutes," Webster said.

"Do you still think," Cole asked, "that I got out of Odessa because somebody *wanted* me to get out?"

That probability had come up during the debriefing, and it had jolted him; until then he had been too exhausted and too euphoric with his escape to think analytically about what had happened in the port city.

"Sam," Richland said, "take a look at it again. You had the MVD after you. The KGB must have known that. Yet they let you walk on board that Turkish ship without so much as a look in the suitcase you stole. You fried a couple of militiamen and killed one more in Moscow, and *somebody* let you go. You can bet it wasn't the MVD. That leaves the K's. You must know there was no other way you could have gotten out, not with that kind of heat on you, no matter what documents or help we supplied you with."

The idea that he'd been helped out of Russia, or at least not interfered with, still infuriated Cole. He looked up at the clock on the wall of the bubble; the jamming equipment hummed softly, just at the margin of hearing. "God damn it," he said.

"But why?" Webster asked. "Apart from what he did to the militiamen, Sam was carrying the microfilm of Winter Palace. They'd never let *that* get out of the country."

"If they knew it was me who met Markelov," Cole said, "they had to believe I was carrying it. So somebody in Moscow wanted that thing to get out. Somebody in the KGB."

Richland nodded. "I've been talking to Langley. They think the same. Somebody high up doesn't like Winter Palace, and by implication doesn't like Ku-

255

lagin. The Kremlin watchers think that whoever let Winter Palace out of Russia is trying to undercut Kulagin's support in the top Kremlin echelons, the Politburo and the Secretariat."

"What good will that do the Soviet Jews?" Webster asked Richland.

"Not much, at the moment. As far as we can tell, Kulagin's firmly in the saddle. How many Jews are out at the transit camp at Kilincli?"

"A hundred thousand," said Webster. "The Turks expect to have six times that by the end of the month, all in by sea."

"Christ," Cole said. He hadn't known there were so many. "Has anybody talked to them yet?"

"Yeah," said Webster, "but only the U.N. relief team supervising the camp. They're hearing a lot of horror stories about the Russian camps. The Russian guards haven't been quite as bad as the Nazis, but there have been a lot of deaths from illness and hunger. Shootings as well, but those haven't been verified. The Kilincli camp's pretty bad, too. What the Turks and the Israelis are going to do when the flood really starts, I don't know. Every last one of those people has to be screened, and even then we won't be able to identify all the plants. Some of those poor bastards could be behind wire for years."

"That's ironic," Cole said. "They get out of Russia, and the West promptly sticks them in camps behind barbed wire."

"That's exactly the effect the analysts say Kulagin wants," said Richland.

"It doesn't seem to be bothering the Turkish government," said Cole. "Letting these people in."

"We've been watching that carefully," Webster told him. "President Celebi leans to the left—a long way to the left. He's been in favor of better relations

256

with Moscow since he took office after the Cyprus war. He makes points with Moscow for letting their Jews in, and he's forced us to lift the arms embargo in return for housing them. We think he's about an inch this side of pulling out of NATO and signing a treaty of friendship with Moscow. Ten years ago the Turkish military wouldn't have let him do it, but they're so pissed off at us for supporting the Greeks over the Cyprus war, and putting on the arms embargo after, that they're willing to listen to Celebi. At least, the Turkish General Staff is."

"When's Washington going to take the lid off Winter Palace?" Cole asked. "It's about time Kulagin had the screws put to him."

Richland and Webster exchanged glances. "I've been talking to Langley," Richland said. "They aren't."

Cole stared at him. *"What?* You mean I risked my butt to get that thing out of Russia, and nobody's going to do anything with it? What about those poor bastard Jews back there? I *told* you about that train. They just let them burn."

"Sam, there's nothing we *can* do just now. Those documents are forty years old. The Russians'll just laugh at us if we accuse them on that basis alone. We've got to wait for more evidence. What the refugees tell us will have to be collated and analyzed before we can make a case."

"A case," Cole said. "Meanwhile, the KGB's doing what it damn well pleases. To people like Alexander Markelov. He's in a cellar somewhere with an electrode stuffed into him and all you can do is talk about *making a case?"*

"There's nothing we can do, Sam. Not right now."

Cole was about to say something about only fol-

257

lowing orders, but was stopped by a soft *buzz*. Webster pressed a button on the side of the table. A voice said, "I have two individuals cleared for entry."

"Go ahead," said Webster.

The steel door at the end of the room hummed open. Two Israelis stepped through it. Webster, Cole and Richland got up.

"Dalia Stein," Webster said. "Mordechai Frank. Both of Israeli External Operations, Turkey."

Frank was slightly chubby, with thinning brown hair and large brown eyes; except for the eyes he was quite nondescript. Dalia wore a severe dark blue suit and navy shoes with flat heels.

Webster completed the introductions. "Let's sit down."

Cole sat across from Dalia. She studied him frankly. Cole thought: I didn't know it was going to be a woman.

"How are you, Mordechai?" Richland said. "I haven't seen you in a while."

"Not since they took you home from Turkey and put you behind a desk," said Frank. "How do you like it?"

"It has its days," Richland said. "You remember Sam Cole?"

"Ah, yes. Your Islamic expert. You also left a few years ago, didn't you, Dr. Cole? Not long after Rich did."

Cole was slightly surprised to find that the Israeli remembered him. "Yes, that's right."

Richland said, "Davis? You've got the floor."

Webster turned to Frank. "Mordechai, you wanted to hear it from Sam directly."

According to Richland, the Israeli government had already been told about Winter Palace and been given a copy of the microfilm, probably on the un-

258

derstanding that they keep silent about it. Mossad, though, wanted as much current information as possible, hence Mordechai's invitation to come and speak with Cole directly.

"Dr. Cole," the Israeli said, "tell me what happened to you in Russia. Please leave nothing out."

Cole began. As he spoke, he felt he was reliving the events, minute by minute, second by second. When he got to the burning train, Mordechai went gray, although his expression didn't change. Dalia Stein listened with her eyes closed. Finally he was done.

Mordechai had regained his color. He looked around the table. "As you can well imagine, my people are very concerned about what was in the microfilm you've given us, as well as what Dr. Cole has witnessed himself. But can I ask just how sure you are of the microfilm's authenticity? That it's not some particularly odd piece of disinformation?"

"Sam brought it out of Russia," Richland said. He glanced at Cole. *One thing, Sam,* he had said before going into the bubble, *I don't want the Israelis knowing our suspicions about KGB involvement in your escape. That's too much of a hot potato at the moment.*

"Given the circumstances he got it under, and what's been happening with the Russian Jews in the last few weeks, I don't think there's any doubt that it's close to reality. It may be forty years old, but the similarities are far too close for coincidence."

"We'll accept your evaluation," Frank said. "What is Washington going to do with it?"

Richland glanced at Cole again. *Keep quiet,* Cole read in the look. "I don't know. That's going to have to be between our State Department and your Foreign Office. That's way above our heads."

"Very well. But something will have to be done,

259

and soon. The news of how these people have been treated is spreading. There will be trouble over it in Israel. Perhaps a great deal of trouble."

"You said there was something else you wanted to discuss," Richland said. "Regarding an unidentified threat from the Syrian Brotherhood."

Frank put his elbows on the table and leaned on them. "Yes. Unfortunately, we do not have a lot to go on. Some little time ago, we removed a man from Damascus; he was a long-term agent of ours and had managed to work his way into military intelligence in Assad's government. Shortly before Assad's regime collapsed and the Syrian Brotherhood succeeded with their Islamic Revolution, he found out that the Brotherhood had for a long time been advised, and at least partially directed, by a German. That in itself isn't too surprising, since many SS officers fled to Syria after the war. This one, however, seems to have been different from the others. He supposedly helped the Brotherhood organize itself into an effective clandestine movement, advised in training its sabotage and military arms, and was at least partially responsible for building the political strength that allowed the Brotherhood to topple Assad. In short, a very dangerous man. The Syrian secret police were trying desperately to identify him, but the country went up in flames before they could do so."

"Surely he's dead," Webster said. "If he was in the SS during the war he'd be an old man by now."

"According to the man we pulled out of Damascus, he was still alive as of a few weeks ago. We would not be quite so worried as we are, except for three things. First, his proven ability. The Syrian police were many things, but they were not incompetent. If they were afraid of him, they had good

260

reason to be. Second, now that the Brotherhood's in power in Damascus, he'll have resources he could only have dreamed of before. Third, and again according to our agent, he had planned a major strike against Israel to take place shortly after the success of the Islamic Revolution.''

"What kind of strike?'' asked Richland.

"That's part of the problem. We just don't know what he and the Brotherhood have worked out between them. A new wave of terrorism? Outright military action by Syria? An assassination campaign abroad? Or something worse? Germ warfare, for example? There's a whole spectrum of things he could have developed. We've been exerting ourselves to find out, but after the revolution, our network in Syria is in ruins, because as far as the Brotherhood was concerned our people were part of Assad's government. What we'd really like to do is locate the German, but we haven't been able to identify him. We would like to ask your assistance in this.''

Richland made a note. "When you've found him, then what?''

"We'll try to kidnap him—or kill him,'' Dalia said.

Except for a murmur during the introductions, it was the first time she had spoken.

"That could be difficult,'' said Webster. "He'll be well guarded, if he's that valuable to the Brotherhood.''

She regarded the station chief coolly. "With the right people and enough determination it could be done,'' she said. "It may have to be.''

"Have you been into Syria before?'' Cole asked.

The long eyes moved to his. "Several times.'' She glanced at Mordechai Frank.

261

"Dalia brought our agent out of Syria," Frank said.

"Could he brief us?" Webster asked.

"No," Dalia said. "He was injured on the way out. He died before I could get him proper medical attention."

There was a brief silence. Then Richland asked, "If this strike is carried out, what would Jerusalem do?"

"Because of the existence of Winter Palace," Mordechai said, "there will be strong suspicion that it was supported by the Russians. Kulagin hates Jews, that much is clear." He shrugged. "What can I say? We will never kneel to another Holocaust, no matter what the price. There are those in our leadership who would pull down the Temple again, rather than submit. The world knows this. It has been one of our strengths. To destroy Israel would be to risk the destruction of much else."

"Even the world?"

"You and the Russians risk it every day," said Mordechai. "You know as well as I do that men do not think clearly when they are under great strain and when there are too many dangerous decisions to make. Human nature demands the relief of action, even if it is the wrong action. That is how the First World War began."

"There's a lot of truth in that," Richland said, noncommittally.

More than you'd like, thought Cole. More than any of us would like. Damn Washington, anyway. But maybe they're right, maybe there's nothing they can do, as there was nothing I could do for Alexander. Nor for those poor burning people on the train. But maybe there's something I can do, here, now.

"Rich," he said, "if Mossad's agreeable, I might be able to help out."

Richland and Mordechai looked at him. So did Dalia Stein, with a quickening of interest in the dark eyes. "Say that again?" asked Richland.

"I know a number of people in Syria. They've been scattered by the revolution, likely. But if I can find out where some of them have gone, one of them might be able to tell us something about the German."

Richland was regarding him thoughtfully. "You were due to go home, Sam. You really want to extend with us?"

I know what's on your mind, Cole thought. If I'm still working for the company, I'm a lot less likely to talk out of turn about Winter Palace. So be it. "Yes," he said.

"Mordechai?"

"We are grateful for all the help we can get," said Frank. "Dr. Cole's knowledge of the Middle East would be exceptionally useful."

"Okay," Richland said. "Sam, you're on. I'll clear it with Langley."

Half an hour later, Cole went to the communications center and got a satellite link to the States, using Webster's authority. He had to try to explain to her, just once, a little of what he was doing, and why. The telephone *burred*, thousands of miles away. Finally: "Hello?"

"Meg, it's Sam—"

The line clicked and went dead. He thought for a moment that it was a transmission fault, but then realized it wasn't. She had hung up on him.

He didn't try again.

Dolinskaya Transit Camp, the Ukraine
April 12

THE COLONEL stood at the bottom of the front steps of the administration block, sniffing the warm air; down here in the south of the Ukraine it was really spring. They'd be chilly up in Moscow for a while yet, but the good weather was coming.

Boots scraped on the fresh raw concrete of the steps behind him. "Comrade Colonel, sir, good morning."

It was the colonel's executive officer. He came down the steps to stand beside his superior. "It's going to be a beautiful day," he said. "We'll be picking mushrooms in the woods, soon."

"If we can find any woods down here," the colonel said. The executive officer was from Leningrad, like the colonel. "The country's as flat as a plate. If we want a woods we'll have to plant it. And maybe the mushrooms, too."

The officer emitted a little chuckle at his superior's humor. "Maybe we should put some of the *Zhids* to work," he ventured. "There are enough of them here to plant a couple of forests."

264

The colonel looked at his watch. "The next train's due in a few minutes. Shall we go over and watch?"

"Certainly, colonel."

They left the steps of the administration block and started along the graveled road. Ahead of them stood the small headquarters guard hut, with its striped barrier; beyond that and to the right, the newly whitewashed clapboard of the guard post at the camp's main gateway gleamed in the early sun. On such a bright gentle morning, even the barbed wire fences surrounding the headquarters compound looked innocuous. Off to the colonel's left lay the main part of the transit camp, with the holding compound behind another barbed wire fence. The camp proper was divided into four quadrants by graveled roads; each quadrant contained rows of raw wood barracks, a mess hall and a bath house. Guard towers were studded along the perimeter fencing.

In the middle of the north side of the main camp's wire boundary was a double gate with another guard tower above it. Just outside the gate was yet another long wooden building, the reception block, and a little way north of this, across an expanse of asphalt tarmac, ran the spur line from the main railway. This processing area was surrounded by another wire fence, which ran off to the east along the north side of the road, ending at the guard post by the main gate.

It was a good five minutes' walk from the administration building to the entrance to the processing area. This entrance also had a guard hut, with a striped barrier. Beyond the barrier, the colonel could see the reception block and the spur line. The KGB guard inside the hut stalked out, saluted, then turned and started to raise the barrier.

265

"Leave it," the colonel called. "We'll watch from here. Carry on."

The guard saluted again and returned to the hut. The colonel looked at his watch again. "Is this the train they lost on that siding in Kiev for a day?"

"Yes, sir."

"I hope you got the disposal team out. There's going to be some trash." This was the term the camp staff used for dead Jews.

"They're ready, Comrade Colonel."

A long whistle sounded from the northwest. Down the railway spur the headlight of a locomotive winked into view as the engine pulled around the bend from the main line. The breeze was also from the northwest. The colonel wrinkled his nose. "Shit," he said. "This is a really ripe shipment. You can smell them from here."

Markelov, Esfir, Irina and Tania were in the third boxcar from the engine. There was nothing to sit on but the floor, and the inside of the boxcar reeked with every odor common to unwashed human beings. The only ventilation was from two small barred windows set into the car's wall, high up at one end. There was a partition at the other end that hid a bucket, but the only way of disposing of its contents was to dump it through a small hole in the floor, and the single bucket had to serve for all the occupants of the boxcar. If it had been summer, the interior would have been suffocating.

They had been on the train for five days; after the second day the Mongol guards, unable to stand the smell, had simply tossed the bread loaves in through the door and left the water cans inside it. By the time the bread and water reached the end of the boxcar there wasn't much left, and the scraps of food that most families had collected the night they were taken were long gone. Everyone was hungry and thirsty. Even the children, from exhaustion and fright, had stopped crying. Four more older people had died during the night; their bodies were piled together near the toilet partition, to make more room.

Markelov was desperately worried about Esfir and Tania; both of them feverish and dehydrated. The child was the worse. Irina and he were all right so far, thank God; Irina was sitting under one of the barred windows, cradling her daughter in her arms.

The motion of the car changed. Irina looked up at her father. Her cheekbones were already prominent from hunger; she'd been giving most of what food there was to Tania. "Are we stopping?"

"I think so," Markelov said. The previous day and the night before it had been terrible. The train had halted, in a freight yard from the sound of it, and then hadn't moved for twenty-four hours. There had been no food or water in all that time. Just before they had started up again the guards had opened the door, grimacing at the stench, and dragged out the bodies of the six people who had died while the train was on the siding. Two of them had been children, and their mothers had shrieked and wept when the small corpses were taken away. That had stopped after a while; energy had to be saved for the living.

They really were slowing down now, almost stopped. Oh God, Markelov thought, will they forget us again, leave us somewhere until we're all dead?

The train halted with the shriek of brakes and the thunder of couplings slamming together. After a moment the door slammed open, admitting sunlight

267

and sweet air. A guard, one of the Mongols the KGB seemed to be using, shouted "Out! Out!" in badly accented Rusian. The mass of humanity in the car stirred itself, slowly, painfully.

There were no steps down to the platform. They clambered out of the boxcar, Irina half-carrying Tania, who couldn't seem to wake up. Esfir was weaker than the previous evening; she leaned heavily on Markelov, who relieved her of the two small string bags containing their extra clothing. The Mongol guard muttered at their slowness in his own language.

They were ordered to line up on the platform. It took several minutes, the guards becoming more and more impatient, their commander, a Russian KGB major, striding up and down with increasing anger.

Markelov didn't see exactly what happened to start the incident; two or three meters away a man began shouting at the guards, swearing, demanding his rights as a Soviet citizen. Two of the Mongol troops raced along the line of transportees and grabbed him, dragging him out into the open. The other guards froze, their assault rifles unslung and pointing at the crowd.

The man was young, maybe twenty. He might have been feverish; he kept screaming at the guards as they dragged him. They started flailing at him with their rifle butts. He tore free, swung wildly, hit one Mongol in the face. Blood spurted from his nose. The Mongol hit him in the back of the neck, driving him to the ground, then backed away, rifle at the ready. The other guard did the same.

The KGB major strode up, red with fury, unsnapping his holster. The young man lay motionless on the asphalt for a moment, then got up on one elbow. Blood poured from a cut on his forehead.

The major had his pistol out. Markelov watched, disbelieving. The young man was sitting up now, staring up at the KGB officer. "No," he said.

The major pointed the gun at the young man's forehead and pulled the trigger. The bullet struck just above the left eyebrow, snapping the head back, leaving a neat round black-edged hole in the white skin. The young man collapsed backward onto the dirty pavement.

The major spun around, waving his pistol at the line of Jews. "Don't any of you," he shouted, "even *think* about doing what he just did. Or you'll end up the same way. Now get inside. Guards! Move them in."

The line moved forward in stunned silence, except for the sound of a woman sobbing. None of us expected anything like this, Markelov thought. They'd just as soon kill us all.

Inside, there were long counters. Everyone had to put their bags and satchels on them. Esfir was leaning more and more heavily on Markelov. When he let go of her to put the string bags on the counter, she stumbled. "Alexander," she moaned. "My chest hurts." Her eyes rolled up and she collapsed onto the cement floor, striking heavily before he could catch her.

"Mother!" Irina screamed. She knelt at Esfir's side. "Somebody find a doctor!"

Markelov looked wildly around. One of the camp staff, a thick man in a gray uniform, sauntered over to them. He prodded Esfir with a toe. "What's this?"

Irina and Tania were crying now. Markelov knelt by his wife. "Can't you see she's sick? There must be a doctor here somewhere!"

269

"Get out of the way," the man ordered. He pushed Markelov aside, bent over, and felt at Esfir's neck. "Doctor's not going to help her," he said. "She's dead."

Washington
April 14

"No, DAMN IT, I can't," Parnell snapped. It was the first time during the meeting that he had shown anger; the four senators sitting in front of his desk in the Oval Office recoiled.

He lowered his voice; getting angry at them wouldn't help. They were doing what they were supposed to do, which was to represent their constituents. He looked at the senator from New York. "Blake, I know the pressure you're under, and I know how you must feel yourself. But this administration can't establish a policy about admitting large numbers of Soviet Jews until all the facts are in. How many of them actually *want* to come here, for example? Maybe most of them want to go to Israel. The Europeans and Turks are still trying to get tents, at least, over these people's heads. Nobody's had time to ask them whether they'd prefer to end up in Tel Aviv or Manhattan."

"When *will* they be asked?" said the senator from Florida. "With respect, Mr. President, there are a lot of Jewish people who voted for you in the last election. You're not doing your administration any good by procrastinating on this issue."

"It is *not* procrastination," snapped Parnell. "Where are you going to put them? On the beach down your way? For how long? We need preparation time."

Cornelissen, who had remained silent for the past half hour, broke in. The members of the senatorial delegation looked at him in surprise; they'd almost forgotten his presence. "Gentlemen, I must remind you that the president has another meeting in a couple of minutes. Could you please finish your presentation in that time?"

There was a short silence. The senator from California spoke. "In short, Mr. President, you're going to send us away empty-handed, exactly as you did last week."

"I'm sorry, gentlemen," Parnell said. "But this administration is not going to be stampeded into commitments it may later regret, or not even be able to fulfill. The welfare and safety of the people of the United States come first, and it's the responsibility of this office to make sure that that is never forgotten."

"That's you last word?" asked the senator from Illinois.

"Not *last,*" Parnell said. "Don't put words into my mouth. There will be policy when there's evidence on which to base policy." He rose. "Thank you, gentlemen."

They filed out. Cornelissen closed the door behind them. Parnell got up from behind the desk, stretched, and went to look out the windows. One of them was ajar, admitting a soft spring breeze. "They're really after my tail," Parnell said. "And I can't tell them the real reason I'm hanging back."

"It's not just the senators," Cornelissen said. "There's another demonstration down on the Ellipse. Open the window a bit more and you'll probably hear them."

Parnell did so, cocking an ear. "I hear them. What are they demanding this weekend?"

"Same as at the demonstration last Saturday. Let the Soviet Jews out of the camps en masse."

"We can't do that," Parnell said. "Not this soon. Nothing's ready. Anyone with any brains would see that."

"Human beings in large groups don't have any brains, Mr. President. That's how politicians survive."

"That's true enough," Parnell said with a wry twist of his mouth. "You should give a few of us some credit, though, Kip, for trying to be a little less cynical than that. What's the crowd composition this time, do you suppose?"

"Maybe sixty percent Jewish, the rest sympathizers. There was a counterdemonstration last weekend by that white-supremacy coalition, what's it called, the Christian America Guard. The police managed to keep the two groups apart, fortunately. The Guard doesn't seem to be around this weekend."

"Good." Parnell closed the window and turned back to his desk. "About Winter Palace—"

The internal telephone rang. Parnell picked it up and listened. "Yes. All right. No, don't do that. Just have them diverted. Good." He put the receiver down.

"What?" Cornelissen asked.

"That was Security. The demonstrators have left the Ellipse. They're heading this way. Banners and all."

* * *

273

The banners were lettered with slogans: FREE THE JEWS OF RUSSIA and NEVER AGAIN. They tossed above a sea of some twenty thousand people, which had now broken through its cordon of parade marshals and was pouring northward along West Executive Avenue toward the White House. The demonstration of the previous week had been smaller and much more orderly, and it had given the police a false sense of security, especially since this time there was no sign of the Christian American Guard being about. There were not nearly enough patrolmen to turn the marchers aside, and the ranking officer on the scene began radioing urgently for help.

It had begun to arrive, in the form of riot police, by the time the marchers reached Pennsylvania Avenue and turned right, clogging the road and stopping traffic, to gather in front of the White House gates. The police, insect-like behind their visors and helmets, deployed in a skirmish line along the sidewalk between the White House grounds and the demonstrators, riot sticks and shields ready.

The crowd, however, seemed relatively good-natured. Someone began chanting, "We want the president, we want the president," which was picked up by a few hundred throats but didn't catch on. The demonstrators were confused, purposeless; they weren't sure, now that they were here, why they had come. A halfhearted attempt at *We Shall Overcome* didn't provide a focus; neither did *Go Down, Moses,* since most people present didn't know all the words. The police were getting a solid cordon around the crowd, preparatory to calling for it to disperse. The captain in charge raised his bullhorn.

The Christian America Guard was better organized than it had been the previous weekend; some hundred and sixty members had infiltrated the crowd while it was in the Ellipse, and most of them had managed to stay together. Many had brought sawed-off baseball bats or lengths of pipe under their coats and jackets, and others had filled pockets and knapsacks with stones. Their leader tore the LET MY PEOPLE GO placard from the pole he'd been carrying, and tied to it a banner crudely emblazoned with an eagle and a cross. As he raised it above his head, he screamed, at the top of his lungs:

"Get the Jews!"

The attackers, although vastly outnumbered, struck from within the crowd, stunning and disconcerting both the marchers and the police. Baseball bats and pipes rose and fell. A shower of stones sleeted out of the crowd and rattled on police armor. The mass of bodies surged involuntarily toward the line of uniformed men in front of the White House fence, threatening to crush them against it. Truncheons lashed out, thudding into flesh. Taken by surprise, the police captain saw not a mass of frightened men and women, but a mob that had suddenly and unaccountably turned murderous. He ordered tear gas.

BRUTAL SUPPRESSION OF
PEACEFUL PROTEST IN WASHINGTON
Washington, April 15 *(TASS)*
—American hatred of its Jewish minority was demonstrated again yesterday in Washington, as a peaceful march of Jews was attacked by neo-fascist thugs and police and dispersed in a cloud of tear gas. Two demonstrators were killed and fifty-eight injured by the clubs. The march was to protest the inhuman conditions

275

in the so-called "refugee camps" the U.S. has caused to be set up to imprison emigrants from the Soviet Union. Needless to say, not one of these camps has been permitted on American soil.

For years, the U.S. has demanded that Soviet citizens of Jewish persuasion be, in the words of the U.S., "permitted" to leave the Soviet Union, and has never ceased its lying propaganda to persuade such people that this would be better for them. Now that the Union of the Soviet Socialist Republics has provided free transport and emigration facilities for all those who have been unable to resist the effects of these lies, the United States has at last shown its true colors of anti-Semitism. No longer able to level such groundless accusations against the Soviet Union, the United States stands revealed in all its lying hypocrisy, as are Great Britain, France, West Germany and other Western countries. None of them, despite all their fine words of the past, has accepted more than a few hundred of these misguided people they once swore they wished to protect.

In the last ten days, there have been peaceful demonstrations in Paris, London, New York and Washington, all of which have been brutally suppressed by the capitalist authorities. Neo-fascist groups have been encouraged by these same authorities to attack the peaceful marchers, and the death toll now stands at 33, with more than 200 maimed or badly injured.

The Zionist government of the so-called State of Israel has behaved no better. As the ideological lackeys of the United States for the past four decades, the Zionists have repeated the capitalist line that Soviet citizens of Jewish persuasion should be "repatriated to Israel," although these people are far better off in the Soviet Motherland. No sooner has this been offered, however, than the government of Israel is content to see, and even insistent on ensuring, that our Soviet Jews remain in camps.

Adana Special Munitions Facility, Turkey
April 15

FOERSTER WAS SITTING in the cab of the lead truck, which was drawn up at the side of the road about five hundred meters from the access gate to the storage site. Over the gate a single floodlight cast a yellow glow onto the road; the rest of the outer perimeter was unlit, and the floods along the inner perimeter were obscured by trees. A quarter moon rode low on the horizon, but because of the trees lining the road the two trucks were nearly invisible. They were Turkish army trucks, freshly painted and labeled with false unit markings the previous night. In the back of each was a combat squad of twelve men of the Soldiers of God, uniformed and armed as Turkish soldiers.

Nadim Haddad, who was behind the steering wheel of the lead truck, flashed a penlight at his wristwatch, shielding the light with his fingers.

"Yes?" Foerster said. His stomach was bad again; he had had to take two of the pills. To really dull the knife-edge of the pain he needed four, but he did

278

not want the drug to interfere with his concentration; not now, of all times.

"0230 hours exactly," Haddad muttered. "We should see his light." Away to the east and the great Incirlik airbase, a heavy jet transport boomed into the night, the thunder of its engines reverberating in the cab. Incirlik was the main American military airfield in southeastern Turkey. It gave Foerster considerable satisfaction to be carrying out his theft under the Yankees' noses, even though they were close enough to prevent the weapons from being slipped across the Syrian border. But they wouldn't react fast enough. By dawn the bombs would be out of Turkey, carried along hidden smugglers' trails by Haddad's men. By afternoon the weapons would have arrived at the secret base camp up in the Syrian mountains.

A brief double flash up the road, just outside the pool of illumination thrown by the floodlight. "There," Foerster said.

"I see," said the terrorist leader, with an edge of annoyance. He had, from the beginning, resented taking orders from the German; Foerster had taken care, usually, to couch them as suggestions and requests rather than commands. This effort, coupled with the advance of his disease, had several times driven Foerster to private rages.

Haddad started the big vehicle and drove slowly along the road in the darkness, the whine of the gearbox grating in Foerster's ears. He put his head out the window to make sure the other truck was following. After what seemed a very short time, they rolled up to the main gate of the storage facility's outer fence, the perimeter controlled by the Turkish army. The inner perimeter and the storage igloos inside it were guarded by American soldiers of the

279

123rd Custodial Unit. Inside the igloos were stored the nuclear shells that would be released to the Turkish army if there were a major war.

Foerster had been studying the custodial units for several years. They and the storage sites they guarded varied considerably in effectiveness and security, respectively. The ones in West Germany, for example, were well-guarded, those in Holland not so well. None of them, however, was safe from a well-organized and determined attack, and the ones in Turkey were decidedly the most vulnerable. Foerster had realized, early, that the best way to reach into a storage site was not by a frontal assault, but by treachery. The Brotherhood's strength was not confined to Syria; it had many sympathizers and adherents in other Islamic nations, including Turkey. When the Brotherhood was still contemplating Foerster's plan, it had needed a Turkish army officer eager to help the cause of fundamentalist Islam, and one who helped guard the Americans' nuclear weapons. Foerster had found such a man, and recruited him.

He was at this moment standing by the main gate, under the dim glow of the floodlight. As Foerster watched, sensitive to every move, two other men came out of the guardhouse and swung the wire gates open. The trucks ground forward again, engines drumming quietly. They were now past the Americans' first line of defense.

The officer who had given the signal reappeared suddenly out of the darkness, climbing onto the running board on Foerster's side of the cab. He wore major's insignia, the gold crescent and stars glinting faintly in the dim light of the floods. "Selim Youssef," he said quietly. "God is great."

"God is great," Foerster replied. "Is all in readiness? You've cut their communications?"

"Yes," said the major. And added: "The Brotherhood prevails."

Foerster smiled inwardly. He had been very careful, when he had contacted and briefed the major a week ago, not to let him guess that he was no longer working for the Brotherhood and Islam, but for Foerster.

"Go on," Foerster told Haddad.

The truck lumbered along the access road toward the gate of the inner perimeter, the major riding on the running board. The gate was better lit than the outer one, and consisted of two steel-framed leaves covered with heavy wire mesh and secured by an electrical lock controlled from the guard hut. The electrified fence was topped by barbed wire and alarm sensors. Just inside the gate was a guardhouse and a pivoting wooden barrier. An armed American soldier came toward them, his weapon still slung.

"Stop," the Turkish major said. Haddad let the truck roll to a halt about ten meters from the gate. The major jumped down from the running board and sauntered toward the American guard.

There are two, Foerster thought. He'll have to get the other one out of the hut.

There was an exchange of conversation, which Foerster could not hear over the noise of the engine. The guard was shaking his head, looking puzzled. The major gesticulated. The American turned and called out to his partner in the guard hut. After a moment he emerged, carrying a clipboard, which both soldiers began to study intently.

The Turkish major drew his pistol and shot each of them in the chest, twice. The shots came as flat

281

dry cracks over the rumble of the truck's engine. The major turned, waving furiously.

One of Haddad's men raced past the lead truck, carrying a pair of huge bolt cutters. In seconds he had sheared a hole through the mesh of the gate and the Turkish major was through it, racing for the guard hut to release the electrical gate locks. He disappeared inside. Foerster waited, nerves strung tight.

After a moment the major reappeared, waving. The man with the bolt cutters dropped them and tugged at the right leaf of the gate. It slid slowly aside in its runners.

"Go!" hissed Foerster. The truck roared through the gate. As it passed the guardhouse, the Turkish major leaped back onto the running board and held on grimly as the vehicle accelerated toward the low curved forms of the storage igloos.

Captain Gerald Morgan, the officer on duty, was sitting with his feet on the desk in the main office of the site control building, reading a lurid paperback novel about the white-slave trade to Saudi Arabia. He was so engrossed he paid hardly any attention to the faint noise of vehicles outside; the Turks on the outer perimeter were always coming and going at odd hours. He was trying to finish the chapter before going out to check the guard posts. In addition to the U.S. troops on inner perimeter duty, there were supposed to be six more patrolling the storage igloos, but the igloo complement was down to four tonight, one man ill and the other away on a weekend pass for some personal reason or other. The storage site was never supposed to be undermanned, but discipline in the 123rd Custodial Unit was flexible, especially when it came to weekends off.

He did look up momentarily, wondering whether he had indeed heard four faint snaps from somewhere outside. At first he thought it was a truck backfiring out on the Adana road, but the noises weren't quite right and had come too close together. He sighed, took his feet off the desk, and went to the window that faced the road to the main gate.

The gate was open, two large trucks already inside the perimeter. Men were leaping out of them even as they moved.

"What the fuck?" Morgan said plaintively. He couldn't remember any security exercise scheduled for tonight. But this—

Holy shit, he thought, it's a goddamned surprise inspection team, they've been sent in to test us, oh fuck, is my ass in a sling now. They'll bust me so low I'll be saluting the Russians.

He had to do what he could: contact the guard posts, call on the emergency line to Incirlik Custodial Unit headquarters.

He took one more glance out the window as he turned for the desk and the telephones. Men from the rear truck—they were wearing uniforms, but in the stark shadows he couldn't tell what kind—were running both ways from the main gate along the inner perimeter. They were carrying weapons. The other truck was careering up the access road, not far away now, moving very fast. This really *was* a detailed simulation of an attack.

My God, Morgan thought suddenly, this isn't a fucking simulation, this is fucking *real*.

He dived for the alarm phone just as the lead truck swung broadside on to the control building. A figure leaned over the tailgate and fired a twelve-round

283

burst from his G3 assault rifle through the window, and through Captain Gerald Morgan.

It had gone perfectly so far, but speed was critical. The inner perimeter sentries and the igloo guards had been wiped out, and the Turkish major had made sure that his own troops would not interfere, probably by telling them that the Americans were carrying out a security exercise.

Speed, speed, Foerster thought as the truck pulled up to the westernmost igloo. The six men of the lift team jumped out of the rear, running for the locked igloo door. Plastic explosives were quickly fitted around the lock and fused. The demolition man for the first igloo twisted the timer, then ran for shelter around the curve of the building. A muffled *crack*, followed in short order by five more. All the igloo doors had been blown.

Foerster trotted to the rear of the truck. One man was still in it, huddled on the bench.

"Come," Foerster said. "Make sure we take the correct items."

The man levered himself over the tailgate and dropped heavily to the ground. In late middle age, he was somewhat overweight and quite bald. He had cost Foerster years of searching and a great deal of money to find. Nuri Alwan was an Iraqi by ancestry but American by birth. Educated at Cal Tech, brilliant in electronics and nuclear physics, he had attracted the attention of the American weapons designers at the Livermore Laboratories. In the late fifties and early sixties he had worked on several nuclear devices and been a trusted member of his design team, with a truly stratospheric security clearance. But in 1967, shortly after the devastating

284

defeat of the Arabs by the Israelis in the Six-Day War, he had fled to the Iraq of his ancestors. He had worked for Baghdad on the Osirak nuclear reactor project until the installation was attacked and destroyed by the Israeli air force. After that he'd gone into retirement, until Foerster had found him.

Alwan hated Israel and the United States with equal passion. He also knew how to identify, assemble and arm precisely the type of atomic weapon that Foerster wanted.

In the first igloo, the demolition team had already snapped on the lights. Alwan looked around, then went hurriedly up and down the aisles, looking at the markings on the locked protective containers which shrouded the weapons.

"No good," he said. "These are W79s. I cannot arm them."

The next igloo was empty. In the third, Alwan found the first set of components.

"There," he said, pointing at a dull metal cylinder a little over a meter long and thirty centimeters in diameter. "M500 container. The shell is in that."

For a few seconds Foerster stared at the long container. Inside it lay a Mark M422 203mm artillery shell, its interior cage built to accept the uralloy explosives package of the W33 nuclear warhead. The assembled shell, including the nuclear package, weighed just over a hundred kilograms. According to Alwan, the shell and its inserted nuclear core could be converted to a manually or electronically triggered atomic bomb, with the destructive power that had incinerated Hiroshima.

"Two of those," Foerster said to Haddad, who had been trailing in their wake, perhaps a little awed by what they had finally succeeded in doing. To Alwan: "What else?"

285

"We need the nuclear materials themselves, and the fuses. They will not be in this building. This is an old type of weapon, and it uses highly enriched uranium, which is unsafe. All W33s have the artillery shell stored separately from the explosives."

"On, then."

The next igloo contained what they needed. The fuses were taken out to the trucks, while Alwan studied the markings on the containers for the nuclear cores that would be fitted into the artillery shells. "Those," he said after a moment. "Be sure you take ones marked 994PW. Those are the high yield ones. The 992PZ and 992TZ are much less powerful."

"What else?" Foerster asked the Iraqi as the lift team began pulling the core containers off the shelves.

"That is all. The rest I must do myself, with the equipment I trust you have provided."

"It's there," said Foerster. "Can you arm them?"

Alwan shrugged. "Yes. I know how they work, which very few other people do. And none, I think, of the Brotherhood."

Foerster nodded. "Only you," he said, thinking: I have done it. Or nearly.

Haddad had come up behind him. "Everything is loaded," he said. "Split between the two trucks, as we agreed."

Foerster nodded. He followed Haddad and Alwan out of the igloo. The Iraqi got into the back and Foerster slid into the cab while Haddad checked the men.

The Turkish major appeared outside the cab window, his face strained and drawn. "You agreed that

286

I should come back to Syria with you. There will be a price on my head, here.''

''Of course,'' Foerster said. ''The Brotherhood will reward you well, and in the sight of God you are one of the bravest of fighters for Islam.''

The major nodded seriously. ''It is as God wills,'' he said.

Haddad got behind the wheel of the truck, slamming his door shut. ''There is one last detail.''

''Yes,'' said Foerster. He reached into his pocket for the Makarov.

Outside, the major was looking worriedly towards the main road. ''There has been no alarm so far,'' he said. ''But we must hurry.''

''Get up on the running board,'' Foerster told him. The truck was beginning to move. ''We may need your authority on the way out.''

The major nodded and climbed up, peering into the cab. ''I—'' he began.

Foerster raised the Makarov and shot him between the eyes.

287

Istanbul
April 16

IT WAS EARLY afternoon, and very warm. Cole stopped by a tumbled block of stone and pulled his sweater off. The breeze from the sea spread a welcome coolness across his back.

"It's too beautiful a day to have to talk about these things," Dalia said. She sat down on the stone and adjusted a shoelace.

They had been walking on the terrace that lay between the great double walls forming the monumental defenses of ancient Constantinople. Above them reared the line of the inner fortifications, studded with huge crenellated towers stabbing some seventy feet into the cloud-flecked blue.

Cole looked down at Dalia. She sat quite still, gazing north along the apparently endless line of the walls. In the distance, muted by the huge masonry barriers around them, there were sounds of traffic, and to the south where the Sea of Marmara lay, the occasional hoot of a steamer horn.

"When the Turks took this city in the fifteenth century," she said, "they didn't get through down here, did they? Wasn't it farther north?"

"Yes," said Cole. "Up near what's now the Edirne Gate. The Janissaries, the Sultan's elite troops, finally managed to breach the inner walls. The Byzantines might have been able to drive them out again—they'd done it before—but a little way north of the breach there was—still is—a postern gate called the Porta Xylokerkou. Somebody had left it unguarded for a few minutes, and a group of Janissaries found it. They got into the inner fortifications, and the line of the walls. The Byzantines were hit from the front and the flank, and they couldn't hold."

"They tried so hard," she said. "But in the end, they lost. No allies, no weapons or money to buy them, not enough men, besieged."

He knew what she was thinking: *Israel*. "They never gave up," he said.

"No," she said. "They never did." She stood up and they set off again.

Several meters on, part of the battlements had fallen from the inner wall, scattering a jumble of stones across the terrace. They scrambled across them, Cole ahead, like a pair of antiquity-smitten tourists. As they reached the far side of the tumbled granite, Dalia, poised on a lip of broken ashlar, tottered uncertainly. Without thinking Cole reached out for her hand and steadied her to the ground. For a moment he felt her palm, cool and dry, against his own. Then she was down on the turf and he let go abruptly.

"Thanks," she said. "My balance is usually better than that."

"I'm sure," he said, suddenly very conscious of her.

"We'd better get down to business," she said. "Let's go over there."

289

The place was a kind of grotto formed of ashlar blocks tumbled from the wall above, overhung by an intact section of the fortifications. Inside it, they were out of sight of anyone more than two meters away. The air held the scent of ancient mortar and weathering stone. They sat down on what might have been a broken lintel, side by side.

"What happened at Adana?" she asked. "Mordechai didn't have much information. Only that it was bad."

"It's worse than bad," Cole said. "They killed the whole American guard complement and a Turkish officer. They got away with two nuclear warheads, big ones. And fuses. Nobody knows where they took the bombs, but it's likely Syria. The border's only eighty kilometers away, and it's mountainous. There's smuggling up there all the time."

She sat very still, looking into space. "Finally," she said. "We know what it is. That's what the German was planning with the Brotherhood all these years. Now he's done it."

"If it *was* him," Cole said. "But it's not likely he can explode the warheads. You can't arm them without the proper codes and equipment. You need an expert. The Brotherhood's got no one like that."

"Are you so sure?" she asked, her voice tight. "Everything else the Brotherhood's tried to do recently has succeeded. Why not this?"

"I admit there's always the possibility."

"I've identified the German," she said. "I think."

He was startled; he hadn't expected her to get results so soon. He had been coming up dry, despite his resources. "That was quick. How did you find him?"

"I went back to Tel Aviv the day after we met in
290

Ankara and started going through our files. We used to keep track of any Germans who ended up in Arab countries after the war, particularly SS. But a lot of the early information in those files is based on suspicion rather than hard evidence. And some of the Germans went native or died or emigrated. Anyway, after three days I found something.

"There was a German who went to Syria just after 1945, an SS officer named Hans Gerhard Foerster. He fought in Russia for several years, and the file said he probably worked at the Dachau extermination camp late in the war, but there was no conclusive evidence, so he wasn't pursued. I don't think the file on him had been touched for thirty years.

"Then I did some more digging, this time into Syrians who might have been connected with either the Brotherhood or with the Syrian security services. I was lucky. There's a man who fits the profile exactly, although we can't be sure he's the one our man Gabriel knew about until we . . . talk to him. His name is Selim Youssef, a merchant in Damascus. Unfortunately, I don't know much more than that. He came to our attention in the mid-sixties, because he did a lot of traveling to Germany and France, and we thought he might have been doing something for the terrorist groups there. But he looked legitimate, so we dropped him."

"You think he could be involved in this." Cole was thinking: It's not possible.

"Yes."

"But there's no direct connection between Youssef and Foerster," he said. "There must be more than one Arabized German who fits the profile."

"Oh, there are. But one thing convinced me." There was a hint of triumph in her voice. "It was a

291

report from 1955, in a dossier on a man named Nazem Saleh. He was in the Syrian Brotherhood even then. In 1956 he dropped out of sight, either dead or gone underground, the file's empty after that. But the report said he had a business associate, to whom he'd lent money to get started.''

Cole said, ''The business associate's name was Selim Youssef. And the file said that Mossad thought he was German.''

''That's right.''

''Jesus Christ.''

''I beg your pardon?''

''Selim Youssef. I've met him. He handled some antiquities exporting for me, three years ago.''

''My God,'' she said. ''Could you identify him?''

''Yes.''

''That settles it,'' she said. ''We have to go into Syria.''

The White House, Washington
April 16

"I WISH YOU were about to tell me this is a late April Fool's joke," Parnell said, "but I don't think you are, are you?"

He was sitting, with the members of the Special Presidential Advisory Group on Middle East Affairs, in the conference lounge adjoining the Situation Room in the White House subbasement. He thought: I suppose we had to expect this. It was bound to happen sooner or later. But I *gave* those orders, goddammit. Security to be upgraded for the weapons storage sites. And nobody seems to have paid any attention.

"Okay, ladies and gentlemen," he said harshly, "this is where we're at. We know the terrorists got two bombs. We've decided to keep news of the theft from the public until they're recovered, but we've informed the Turkish and Israeli governments, since they're the most likely targets. Any terrorist group that's pulled off a coup like this one isn't going to hide its light under a bushel for long, though. It's going to tell the world about it. How much time might we have before they do that?"

Secretary of State Cornelissen looked at John Lusby, the secretary of defense. Lusby nodded at him. "You go ahead, Kip."

Cornelissen said, "We believe that whoever took the weapons will delay making it public until they've put the bombs where they want them."

"Have we *any* idea who's responsible?" Parnell asked. "The Syrians?"

"We don't know that, either. Since we're trying to keep this—disaster under wraps as long as possible, we can hardly ask the Brotherhood government in Damascus. But the raid was very well planned and competently carried out. This isn't a splinter group of four or five fanatics. It's bigger, and it's well-led, by somebody with a good deal of military experience. That could point to Syrian involvement."

"If the story gets out before we recover the weapons," Lusby said, "we're going to have every antinuke activist on the planet saying 'I told you so'."

"It's going to be worse than that," said Cornelissen. "A lot of people who trusted us not to let this happen are going to be very angry indeed. We're going to lose a lot of that trust."

And maybe the next election, thought Parnell. *Probably* the next election. *"Why,"* he asked furiously, "weren't the security systems improved as we ordered? We've been fortifying our embassies for years, for Christ's sake. Surely our nuclear weapons storage is at least as important."

"Money, Mr. President," the secretary of defense told him. "The appropriation for that was part of a package that got stalled in the House. Work was supposed to have started this summer, but. . . ." He trailed off.

"It's a little late now," Parnell snapped, "but it

better begin right away. Now that one terrorist group's done this, all the others will think they can pull it off, too. This could turn into a catastrophe. Dammit, it already *is* a catastrophe." He paused for breath. There was no point in belaboring the guilt question further.

"Okay, that's enough of that," he said. "We'll let heads roll later. Now. I've always been told that these weapons couldn't be exploded unless you knew the arming codes, which, I've been *told,* are several grades above Top Secret. Did they get the arming codes?"

"No," Secretary of Defense Lusby said. "They didn't."

"Thank God for small mercies. You're sure?"

"We're sure, Mr. President." There were tiny beads of perspiration on Lusby's upper lip. "But, unfortunately, I must draw your attention to Dr. Edmund Shapiro's report on the bombs. As you recollect, he's the top-ranking expert in our nuclear weapons research program."

"What's he got to say, John?" Christ, Parnell thought. Not another surprise.

"It seems, Mr. President, that they are not actually bombs. The W33 devices which were stolen are artillery shells for the 203mm howitzer first fielded by Turkey in 1956 as part of their NATO armament. The W33s are now nearly obsolete. They have three different components: the shell assembly, the uralloy nuclear charge and the fuse. They are designed to be assembled in the field, and to be armed and fused at that time." Lusby paused and looked around. All eyes were on him. "Nowadays all of our air and land based nuclear weapons are protected by safety devices, especially if they're deployed in foreign countries. The safeties are called

295

Permissive Action Links, PALs, and they've been becoming more sophisticated for years. Dr. Shapiro points out, for example, that the B61 bomb is protected by a multiple code, twelve-digit entry pad, nonviolent command disable and weak-link-strong-link switches driven by a unique signal generator.''

"You just left me behind, John," Parnell said. "Would that mean it's hard to explode, or easy?"

"Very hard, Mr. President. Virtually impossible."

"What protects the weapons that were stolen?"

"Very little. As I told you, the W33s are almost obsolete. A W33's arming mechanism is protected by a mechanical combination lock, and nothing else. A technician trained in the early days and provided with the right equipment could arm one quite easily."

"Jesus Christ," Parnell said, as a murmur went around the table. "Does Shapiro think these terrorists could have found someone like that?"

"I don't know, Mr. President. But we can't dismiss the possibility."

"Then the bottom line is that this group not only has our warheads, but also that it can probably use them."

"That's it, sir. Shapiro says that once a shell was armed, it would be relatively simple to install a timed detonation system, or a manual trigger. A technician who could arm the bomb would know how to do that."

Worse and worse, Parnell thought. It's finally happened, it really has. "John, what, to your knowledge, would the effect be if one of these warheads exploded in a city?"

"The device has a yield of about twelve kilotons, Mr. President, not much less than the bomb that

296

destroyed Hiroshima. The weapon there flattened most of the city, with severe damage to, and fires in, the suburbs. In the case of Israel, the areas around her major cities are heavily populated. If there were no evacuation, we estimate fatalities, from the explosion itself and from immediate fallout, of two hundred and fifty thousand people. That's just from one bomb. In addition, the fallout would cause serious health effects for decades after. Croplands in the fallout pattern would be unusable indefinitely."

"Could Israel survive it?" Parnell asked.

"Possibly," Lusby said, after a moment's thought. "If enormous amounts of aid were poured in, medicine, food, medical personnel, heavy equipment for reconstruction. Remember, most of the medical facilities and industrial plant and housing in the affected area would be destroyed or rendered unusable. It would be years before Israel could rebuild her economy, or muster the military strength she now has."

"And if she were attacked by another nation—Syria, for example—in the period following the bomb?"

"She would be destroyed. The Israelis would almost certainly use their own nuclear arsenal in retaliation, but that would be too late as far as her long-term survival was concerned. She would take her enemies down with her, that's all." Lusby paused. "That is, unless she were helped by foreign military intervention, which I suppose means ourselves. I hesitate to consider the implications of that, especially if the Israeli government insisted on using its own atomic weapons against, for example, Syria. A nuclear war in the Middle East has always been one of our worst-case scenarios, since it logically leads to global thermonuclear exchanges between ourselves and the Soviet Union.''

"Is there any way out of this?" Parnell asked the assembly around the table.

"Only to retrieve the bombs," Cornelissen said.

No kidding, Parnell thought. Ye gods, Kip, talk about stating the obvious. "Okay," he said, "exactly how do we do that? Do we have any latitude for military action? General Haslett?"

"Not until we know who took them," the chairman of the Joint Chiefs of Staff said. "Even then, we're in a hostage situation. If we go military, they might set their weapons off."

"How are the Israelis taking it?" Parnell asked Cornelissen.

"They went right up in the air at first," he replied. "They've calmed down a bit now, but they're still very angry and very frightened. If the Brotherhood in Syria really does get those bombs, and can fuse them, Israel's existence could be measured in days. The only thing holding Jerusalem back at the moment is uncertainty that Damascus has the bombs. Since they were ready to go to war with the Syrians before this, anyway, what's happened has made them that much edgier. If they find evidence that Syria has the weapons, I wouldn't rule out an Israeli nuclear first strike against Damascus. That would bring in the Russians. Kulagin may not like the Brotherhood government much, but he would certainly back the Syrians to the hilt." He stopped, drew a deep breath, and looked out into the Situation Room, where the military symbols glowed on the wall screens. "We were already worried about the Israelis' response to Winter Palace. Now this."

"Is there any chance," Parnell asked, "that the two schemes are connected? That it's Kulagin and the Russians who backed up the bomb theft? Coop?''

Cooper Tarkington hunched forward in his chair. "God help us if the Israelis convince themselves of that. They've never admitted it, but they've got nearly two hundred nuclear weapons, air-deliverable, in their arsenal now. That's bigger than their deterrent force ever needed to be. With that many warheads, they even threaten the Soviet Union. And with midair refueling, their planes could reach all the way to Kiev. One way, even to Moscow.''

There was a brief silence. Parnell spoke into it. "Kip, would they do that?''

Cornelissen said, "Israeli policy has always been an eye for an eye, or two eyes for an eye if they can manage it. There's an unbelievable emotional factor associated with Israel, for the Israelis. If they thought the Russians had helped somebody destroy their country . . .'' He shrugged. "I'm sure they'd go all the way. Rationality would fly out the window. 'Never again', remember? I think they'd pull the rest of the world down with them, rather than submit to another Holocaust.''

"That bastard Kulagin,'' Parnell said. "If he's engineered this. . . . He'd have to be crazy.''

"He may be,'' said Tarkington. "Extreme anti-Semitism, as he seems to be exhibiting, is a form of mental illness. It distorts reality. But that doesn't rule out his being very cunning. He didn't get to be general secretary by being stupid. Why the rest of his government's going along with Winter Palace, it's hard to tell, except to say that the ones in the Politburo who matter are all getting something out of it. But I doubt if the Kremlin's behind the bomb theft. It's more likely a really bad set of coincidences."

"Let's hope the Israelis see it that way. What are we doing about finding the people who stole the bombs?"

"Mr. President, Mossad knew that something was in the wind even before the Brotherhood's revolution succeeded in Syria. They've now tentatively identified the man who could have arranged it. They believe he's in Damascus, and are planning to go in and get him. But it's difficult even for Mossad to work in Syria at the moment, since the revolution. It will take five days, at the minimum, to get a team in."

"No chance of less?"

"Apparently not."

"We may not *have* five days."

"Yes, Mr. President. I know."

Parnell sighed. Too many things going wrong at once, he thought. The old nightmare. One big crisis at a time, we can handle, but two . . . A bad set of circumstances, Coop said.

We all knew that that could happen. That sooner or later it *would* happen, but we all hoped we wouldn't be around, or, at least, responsible, when it did: when events ran out of control, and no one knew how to stop them, how to step back from the abyss. Maybe Winter Palace and the bombs *are* connected, maybe Kulagin is behind the theft somehow. But that doesn't matter. Events are going to jam the two together.

And there are hundreds of thousands of Jews over there in camps on the other side of the world, and there are also two nuclear bombs in the hands of people who are willing to use them, and who hate Jews. The two crises are going to intersect, and there

300

seems to be nothing we can do about either. With Winter Palace, our options are zero. If we accuse the Russians of anti-Semitism, using documents forty years old, and do so before we flush a substantial number of Soviet moles out of the refugee camps, Kulagin will just laugh at us.

But if we take in the Russian Jews en masse, we'll lose all control of them. There may be fifty thousand KGB agents waiting for a ticket to the United States. That's the equivalent of a Soviet army, four goddamned Russian divisions, on American soil. But if we refuse the Jews much longer, the Soviets will accuse *us* of anti-Semitism, and with the present emotional climate, they'll be able to make it stick. We can't even ask Moscow to slow down the flow because that would make it look as though we wanted the Russians to keep the Jews. Christ! Kulagin's really got us this time.

And then there's the bomb. Two bombs. There's a chance there—a success would make us look a little better. If we got them back it would at least prevent two dreadful crises from becoming a single, monstrous, uncontrollable one.

"This Israeli team," he said to Tarkington, "the one going into Syria to find the man who stole the weapons. It would be politically expedient to have an American with them. I don't want the perception that the Israelis are saving our asses for us. We look bad enough without that."

"One of the team *is* American," Tarkington said. "Dr. Samuel Cole, the man who brought the Winter Palace documents out of Russia for us."

A glimmer of hope, Parnell thought. "Okay," he said. "That's a start. One other thing, Coop. You said there was some evidence that somebody in Russia may have let Dr. Cole out of the country even

301

though he had the Winter Palace documents with him. Any more on that? It might give us the edge we need, if Kulagin's got adversaries at home.''

Tarkington shook his head. ''Nothing. We're doing everything we can think of to find out, but nothing so far.''

''Okay,'' Parnell said. ''I suppose it was a real shot in the dark.''

North Syrian Coast
April 20

THE MOON was down, leaving only a faint pale glow on the horizon. Foerster stood on the beach next to the boat, scanning the low waves through a pair of night binoculars. Haddad was beside him, shifting restlessly from one foot to the other. Behind them, the four *Jund Allah* soldiers squatted on the beach, their camouflage uniforms barely visible in the starlight. Their faces had been blackened, like Foerster's and Haddad's.

"Are you sure he will come?" Haddad asked in a low voice.

"He'll come," Foerster said. And he'd be wise to, the old man thought. I paid him well. If he doesn't show up I'll kill him myself when he goes back to Istanbul. And he knows that. He'll come.

Foerster glanced into the boat. It was old, wooden, about five meters long, with curved gunwales and two sets of oarlocks, no motor: an unremarkable coastal fishing vessel. The oars were piled on the beach beside it. Inside the boat, well lashed down, lay the bomb container in a wooden crate.

The Iraqi bomb expert had wanted to watch the

303

transfer, but Foerster had refused; he wanted the expedition to be no larger than absolutely necessary. Now he looked at the dim shape of the crate that held the bomb container, nestled in the boat's interior. Alwan had managed to fit the timer into the container, after arming and fusing the weapon. He had also shielded the warhead with thin lead plates, to reduce the chance of the bomb being detected by its radiation. Inside the container, the timer was ticking off the seconds in its electronic innards, and it would reach zero at precisely 6 A.M. on April 28.

Foerster swept the waves again with the binoculars. Five hundred meters out was a long black shadow that hadn't been there before.

"The *Konya,*" he said. "She ought to signal."

A light winked, one long, two shorts, from the vessel. "Answer," said Foerster.

Haddad clicked his lantern. A glimmer from the ship.

"It's the right response," Haddad said. He turned to his men. "Get the boat into the water."

They grunted and strained at the broad hull until it slid, grating and rumbling, over the shingle and into the waves. With Haddad and Foerster aboard, they began to pull toward the blacked-out vessel offshore. Foerster kept sweeping the horizon to the north with the binoculars, but there was no sign of Syrian patrol boats.

The ship drew closer, taking on shape in the starlight: a coaster of about eight hundred tons, high stem, well-deck aft of it, high bridge and stern deckhouse, tall antiquated funnel, stub mast. Even in the darkness she exuded dilapidation and age; built for the British coastal trade before the war, she now belonged to a consortium of minor Turkish traders. She had spent the previous eight years of her decaying life steaming smokily from port to port in the eastern Mediterranean, hauling anything and everything. Her destination this voyage was Haifa, to collect a consignment of specialized aluminum castings.

She would also deliver a nuclear bomb.

Two of Haddad's men, with false seamen's papers, were to join her to conceal and guard the weapon on the voyage. When she docked at Haifa the following evening, they were to ease it over the side. It would lie in the silt of the harbor bottom, unsuspected, until the timer reached zero. The *Konya*, with her load of castings, would be on the way back to Turkey long before that, dropping the *Jund Allah* men at the cove as she passed.

The Turkish captain, an eminently bribable man, did not know what was in the crate. Should he develop any doubts about the cargo, Haddad's two men were on board to ensure that he suppressed them. As for the *Konya*'s crew, they were the sweepings of every port in the Mediterranean and the Persian Gulf; there was nothing to fear from them.

The boat swung, bumping against the *Konya*'s scabbed plates. A cargo net had been rigged over the bulwarks; Haddad's two men scrambled up. A minute later a cargo sling dropped into the bottom of the boat. Haddad and his other two men unlashed the crate and loaded it into the sling. Up on deck a winch clanked, and the crate rose, swaying, up the side of the ship. It reached the well-deck rail and swung inboard, disappearing from Foerster's sight.

A head appeared at the rail, outlined against the stars. "The money?"

Foerster took the canvas packet out of his *galabiyeh* and tossed it up into the darkness. The head disappeared, to reappear a moment later.

"It is satisfactory."

305

"Good," Foerster called quietly. He could hear the faint thud of the *Konya*'s engine. "The rest will be paid in Istanbul when you return."

"I will be there."

"Make sure of it," Foerster called. "If you do not carry out your instructions, you know what will happen to you. And to your family."

"I understand. Go with God."

"And you," said Foerster. To Haddad he said, "We can go back."

Haddad's two men unshipped their oars, pushing off from the *Konya*'s black bulk. Foerster and Haddad sat in the bow, looking back at the coaster. "Soon," Haddad said, over the creak of the oars.

"Yes," said Foerster absently. He'd been humming again, almost without realizing it, but he didn't care. He was thinking: One weapon I have used. The other I will not be able to get into Tel Aviv; Haddad doesn't have the resources to manage it by land, and I cannot find another ship in time.

But there is still the target I thought of last night.

"Nadim Haddad," he said to the dark figure beside him, "I want to discuss something with you."

306

Damascus
April 21

THE TELEPHONE was ringing. Khalil Dirouzi, head of the Inner Council of the Muslim Brotherhood and Protector of the Islamic Revolution of Syria, woke instantly, throwing off the single rough blanket. A night breeze filtered through the louvers of the open window, striking cool against his chest as he picked up the receiver.

"Dirouzi."

"Mahmdou Ubari," a voice said in his ear.

Something had happened for the chief of security to be calling him in the dead of night. Dirouzi's alertness increased a level. "What?"

"I have serious news." Ubari sounded agitated. "It is regarding the raid several days ago that was carried out against the American nuclear weapons site at Adana. All the American guards were killed, as you recollect."

"The attackers were not of the Brotherhood," Dirouzi said. "We can disclaim any responsibility. Have you been able to identify them?"

"Not as yet," Ubari told him. "They left three dead, but there was naturally no identification. The

Americans reported the raid to be a failure. But it was not. As you know, we have a source in the Turkish General Staff. He has informed us that the attackers succeeded in escaping with two nuclear bombs. That has not been made public, and the Americans will doubtless try to keep it that way. The loss makes them look very stupid. However, I thought you should know as soon as possible.''

Dirouzi was cursing inwardly. When he had first learned about the Adana raid, he had instantly thought of Youssef, or rather Foerster. But the man was old and sick, surely too frail to engineer such a thing. Besides, where would he find soldiers and logistical support?

"You said two weapons? Have you any idea where they've been taken?''

"No.''

"Could they have been brought across the border? Here into Syria?''

"Maybe. It is impossible to seal that terrain east of Adana against men who know the area. You know how much smuggling takes place.''

"Yes,'' Dirouzi said. Then, more or less to himself: "He did it. I don't know who helped him, but someone did. He may wreck everything.''

"Who?''

"The German. The one Saleh brought into the Brotherhood years ago. He must have been planning this since I released him from the Brotherhood.'' *Foerster*, he thought. The Brotherhood should have rid itself of him long ago, when Saleh died. The man had outlived his usefulness, twice over. That plan of his, to use nuclear weapons. Madness.

Foerster. Where is he?

"Protector, are you still there?''

308

"Yes. You must locate Foerster. As soon as possible. I believe he did this thing."

"We will find him, if he's in Syria," Ubari said. "And the weapons as well."

"You understand what hangs on taking him? With the Americans we can deny, they won't react immediately, but if the Israelis believe we have the weapons—"

"I understand, Protector. We will find him."

"See that you do," Dirouzi said.

Turkey—Syria
April 21

AFTER LANDING at Gaziantep, Cole took a *dolmus* into the city. It dropped him in a street not far from the old Byzantine fortress built by Justinian the Great, in a quarter of narrow flagged streets, tumbledown houses whose plaster was crumbling away to reveal the brickwork beneath, wooden balconies in the last stages of dry rot, the alleys full of dust and broken bottles. It was six o'clock, the sun declining rapidly into the west.

He paid the driver and got out, lugging his flight bag, then walked half a block to the entrance of a narrow side street that ran north and south. The declining sun had cast it into shadow; fifty meters farther along it, half a dozen children were playing some kind of game with a hoop. Their shouts echoed and reechoed from the crumbling facades.

Second alley on the right, she had said. Cole turned into it and found himself in a narrow passage between two buildings. A dozen meters along, a door was set into a stone wall topped with broken glass laid in mortar. He tried the door; it wasn't locked. Stepping over the threshold, Cole found himself in a small courtyard behind a decrepit-looking house. He pushed the bolt of the door home and locked it.

The courtyard was deep in shadow by now, the air cool. Cole went to the only other door—there was a curtained window beside it, protected by a rusted iron grille—and knocked. After a moment he heard soft footsteps inside. The window curtain twitched. After another couple of seconds the door rattled, opening.

"Hello," Cole said, in Turkish.

"Come in," she said.

He entered quickly and Dalia closed the door, locking it. They were in a narrow passage, stone-flagged, dim. The walls were covered in what could only be silk, blue-green and covered with intricate floral designs. Cole blinked in surprise.

"The owner of the house is a Jew," she told him. "His family has been in Turkey for eight generations. They have been helping us for two. Like many other things, the outside doesn't well represent the inside."

Cole nodded. He followed her along the corridor and up a stairway, whose bannister was carved of some dark wood polished to a deep lustre. Under Cole's palm its surface was as smooth as oil. He realized that part of him was noting the sway of Dalia's hips as she went up the stairs.

The old Adam, he thought with a touch of bitterness, thinking of Megan. No matter what else is going on, he's always in the background somewhere.

At the top of the stairs was a small sitting room, furnished with a divan, a brass tray on legs, Kashan carpets and delicately embroidered cushions. A small slender man was sitting on the divan, smoking a cigarette.

"This is Avi Maoz," Dalia said. "Transport and

311

logistics. He'll be taking us and the ultralights up to the takeoff area.''

"Hello," Avi said without expression. Whatever he thought of Cole was hidden behind the mask of his dark, thin face.

"Hello," Cole said, just as expressionlessly.

"Have you eaten?" Dalia asked.

"On the plane. Not much."

"That's just as well. It may be a little bumpy, going through the mountains. Ever been airsick?"

"No," he said truthfully. Even if he had been, he wouldn't have admitted it in front of Avi.

"Fine." She had sat down on one of the cushions, next to the brass tray. "We'll leave here as soon as it starts to get dark."

He had found the flight exhilarating until Dalia flew the ultralight into the mouth of a canyon that was becoming disturbingly narrow.

Christ, he thought. I hope she hasn't picked the wrong one. We'll be like a nut in a nutcracker if it doesn't open out soon.

But it did, suddenly and surprisingly, the canyon floor leveling out at the same time and transforming itself into a plateau that quickly began to fall away to the south, where it ended at another range of crags. The faces of the peaks were faintly luminous in the moonlight. Between two of them there was a gap; Dalia flew toward it, keeping the little machine no more than ten meters above the stony land. Cole wondered whether, if the engine stopped, she would be able to get them down alive; the ground below them was appallingly rough.

The ultralight reached the gap and passed through it, lifting to follow the contours of the terrain. On

312

the far side of the gap the ground sloped steeply away, into a wide valley. Off to the east Cole saw faint lights: the Turkish border post of Ackacale.

The ultralight skimmed over the land, Dalia swinging its nose more to the west. On their right a line of mountains loomed, paralleling their line of flight, less than half a kilometer away. Dalia raised her left hand, giving the thumbs-up sign. They had penetrated into Syria.

So far, so good, Cole thought. Now if we can just get out again. And with Foerster, into the bargain.

That was going to be the hard part. Once they'd captured him, they would have to find a way to get him to Turkey for interrogation. If they couldn't get him out, the details of his intentions were to be extracted by any means necessary.

The ultralight was turning, climbing again. A great dry cove opened in the wall of mountains on the right. Dalia flew into it. A precipice of stone rose in front of them, iron, impenetrable.

What in Christ's name is she doing? Cole thought. Jesus, she's lost her way.

A tall moon-thrown shadow suddenly transformed itself into the mouth of a wadi. The dry valley might have been twenty meters wider than the ultralight's wingspan. Cole realized that he was biting his lower lip, painfully.

The ultralight began to sink. The wadi floor widened, leveled out. Dalia cut back the throttle, settling the little machine lower. The ground, fissured and strewn with boulders and scree, slid upward toward the aircraft's wheels.

A clear patch appeared, its dimensions indefinable in the moonlight. Dalia chopped the throttle; the plane was no more than half a meter up. The wheels sank, touched, a slight bounce, they were down. The

313

engine's hum faded into silence, the wheels jolting over pebbles and small ridges of stone. They came to a stop.

A moment of moonlit silence, then they were out of their harnesses, grabbing the Scorpions from the clips beside their seats, running toward the wadi sides and the litter of rockfall. It was unlikely that anyone was waiting in ambush, but they could not take the risk.

Cole reached a boulder and crouched behind it, scanning the moonlit wadi floor and its far wall. Dalia was a dozen meters away on his right. They waited for a couple of minutes; nothing.

"Good," Dalia said in a low voice, standing up. "Let's get the plane hidden."

They removed the cargo canisters from the ultra-light and rolled the little aircraft to a cleft in the wadi's side. In five minutes the wings were off, stowed in the cleft; then the camouflage sheeting went over all. Cole looked at his watch, tilting it to catch the moonlight.

"He should be here soon."

Dalia nodded. "Always assuming the best."

"You're a superb flier," he told her.

"I've had lots of practice. I've used this landing ground before."

"Often?"

"A few times. There's another one on the other side of the range, but we can only use it in the dry season."

They got out of the survival suits and put on Syrian clothes. It was a curiously intimate moment; Cole avoided looking at her, although she seemed quite unself-conscious. The suits went back into the canisters, which they slipped under the camouflage net. After that there was nothing to do but wait, so they sat in shadow with their backs against the cliff face, Scorpions beside them, and waited. The air was very still, and cold with the chill of the desert night. The moon was sinking toward the horizon. In the vault of the sky, meteors traced occasional scratches of light.

"It's very beautiful," she murmured after a while. "I've always loved the desert, especially at night. Everything here is stripped to its essentials, completely honest. It will kill you quickly if you do not understand it, but if you do, it will not betray you. Everything is exactly itself."

"Unlike people," Cole said.

"Yes. Unlike people."

He heard the faint clink of a pebble as she stirred. Her elbow brushed his.

There was a long silence. The night was so still that he could hear her breathing. It was deep and regular.

"Are you warm enough?" he asked.

"Yes. Are you?"

"Yes."

Another silence. It was probably an illusion, but he thought he could feel a warmth along his arm, from her nearness.

She shifted. Her arm touched his again, stayed. They were miles from anywhere, from anyone. He was suddenly and intensely aware of her femaleness. Megan's gone, he thought. Gone for good, and by my doing. I loved her, love her, but she's gone. Why not this?

She stirred again, half-turning to face him. "Are you afraid?"

"Yes," he said. "I'd be a fool not to be. Are you?"

"As you say, I'd be a fool not to be." She leaned

315

toward him a little. Her breathing changed, became more rapid. He felt a very soft pressure against his arm. He moved a little, but the pressure didn't go away; it seemed to increase.

"We're a hell of a long way from anywhere," he said. "Does Avi come with you on these runs?"

"Sometimes."

"Are you and Avi—"

He thought she smiled. "No. He's like a brother. We aren't lovers, we have never been. It wouldn't work."

"Oh. There's nobody, then?"

"No. This business doesn't make that sort of thing easy."

He turned a little to face her more directly, knowing now what was touching his arm; her left breast. "There's no point in dancing around it," he said. "I want you."

"You mean you want to make love to me."

"You wouldn't believe me if I denied it."

"No."

"You?"

"I've been thinking about it."

He was erect. He reached over with his left hand and touched where the pressure lay against his arm. She didn't stop him. Under the *galabiyeh* her breasts were free. He felt her nipple harden under his fingers.

"One thing about Syrian clothes," she said. "You don't have to wear much underneath."

It happened quickly, urgently; they knew they didn't have much time left. She was completely ready when he touched her, so close to the edge of orgasm that she thrust involuntarily against his fingers. Moments later he was buried in her, her arms and legs locked around him as though to squeeze

316

him dry. They reached climax almost simultaneously.

Afterward, they lay entwined in the cold light of the declining moon. Cole kissed the side of her throat, just below the curve of her jaw. "We'd better get our clothes back on," he said.

When they were dressed again, they sat down to wait. It could have been an awkward moment, but somehow wasn't. She leaned against him quite naturally, now that the sexual tension was gone. There didn't seem to be any need to talk about what had happened between them; it had occurred and could now be set aside.

"What time is it?" he asked, after a while.

"Five to three."

"Mustafa—" he began, and then: "Listen."

Floating up through the wadi, barely audible, came the muted hum of a truck engine, the whine of a gearbox in low ratio.

"He's come," she said.

"Or Syrians. We'd better move."

Dalia picked up the signal lamp, testing it momentarily with her fingers over the lens. Then they chambered rounds in the Scorpions and ran a hundred meters down the wadi, stopping a little short of its entrance, where they separated, positioning themselves behind boulders to establish a cross fire on whoever came up the wadi floor. Cole waited. He could smell the Scorpion's machine oil, mingled with the scent of their lovemaking.

A light blinked dimly from the wadi entrance. Cole relaxed a little. It was the right code, without the error that would indicate that Mustafa was acting under duress. With his night-adapted sight he caught a faint glow from Dalia's position, answering. The glow cut off, and he saw her stand up and

317

hurry toward the origin of the other light. As insurance, Cole kept the Scorpion trained on the place until she reached it. She disappeared into the shadows, the gray of her *galabiyeh* merging with that of the rock walls.

A minute later she reappeared, followed by a burly figure. The moon was almost down, but in its last light Cole could see that Mustafa was wearing a camouflage smock over military trousers and boots. An army forage cap was on his head.

"Sam. You can come out now."

He put the Scorpion on safety and left his hiding place. Mustafa watched as he approached. Beside him, even in her voluminous *galabiyeh,* Dalia looked slight and frail.

"Samuel Cole." It was a statement, not a question.

"Yes. Mustafa?"

"That's the name you'll know me by. From here on in, you've got Syrian identities. But not the ones you were issued." He fumbled in his shirt under the camouflage smock. "New ones. Here."

"But the others—" Dalia began.

"Forget them. These are better. For the last day and a half Aleppo and the north have been like a kicked anthill, so is Damascus apparently. The Brotherhood's looking for somebody. I couldn't warn you, I hardly dare use the radio, even on burst transmission."

"Looking for us?" Cole asked.

"I doubt it. But it makes things harder, there are roadblocks all over the place."

Cole peered at the identity card Mustafa had given him. The Israeli clicked on his light, shielding it. Cole's new name, Hasan Abdullah, had been neatly typed in. There was, surprisingly, no photograph.

318

Dalia had been reading hers as well. "We're Islamic Revolutionary Guards? How far will that get us?"

"Far enough, as long as you're with me." Mustafa chuckled, but with little humor. "In fact, you're looking at a lieutenant in the Islamic Guard. I managed to join up after the Brotherhood got Aleppo organized. We run around looking for suspected Assad supporters, or anyone else the Brotherhood chief in Aleppo doesn't like, and throw them in jail. I must say," he added in a sardonic tone, "that it gives me a certain amount of satisfaction. Also it means you'll be able to bring the Scorpions. The Guard's got a dog's breakfast of weapons, right back to British Lee-Enfields. The guns may give us an edge, if we need it."

"We need more than these cards," Dalia said. "Residence registration—"

"They're in the truck. You'll have to memorize the information on the way back. Now, listen. We haven't much time. The Guards identification will get us through army roadblocks. The soldiers are scared stiff of the Guards, but if we hit a Guards block, let me do all the talking. Those bastards are crazy. I've seen women shot at the side of the road a couple of times, the Guards don't give a damn. The Brotherhood'll probably have to suppress them later, but right now Damascus is letting them run wild. Got all that?"

"Yes," Dalia said. Cole nodded.

"We'd better go," Mustafa said.

Haifa, Israel
April 21

IT WAS EARLY afternoon. The *Konya* wallowed in the long swell riding out of the northwest. Beyond her bows lay the entrance to Haifa's great harbor, Israel's largest, the horizon webbed with huge cargo cranes and punctuated by the long pale bulk of the Dagon grain elevator.

The Israeli pilot launch was drawing alongside. From the stern deckhouse, Madhat, the senior of the two *Jund Allah* men Haddad had put aboard to lay the bomb, watched with mounting tension as the Israeli harbor pilot, a customs officer and two well-armed harbor security police clambered onto the deck. They were carrying some kind of electronic equipment. The crate containing the weapon was well-hidden in the engine room bilges, under water in the smuggling compartment, but if the Israelis had any suspicions at all they would dismantle the *Konya* rivet by rivet and plate by rusting plate.

Israeli regulations were that all crew had to pass an identity check. Madhat scrambled down the ladder from the deckhouse, joining the other hands in a short ragged line just aft of the cargo hoist. Adib,

320

the second *Jund Allah* man, stood at the other end of the rank.

Madhat's papers were ready and, he hoped, in good order. He was supposedly a seaman from Jiddah, in Saudi Arabia. The papers were suitably creased and stained; for all Madhat knew, they might have been real. The passport was equally dogeared. He hoped that the *Konya*'s master had remembered to enter his false identification in the log as having signed on at Istanbul.

The Israeli security man, Uzi slung over his shoulder, started with the man on Madhat's left. Everything in order. Then he stepped in front of Madhat, hand outstretched, tanned, clean. Madhat felt the old fury surge in him. He passed over his documents. The Israeli inspected them minutely. Then he said, in Arabic:

"How long have you been with this ship?"

"This voyage only," Madhat said evenly.

"Before that?"

"A coaster in the Black Sea." He had had this story drummed into him before he left. "But she went aground off Kilimli so I was paid off."

"What was her name?"

"Yildiz." The vessel really did exist, and had in fact gone aground the month before.

The Israeli handed the documents back, satisfied. Now, Madhat thought, if only Adib remembers his tale.

He did. Instead of letting the crew go, however, the Israeli kept them in the well-deck. The others didn't appear to find this unusual, but it increased Madhat's anxiety a good deal. He imagined the customs man and the other security officer raising the footplates in the engine room, peering under them, their electronic instruments sniffing for the

321

bomb. . . . The *Konya*'s master had built his smuggling compartment back there, up against the sternpost, it looked like part of the bilges in the dark, but even so, if their detection equipment was good enough. . . .

There was nothing Madhat could do about it. He could only wait.

Twenty minutes passed. The crewmen smoked, muttered to one another, fidgeted, spat. Finally the customs officer and the other security man came out of the deckhouse and went up to the bridge. They spoke to the *Konya*'s master for a couple of minutes. Madhat watched them through the glass of the bridge windows, hands aching for a weapon. But they hadn't been allowed to bring any. If they were to be betrayed, it would happen soon.

It did not. The Israelis left the bridge and came down to the well-deck, moving toward the companionway. The security man who had been watching the crew gestured, half-contemptuously, and joined the Israelis. The crew dispersed.

A minute or two later the bridge telegraph jangled, the *Konya*'s engine thumped more loudly, and the coaster swung her bows toward the entrance of the Israeli harbor.

The *Konya* loaded her cargo in the late afternoon, and the crew went ashore. Madhat and Adib waited in the hold until just after midnight; then Madhat went on deck to observe the situation. After taking on cargo, the coaster had been moored alongside another one, of slightly more tonnage, alongside the outer quay. The Arab leaned against the taffrail, smoking, watching the patrols move up and down the quays, timing them.

After an hour, Madhat knew what he was going to do. The dangerous part of the operation lay between the time they got the crate on deck and the moment they put it over the side into the water. The sight of a pair of seamen dropping a large object overboard would invite immediate investigation. But their berthing had been a stroke of luck. There were a good two meters of water between the *Konya* and the other coaster, and Madhat had decided that they would drop the bomb into that gap, so that their actions would be hidden from the near quay by the other ship, and from the harbor security launches by the *Konya*'s own hull. It was time to act.

He left the taffrail and went below. Adib was waiting in the hold, leaning up against one of the crates the *Konya* had loaded that afternoon. Adib was nervous, that was clear, but he had been with the *Jund Allah* for a long time. He would do whatever was necessary.

"We can go ahead."

Adib nodded and got to his feet. Together they went astern along the passageways into the engine room. They lifted the footplates by the sternpost and descended into the bilges. With a little difficulty, they got the captain's smuggling compartment open; the lid was so tightly fitted and disguised with grime that even though they knew it was there, they had to search for the edges of the cover.

The crate was heavy, nearly a hundred and forty kilos in all, but the two Arabs were used to brutal loads. The difficulty was in the awkwardness of the thing. By the time they got the dripping crate up onto the engine room floor they were sweating, tense and angry. But getting it on deck was less difficult than Madhat had expected. The *Konya*'s masthead lights had been switched off, and there was deep shadow under the well-deck bulwarks. They put the crate down, panting. Madhat rubbed his hands together, loosening the cramped muscles.

An Israeli patrol was coming down the quay. Lights flashed. They were shining hand spotlights over the moored ships. A random patrol. He should have known they wouldn't be entirely predictable.

Allah preserve us, Madhat prayed. "Get down!" he hissed at Adib.

The two men crouched under the rail. The lights flashed over *Konya*'s cargo derrick, across the front of the wheelhouse, then swept on.

Madhat waited. Nothing.

He risked a peep over the rail. The two Israelis were moving steadily away.

"Get ready. We'll wait until they're a hundred meters on."

They kept going, never a backward glance.

"Now," whispered Madhat.

The two Arabs grabbed the ends of the crate, lifted. They steadied the crate on the top of the rail.

"Let it go."

An endless second while the bomb fell. Then a splash, which to Madhat sounded as though it should be audible all over the harbor. He waited for the explosion.

The bomb didn't go off. Madhat looked up the quay. The Israelis hadn't stopped.

Thirty feet down, the crate nestled deep into the harbor silt.

Istanbul
April 24

FOERSTER HAD BEEN awake since three in the morning. The stomach pains had gotten him out of bed to begin with, and despite taking four of the painkillers he had been unable to get back to sleep. Finally he had given up, switched the bedside lamp back on, and lain on the bed in his underwear, alternately staring at the ceiling and glancing at his watch and at the telephone. At least in the Etap Marmara Hotel he could be sure that the phone would work; it was the most expensive hotel in the country. He would have preferred to stay in a more obscure establishment, but for this day at least he had to have good communications.

Ten to six, by his watch. The minute hand seemed hardly to move. Often it had been like this in Russia, waiting for an attack to begin: at first it would seem that time had become somehow *thick,* viscous, that it would not flow as it normally did; and then, in the last few seconds before the guns opened up and the tanks and infantry began to move toward the Russian lines, it would seem that the hands of his watch raced, and that all the hours of waiting had been compressed into a moment's duration.

Call, God damn you, he thought, staring at the silent telephone. It's time.

He had always, in the old days against the Russians, been proud of his ability to organize an attack at a moment's notice, welding a few scraps of men and equipment into a hard-edged combat group, throwing it into the teeth of the Russians, overrunning them, smashing their resistance. He still possessed the ability, as his experience with Haddad and the *Jund Allah* men over the last few days had demonstrated, even to Foerster's own satisfaction.

At first Haddad had told him that it would be impossible to move one of the bombs as far as the Jewish transit camp outside Istanbul in the time Foerster wanted.

"Nadim Haddad, you have contacts with the smugglers, the Society of Merchants. I know how you get your guns and supplies. It wasn't from Damascus, even when Assad was there. Your guns came from Bulgaria, and they were carried here by the Society. They can move the bomb, if anyone can, in the time I told you."

"The Society is expensive," Haddad had said, irritably. "Especially if they are only moving cargo, without a profit share."

"I will pay," Foerster said, "if necessary. But you also have funds. Think! We will be able to threaten Jews from two directions. If they find the bomb in Haifa, which, if God wills, they will not, we will still have the other one. Find out if the Society will talk to us, at least."

Privately, he had hoped that Haddad would finance the operation. Before disappearing from Damascus, Foerster had moved large amounts of his

326

own money out of the country, into various foreign banks, but there was always the difficulty of reaching the accounts, and he had already drained a couple of them.

Eventually, however, his arguments had convinced Haddad. The *Jund Allah* leader had even begun to be enthusiastic about the project, but had extracted from the German one concession: when the time came to threaten the Israelis, Haddad would set the conditions.

Foerster had agreed. He had already guessed what Haddad was thinking about doing. The man wanted to assume the leadership of the anti-Zionist fight from Khalil Dirouzi and the Brotherhood, and Foerster had presented him with the means to do so. A successful attack on Israel, especially with a nuclear bomb, would elevate Haddad's reputation far above that of any other Islamic leader, including Dirouzi. Foerster was certain that Haddad would let the Haifa bomb explode anyway, whether Jerusalem caved in or not. He also considered that the terrorist, for all his short-range cunning, was a fool; the man had not thought beyond the time the weapon detonated. Dirouzi and the Syrian Brotherhood would never let Haddad assume leadership of the war against the Jews, no matter how strong the *Jund Allah* was. Dirouzi led a nation-state; Haddad was a landless terrorist.

No matter. The terrorist leader was serving Foerster's purpose: to kill as many Jews as possible before he died himself.

He looked at his watch again. By now the bomb destined for the transit camp should be over the Syrian-Turkish border, lugged across the mountains by *Jund Allah* men, for the rendezvous with a truck driven by two men of the Society of Merchants, the

327

smugglers. Haddad had carried out the negotiations by means of which Foerster was not certain; the man was extremely secretive about his contacts with other organizations, which was as it should be. There was always the chance that Haddad would betray him, but Foerster did not think that this would happen, at least not yet.

The return of the *Konya* to the cove at 4:00 A.M. on the morning of the twenty-third, reporting success in placing the bomb and dropping off the two men who had placed it, precipitated Haddad's decision to go ahead. He had gone into Aleppo and come back with an agreed price and delivery time, the truck to be driven nonstop from the pickup point inside Turkey to Istanbul. The Society would supply the drivers, experts who knew the roads and how to avoid towns and the sporadic military checkpoints. The trip would take no more than thirty-six hours, which was within the time frame Foerster had specified.

That, he thought, still looking at the telephone, will bring the bomb and Haddad and his two men here in the late afternoon tomorrow. Then we have to get everything into the transit camp. It shouldn't be too difficult, there's no organization over there, it's an anthill, a dungheap full of beetles. Jews.

He had gone out to reconnoiter the camp the previous evening, just after flying into Istanbul and checking into the Etap Marmara. He had been desperately tired, from having crossed the mountains back into Turkey that morning and then busing into Adana and the airport, worrying about the integrity of his false passport and the forged entry stamps. He had already used the passport and the other papers more often than was safe; he had another set concealed in the bottom of his suitcase but was saving them for an emergency.

328

Because of his fatigue he had not made a really thorough inspection of the camp, but enough to be certain that it had terrible security—a single fence surrounding acres of tents and ramshackle prefabricated buildings, a warren full of Russian Jews as thick as lice. There were, apparently, about 600,000 Jews, with more coming in every day as others—a trickle—left for Israel or other Western destinations. Foerster wondered how they were being fed, if at all. He hoped they were. A truckload of dried milk would be more than welcome.

Even if, underneath it, was an armed and fused American atomic bomb, with a manual trigger.

He mused on that, in delectation.

Of course, it might all be false hope. If Haddad and his men had been picked up by border patrols as they crossed the mountains—

The telephone rang.

Savoring, Foerster picked it up. "Yes?"

The line wasn't good, but it was Haddad's voice. "We've finished the first phase," he said. "The shipment will arrive on time."

"Good," Foerster said. "We'll be ready to receive it."

The line clicked and went dead.

The old German replaced the receiver, the rush of elation masking, for a moment, the pain in his belly. They had reached Osmaniye, with the bomb. Less than thirty-six hours.

Now he could begin the next step, the first delight of several he anticipated.

At six minutes past nine that morning, the telephone rang in Andrew Paige's office in the American Consulate in Mesrutiyet Street. Paige was head of security for the consulate, and was used to nuisance calls, most of which were filtered out by his deputy head.

"Andy? I've got a strange one on the line."

"What language?"

"Turkish. No accent."

"What's on his mind?" Paige, who had a good deal of paperwork to get through, kept scribbling on the form in front of him; he didn't want to spend time on the phone with another Islamic fanatic, no matter what the man was threatening to do.

"He said, 'If you want nuclear bombs to go off in Israel, by all means ignore this call'."

Paige stopped writing. He was the only one in the consulate, barring the consul himself, who had been told about the theft from the Adana storage site. He realized that he was gripping the receiver too tightly. "Anything else?"

"He's calling from a public phone. I can hear street noises in the background. But he's calm, not impatient."

"Just a second." Paige laid down the phone, opened the right drawer of his desk, and turned on the tape recorder. "Date and time of following conversation," he said, looking at his desk clock. "Oh nine oh eight, April twenty-fourth." He picked up the receiver. "Okay, put him on."

Clicks, then a hum of traffic sounds in the receiver.

"Yes?" Paige said.

"May I ask to whom I speak?" said a voice. Even over the noisy telephone line it had a light rasping quality, like an old man's.

"An American consular officer," Paige said.

330

"Very well. I have a statement to make. I presume you have a recorder running?"

"I do."

"Good. The statement is as follows. The organization I represent has taken two Model W33 nuclear weapons from the storage facility outside Adana. Despite the presence of their safety devices, they have been armed and fused. They will be used unless certain conditions are met by the Zionist government in Jerusalem. These conditions will be made known to you in a moment. Do you have any questions at this point?"

"Yes," Paige said, trying to think quickly. "I am not convinced that your organization actually has possession of such devices. The attack on Adana is public knowledge, and although no weapons were stolen, you may be trying to take advantage of the rumors."

"You may say that," replied the voice, with a tinge of amusement, "for your own purposes. But I believe you know better. We have the following components: shell casings with nuclear cages installed, nuclear materials packages, and fuses. I will now read to you the serial numbers of each of the components in our possession. Perhaps that will help you convince your elders and betters. Listen carefully, and keep your recorder going. I will read slowly, so that you can write the numbers down as well, in case your recorder is defective."

The voice read off strings of letters and numbers while Paige wrote them down and the recorder turned. They may be fakes, he thought. God, I hope they are. But I don't think so. This one isn't like the others I've heard.

The voice finished. A short silence. "Are you sure you have that?" it said.

331

"Yes."

"Good," the voice continued, "Now to the details. One of the weapons has already been placed in Israel. It will detonate, automatically, in a number of days, unless the Zionists meet certain conditions by a certain deadline. There is no point in searching for the device. The Israelis will not be able to locate it in the time allowed."

The bastard is enjoying this, Paige thought. "What are the conditions?"

"Please ensure that your recorder is operating properly."

Paige had been watching the signal-level meters. "It's running." He took a cigarette from the open packet next to the phone, and lit it.

"Good. Here are the conditions. There are nine of them.

"First. The Zionist government is to accept the principle of repatriation and property restoration for all Palestinians who resided, or whose ancestors resided, in what is now the so-called State of Israel.

"Second. The Zionist government is to commit itself to the immediate establishment of a joint Jewish-Palestinian parliament.

"Third. The Zionist government will immediately sever all military, trade, cultural and diplomatic ties with the United States.

"Fourth. The Zionist government will immediately sever all diplomatic, economic and cultural ties with the anti-Islamic government of Egypt.

"Fifth. The Zionist government will commit itself to expelling from its stolen lands all Jews who were not born in the country, or who have been in residence there for less than fifty years.

"Sixth. The Zionist government will immediately

remove all Jews from the stolen territory of the Left Bank of the Jordan River.

"Seventh. The Zionist government will immediately withdraw all troops from the illegally occupied territory of the Golan Heights.

"Eighth. The Zionist government will suspend all production of nuclear weapons, and deliver those it already possesses to a place which will be specified later.

"Ninth. The Zionist government will admit observers of my organization to ensure that points six, seven and eight above are being complied with.

"Those are the conditions. The sanctions now follow."

Paige thought: This bunch is crazy. The Israelis won't agree to *any* of those things, let alone all nine. They'll nuke Damascus first. "Go on," he said. "The tape's running."

"Do not interrupt. If the above conditions are not met, negotiations will be broken off, and at six A.M. on April twenty-eighth a twelve-kiloton nuclear weapon will detonate in Israel. If the Zionist government is willing to meet the above conditions, it must do so within the next twenty-four hours, in order to admit the observation team. It will signify its acceptance by publicly announcing its position on its national radio and television networks. At that time, further details will be provided. As these demands cannot be negotiated, the consequences of failing to comply with them are obvious."

Paige's index finger stung. The cigarette had burned down almost to the flesh. He jammed the butt into the ashtray.

"Communicate this to your government," the old dry voice said in his ear. "But do not try to keep it

333

secret. We will be informing others." A desiccated chuckle. "Including the Jews."

"Wait," Paige said, trying to remember all he had been taught about these things. "Why don't you stay on the line? I can arrange for talks to begin with—"

The old voice cut him off. "Do as I have said. I will be in contact again."

The line clicked and went dead.

Washington
April 24

THE SITUATION ROOM again, Parnell sighed. I seem to be living down here these days. "Give us the news," he told Cooper Tarkington.

The director of central intelligence cleared his throat. "First of all, unfortunately, this is unlikely to be a bluff. The man who called our consulate in Istanbul had the correct serial numbers for the stolen warheads and fuses. He is almost certainly part of the organization that has the weapons."

"Which organization?" Secretary of State Cornelissen asked.

"We can't find out. Whoever they are, they have extremely good security."

Parnell asked, "Could they really have gotten a nuclear weapon into Israel?"

"We have to assume that they've succeeded in doing so. It's far too serious a possibility to dismiss out of hand."

"And the caller said that six A.M. on the twenty-eighth was the deadline."

"Yes, Mr. President."

335

"That gives us four days. Can we find the one in Israel and get the other one back in that time?"

"We have to," Cornelissen said. "The Israelis are blaming the Syrians for this, or at least accusing them of not controlling whatever terrorist group it was. Damascus has denied everything, and Jerusalem's getting ready to go to war. If the deadline gets too near, they may carry out a full-scale invasion of Syria."

"What're they going to do in the meantime?" Parnell asked the secretary of defense.

"Probably air strikes to intimidate the Syrians into doing something about the bombs," Lusby said. "That is, if they've got them, or know who does. But if the Syrians really are telling the truth, that they didn't have anything to do with it, that's not going to help Israel one little bit. And there are still a lot of Russian advisers and technical support troops in Syria. Israeli strikes on military installations will definitely cause Russian casualties. If Kulagin wants to make an issue of that—" Lusby spread his palms. "The situation could get very bad very quickly."

"We've got one other difficulty," Tarkington said. "You remember that Mossad thought it knew where to find the man—his name's Foerster, a German SS officer during the war—who engineered this whole catastrophe. He was supposed to be in Damascus. Unfortunately, the consular officer who took the phone call in Istanbul says the caller sounded like an old man. Foerster's an old man. So he may very well not be in Damascus at all, but in Turkey."

"Then we should be looking there," said Lusby.

"We are," said Tarkington. "But the team looking for Foerster in Damascus has already gone in. It's unlikely we'll be able to contact them before they carry out the operation."

336

"Damn," said Parnell. "You sent Dr. Cole. Who's with him?"

"Mossad's operative is a woman named Stein. They'll have support on the ground in Damascus, apparently, but communications between Mossad headquarters and their network in Syria—what's left of it—is very poor."

"So we have to let them run."

"As far as I can tell you."

"Very well," Parnell said decisively. "Let's leave the intelligence operations aside for a moment. John, what military actions might the Russians take in the Mediterranean area if the situation gets any hotter?"

Lusby rubbed his jaw. "Their major strength in the Med itself is their Fifth *Eskadra*, the Fifth Flotilla. It has an assortment of ships and submarines, but on its own it isn't a match for the two carrier task forces and the submarine groups we have there. The force we would be worried about, if it could break out into the Mediterranean, would be their Black Sea fleet. It's based around their new supercarrier, the *Admiral Gorshkov*, and it has a lot of combat support ships. That force, if the Russians could get it through the Dardanelles, would tip the balance against us. Its presence anywhere near Israel would also be very intimidating for the Israelis. If things really got hot, and the Israelis were defeating the Syrians, the *Admiral Gorshkov* might intervene. Without a doubt, the Israelis would attack her. The Russians would strike back at Israel. And you know what the worst-case scenario is, where the Israelis decide to take an attacker down with them. They might consider a nuclear strike against the Soviet Union itself."

"Jesus Christ," said Parnell. "Nobody ever bar-

337

gained for *that*. But we can't let them down. Or even be perceived to be doing so."

Cornelissen exhibited a wry smile. "Exactly. They're the only ally we've got at the end of the Mediterranean, barring the Turks."

"Would the Turks let the Black Sea fleet through the Bosphorus and the Dardanelles?" asked Parnell.

"President Celebi probably would. A government with a less leftist leader would probably be a lot more reluctant. Celebi might also take the opportunity, if Israel and the Russians were nose to nose, to declare neutrality, which would imply leaving the NATO alliance. That, of course, would leave Turkey vulnerable to all sorts of Soviet pressures."

"That," said Lusby, "is something we can't afford strategically."

"If there were a coup, and a center or rightist government took over in Ankara, what would happen?" Parnell asked Cornelissen.

"It would depend on how close Celebi'd brought Turkey to the Russians. If the Soviets really wanted to get the *Admiral Gorshkov* task force into the Mediterranean, they might carry out a limited military action to seize the straits and pass their ships through. But they'd need a very good excuse, and they'd be risking our intervention, as well as a Turkish military reaction."

"We've got to cool the Russians off somehow," said Parnell. "Can we use Winter Palace?"

Cornelissen toyed with a pencil. "We originally intended to break the nastier details of their operation publicly, to embarrass Kulagin's government and undercut their claims about letting the Jews emigrate. That would also have bought us time to absorb the refugees while checking which ones were planted agents. Now, though . . . if we back the

338

Russians into a corner by doing that, their reactions are unpredictable. There's too much tension at the moment to aggravate it further."

"If I might make a suggestion," began Tarkington.

Parnell nodded. "Go ahead, Coop."

"We all know how that microfilm came into our hands. Somebody in the Soviet Union wanted to put Kulagin's regime in a very awkward position."

"Who?"

The DCI looked around the table. "The CIA analysts suspect it was the KGB."

"*What?*"

"There was no way that Dr. Cole could have gotten out of Russia with the criminal police after him, if it hadn't been for KGB intervention at the very highest level. Whoever it was wanted us to make this thing public, for reasons we can only guess at. Before the bomb theft, I would have said we should oblige him. But I agree with Kip, that we shouldn't turn the heat up any more than we absolutely have to. I'd suggest we contact the Soviet ambassador here and tell him what we've got, and what we may do with it if the Kremlin doesn't moderate its treatment of the deportees. You can bet that will be in the Kremlin and KGB headquarters half an hour after the ambassador leaves the State Department. If there is somebody over there in Dzerzhinsky Square who'd like to get rid of Kulagin, I think we should give him all the help we can."

Cornelissen nodded slowly. "It makes sense. Mr. President?"

"I—" Parnell began, only to be interrupted by a knock on the glass conference-room door. Cornelissen got up and opened it. An aide handed in a folded Telex printout.

339

"It's for you, Coop," said Cornelissen, handing the printout to the DCI. "Highest priority."

"Excuse me, please, Mr. President," Tarkington said. He unfolded the sheet of paper and read it, then looked up slowly.

"Mr. President," he said, "this reports the processing of the latest batch of NSA intercepts from the area we've been talking about. The Israelis have laid air strikes on four military targets in Syria." He paused. "And also, the Russians have put their Black Sea fleet on movement alert. They may be getting ready to come out."

Damascus
April 24

IT WAS HOT in the courtyard, even under the vine-shaded trellis. The house surrounding the courtyard was just outside Damascus, on a green slope above the Barada River; it belonged to the man named Ibrahim, who had brought Gabriel to Aleppo. Ibrahim had been one of Mossad's deep-cover people in Syria for decades.

"He may not be here," Ibrahim was saying now across the wrought-iron table to Cole, Mustafa and Dalia. "I can't be sure." He sounded angry. "If I'd known earlier—"

"None of us knew earlier," Dalia told him. "Even now, I'm not quite certain. But we must try to find him. You've found out where he lives, and that Sam can identify him, but there's no other lead."

"Could we get into his house?" Cole asked. "There might be something incriminating there."

"You could break in, I suppose," Ibrahim said. "But he's a big merchant, so there may be alarms."

"You say he may not be there to hear them," Mustafa pointed out.

"It's still dangerous. The curfew's been lifted, but

there are lot of Islamic Guard patrols about, and army too."

"We have to try," Dalia said.

Mustafa poured himself another glass of mineral water. A fly buzzed up off the table and the Israeli waved ineffectually at it. "I agree," he said.

Ibrahim threw up his hands. "Very well, if you're determined to go after him. But I don't believe anything will come of it."

"Tonight," Dalia said, ignoring his remarks. "Can it be arranged for tonight?"

"What will you need?"

"Ropes," Mustafa said. "Hemp, not nylon, it's too slippery. Two electric lanterns. A pair of grappling hooks, padded so they won't clang. Cole and I will get in by the roof and the courtyard while Dalia guards our escape route."

"I'm going in," she said. "Mustafa, you'll guard."

"But—"

"Mordechai put me in charge of this. I am going in."

After a moment he said, "As you wish."

"I can get all the equipment by tonight," Ibrahim said.

He didn't return with the equipment until after dark. Cole, Mustafa and Dalia loaded everything into the Toyota—the Aleppo license plates had been removed and replaced by false Damascus-registered ones—and left a little after eleven. Mustafa drove. They were all armed with silenced Walther pistols that Ibrahim had procured for them.

The highway followed the line of the Barada River south into Damascus. Mustafa skirted the Citadel

342

area and the warren of ancient lanes around the al-Hamadieh suq, pulling up finally in a side street near the Jawzah Mosque. They had several times passed groups of Islamic Guards and, twice, army patrols, but no one had shown any interest in the dusty Toyota. The street was dim, the shops and houses shuttered and dark, except for one bravely lit sidewalk cafe in which two old men were smoking water pipes and playing backgammon. Yellow light spilled from the cafe into the street.

Mustafa consulted the map Ibrahim had drawn for them. Foerster's house was east of Sarouja Street, almost backing onto the mausoleum of Ibn al-Muqaddam.

"That way," he said.

They turned left, then right, then left again. Back here the streets were truly deserted. Mustafa went ahead, Cole and Dalia walking side by side behind him. Cole wore a scruffy Western suit jacket over a *galabiyeh*, as many Syrian men did, with the Walther in its right pocket. The gun with its awkward silencer bumped against his hip as he walked. He felt tuned, ready, the inevitable fear giving his alertness a sharper edge.

The street narrowed suddenly, passing under an archway. "Here," Mustafa said, looking up at a two-story wall. An ironbound door was set into it. In the upper story were two small windows, each protected by an iron grille. The house was turned inward on itself, away from the street, the windows dark and blind.

"Now we go around to the back."

The rear of the house lay along a cobbled alley. It had one window, on the second floor, which was protected by a filigreed iron grille. Cole pulled the coil of rope and the grapnel out of the burlap bag

343

he carried, and checked the knot and the padding on the hooks.

"I will wait here," Mustafa whispered. "If a patrol comes I will avoid it, but I don't think there will be any back here. When you come back out on the roof, give me one flash. If it is safe, I will give you one flash back from the penlight. If I don't answer, there is danger and you will have to make your own decisions. You have thirty minutes. Good luck."

Cole nodded and swung the grapnel. It curved up into the night, over the edge of the roof. He heard a soft thud from above.

Cole tugged; the rope was slack. There should be a raised masonry lip running around the edge of the flat roof, he thought. He tugged again. The rope tightened. He yanked; the iron above him held.

"Go," Mustafa whispered. "I will send the lantern up when you're on the roof."

Dalia had placed her own grapnel and was already starting to pull herself up the rope, digging her toes into the cracks between the masonry. Cole followed suit, grabbing the rope with his knees, levering himself up hand over hand. Once the grapnel slipped fractionally and he thought he would plummet back into the alley, but the hooks held.

He pulled himself over the edge of the roof and shook the rope. Below, Mustafa tied its end to the handle of one of the lanterns and tugged. Cole pulled the light up, carefully coiling down the rope as he did so. When the end of the rope and the light came up he untied the knot and then checked the grappling iron. Even without tension on it, it was securely rammed into a joint between two stones of the parapet. They would be able to get off the roof in a hurry, if necessary.

344

Dalia came over to him, her own rope and grapnel coiled over her arm. "Secure?"

"Yes."

"Come on."

They trod softly across the flat dusty roof toward the dark rectangle of the courtyard opening. Around the opening was another low parapet.

"There's probably a trapdoor up here that leads into the house," he whispered. "It might be better than this way."

"I don't think we've got time to look for it," she whispered back. "And it would be locked."

"You're right."

She lodged her grapnel into a cleft in the masonry, then fed the rope over the parapet. Below, the courtyard was shrouded in blackness.

"Is there a trellis?" he whispered, remembering Ibrahim's house.

"Not this side. It's over there."

He remembered how good her night vision was. "Anything else down there?"

"I can't see anything."

"No electronic alarms, so far."

"No."

Cole took her rope and bellied over the parapet, letting himself down slowly. Somewhere overhead a helicopter was beating through the night.

His feet touched the courtyard floor. He tugged the rope. In a few seconds Dalia was down beside him. He took out the Walther and clicked off the safety.

"Dare we use the lights?" she whispered. Ibrahim hadn't been sure of the layout of the courtyard, but he had thought that the entrance to the *haramlek*, the private quarters, was in the wall under the trellis.

"Not yet. Let's find the door and try it. We'll use the lights when we're inside."

They crossed the courtyard. On the far side there was a raised platform, the *diwan,* where one could sit in the shade in the heat of the summer, under the trellis. The shadows there were pitch-black; Cole couldn't even see the courtyard wall, or where the door might be.

They reached the platform. Cole stepped up onto it, moved a meter farther on, past the wooden pillar supporting the trellis.

"Stop," said a voice in the shadows ahead of him. "Do not move."

Cole had been carrying the Walther ready, muzzle searching instinctively in front of him, like a snake's head. Without thinking, he fired toward the voice. The silencer reduced the report to a low *phutt,* and he heard the flat slap of a bullet striking flesh.

Then something struck him in the back of the head, and he fell into blackness.

Damascus
April 25

HE WAS DREAMING, a dreadful dream, full of horror. He lay in a dimly lit courtyard somewhere, in the hands of his enemies, trying to move but unable, his body unresponding. The courtyard seemed small and distant, as though he were seeing it through a distorting lens. On the far side of the court were two men. One of them was holding Dalia by her upper arms. The other was hitting her across the side of the face, snarling unintelligible words. She struggled, ineffectively.

The man holding her arms threw her down on the pavement. She struck heavily, stunned. The man who had been hitting her stooped, fumbling at the hem of her *galabiyeh,* dragging it up.

I'm not dreaming, Cole realized suddenly. This is real. It's happening. Syrian security. They caught us.

The man who had been holding Dalia was forcing her knees apart, snatching at her thighs. She kicked at him, twisting onto her stomach. He swore as her foot connected with his shin, and wrenched at her. The *galabiyeh* fell up over her, above her waist.

347

"Like that," the other man said, voice thick and urgent. The one holding her ankles grinned and pulled her legs up off the courtyard pavement, spreading them. Dalia struggled, but there was nothing to grasp on the smooth stone. She stopped, seeming to wait for the inevitable, the nightmare.

The other man fumbled at his trousers, opening them, took one of Dalia's ankles from his compatriot, spreading her legs even farther, more vulnerable yet. One hand slipped down, felt, came out. "I like the back door," he said. He knelt at Dalia's buttocks, erect and ready, preparing to insert himself.

Fury helped clear Cole's head. He tried to get up on one elbow. The Syrian had begun to hunch over Dalia—

"Stop! Get on your feet!"

The man leapt up from her, rearranging himself with all the speed he could muster. A Syrian officer was standing at the entrance to the *haramlek,* high polished boots gleaming in the courtyard lights. He wore major's insignia. Dalia turned onto her side, pulling the robe into place. Cole saw blood at the corner of her mouth.

"You dungheaps," the major said. "Both of you." He crossed to the pair of security men and struck first one, then the other, across the mouth. "What were your orders?"

The one who had been about to rape Dalia said, in a shaky voice, "Major, to hold anyone we caught for interrogation."

"And hold *intact.* Or had you forgotten?"

"No, Major, but the man shot Hasan, and the woman tried to kill me—"

"Be silent. You are lucky I came back when I did. If you had gone any farther, I would have had you

shot for disobeying orders. Handcuff the woman. Then get the van." He turned and walked over to Cole, who had managed to sit up. "You shot one of my men," the major said. "It was only a flesh wound. You are both fortunate."

Pain roared through Cole's head. He wanted to vomit. The major prodded him with the toe of his boot. "Who are you?"

Cole realized that he was concussed. He couldn't remember his cover name. "No," he said.

Again the tip of the boot, harder this time. "Who are you and what are you doing here?"

"We knew the house was empty," Cole said. "We came to rob it." It was the best he could do.

"I doubt that. I think you came here looking for someone."

Of course, Cole thought. How could we have been so stupid? The Syrians are after the German too. They've been in this place for days, waiting for him to come back.

"I don't know what you're talking about," he said.

"You will," the major observed.

A voice called from the door into the *haramlek*. "Major, the van's ready."

"Get up," the major said.

Cole got up. The major pulled an automatic pistol out of his belt holster, covering him warily. "Handcuff him," he ordered one of the security men.

The man obeyed with grinning enthusiasm. "Through the house," the major said. "If either of you tries to escape, we will shoot to maim. Do not do anything unexpected."

They passed through the house in a grim procession. Outside, the major opened the rear door of a parked Mercedes van.

"In. You first," the major told Cole.

There was a metal bench running along each side of the van's cargo space. Cole sat down. The major put the muzzle of his pistol to Cole's temple and said, "Do not move."

One of the security men got in and shackled Cole's wrists to a bracket welded to the bench. Then he went out for Dalia and repeated the performance, placing her at the far end of Cole's bench so that they could not communicate with each other.

"Let's go," the major said. "Get on the radio and tell them we have somebody. Also get another team over to the house immediately." He sat down across from Cole, revolver still drawn. One of the other security men positioned himself opposite Dalia.

The van began to move. Cole's head throbbed.

"Where are you taking us?" Dalia asked. It was the first time she had spoken since their capture. Her voice was calm and even.

"Be silent. Do not speak to or look at each other, or you will be blindfolded and gagged."

That was clear enough. Cole thought they would probably be taken to the old *Muchabarat* headquarters in As-Salihiyeh Street. There, if normal procedure were followed, they would be put into separate holding cells and left for a while, to build their anxiety. After a few hours they would be taken to the interrogation cellars. The Syrians would use them against each other, probably beginning with Dalia. They would do things to her, in front of Cole, until he told them what they wanted to know. Or he could let her die, and then they would begin on him.

He tried to estimate the travel time from Foerster's house to *Muchabarat* headquarters. After a while he began to wonder why the van was following such a circuitous route, turning, stopping, starting. After

350

twenty minutes he began to suspect they were not headed for the security headquarters at all, but by then he had lost all sense of direction.

After another period of time the van stopped. Cole heard an unintelligible exchange between the driver and someone outside the cab. Then there was a slow creaking, like that of unoiled hinges, and the van pulled slowly forward. It traveled at a walking pace for another second or two, and then stopped again.

"Unshackle them and get them out," the major said to the other man. "One at a time, the woman first."

Clinks of metal, then the scrape of the van's doors being opened. The major got up and followed Dalia out of the vehicle. The other man came back for Cole.

They were in a small courtyard, lit by a single bulb under a circular metal shade. In the wall before them was a massive wooden door, with a small grille set into it at eye level. There was nothing else in the court.

The major walked over to the door and knocked. Someone answered from the other side of the grille. A guard, probably. Cole was regaining some of his equilibrium. He found that he could now remember his cover story. Not that it would hold up for long under determined questioning; it had been intended only to get him past random identity checks.

"We radioed in half an hour ago," the major was saying.

"Enter."

The door swung open, revealing a plastered corridor flagged with large smooth stones. Cole and Dalia were escorted along it, past the uniformed guard who had let the major in. The corridor ended at another door. The major opened it, to reveal another, much larger, courtyard. It was dark, but Cole could make out the shapes of trees and flowerbeds. The air was heavy with the scent of orange blossoms and cedar.

They reentered the house—although, with a courtyard of that size, it was closer to a palace—on the far side of the court, passing under a colonnade of Moorish arches. Cole blinked in the sudden light.

"Stop," the major said, closing the door behind him. "Be quiet and wait."

Cole had a chance to study their surroundings. The room was lit by electric lights in delicately fluted wall sconces, probably a modern improvement, since the rest of the room obviously predated electricity. Half of the floor space was formed of a raised platform, covered with richly colored carpets. The remainder of the floor, on which Cole and Dalia stood, was pale veined marble. In its center was a large stone water basin, the pool within it unrippled. Around the sides of the room were low divan seats strewn with cushions; above the seats the walls were paneled in dark gleaming wood.

Cole waited. The major and the single guard he had brought along shifted nervously. Cole was regaining a little of his confidence; this was far from the dank cellar he had expected.

One of the panels in the wall behind the raised platform opened, and two men came through it. The first seemed to be in his mid-sixties, face seamed, a short gray beard hiding his chin. Above the high cheekbones the eyes were very dark, penetrating. He wore a gray *galabiyeh* the same color as his beard. The second was younger, by perhaps ten years, coppery skin, a gaunt face. But his eyes, too, were used to power. He wore a Western business suit.

They stood for a moment, looking at Cole and

352

Dalia. The first man said, "You caught them in Selim Youssef's house?"

"Yes, Protector," the major answered. His voice betrayed nervousness. "They came over the roof into the courtyard."

"What have they told you?"

"Only that they came to rob. My orders were to bring anyone who came to the house directly here, so they have not been questioned."

"Good. You have done well. Leave us."

"Protector—" the copper-skinned man began.

The old man waved a hand. "We are in no danger, Ubari, and you are armed in any case. You may go, Major. *Salaam alaikum.*"

"*Alaikum salaam,*" the major responded.

Cole heard the door close softly behind him. He and Dalia were alone with the two Syrians.

"If you are who I think you are," the man named Ubari said, "you do not need weapons to kill. Do not attempt it. If you cooperate, you may live. Take cushions from the benches and sit down."

Cole and Dalia did as they were told. There was a silence, while the older man studied them.

"We would usually offer guests refreshments," he said after a moment, "but those who will not identify themselves are not guests. To show our good faith, I will tell you who we are. I am Khalil Dirouzi, protector of the Islamic revolution of Syria and head of the Inner Council of the Muslim Brotherhood, and this is Mahmdou Ubari, the chief of our security services. Who are you?"

"We are Syrians," Cole said. "We—"

Dirouzi raised a hand. "I think you are not. But I think we may be looking for the same person. A German, perhaps?"

353

"Perhaps," Cole said. There was the smell of negotiation here.

Dirouzi exhibited a tiny smile. "We have an interest in him, as well. Do you know who he is?"

There was no point in being elusive. "Yes," Cole said. "His Syrian name is Selim Youssef. His real one is Hans Foerster."

"What is *your* name?" Ubari asked.

"Samuel Cole."

"And yours?" Directed at Dalia.

"Dalia Stein."

"An Israeli," said Ubari.

"No doubt," Dirouzi said. "Do you know," he asked Cole and Dalia, "what has happened in the last twenty-four hours outside this country?"

"No," Cole said.

"First I should tell you that the man we are looking for is indeed Foerster. He lived here for many years and assisted the Brotherhood in the planning which led to our revolution. He also planned to use stolen nuclear weapons against Israel. We are sure that he organized the theft of the bombs from your base in Turkey."

"That's public knowledge?" Cole asked. Christ, he thought. They'll be going nuts in Washington.

"It is. Yesterday he announced, through the international press, that he has placed one of the stolen bombs in a city in Israel. And that it will go off on the twenty-eighth of April, by your calendar, if Israel does not submit to his demands."

Cole looked at Dalia. Her face was white, stricken. "How could he have done this, alone?" she managed.

"We believe that he was helped by a group called the Soldiers of God, the *Jund Allah*. They have been based in Syria for many years, and until now we

354

have left them alone, since they are strong and dangerous. They have a base camp in the north, and we are preparing to attack it. There will be heavy fighting, but I do not think that we will find Foerster. We think he is in Turkey, coordinating his plans from there."

"What are the demands?" Dalia asked.

"Jerusalem will never accept them," Dirouzi said. "But Jerusalem will believe that the Brotherhood is responsible for the German's action. So, if Foerster's bomb does go off, Israeli jets will be here immediately afterward, carrying Israeli nuclear weapons. Compared with that, the exact nature of the demands is of no importance."

"Why are you telling us this?" Dalia asked.

"Not because we are friends," said Dirouzi. "The Brotherhood will one day destroy Israel. But not in this way, at the expense of our own survival." The black eyes were intent; although the old man's words had been reasonable so far, Cole suddenly glimpsed the fanaticism and the obsession that drove him.

"Perhaps," Dalia said. "Perhaps not."

"It is the will of God," Dirouzi said. "It will happen."

Ubari coughed. "Protector," he said, "there is little time."

"You need to know nothing else about Foerster or what we are doing about him," said Dirouzi, returning to his pragmatic voice. "Except this. If he is following the plans he made before the Inner Council canceled them, the bomb is in either Haifa or Tel Aviv. He had several alternate delivery routes. But those two places are where you must look. I am telling you this because I want your people to know that we have had no hand in this matter."

"Why not call Jerusalem direct?" Cole asked. "Why do you need to use us?"

"Because there are many naive members of the Brotherhood who would applaud the *Jund Allah* for this. If I am seen cooperating with Jerusalem, even for the most urgent of reasons, many will believe that the *Jund Allah* is right in what it has done."

"I see," Cole said. He thought: We may get out of this alive yet. "What do you intend to do next?"

"I am sending you into Israel. You must tell your people, immediately, what I have told you. Jerusalem is supposed to respond to the *Jund Allah* demands by nine o'clock this morning. I do not need to tell you what Jerusalem will say."

"No," Cole answered. "You don't."

"Go," Dirouzi said. "Ubari, see to it. Send them by the U.N. border post at Kuneitra. The U.N. troops will get them to the Israeli side of the border fast enough."

The Black Sea
April 25

THE AIR in the freighter's hold was thick, almost viscid. It dragged in Markelov's throat when he inhaled. Above him, only a few centimeters away, the slats of the next bunk up sagged with Irina's weight. Tania had the one underneath Markelov's; she was sleeping at last. All day she'd been burning up with fever, and the only thing the ship's doctor would give her was aspirin; probably it was all he had to give now. Almost everyone in the *Sokol*'s forward hold was ill with something; in the three days they'd been at sea there had been fourteen deaths. Markelov lived in dread of something really terrible breaking out, like typhus, or even cholera from the bad water they were given. Tomorrow, though, the freighter should be docking at Istanbul. They'd been told by the captain of the guard contingent that a camp was ready for them there, with many Jews already in it. Markelov hoped he was telling the truth; many Jews in the Nazi holocaust had gone willingly to the transport trains on the promise that they were to be sent to work camps, or to new settlements. They had been, but the camps had borne

357

names like Treblinka and Sobibor and Belsen. There wasn't, really, anything to prevent the Russians from throwing them all into the sea. This far from land, nobody would ever be any the wiser.

He closed his eyes for a moment, thinking of Esfir. He could hardly believe she was gone, erased from the world, no, from the universe, as though she'd never been. So near to freedom, and then to die; although he was not sure she would have survived *Sokol*.

It hadn't looked too bad at first, when the transportees had boarded the freighter, at night, back in Odessa. The hold had smelled of disinfectant, although there'd been something underneath the antiseptic odor even then, something vile and putrefying. At first they'd all been terrified of the echoing metal cavern anyway, before realizing that the sharp smell really was disinfectant, and that the bunks really were there to be used. Markelov and Irina and Tania hadn't been the first into the hold, nor the last, so they were neither in the favored tiers near the ventilator outlets, nor in the really bad ones, those next to the steel drums with wooden lids that served as toilets. The drums were welded to the deck, and there was no way of emptying them. A chemical had been put in them, but by the end of the second day it had lost its effectiveness, and the hold had begun to reek. Added to that was the stench of vomit, the retchings of those who'd been seasick. The seasickness had had one positive effect, though; there'd been a little more food for those who could keep it down. It was a kind of thin fish gruel, with fins and bones and heads in it, brought by the Mongol guards in filthy tubs and left for the transportees to ladle out among themselves, using the tin dippers they'd been given when they boarded. There was

358

bread once a day, rough black stuff filled with barley husks: prison bread. It tasted as bad as the air smelled. Only a grim determination to survive enabled Markelov to get it into his stomach and keep it there. Irina and Tania couldn't eat it; although they weren't seasick, all they could manage was the gruel. Tania hadn't even had that since this morning, when she'd become really ill.

Markelov opened his eyes, looking up past the tier of bunks. He could just make out the underside of the cargo hatchway overhead, as the shadows cast by the feeble bulbs swayed across it. Up there, only a few meters away, was evening light and sky and air, clean and cool and salt. Down here, three days of vileness, the dim light, the smell, the shadows, the hunger and thirst and nausea mixed, fouled clothes and filth and sickness, the sounds of men and women and children retching with nothing left to bring up, groans and sometimes screams as bowels wrenched with dysentery, the constant fear of the guards and what might yet happen (the ship stopped and silent, echoing, and then the rush of water pouring through the seacocks). Somewhere on the other side of the hold a woman was babbling in fever.

He wondered how many Jews they'd been able to cram into the holds. The ranks of bunks were less than a meter apart, and they were tiered six deep, so that you had to climb up the frame if you were in the topmost one. The air was worse up there, too; at least poor Tania was closest to the floor. He counted again; there were four holds, with so and so many bunks . . . he'd worked it out before, but his memory wasn't good. At least three thousand people jammed into the freighter, and she wasn't a big one, either.

Part of the horror was that, although some of the

transportees in the hold were glad to be leaving Russia (or had been glad, at the beginning of the voyage) this wasn't true for the majority. Most wouldn't have tried to leave earlier even if it had been permitted; with all its flaws the Soviet Union had been their home, and they wouldn't willingly have exchanged its certainties for the enigmatic and alien West. For Markelov, on the other hand, despite the present circumstances, it was a gift of life. He still did not understand why he hadn't ended in the cellars of the Lubianka, with electric prods inserted into him—or worse, into one of his family—while the interrogators tried to find out where he had got the documents and where the original film was. He would have held out as long as he could, to give Samuel enough time to get away, but he knew he'd have talked sooner or later. Especially if they had tortured Irina or Esfir or Tania in front of him.

Samuel, he thought, *did* you get away? Does the world know what they are doing to us?

The lights dimmed; five minutes to curfew. The guards would be in shortly, to make sure it was obeyed. Markelov was afraid of them; they were Mongols, like the ones on the train platform back at the camp, and they weren't much cleaner than the transportees. Yesterday evening they'd grabbed a teenaged girl from one of the other tiers and began pulling her about, and had only stopped and left the hold when they heard one of their officers shouting for them.

Above him, Irina stirred. He saw her feet and calves appear and then the rest of her as she dropped to the floor. "Father? Are you all right?"

"Yes. Remember, tomorrow it will be finished. We'll be out."

360

"And into another camp. Will there be medicines there for Tania? She's not getting better."

Dear God, he prayed, don't let my granddaughter die in sight of the promised land. Please, if you love any of us, let her live. "Of course," he said. "The Americans and the Israelis will take care of that, they won't treat us like the Russians do. Tania can grow up to be an Israeli. Think of that."

"I'm going to get some water for her. She's so hot."

"We're not supposed to be out of the bunks now. I wish you wouldn't go."

She shrugged. "What will the guards do about it? Put me in a camp? I'll only be a minute, anyway." There was a trace of the wry humor yet.

Markelov smiled at her. She was taking the death of her mother better than he had thought she would; or perhaps she was only waiting until she had the privacy to grieve. He looked after her as she left for the after bulkhead, where the water tank was. Even with the dirt and the hunger, she was still a beautiful woman. He rolled onto his back again and closed his eyes.

"Hey! What d'you think you're doing? *Stop it!*"

It was Irina's voice. Markelov's eyes flew open.

"Let *go,* you pig—" Sound of a blow, flesh on flesh, then cursing, not in Russian.

The guards. Markelov hurled himself off the bunk, ran around the end of the tier, banging his shoulder painfully on one of the metal supports, past the next tier and into the aisle. Irina's voice came through an open bulkhead door and through it Markelov saw a uniformed Mongol tearing at her blouse while another held her with his arm locked around her throat.

"Let her go!" Markelov yelled, as he raced down the aisle toward the door.

361

One of Irina's attackers hit Markelov in the stomach as he stumbled through the opening, throwing him back against the bunks. The steel door slammed shut. Markelov pounded at it in vain as Irina's screams rose beyond it. He closed his eyes hopelessly, and tried not to hear the sounds his daughter made for the next ten minutes. No one came to help; no one at all.

Jerusalem, Israel
April 25

COLE WOKE to the jangle of the telephone and grabbed for the receiver. "Yes?"

"Your wake-up call," the hotel operator said. "It's half past six."

He was disoriented. "Oh. Morning or evening?"

"Evening, sir." Flatly.

"Thank you." Cole hung up and turned over onto his back. On the other bed, Dalia breathed evenly, still sound asleep despite the telephone. Quietly, Cole raised himself on one elbow and looked over at her. Like him, she still wore the clothes Mordechai had supplied. After the debriefing that morning, he had taken them to the Jerusalem Tower Hotel and booked them into separate rooms with a connecting door. They had each cleaned up and tried to eat, but soon gave that up, collapsing onto the twin beds in Cole's room to fall instantly asleep.

The captain of the U.N. detachment at Kuneitra had turned them over to the Israeli frontier post easily enough, but the soldiers on duty there were deeply suspicious, especially on learning that neither Cole nor Dalia had any identification—the Syrian security men had taken their false sets. Finally, after an hour, an Israeli major arrived, recently awakened and short of temper. Dalia repeated, for the third time, that she had information about the nuclear bomb threat. The officer tried to bully her into telling him what she knew and how she knew it, until she finally lost her temper and cursed at him in rapid-fire Hebrew.

Grudgingly, the major let her call Mossad headquarters in Jerusalem. It was not yet 6:00 A.M. and the duty officer there wasn't sure what to do about her call; he knew nothing of an operation mounted "from outside the country," which was all Dalia would tell him over an unsecured line, and he was as suspicious as the soldiers. In desperation, she told him to contact Mordechai Frank in Ankara.

Mordechai wasn't in Ankara. Miraculously, he was in Jerusalem, called back because of the threat of the bomb. Half an hour after her contact, he was on the line to the frontier post. An hour after that, a helicopter picked them up to fly them to Jerusalem. Mordechai drove them from the military airfield to Mossad headquarters, where they relayed the whole story for the emergency team that had been assembled to deal with the bomb threat. The search had already begun, but it was hampered, at least temporarily, by the lack of suitable equipment and the sheer number of places that had to be searched. To add to the confusion, Israel was in an uproar over the fate of the Soviet Jews. There had already been riots throughout the country, started by ultra-orthodox factions who wanted wholesale immigration to start at once, and never mind where the refugees would be housed or how they would be fed; God would provide for his people somehow. The Israeli government wasn't nearly so willing to trust to divine intervention, and so far only a trickle of a few thousand refugees had been allowed into the country. But the situation was causing political strains that could easily fragment the government and deprive Israel of united leadership, exactly when she needed it most.

Dalia stirred. Cole turned onto his back, closing his eyes. There's not going to be anything between us, he thought. No matter what happened up there in the desert. We both knew it as soon as we got here, maybe even as soon as we got out of Syria. It wasn't even necessary to say anything. Megan, Megan, what are we going to do, what are you going to do? For an instant he felt lost, desolate, wretched.

He heard Dalia sit up. "Mordechai's due in fifteen minutes," he said, not opening his eyes.

She got off the bed. "I'll be back in a minute."

When she returned from the bathroom, there was a rap at the door, a pause, then two more.

"Mordechai," she said. "Early."

She went to the door and let the Israeli in. Mordechai looked exhausted, heavy pouches under his eyes. "Did you two get some rest?" he asked.

"We just woke up," Cole said.

Mordechai put a shopping bag on the table next to the door. "I brought you some shaving tackle and more clothes." He looked around for a moment. "We'd better sit down. There's a lot to get through."

Dalia curled up on her bed, resting on one elbow. Cole sat down on the other. Mordechai took the black swivel chair next to the window. "This is

365

what's happening," he told them. "We naturally refused the demands the terrorists made. There hasn't been any more communication from them, and that's a bad sign. We agree, by the way, with Dirouzi's identification of the group as the *Jund Allah*. That doesn't necessarily mean that the Brotherhood isn't supporting them, though. In any case, our analysts think that they're planning to let the bomb explode, no matter what we say or do. They're one of the most vicious groups around."

"Will you be able to find the bomb in time?" Dalia asked.

"There's no telling," Mordechai answered. "We've only just managed to get our hands on some underwater radiation detection equipment. We're also using metal detectors in the harbors, but there's so much junk on the bottom . . . We've got divers down in Tel Aviv and Haifa, but visibility's poor and if the thing's silted over it's going to be very hard to spot. That's in addition to the land searches."

"Can you disarm it, once you've found it?" Cole asked. "They might have fitted it with anti-tampering devices."

"Some of your experts are on the way from the United States. They're supposedly capable of making the things safe."

Dalia asked, "What are we doing about the civilian population?"

"If the thing isn't found by twelve hours before the deadline, we're going to have to start evacuating Tel Aviv and Haifa. But we'll need a firm wind forecast before we know the safest places to send people. The weather patterns are unstable at the moment. Bad luck."

"What're you doing militarily?" Cole asked.

366

"We've mobilized. The Syrians are doing the same. We've also started air strikes against Syrian military targets to clear the way for a nuclear strike of our own, if that bomb goes off."

"Despite what Dirouzi said?" Cole asked. "That it isn't the Brotherhood?"

"He may be lying. In any case, we would have to do it, for strategic reasons. If either Tel Aviv or Haifa is destroyed, we lose most of our industrial and service infrastructure. We'd be wrecked militarily, and the Syrians would have a good chance of defeating us within the next couple of weeks, whether they planted the bomb or not. We'd have to destroy them first."

"Have you told Damascus this?" Cole asked.

"No. Only Washington. At this moment, the more uncertain our enemies are about our reactions, the more advantage we have."

Dalia asked, in a voice tinged with despair, "Would we *have* to do it? How could we face ourselves, afterwards?"

"There might not be an afterwards," Mordechai said grimly. "Anyway, it's what the Cabinet and the General Staff decided, after the Mossad briefing."

"Don't they realize how fast it could escalate?" Cole asked. "The Russians still back Syria. If Moscow supports Damascus all the way, and we're drawn in—" He spread his hands. "It could be the end."

"Jerusalem is willing to take that risk," Mordechai said.

There was a silence. Then Cole said, "I should contact Richland."

"I already did. He knows what has happened, and what may happen."

"Did he give you instructions for me?"

"You're to go back to Turkey, to Istanbul, with Dalia. Foerster must be found. There is still another bomb out there, somewhere."

"Foerster's in Istanbul?" Dalia asked. "Are you sure?"

"We're pretty certain. We were able to identify the trunk line used for one of the calls to Ankara, with Turkish help. It was an Istanbul line."

"How much help *have* we been getting from the Turks?"

"They appear to be looking as hard as we are. But their security services have a lot to deal with. The Left and the Islamic fundamentalists are both rioting. They're demanding that Turkey pull out of NATO before she gets dragged into a war to support Israel."

"How are you getting us back into Turkey?" Dalia asked.

"By air," Mordechai said. "There's an American carrier group moving east, centered on the *John F. Kennedy* and the *America*. We're sending you out to the *Kennedy* in a helicopter tomorrow morning. Arrangements are being made to put you on a S3 Viking sub-hunter plane. It'll fly you to the base at Incirlik. Your passports will be waiting there."

"Then?" Cole asked.

"Istanbul. Check into the Dedeman Hotel and wait for me to contact you."

Turkey
April 26

THE TRANSIT CAMP had been laid out on a level stretch of the coast some thirty kilometers east of Istanbul, just off Highway 25 not far from Kilincli. Foerster's van sat on the highway's shoulder while Haddad's three men made a last check of the cargo.

On the far side of the highway, toward the sea, Turkish military engineers had erected a wire fence, complete with observation towers. Beyond the fence the tents began, hectare upon hectare of them, of all shapes and sizes and colors, ranging from army olive through bone-white canvas to the bright orange fabrics of mountaineering shelters. Here and there among them rose wooden prefabricated buildings that served as mess halls and bathhouses. Among the tents the Jews wandered, awaiting whatever destination fate would deal them. The breeze was off the sea, blowing into Foerster's nostrils from the direction of the camp. The Jews had been there for some time and on packed ships before that, and Turkish sanitation standards were at best minimal: even from here the air smelled foul. Foerster took a certain

369

pleasure in imagining conditions inside. The Jews were finding their natural level.

"Are you not yet finished?" he asked, turning to look over the back of the seat, into the van's cargo bay. Haddad's men were rearranging the boxes of dried bagged milk over the crate that held the bomb and the one that contained the guns. Foerster had disposed of his false Syrian passport and was now using the West German one, the one he kept back for emergencies.

"Done," said the *Jund Allah* soldier brusquely. He was the tallest of the three and the most truculent; his name was Madhat, and he plainly resented the fact that Haddad had put him under Foerster's orders. The other two, Adib and Salim, didn't seem to care. Their eyes had already taken on the depersonalized sheen of men who were prepared to die. Others like them had intentionally blown themselves up in explosive-laden trucks from Beirut to Morocco. They could not be reasoned with, but they would obey as long as they believed they acted in the cause of God.

"We should go in, then, if you're finished," Foerster said mildly.

Madhat slipped between the two bucket seats of the cab and got behind the steering wheel. Down the highway on the left was the main gate of the transit camp. A steady stream of trucks was moving sluggishly in and out of it. A wooden guardhouse stood to the east of the gate. The gate, as far as Foerster had been able to determine from his observations, would be the only hard part. Once inside the camp, no one would be able to get them out, except on their own terms.

Madhat moved the van into the line of vehicles approaching the gate, behind a flatbed truck loaded

370

with sacks of rice. One of the sacks had broken open and a thin stream of silvery grain dripped off the tailgate. Foerster watched the rice fall absentmindedly, his silver-headed cane between his trembling knees. The excitement and tension were making him young again; it was the way he remembered Russia.

This time, though, he knew he was moving toward his death. When the Israelis had refused Haddad's demands the previous morning, he had decided to accompany the bomb into the transit camp himself, leaving the terrorist leader outside to watch for countermeasures. Two other men would make sure the Turkish authorities didn't try to move the Jews out of the camp under cover of darkness. Foerster didn't think the Israelis would find the Haifa bomb in time—there was no way they could know that it *was* in Haifa, they'd have to search everywhere. But if they did, he would still be able to strike one last blow. Better to end like that than clawed to shreds by the demon growing in his belly. The pain had become much worse now; for two or three minutes that morning in the hotel room he had been unable to stand upright. And he was running out of the tablets, without the prospect—now—of getting any more. At the rate he was using them, there were only enough left in the vial for another day and a half.

Perhaps, he thought, when they are gone, I will go too. Forever.

Ahead, the truck bearing the sacks of rice halted at the guardhouse. A Turkish soldier walked around to its rear and prodded lackadaisically at the cargo, then shouted. The truck moved on, into the camp.

Madhat engaged the van's clutch and the vehicle rolled ahead. Foerster felt beads of sweat gathering

371

on his upper lip. None of them was armed; all the guns were in the case under the dried milk.

The Turkish soldier peered into the cab. "What're you carrying?"

"Dried milk," Foerster said. "From the West German relief mission. It's the first time we've been here."

"Identification?"

Foerster took his West German passport out of his pocket and showed it to the soldier. The man looked at it without much comprehension. "You are German?"

"Yes. We've hired these men to help unload. We're going back for more supplies as soon as that's done."

"I spend some time in Germany," said the soldier, in atrocious German. "I work there."

"Good," replied Foerster, in the same language. "Did you bring back plenty of money?"

"Plenty. But then I have to go back into army, can't spend it."

"I sympathize," Foerster told him. He returned to Turkish. "As I said, I haven't been here before. I should check in at the administration building. Where is that?"

The soldier also reverted to Turkish, with clear relief. "Straight ahead, it's the one with the flagpole. But first I have to look at your cargo."

"Go ahead," Foerster said.

The soldier went around to the van's rear. Salim opened one of the doors. The Turk looked at the containers of milk and nodded. "Go on."

Salim closed the door. Madhat started the van moving again. When they were well away from the guard post, Foerster permitted himself an exhalation

372

of relief. "Open the guns," he said over his shoulder. "But don't get them out yet."

On either side of the road, people were sitting in front of the tents, or talking in small groups, or walking aimlessly about, their faces bearing the blank expressions of the uprooted and homeless.

Jews, Foerster thought. And Russians to boot. How the wheel turns, full circle. I have them at my feet again.

"Where are we going?" Madhat asked, irritably. "In the name of God, give me some instructions, if that's what you're supposed to do."

"You can see the flagpole up there as well as I can," Foerster said. "Drive there and stop in front of the front door. If there's a guard, Salim will deal with him as we planned, but only after I'm inside, and only when I give the signal."

They were still following the rice-laden truck. Just before the administration building, the truck turned off, presumably headed for the supply dump. Foerster could see one army guard, stationed outside the building.

He half-turned. "Give me the Makarov." Salim handed it to him and he slipped it into his coat pocket.

There is one advantage to being an old man with a cane, he thought. The young will not believe that I am dangerous. Until it is too late. There is advantage in anything, if one knows how to look.

The van stopped in front of the administration building. It was a one-story wooden structure, unpainted, with four windows along the front and a door in the middle. The guard studied the vehicle suspiciously, then caught sight of Foerster's lined and emaciated face and relaxed. The German got out, moving very slowly and stiffly, supporting himself on the cane. From the van's rear he heard the sound of a door opening and closing. That would be Salim, also carrying a concealed pistol, acting as backup.

"Good afternoon," Foerster said to the guard. "I would like to speak with the camp organizer. I am from the West German relief agency."

"Your identification?"

Foerster showed him the passport. The guard nodded. "Go on in. They will tell you who to see."

Foerster went inside, leaving the door open behind him. The interior was one large room, partially broken up by partitions. In front of Foerster was a rough wooden counter about three meters long. Beyond it, at a score of desks and tables, a collection of harassed-looking civilians of half a dozen nationalities were at work over typewriters and reams of paper. Telephones jangled. The civilians were members of the U.N. relief team set up to care for the Soviet Jews until they could be moved to more permanent residences.

Foerster stepped up to the counter, one hand resting on the butt of the cane, the other in his jacket on the Makarov. A young stocky Turkish woman got up from a desk and came over to him. "May I help you?"

"I'd like to see the person in charge—Dr. Langstrom." Langstrom was a Swede on the U.N. staff, who had been given the thankless task of running the camp; Foerster had found out his name from the newspapers.

"Dr. Langstrom is very busy."

"I'm sorry, but this is extremely urgent. I've come a long way, from West Germany. We are trying to locate a particular Jewish family."

"Why?"

"I must speak to Dr. Langstrom."

"I will find out if he'll see you."

She left the counter and walked among the desks to the far corner of the room, where a man was seated at a large table, talking on the phone, obviously annoyed at being disturbed.

Foerster couldn't hear what she said over the office noise, but after a moment, Langstrom put the phone down and threw up his hands in a gesture of resignation. As he approached the counter, Foerster's grip on the Makarov tightened. He slipped the safety catch off with his thumb and moved to the end of the counter, so there would be no barrier between himself and the Swede.

Langstrom's face showed barely concealed irritation at Foerster's demand to see him, but he remained polite. "How can we help you?" he asked in stilted German.

"I'm quite comfortable in Turkish," Foerster said. "We are trying to locate a particular family that we believe is here." He had to get the man closer, without being obvious about it. He leaned the cane against the counter. "I have documents—"

As he had intended, the cane slipped and clattered to the floor. Langstrom stepped forward to pick it up for him.

Foerster yanked the Makarov out of his pocket and rammed it underneath Langstrom's chin. "Still," he said. "Very still. Or I will kill you." He raised his voice. *"Jund Allah!"*

The room fell silent. From outside Foerster heard three flat cracks of a pistol, Salim dealing with the guard.

"All of you," he called out. "Stand up, very slowly, and clasp your hands on top of your heads. *Now.* Or I will kill Dr. Langstrom."

375

Only now was the realization beginning to strike home, the faces stunned, disbelieving. "Move!" Foerster screamed at them. "Anyone using a telephone, hang it up. We will slit the throat of anyone who tries to keep speaking."

One young woman fumbled the receiver she had been holding, dropping it on her desk. She looked at Foerster, wide-eyed, stricken. He did not want to start killing them unless he had to.

"Hang it up," he barked at her. "One chance." She did so, her face white with terror. Foerster transferred the muzzle of the Makarov to Langstrom's temple. Behind him he heard thumps on the steps: Salim joining him, after throwing the guard's body into the van. The terrorist was armed with a G3 submachine gun, courtesy of the Society of Merchants. He took up a position to the right of Foerster, covering the hostages. Less than two minutes had passed.

Through the open door behind him he heard more scrapes and thumps. Madhat and Adib entered, straining under the weight of the crate containing the weapon. They set it on the floor beside the counter. Langstrom looked down at it, uncomprehending.

"Dr. Langstrom," Foerster said, "I am going to let you rejoin your people. Move very slowly, with your hands on your head. Do you understand?"

"Yes," Langstrom said in a choked voice. Good, Foerster thought, as Langstrom backed away. He's their superior, and they see he's frightened. There won't be any trouble.

"Now, listen to me very carefully, all of you. One at a time, go to the back wall and stand facing it. Keep your hands on your heads. Do not talk. Do not go closer than a meter to the windows. If any of

376

you is thinking about trying to get out a window, don't. For each person who tries, we will shoot two others, starting with the women.'' He pointed the pistol at the girl who had met him when he first came in. ''You first. Over to the wall.''

He had them arranged to his satisfaction when Adib and Madhat returned with weapons for themselves, a G3 for Foerster and a dozen fragmentation grenades. They closed the door behind them. Foerster wondered how long it would be before the camp guards found out what was going on and responded. The Jews outside could not have failed to see what had happened, but they would likely have trouble making themselves understood. There were a few minutes yet.

The three *Jund Allah* men dragged the bomb crate around behind the counter and began levering it open with a crowbar they had brought from the van. Only the top needed to come off; the pair of manual triggers Alwan had constructed back at the base camp were fixed to the top of the bomb container with plastic resin. One more step.

''Watch them,'' Foerster told his men. He went around the counter and knelt beside the crate, putting the G3 on the floor beside him. He studied the wiring and the batteries. Alwan had shown him a dozen times how to connect the triggers, and Foerster had burned it into his memory, but he wanted to be mentally prepared.

Very carefully, he screwed the first set of wires onto their contacts. Then, gingerly, he pressed the black test button. The voltameter needle swung; the batteries were still fresh. He released the button. With exact precision, he connected the remaining wires. The last one went into place without incident.

Not, Foerster thought, that I would have known

377

anything about it if there had been a flaw in the circuit. I would simply be gone.

He surveyed the weapon. The trigger buttons were red, cemented to the bomb's casing about thirty centimeters apart. You needed two hands to fire the bomb; Alwan had been insistent on that, and Foerster had to let him have his way.

He picked up the G3 and got to his feet. There couldn't be much time left. "Dr. Langstrom," he said. "Come over here. Not too close. Just by that desk."

Langstrom came, moving like a man under water. "Do you see this weapon?" Foerster asked.

"Yes." Dully.

"Do you know what it is?"

"I suppose that it is a bomb."

"That's correct. It is, to be exact, an atomic bomb. You probably have heard about the theft of the weapons from Adana."

"Yes."

"This is one of them. The other one is in Israel. I want you to do one thing, and do it exactly as I tell you to."

Langstrom nodded.

"Do you have a direct line to the guard post at the main gate?"

Another nod. "On my desk."

"We will go over to your desk, you and I. You will call the post. You will tell them who you are, and that we have taken the headquarters staff hostage, and that we have an armed nuclear bomb here. Then you will tell them that if *any* approach is made to this building, we will not negotiate, we will simply detonate the bomb. Furthermore, this: we have observers outside the camp. If there is any attempt to evacuate the camp, we will also detonate the bomb.

378

Finally, if two hours have passed without interference, we will release some of our hostages. We have no quarrel with them, only with Israel. After that, we will open further negotiations.''

"I can't remember all that," Langstrom said helplessly.

"I will prompt you. Now come."

Israel—Western Mediterranean
April 26

HIGH OVER NORTHERN Israel, the Boeing 707 with the Star of David insignia orbited in lazy circles. It was packed with computers, electronic radiation sensors and jamming transmitters. Its crew had been monitoring Syrian anti-aircraft radar emissions for the past fifteen minutes, ever since the Arabs had been fooled by the decoy drones into switching their instruments on. They didn't seem to have learned from the catastrophe their air defense system had suffered during the Lebanon war in 1982; they were keeping the radars on continuously, even when they didn't need tracking information.

The Boeing's crew had completed their signal analyses when the clocks reached zero hour. They turned on the jammers, and the Syrian radar displays in the air defense positions southwest of Damascus dissolved into a fog of green blots and spikes.

Several kilometers from the Boeing, closer to the Syrian border, an E2C Hawkeye airborne command post began to vector Israeli F16 and F15 interceptors toward the Syrian Mig fighters rising from the air bases around Damascus. Simultaneously, a second Boeing 707 began to jam the communications links between Syrian ground control stations and the pilots they were supposed to guide. After a minute or two the Hawkeye's radar scopes began to display the result: the Syrian planes were losing formation. Bereft of direction from their bases, they would be easy targets for the Israeli jets flying cover for the ground attack aircraft.

Captain Benjamin Engle held his F16 fighter at fifteen meters above the ground, coming in under the Syrian border radar. The underside of the delta-winged jet was jagged with cluster munitions and bombs. Off to the right, his wingman Alex Hofi maintained an even distance, as though the two aircraft were linked by an invisible iron bar.

Two minutes to the target. One minute from now the Kfir C2s should be firing their anti-radar missiles at the Syrian SAM-6 missile battery that was Engle's and Hofi's target. The two Israeli pilots had been training for this attack for the past three days, using simulated air defense sites down in the Negev. Assuming no Syrian opposition, the battery had two minutes of existence left.

The F16s screamed over the landscape of dusty brown villages, dark lines of roads and irrigation ditches. Engle heard snatches of conversation on the general frequency, although he and Hofi were maintaining radio silence. Somewhere up above, there was a big air battle going on.

The pair of aircraft swept over a low ridge. There they were, right ahead, the wheeled transporters still loaded with their missiles. As usual, Syrian camouflage was poor; it was hard to conceal a SAM position. A column of smoke rose from the northwest of

381

the site. The Kfirs had already done their job against the tracking radar. Engle wondered briefly if any Russian advisers had been killed. Probably.

He touched a switch on the left control panel. A chaff-dispensing missile shot out from under the F16's wing, spreading clouds of tiny aluminum ribbons to confuse any remaining radar. The two planes screamed over the SAM position, barely clearing the pointed snouts of the missiles, climbed sharply, and howled back down. They were now coming in from behind the battery, and the SAM transporters wouldn't be able to track quickly enough to engage them, even under manual control.

Engle squeezed the ordnance release switch and pulled back on the control lever. The F16 leveled out, its bombs and cluster munitions falling away, right into the center of the battery. The Syrian position dissolved into a great mottled bloom of flame and smoke.

The Bear was flying very low, almost on the wavetops. Lieutenant Ray Shannon slid his F14 Tomcat fighter outboard of the big Russian reconnaissance aircraft's starboard wing and took up station there, some ten meters higher. The Bear's long silver fuselage gleamed in the early morning light, the whirling blades of the huge propellers catching an occasional flash from the just-risen sun.

"Sucker's trying to come in under the radar again," Shannon observed to Keith Rutledge, his radar intercept officer in the seat behind. "Don't they ever learn?"

"He's climbing," said Rutledge. "Okay, picking up speed too. He's going to go in for a look at the battle group. He's been vectored by choppers off the *Moskva,* lively.''

''They're all over the goddamned place today,'' Shannon said. ''You think they're going to do something?''

''Who knows with Ivan?''

Shannon lifted the Tomcat and edged the throttles forward to maintain station off the Bear's wing. There was nothing they could do to keep the Russian reconnaissance plane from hanging around the carrier task force centered on the *Kennedy,* short of edging so close that the Bear's pilot would lose his nerve and turn away. Some pilots, including Shannon, did that from time to time, although it was officially frowned on. At the flight briefing this morning, however, the orders had been not to give the Russians any provocation whatsoever. Their Fifth Flotilla, composed of the helicopter carrier *Moskva,* the small aircraft carrier *Novorossiysk,* eight attack submarines, two missile cruisers, six frigates and twenty-three support craft, was steaming eastward only a hundred kilometers away, paralleling the course of *Kennedy*'s battle group. Because of the renewed outbreak of fighting between the Israelis and the Syrians, both fleets were nervous. American reconnaissance planes were shadowing the Russian ships, just as the Bears were watching the battle groups of the *Kennedy* and of the *America,* which was some kilometers farther north. Soviet trawlers— actually intelligence-gathering vessels—trailed both American task forces.

The Bear and the Tomcat reached a thousand meters' altitude. The Bear leveled out. Shannon kept his Tomcat at a safe distance, barely. Christ, he thought, how I'd like to edge that bastard off. Not today. Orders.

383

"Jesus Christ," Rutledge said in Shannon's earphones. "What's that asshole think he's flying? A Mig?"

The Bear had suddenly edged closer. The two planes were flying at 300 knots.

"He's pushing," Shannon said. He backed off a little. "Tell home plate."

"Henhouse," said Rutledge. "This is Mustang 204. Our target wants to play chicken."

"Mustang 204," came back from the *Kennedy*. "Maintain your distance. Acknowledge."

"204. Roger, maintain distance."

The Bear's pilot tried it again, perhaps encouraged by the Tomcat's earlier withdrawal. Shannon pulled away, not quite so far this time. He could see one of the crewmen on the Bear's flight deck staring out at the Tomcat. The bastards think they've got us on the run, thought Shannon.

Once more the Bear edged closer. "Fuck him," Shannon said. "I'm not moving." The Russian, with his far bigger and clumsier aircraft, would have to back away first.

The Bear's wingtip slid closer. Shannon stayed put. He was still a littler higher than the Bear, but not much.

Rudledge said, "You want to think this one over a little, Ray?"

Shannon didn't answer. The Russian wouldn't dare go much further.

But he did. The Bear's wingtip slotted in under the Tomcat's as though they were flying formation at an air show. There was no more than two meters of separation between the two aircraft.

Shannon had just decided to start backing away after all, when they hit the wind shear. The sudden and violent downdraft had far more effect on the lighter Tomcat than it did on the lumbering Bear; the fighter was smashed down hard on the Russian aircraft's outer wing. The Tomcat's port wing ripped off just outboard of the pivot, and the fighter began to tumble.

"Eject! Eject!" Shannon yelled. He yanked hard on the ejection handle. The wind blast as the canopy blew off and the seat shot out of the cockpit stunned him for a moment. Then he separated from the seat. Because of the low altitude his chute opened automatically. Rutledge had also got out; Shannon could see his parachute not far away.

Where was the Bear?

Oh, Christ, Shannon thought through his daze. We're fucked.

The Bear was spinning down out of control, twenty feet of its starboard wing torn away. There were no parachutes. The huge plane hit the water almost upside down and disintegrated in a towering pillar of white foam.

Incirlik—Istanbul
April 26

COLE PEERED OUT of the S3's canopy as the sub-hunter rolled to a halt outside one of the giant hangars of the great Incirlik air base. A pair of F16 jets, loaded with bombs and rockets, howled into the sky, followed promptly by two more.

This doesn't look good, Cole thought. Out on the *Kennedy,* the tension had been palpable; early that morning one of her planes had disappeared off the radar scopes along with a Russian reconnaissance aircraft. Since the incident, the *Kennedy*'s battle group had been in combat formation and the carrier herself at full action stations. Everyone was half-expecting a violent Soviet response to the loss of their aircraft. What that might lead to, Cole didn't want to imagine.

A black Renault pulled around the corner of the hangar and stopped. A man got out of the driver's side: Avi Maoz.

"Sam," Dalia said, "something's wrong. Avi's here."

They got out of their flight suits and left the plane. Avi waited impassively as they walked over to him.

"Avi," Dalia said. "Mordechai sent you?"

Avi nodded at Cole. "And the Americans in Istanbul. I have your passports."

"What's happened?"

"You haven't heard?" Avi said. "I thought the news might have got to you on the plane. The Turkish president's been shot."

"What?"

"Celebi's dead. In Ankara. He declared Turkish neutrality this morning, and one of his own bodyguard shot him. There's fighting in the capital between the leftists and the army."

"When was he killed?"

"Four hours ago. Everything is in an uproar. I brought a plane to bring you to Istanbul." The Israeli's face turned even more somber than it normally was. "I have some very bad news. Foerster—"

"He's placed the other bomb," Dalia said, as though she had already known. *"Where?"*

"Foerster," Avi said in his precisely accented English, "has managed to get the weapon into the Jewish transit camp at Kilincli. He is holding the entire camp population, and its director, hostage. He has three *Jund Allah* men with him, he says, and others outside."

There was a silence. Two more F16s boomed into the sky, trailing thin skeins of exhaust from their engines. "Have any ransom demands been made?" Dalia asked.

"Not yet. The Turkish military from First Army headquarters in Istanbul has sealed off the camp, but with the situation in Ankara—well, the Turks have other things on their minds than Russian Jews. They have a direct telephone line into the camp, but at the time I left, no demands had been made."

387

"The bomb that's supposed to be in Israel," Dalia asked. "Have we found it yet?"

"Not yet," Avi said. "We're moving armor and artillery up to the Golan area, and into the South Lebanon zone. We're still putting in air strikes against the Syrians. Some have apparently hit targets manned by Russians."

"We should talk on the plane," Dalia said. "We may not have much time. Where are we supposed to go?"

"The American consulate in Istanbul."

The flight to Istanbul's Yesilkoy airport was uneventful; Cole even drowsed while Dalia and Avi talked. At the airport a driver was waiting for them, but it took considerable time to reach the consulate; there were army detachments on every other street corner. Twice they were stopped at military checkpoints, but the car's diplomatic license plates and the driver's pass got them through. Finally, the car stopped in front of the consulate. Its fortified entrance had been reinforced with layers of sandbags. The three passengers got out and went through the entrance checkpoint.

"We're reporting in," Cole said to the receptionist. "Stein, Maoz, Cole."

"You're expected," she said. "Go on up the stairs."

The communications center was on the top floor, really just a large room with several telephones on desks, a teleprinter, and a terminal for a satellite data downlink. There were four people already there: Davis Webster, the CIA station head from Ankara; Mordechai Frank; the consul himself, Michael Kirkpatrick; and a Turk in general's uniform.

Kirkpatrick, a tall angular man with a prominent Adam's apple, was wearing an agitated expression. "Dr. Cole?"

"Yes," Cole said.

"This is the rest of the crisis management team?" Kirkpatrick sounded doubtful.

Cole was taken aback. This spoke of bad organization. "I thought one had already been put together."

"This is the liaison end of it," Kirkpatrick said. "But I was under the impression that a specialist counterterrorist force was coming."

"I've had no information on that," Cole said. Jesus, he thought, a screwup. Where's Rich, now that we need him? "Who's been put in charge?"

"It's joint, at the moment," Kirkpatrick told him. "CIA, Mossad, and," he added hastily, "liaison to Turkish First Army headquarters. This is General Tobur."

"You're not in Ankara?" Cole asked Webster.

The station chief grimaced. "I ought to be. But Rich called from Washington. He says this bomb situation takes priority. So here I am."

Cole nodded. "What's the situation?"

Mordechai answered, looking far from pleased. It was obvious that he had little patience with the way the operation was moving so far. "There was a call made from the transit camp twenty minutes ago. It was Foerster; he identified himself this time, SS rank and all. The demands are the same as before, no change. Also, he reminded us that if there's any move made toward evacuating the camp, he'll detonate the warhead. He says he's got accomplices outside to tell him if that's being done. We don't really know whether he does, though. Except for the

389

camp director, Langstrom, he's released all the staff."

"Has a tactical headquarters been set up?" Cole asked.

"Our commander out there has established one in the guard post at the main gate," General Tobur said. He spoke excellent English. "We also sent out one of the Milstar communications vans you sent our military before the, ah, embargo. Our communications are good."

"Negotiations?"

"The West German embassy is sending one of its specialists," Kirkpatrick said. "He's supposedly experienced. We also need a tactical team, but none seems to be available."

"Events in Ankara are very chaotic at the moment," General Tobur said. "General Munir Orhan has taken over as acting president since President Celebi was assassinated. But there have been disturbances. It means, unfortunately, that our special tactical squads are committed elsewhere at the moment."

"What about moving in a NATO unit?" Cole asked. "The SAS or the West German GSG9, for example. Or our own Delta Force?"

"No one will do anything without permission from Ankara," Kirkpatrick said. "But we can't get hold of the acting president or the foreign minister. Celebi's murder has knocked everything to hell."

"You mean," Dalia said, "that there isn't *any* strike unit available?" She sounded incredulous.

"Not at the moment, I'm afraid," Kirkpatrick said. "Perhaps by tomorrow—"

"It's early evening now," Dalia told him in an angry voice. "By that time those people out there may all be dead."

390

"The negotiator will be out at the camp by nine this evening," Kirkpatrick said. "That'll buy us some time."

"Doesn't anybody take this seriously?" Cole barked. "There's a *nuclear bomb* in that camp. It's nearly the size of the Hiroshima one."

"Too many things went wrong at once," Kirkpatrick said. "Celebi's murder. The bomb that's supposed to be in Israel. The Israeli and Syrian mobilizations. And there's something that's possibly even more dangerous. The Russians are saying that they will take whatever actions are necessary to protect their citizens abroad. It's obviously about the Jews in Kilincli."

"*Citizens?*" Dalia exclaimed furiously. "What the hell! Kulagin and the Russians threw them out. They didn't care how many died on the way. Now they talk about *protecting* them?"

"Their position has always been that these are voluntary emigrants. They can't be seen to ignore the threat."

Webster was looking on dourly.

"Davis," Cole said evenly, "what about your people? You must have somebody who can get into that camp and take on Foerster."

"I've got nobody," Webster said. "We could get some people from Langley, but they'd be sixteen hours getting here, and the same problem applies as with the foreign tactical units: we'd have to have permission."

"So that, for the moment, leaves us."

"I'm afraid so. But as Mr. Kirkpatrick pointed out, too many things have gone wrong at once."

One of the telephones warbled. The consul picked it up. "Kirkpatrick."

He listened, and then handed the receiver to Webster. "It's for you."

"Webster here." The station chief nodded. "Yes. They just arrived. All right. Right away. Talk to you shortly."

He hung up. "That was Rich. He's in the Situation Room with the president and a crisis management team. We're to go out to Kilincli right away and wait for instructions."

Moscow
April 26

THE EMERGENCY MEETING of the Soviet Main Military Council was assembling. Kulagin had ordered that it be held in the deepest bunker of the Moscow Central Command Post, a complex of communications and living facilities buried nearly a hundred meters underneath the small military airport of Khodinka, a kilometer and a half northwest of the Kremlin. From there, communications lines ran to every Russian military headquarters and Soviet embassy in the world.

This latter fact suited KGB Chairman Viktor Frolov very nicely. He had been able to ensure that the message concerning the Americans' possession of the Winter Palace plans had gone directly to Kulagin, via Dzerzhinsky Square; if he'd had to delay until it was filtered through the diplomatic apparatus and Foreign Minister Truschenko, he might still be waiting. He was also able to keep in close touch with Osipov, whom he'd sent to Turkey for two reasons: partly to monitor the search for the American bombs and partly to get him out of the way, just in case his loyalty to Frolov was not quite as perfect as it

393

seemed. Osipov did in fact realize that his fate hinged on that of his superior; it couldn't be otherwise, since he'd been directly responsible for Cole's escape. The KGB chief had told Osipov exactly what was going on, and then added, "Don't forget you're in this with me, now. I'm going to need you, Major-General. And you're going to need me. If we mess this up, don't forget what I've told you. We'll both end up in one of our own cellars."

Still no sign of Kulagin. Frolov glanced at Truschenko, who was sitting nearly across from him. The diplomat wore a harried expression, which was not surprising. It was going to be his responsibility to manage the campaign that described the Americans' allegations as lies. Normally, he would have the full support of the KGB disinformation organs to do that; but not this time. There wouldn't be any disinformation campaign at all, at least not until Kulagin was . . . out of the way. Frolov had virtually completed his plans, but they were going to depend on very delicate timing.

A guard opened the door to the bunker. "General Secretary Kulagin," he announced.

Kulagin entered the room. There was a feverish look about his eyes and a lighted cigarette dangling from the fingers of his right hand. Frolov noted that the index finger was nicotine-stained; the general secretary was smoking even more than usual. Good.

Kulagin sat down at the head of the table and flicked his gaze over the other members of the Military Council: Defense Minister Lesiovsky; Foreign Minister Trushenko; the Chief of the General Staff Marshal Tyurin; the head of military intelligence; the minister of armaments; and Frolov. To the KGB chairman it seemed that Kulagin's eyes rested on him a fraction of a second longer than on the others.

"This is an extremely critical and dangerous time," Kulagin said, lighting a fresh cigarette from the old one and extinguishing the butt in a glass ashtray. "First item of business. I am sure the council would like to hear Comrade Frolov's explanation of *how* the Americans discovered the truth about Winter Palace? This is a serious dereliction of duty." The general secretary's eyes were like black ice.

Frolov was ready for this one. "The KGB *rezidentura* in Washington has examined the exact text the Americans provided to our embassy. There are significant differences between it and the existing operational orders for Winter Palace. In fact, the text the Americans possess is exactly the same as that of the original plan, which was, as you know, drafted under Stalin and signed by Beria." Frolov paused and sipped at his water glass. "It is clear that the Americans obtained the material a very long time ago and have been waiting for an opportunity to use it."

"You have proof of this?" asked Kulagin.

"I have very good evidence. In June, 1953, one of Beria's section heads, a certain Igor Ilyich Yatsenko, attempted to defect to the Americans with a microfilm of Winter Palace. He was caught and killed by border guards before he could reach Finland, but the microfilm was never recovered. It seems plain now that he managed to get it to the CIA before he attempted his escape. If necessary, we can undercut the Americans' allegations by pointing out that this 'evidence' is nearly forty years old. They know they are on shaky ground, since they have not threatened to make their accusations public just yet. Our disinformation campaign will easily deal with the accusations, if the Americans elect to release the document."

Kulagin regarded the KGB chief with stony eyes. "You have proof of all this?"

"I can supply it to the Politburo and the Secretariat whenever required."

"Are the rest of you satisfied with Comrade Frolov's defense?" asked Kulagin.

This was the critical point. Trushchenko and Lesiovsky were on a knife-edge between committing themselves to Frolov, and remaining with Kulagin. Frolov had had obtuse conversations with other members of the Secretariat and Politburo over the past couple of weeks, and he was confident that if he had the foreign minister and the defense minister on his side, Kulagin's days were numbered; especially if he elected to carry out the military operation in Turkey. Frolov hoped fervently that the secretary wouldn't lose his nerve at the last moment.

No one at the table seemed to question Frolov's reasoning, to his enormous relief.

"Very well," Kulagin said. "Now, to the main order of business: the question of the nuclear bombs in Israel and in the Kilincli transit camp in Turkey. Defense Minister Lesiovsky?"

"President Celebi's assassination has destabilized the entire affair," Lesiovsky said. "We had intended to move the *Admiral Gorshkov* and her task force through the Dardanelles within the next two days, but we can no longer be sure that the Turks will allow us free passage. Getting the carrier group out of the Black Sea is essential. There is every potential for nuclear war in the eastern Mediterranean, which could escalate rapidly into global war with the Americans. If that bomb explodes in Israel, the Israelis will almost certainly carry out nuclear attacks on Syria. The Americans will then be expecting us to strike at Israeli military targets in retaliation. They

396

may very well decide to preempt with strikes against our navel forces. We all know where that will likely lead. With the Black Sea fleet in the Mediterranean, though, the United States will face the likelihood of a severe defeat at sea. We think that Washington will exercise more restraint if the *Admiral Gorshkov* and her fleet are there."

"We need to ensure that the ships pass through the Dardanelles without being attacked," said Kulagin authoritatively. "They do not have enough room to maneuver in those restricted waters, and even the Turkish military could cause severe damage."

Well, Frolov thought to himself, catching Lesiovsky's eye. Now you think you're a warlord and a military genius. Lesiovsky doesn't like that, neither does Tyurin. A little more rope.

"We therefore," Kulagin was saying, "have to have a very good reason to secure the straits by parachute drops and amphibious landings. I believe I have found the solution."

He looked challengingly around the table. "We will portray the action as a mission to rescue our Soviet citizens from the threat of the nuclear bomb in the Kilincli camp. No one, least of all the Israelis, can object to that. They have done exactly the same kind of thing in the past. While the rescue is going on, we will secure the straits and pass our ships through. Afterwards, if the situation warrants it, we can withdraw our troops. Or, if general war is unavoidable, we can use the bridgeheads to ease our overland invasion of Turkey."

Now, Frolov thought. "Secretary, may I be the first to offer my support for this plan. As you know, we also have nearly twenty thousand of our agents in the transit camp. Their safety is of great concern

397

to the KGB and is critical to the success of Winter Palace. A rescue operation will also show the world that the Americans' accusations about our treatment of the Jews are groundless."

Kulagin glanced indifferently at him. "That also is true. But at the moment my greatest concern, as yours should be, is that we not be caught unprepared if it becomes necessary to fight in the Mediterranean. Are we all agreed that we should carry out the rescue mission in Turkey?"

Everyone nodded. "Good," Kulagin said. "See to it."

Now, Frolov thought, all depends on timing. I have to wait until Kulagin is committed to his military adventure, and then strike. Timing.

I hope the Israelis find that bomb. If they don't, there may be no point in any of this.

The Black Sea—
Odessa Military District
April 27

IT WAS JUST before dawn, but the sky was still lit by moon and stars, the dark rolling waves touched by silver, luminous foam at their crests. Even on the enclosed bridge of the *Admiral Gorshkov,* it was possible to smell the sea air, fresh after the various stinks of the Sevastopol naval base. The task force had been at sea for an hour.

Captain First Rank Sergei Petrov looked out of the bridge windows, down the long angled flight deck, past the bows of the great aircraft carrier to the path of light the moon had laid down on the surface of the sea. He was not usually a fanciful man, but he found himself musing as to whether the pale gleaming band stretching away toward the southwest had some kind of hidden significance. After a few moments he decided it did not. Just moonlight reflected on water, that was all.

Off to port steamed the *Zhdanov,* the battle group's command cruiser. Petrov wondered whether the Vice-Admiral was gazing from the *Zhdanov*'s bridge at the huge bulk of the carrier, and what she looked like under the moon. The *Admiral Gorshkov* was the pride of the Black Sea fleet, and perhaps of the Soviet Navy itself; nuclear-powered, she was a carrier fit to match the great attack-vessels of the United States. Like most Soviet warships, she carried a huge armament for the size of her hull, much of it in the form of the new Yak-40 attack aircraft and Mig-23Ts, the naval version of the land based interceptor. In addition, she loaded a complement of anti-submarine helicopters, and a pair of tanker aircraft for midair refueling of the strike planes. For close defense she was studded with anti-aircraft missiles and rapid-fire automatic guns.

She might need them, and soon. The Americans were being extremely aggressive; that was proven by the way their fighter had rammed the reconnaissance plane watching the *Kennedy,* the previous day. Petrov was still angry about that, and worried. He hadn't really thought the Americans would go that far. Yet.

He looked through the other bridge window. Visible out there were a few of the ships of the escort group, light cruisers and destroyers. Out of sight, following the *Admiral Gorshkov* in line astern, were the helicopter carrier *Leningrad* and the heavy nuclear cruiser *Kirov.* Behind the core of the battle group were the vessels of the amphibious assault squadron, spread over kilometers of ocean: two big *Ivan Rogov*-class landing ships, five tank landing vessels and a dozen medium assault ships, all packed with naval infantry and their vehicles and equipment. These men would support the paratroop landings in the Bosphorus and the Dardanelles straits, and hold that passage past Istanbul until the ships reached the Mediterranean and the open sea. Then, perhaps, the Israelis would think twice about invading the Soviet Union's Syrian ally, and the Americans reconsider attacking the vessels of the Fifth Flotilla.

But perhaps they would not. If they didn't, and fighting began between the two fleets, Captain First Rank Petrov knew his ship would savage the Americans bitterly; but he also knew she would likely never come home again.

General Oleg Retzov, commander of the 105th Guards Airborne Division, peered out of the cockpit window. The Ilyushin-76 jet transport was sliding into its final approach to the forward staging base; there had been a thaw in the night, and a fine pearly mist hung over the meadows below. Through the window, just visible ahead, Retzov could see the ranks of transports dispersed along the base taxiways: more Ilyushins, medium Antonov-12 paratroop carriers, and the monstrous humped fuselages and long tapering wings of the Antonov-22 heavy transports. With the heavies, there would be enough planes to get the whole division to the target, along with its vehicles, in one lift. Then the planes would return to pick up the 103rd Guards. It would have been preferable to drop both divisions at once, but there simply were not enough planes immediately available; the crisis had come to a head too fast. Fortunately, General Retzov had kept his division up to a high pitch of readiness ever since taking command of it; he and his staff had been able to cut the orders in what must have been record time.

The Ilyushin thumped onto the runway and the engines howled in reverse thrust. Back in the troop compartment, his staff would be shoving the operational plans back into their briefcases. The divisional troops, all eight thousand of them, had already been

401

lifted with most of their vehicles into the staging bases. The rest of the vehicles—transport, communications and combat—would follow during the day. Retzov and his division would sleep rough tonight, in the planes, but they'd be up and on their way not long after midnight, unless orders were canceled or there was some kind of a delay.

A night drop, Retzov mused as the Ilyushin rolled along the taxiway. That'll surprise the Americans and the Turks, all right. They don't know how long we've been practicing this sort of operation. Two regiments to hold the Bosphorus Bridge, one outside the transit camp for the rescue operation—not that that matters. Then, on the second lift, Kirilenko's 103rd airborne boys to seize the Turkish shore defenses along the Dardanelles.

Retzov's orders had been very precise: the regiment dropped at the camp was a cover operation, designed to slow and confuse Turkish reactions. It was supposedly intended to rescue Soviet Jewish citizens from nuclear-armed terrorists. Whether or not the Jews were actually rescued or the terrorists set the bomb off, was of little importance. The real task of the two airborne divisions was to hold the straits of the Bosphorus and the Dardanelles until the main strength of the Black Sea Fleet, centered on the *Admiral Gorshkov,* penetrated into the Mediterranean.

If there were going to be a war, the Admiralty didn't want its biggest and best ship bottled up in the Black Sea. Retzov and his men were to make sure that did not happen.

Kilinchi Transit Camp, Turkey
April 27-28

COLE STOOD by the sea, looking through the barbed wire fence into the camp. The tents marched endlessly away inland, under the morning sun; there were nearly six hundred thousand people in there. On the other side of the wire a group of Soviet Jews looked back at him. One of them, a young woman who would have been pretty under other circumstances, called out to him in Russian, gesturing. He waved back to her. She waved again, beckoning.

He didn't want to face her, but felt he had to. He walked the fifteen meters to the gate in the fence, which ended here at the edge of the sea. The Turkish army guards looked nervously at him, but they had orders from Tobur to let him enter the camp. They were here only to make sure the refugees stayed in.

Close up, the woman was not as young as he had thought, or perhaps it was fear that made her look older.

"Are you coming to help us?" she asked, in Russian.

He answered her in her own tongue. "Yes. We're here to help you."

"Then you can answer some of our questions." Anger flickered in her face. "When are you going to let us out? Why are you letting these people threaten us? We thought we were finally safe."

"We're trying," Cole said, knowing how useless it sounded.

"There is really an atomic bomb here?"

"Yes."

"Why do they want to kill us? We never have done harm to them."

"They want to destroy Israel," Cole said. "They've told us that if we do not agree to what they want, they will explode the bomb. They will also do that if we try to let you all go."

"So you cannot help us."

"Not right now," Cole said. "But we will get you out."

"How?"

"I'm afraid I can't tell you that," Cole said. "Can you take me to the camp committee headquarters?" As well as the U.N. administration, there was a committee of refugees that controlled the internal affairs of the camp. Its headquarters was some distance from the U.N. block, and Cole wasn't sure he could find it, coming in from this direction. It would have been easy enough from the main gate, but he couldn't take the chance that one of Foerster's outside men—if there really were any—might see him enter. So he was beginning his reconnaissance from down here, where the edge of the camp met the sea and Turkish patrols made surveillance impossible.

"You want to see the committee?"

"Yes."

"I'll take you."

Cole nodded to one of the guards and the barrier swung open. "I can't be conspicuous," Cole said to the young woman. "Can you take me alone, please?"

She nodded. The rest of the group, overhearing, dispersed. She set off into the camp, Cole tagging behind. He was wearing battered, nondescript clothes and could have been a refugee himself; except that he wasn't gaunt enough.

Once among the tents it was easy to lose any sense of direction; whichever way Cole looked, the aspect was the same: guy ropes, dusty paths worn in the tough grass, more dust blown by the sea wind, tents everywhere one looked. But despite the number of people in the camp, it was remarkably quiet, with few out in the paths and dusty lanes. Cole mentioned it.

"Most of us stay inside in the morning," the woman replied, "until it gets too hot. No one has enough to eat, so we rest as much as possible. Later, when it's too warm, we open the tent sides. There isn't much to do yet, but we are getting organized. There are schools for the children, that was one of the first things we started. Some rabbis were sent out in the first ships, so we can at last have religious instruction and lessons in Hebrew without trouble from the authorities. Some of our craftsmen have begun working, mending shoes and clothes, making tools out of whatever they can find. There are a few books, but not many good ones in Russian. The children are being taught mostly from memory."

"Do you have children?" Cole asked, and immediately wished he hadn't. A look of anguish passed over her face.

"Yes. Two. But my husband wasn't a Jew. So

405

when they came for me, he kept the children. We were going to be divorced, anyway.''

"I'm sorry."

"Everyone here has something like that, some better, some worse.''

They went on in silence. The sun was higher and Cole felt perspiration gathering on his forehead. He studied the faces of the people he passed. Some were dispirited, but many held a look of guarded optimism. Russians are tough and Jews are survivors, Cole reminded himself. And these people are Jews, *and* they're Russians. Maybe the most resilient people on earth.

"It's there," she said, pointing. Ahead, in a less congested area, was a large green Turkish army bell tent. Two of its sides had been rolled up. Under the canopy were trestle tables, chairs, people working. Cole heard the noise of a typewriter.

"Who do I ask for?''

"Anyone will help you. Good-bye.''

"Good-bye. Good luck.''

"Try to save us.''

He didn't know whether she meant from the bomb, or from everything. "I will.''

She was gone. He went on to the bell tent. To the southwest he could make out the flagpole by the U.N. building, half a kilometer away, where Foerster and the bomb were. Safe enough.

No one seemed to take much notice of him. Three men of varying ages and an older woman were bunched at the far side of the tent, leafing through a stack of papers. Two other women, younger, were working at the tables. Next to one of them was an older man tapping at the typewriter, his back to Cole, white hair disarrayed in the breeze. Cole's

406

shadow fell across the typewriter. The man turned and looked up. Cole stopped, transfixed.

"My God," Alexander Markelov said. "It's Samuel. Samuel. How in the name of God did you get here?"

It was a moment before Cole could speak. "Alexander. You got out. How?"

But Markelov was already on his feet, nearly knocking the typewriter off the table, throwing his arms around Cole in a great bear hug. Cole returned the embrace. After a moment Markelov released him and stood back. His eyes were wet. The others in the tent had stopped working and were staring at them. "They shipped me out with the others," he said. "I don't know why. None of it might ever have happened, the *dacha*, the papers . . . They didn't question me at all."

I'm beginning to know why, Cole thought. What we suspected is true. Someone in the Kremlin doesn't like Winter Palace.

"You had no trouble getting away?" Markelov asked. "I was terribly worried about you."

He'd tell him later. "No trouble. Alexander, I'm sorry, but we're very short of time. I'm with the team that's to deal with the terrorists and the bomb. I came in this morning to reconnoiter."

The others had moved closer. One of the three men said suspiciously, "Alexander, who's this?"

"Samuel? I've already told these people about Winter Palace. Only these people."

"That's all right."

"Samuel Cole took the documents out of Russia for us," Markelov told them.

The suspicion in their faces vanished. There were introductions, and explanations of what they did on the camp committee. Alexander was in charge of

407

education. One of the other men, Gennadi Kovalev, was in charge of policing the camp. Cole didn't catch all of the rest.

"You know about the bomb deadline," he said.

"Yes," said Markelov. "There are a few radios here." He looked at Kovalev. "Gennadi, we can tell him."

"We've made plans to deal with the terrorists ourselves, if no help comes from outside," Kovalev said. He was younger than Cole had at first thought. "We were going to give you people until four tomorrow morning. Then we were going to try ourselves."

Cole looked at them, aghast. "But you've no weapons, no training. How—"

Kovalev held up a hand. "There are a few of us here with recent military experience. My rank in the army was captain. I led a counterinsurgency company in Afghanistan, fighting the guerrillas. For two years." A grim expression crossed his face. "As for weapons, we were planning to take them from the Turkish guards, just before the attack."

They mean it, Cole thought. And why shouldn't they? Their lives are at stake. "You need other equipment," he said. "To have a reasonable chance of success. Silencers, sniping rifles, stun grenades."

"We were going to try with what we had. We won't lie down any more."

Cole turned to Markelov. "Alexander, there are negotiations—"

"Captain Kovalev told you, Samuel. We won't lie down any more. When you saw me last I had waited, waited for years, to do something about Winter Palace, hoping it would go away. It did not. It's killed my wife and my two sons. My daughter has been raped by Russian soldiers, and my grand-

408

daughter may die of fever in this camp. No more. We will not lie down for this.''

The courage of men with nothing to lose, Cole thought. They really mean it. They'd go after Foerster and his bomb with their bare hands, if that was all they could do.

"We'd better combine forces on this," he said. "We don't want to get in each others' way."

When Cole reached the guard post at the main gate, Webster was standing in the doorway. "You made it in and out okay."

"Yeah. Alexander Markelov made it out, too. Out of Russia. He's here. And they were all set to go after Foerster themselves, tomorrow morning."

"Jesus Christ."

"I know."

"Peiper's going to start the briefing," Webster said. "We couldn't wait for you any longer." Peiper was the negotiator and counterterrorist expert from the West German embassy. "Foerster called at noon, but he just made the same demands over again. No change since we got here."

The team had come out from Istanbul from the consulate the previous evening; it consisted of Cole, Dalia, Avi, Mordechai, Webster, the Turkish commander of the guard unit, General Tobur and Fritz Peiper. No one had slept well; the waiting was beginning to wear on their nerves and they were beginning to feel claustrophobic in the tiny building.

Peiper was standing at the head of the trestle table upon which lay a sketch map of the inner camp and a penciled floor plan of the headquarters hut. He was a big man with a sharp mind, an acerbic wit and a quiet friendly voice. He inspired confidence,

409

an invaluable asset in someone who negotiated with desperate men. He nodded to Cole as Cole and Webster came inside. "Are we ready?" he asked.

"Yes," said Webster. "Let's start."

"Very well. In the camp there are Foerster and three *Jund Allah* men. We know that we have problems, but the terrorists do as well. They are not in an airliner or a solidly constructed building, which makes them vulnerable, because approach is relatively simple for us.

"Also, there is the fact that there are windows only in the front and back of the building. The two side walls are blind. For this reason, we think, two of them always mount guard at the opposite corners of the building, so that they can monitor the approaches. The third one watches the generator hut, which powers the lights in and around the administration building. They are at some disadvantage at night, because the lighting is poor. Because of this, they do not turn the lights on in the headquarters hut after dark. They can see out, but we cannot see in. This makes approach to the hut difficult, but I believe it can be solved provided we can shut down their electrical power for a few seconds, and then turn it back on. This operation of theirs shows signs of being hastily planned. If it were not for the presence of the bomb, we could have them out of there in short order."

"Unfortunately," Mordechai put in, "the bomb *is* there."

"Yes," Peiper agreed, unruffled. "It is. Now, as to the arrangements inside the hut. The hostages the terrorists released say that the bomb in its crate was placed here, behind the counter inside the front door. The telephone being used by Foerster is on this desk, here, about two meters away. We know this because

410

it is the only one in the hut that has a direct line outside. Now, one of the hostages risked a look at the bomb as they were letting her go. It appears to have a pair of firing buttons, mounted somehow on the upper side of the casing. I made a sketch from her description. It looks like this." He pointed to a drawing beside the floor layout of the hut. "The buttons are between twenty and thirty centimeters apart. There was also a battery, so I believe that whoever armed the weapon has built an electrical firing circuit into it somehow, connected to the warhead fuse. Unfortunately, since I do not know much about the construction of American nuclear weapons, I cannot tell you more than that."

Webster said, "Dr. Hoffmann, one of our experts, is on his way here with his specialists."

"Good," said Peiper. "We may need them. But I am worried that we do not have much time. From my experiences in other events of this nature, I judge that Foerster is not really interested in negotiating, but merely going through motions until something precipitates his decision to detonate the bomb. What that might be, I do not know yet. In my conversation with him at noon, he merely reiterated the original demands. Normally, if I can form a relationship with the leader of a terrorist team, I can persuade minor concessions at first, and later, sometimes, larger ones. But if they will not talk to me, I am at a very great disadvantage. I think that Foerster is seriously unbalanced, but not in the way that most hostage-takers can be said to be. I believe that he is following his own agenda, and that the *Jund Allah* is simply a means to an end."

"Do you mean that Foerster could detonate the bomb at any time, without warning?" Dalia asked.

"Yes."

411

"What can we do?"

Peiper looked at her, apparently unperturbed. "I still advise patience. I do not think that Foerster is ready to act yet. He has us and the Jews at his mercy, and I believe he will continue to enjoy that in his twisted way for some time. The deadline is six A.M. tomorrow, like that of the Israel bomb. It is still possible that there will be negotiations."

General Tobur spoke. "Ankara has promised a counterterrorist tactical squad by three A.M. tomorrow. There will be enough time to brief them, and they can go in just before dawn."

Cole looked at the Turk. The acting president, General Orhan, seemed to have gained control of the capital, but at the cost of affirming Turkish neutrality if war broke out between the United States and the Soviet Union over the escalating conflict between Israel and Syria. It was tantamount to declaring that Turkey would no longer support the NATO alliance. Cole was certain that the Kremlin had taken careful note of the decision; it could play into their hands politically and perhaps militarily. To increase the tension even further, the Israelis had shown no desire to back away from their confrontation with Syria. They wouldn't, either, until they found the other bomb; if they did.

"Suppose the tactical team doesn't get here?" Cole said. He didn't want to mention the attack the camp committee had been planning, yet. "Or if we think Foerster's going to jump the deadline?"

Peiper looked down at his plans. "We need to be prepared for that. Dr. Cole, did either your reconnaissance or the camp committee provide us with anything useful?"

Webster was looking at him. "In a sense," Cole said. "The approaches from inside the camp are no better than from out here, so that's not a factor. But there's something we have to take account of. The Jews in Kilincli are planning an attack on Foerster themselves.''

They all, except Webster, stared at him. "What?" Peiper said.

Cole recounted what he'd been told. When he finished, Peiper frowned worriedly. "We can't have that. A premature move could be disastrous.''

"I told them that,'' Cole said. "They agreed to put their plan on hold until I came back and told them what we're going to do.''

"Hmm.'' Peiper rubbed his chin, looking down at his plans again. "Very well. Let's leave that aside for the moment. This is what I was going to propose. We require seven people. Two will slip into the camp from this position.'' He touched the map with a pencil tip. "They will be armed with silenced sniping rifles, with night fighting telescopes. There are positions, here and there, where the snipers can lie well back and yet have clear lanes of fire at the two terrorist guards at the corners of the building. The next three members of the team will remain in concealment behind the rows of tents here, here and here, twenty meters from the administration hut. The remaining two will cover the generator hut: one to snipe the guard, the other to shut off the power momentarily.

"We will begin with a distraction. I will telephone Foerster. As soon as he answers, someone here at the command post will fire a white flare. That is a risk, but we have to take it. As soon as the flare ignites, the sniper at the generator hut will kill the guard there. The *instant* that happens, our second man will enter the hut and shut off the main power switch, which is here, as you can see from the plan.

413

To reach the hut and do that will require five to six seconds, before the lights go out. I will be speaking with Foerster by then.

"As soon as the lights go down, the other two snipers will kill the guards at the corners of the administration hut. Foerster will not be able to see anything if he looks out the window. A power failure will not likely make him trigger the bomb immediately, and remember that inside the hut it will be pitch-black, so he won't be able to reach the weapon quickly.

"The power will remain off for five seconds. Right after the guards are killed, the other three members, who will be armed with submachine guns and concussion grenades, will run to the door and to the window on its left. One will shoot out the window and a second will throw in two concussion grenades with two-second fuses. The third member will break through the door as the grenades explode, and begin firing. The other two will follow him in, one of them turning on the interior lights; the power will be back on by then. The light switch is at shoulder level, just inside the door on the right. It moves up to turn on. Foerster will be stunned by the concussion grenades and unable to react effectively for another five seconds or so. That should give you enough time. It all requires precise coordination. We will have to begin run-throughs immediately. Who do you suggest to take what position?"

"Who's a good shot?" Cole asked. Seven people, he thought. We only have five.

"I'm not bad," Webster said. "I had sniper training in the Marines, and I've kept my hand in. I'll take one of the guards at the administration hut."

"I can deal with the other," said Mordechai.

414

"Okay. Sam, I suppose you want to go inside," Webster said.

"Yes."

"Mordechai? Who else for the inside team?"

"Dalia. And Avi Maoz, here."

"This is the problem I was coming to," Peiper said. "We are lacking two people for the generator hut. General Tobur? Can you assist?"

The Turk looked troubled. "The men here are line infantry. They are tough in an outright battle, but they're not trained for this sort of thing."

"Damn," Peiper said. "We can't go in with the lights on. Foerster will be able to react."

"Let the men in Kilincli help," Cole said. "There are trained counterinsurgency troops in there, a few at least. I told you what Kovalev was planning to do."

"They only speak Russian."

"I can translate. We need more people, and that's the only place we're going to get them if the tactical team from Ankara doesn't get here in time." Cole was getting annoyed. "We've got trained men in that camp, and we should plan to use them if we have to go in. Otherwise we can just sit on our hands and let Foerster do what he wants."

Peiper tossed his pencil onto the map. "Very well. You put it very persuasively."

"Davis?" Cole asked.

"Makes sense to me," Webster said.

"Is the equipment available?" Cole asked Tobur.

"Yes. There is a pre-positioned stockpile in Istanbul for this sort of eventuality."

"How long to get it?"

"Four hours. I will leave immediately."

Tobur departed. Webster looked at his watch. "I want to get a situation report," he said. "Let's go

415

out to the van. Sam, as soon as we've done that, you'd better get back into the camp and tell them what's going on.''

Communications from Kilincli were better than Cole had dared hope. The command vehicle was one of the new large ones supplied to the Turkish army by the United States. It pulled a trailer with its own electrical generator, and its roof was crowned with whip antennae and a parabolic dish, which could receive and transmit messages through the Milstar communications satellite network without fear of eavesdropping or jamming. From the consoles inside the van, they could talk to anyone they needed to. One line was kept open to Washington and the Situation Room under the White House.

Cole, Webster and Mordechai climbed into the vehicle. The two Turkish radio specialists discreetly left; Webster, who seemed to know a surprising amount about the vehicle's operation, sat down in a swivel chair in front of one of the consoles. He made sure the scrambler circuits were on, pressed a button and said, ''Baseplate calling High Tower. Over.'' High Tower was the Situation Room.

The response from the console speaker was immediate, in Richland's voice. ''High Tower to Baseplate. What is your situation? Over.''

Webster described what had happened in the meeting. Then he asked, ''Can you give us present background? Over.''

''Baseplate, we have some bad news. Six items. One. We have signs the Russians are moving two airborne divisions south. Two. The Soviet Black Sea fleet, with the *Admiral Gorshkov,* left port just before dawn today, headed for the Mediterranean. Three. The Soviets have informed Ankara that they will take any measures necessary to protect the lives of their

416

citizens now in Turkey. Four. Jerusalem has stepped up its air strikes on Syria. Five. The President has had no response from Kulagin on cooling the naval situation. It's clear Kulagin will try to get the Black Sea fleet into the Mediterranean to support the Syrians, and make the Israelis and us back off. Six. The President indicates that, if possible, the weapon over there should be recovered before the Soviets use it as an excuse to attack Turkey. Over.''

"Lovely," Webster said. "Have you got anything really depressing? Over.''

"That'll have to do for the moment. Anything else? Over.''

"Not at this time. Will monitor this line. Over.''

"Good luck. Out.''

Webster got up from the console. "You heard," he said to Cole and Mordechai. "It doesn't look good. This is how accidents happen, when you're nose to nose. Parnell wants that bomb out of the camp. Should we go in when it's dark?''

Peiper was standing in the doorway. "I heard the last part," he said. "I would advise against it. Much as I have respect for your people's abilities, we would be better off to wait for the tactical team.''

"Okay," said Webster. "We'll wait.''

It was almost dark. Cole and Dalia walked along the wire some distance from the guard post. "Are we going to succeed?'' she asked.

"We have to," Cole said. "There's no one but us, and Captain Kovalev and his lieutenant.''

"Sam, what if we fail?''

"We can't think about that," he told her, looking through the wire at the camp, whose sparse lights were brightening in the gathering dusk. There was

417

now a curfew, and all the refugees had disappeared. "We'll do it. Look at what we're up against. One old man, and three incompetent terrorists."

"They're not so incompetent," she said. "And they have an atomic bomb."

"Yes. I know. But we have to keep up our confidence."

"Let's go back," she said.

They reached the hut, walking in silence. Inside, the air smelled of Turkish cigarettes and nervous sweat. Peiper had just got off the line to Foerster. "He talks a little," he said, "and then breaks it off. He's making it into kind of a game. He's also becoming somewhat disjointed in his conversation, goes into digressions about fighting in Russia, almost reminiscing. It's worrisome. I have to phone him occasionally, so that he won't be suspicious if we have an emergency and I have to distract him with a call, but I don't dare do it too often, in case he starts to refuse to answer."

"Any word on the Turkish tactical squad?"

"None. They're still expected at three."

"How about somebody to defuse the damned thing?"

"Hoffmann's team is on the way. Shapiro's is closer but we don't dare pull them out of Israel."

"They'd better be here when we need them," Cole said.

It felt very late, or very early. The interior of the command vehicle was dim, the red, green and amber lights on the consoles shining steadily in the half-gloom. Webster was slouched in front of the console with the direct Washington line. In another swivel chair behind him, Mordechai stared into space. Dalia was sitting on the floor at the front of the communications bay, head leaning against the back of the driver's seat, arms linked around her knees. Avi had gone outside to smoke, accompanied by Captain Kovalev and the lieutenant who was sniping for him. Everyone was ready, their faces blackened with greasepaint, the sniper rifles and G3 submachine guns cleaned and loaded. There had still been no confirmation that the Turkish tactical squad was on its way.

Cole, in the chair next to Webster's, watched the red digital display on the console count off minutes and seconds. It was ten minutes to two in the morning. The last situation report from Washington had come in twenty minutes ago; the Soviet Black Sea fleet with the *Admiral Gorshkov* was steaming southwest at eighteen knots, and would be off the entrance to the Bosphorus just before dawn. Cole had asked Mordechai what the Israeli Air Force would do if it decided that the *Admiral Gorshkov* and her escort group were about to break out into the Mediterranean.

"We'd strike at them, likely," Mordechai had said. "That is, if your people wouldn't. We can't afford to have a ship like that operating off our coast. Our air bases and cities would be naked."

"No matter what the consequences?"

"I don't know what Jerusalem thinks. But I think, no matter what."

We're looking into the throat of the volcano, Cole thought, watching the eyes of the consoles. And no one dares stop, because if they do, they make themselves vulnerable.

He began to sit up, his back cramped. Webster's console bonged. Webster shot out of his slouch and hit the transceive button. "Baseplate. Over."

Even through the scrambling, Cole thought he sensed the apprehension in Richland's voice. "Baseplate, this is High Tower. We have an intruder

419

report for your position. A large number of aircraft are flying in your direction, from the northeast. We estimate a Soviet airborne division. Over."

"High Tower," Webster said, his voice very cool. "How much time have we got? Over?"

"Baseplate, they will be crossing your coastline within ten minutes. The President wants you to move on the camp weapon immediately. Over."

"Jesus," Webster said, forgetting signals discipline.

"Baseplate, repeat? Over."

Webster looked at Cole. The others were listening, faces shadowed in the subdued light.

"High Tower, sorry, we copy. Will proceed. Over."

"Baseplate. If we get jammed, go to hop transmission. It's getting hot over your way. Over. Anything else?" Even Richland was dropping his signals discipline.

"High Tower," Webster said. "We'll be okay. Baseplate out."

He turned to the others, away from the microphone. "You heard the man," he said. "Let's tell General Tobur and get going."

The night sky was still quiet, deep indigo around the moon. Cole bent low in the crouch, gliding from tent to tent along the lanes of the camp. Through the thin canvas walls he could hear hushed conversation, occasional weeping, the small voices of children. Oddly, very few of the children were crying or complaining, although they must have been very hungry and thirsty by this time. Foerster had refused to let any provision trucks into the camp since the takeover.

He saw Dalia, momentarily, as a flitting shadow between two tents on his right. Avi would be on her far side somewhere. They were wearing black slacks and sweaters in addition to the greasepaint. Around Cole's waist was buckled an ammunition belt with pouches containing spare clips for his G3 assault rifle and two concussion grenades.

He couldn't see Webster or Mordechai; they were off somewhere to the northeast and the northwest, heading for their sniping positions. Kovalev and his man had also disappeared. They'd be halfway to the generator hut by now.

Ahead of him, through a narrow gap between two tents, he could see the front wall of the administration hut. The windows were dark, as they had expected. He checked the ground in front of him for obstructions. Dalia would be on the far side of the tent on his right, Avi beyond her. He couldn't see the two guards, but that didn't matter; as soon as the lights went out he and Dalia would start running, on the assumption that Mordechai and Webster would simultaneously shoot down the *Jund Allah* men.

He took the two concussion grenades out of the pouch and held them in his left hand. The waiting began. They must have penetrated the camp more quickly than expected. The tents here were empty, cleared of refugees on the first day of the terrorist attack.

If they'd been thinking better, Cole mused, they would have ordered the tents taken down for a hundred meters around, to give them a better field of observation. Foerster's been very clever so far, working on a shoestring, but maybe he's slipped.

The thought gave him a small amount of comfort, but then he heard the sound. It was out of the north-

421

east, like the grumble of distant thunder. But it was moving too swiftly for any storm. Cole recognized it: the drum of hundreds of heavy aircraft engines.

Foerster heard it as well. Like Cole, he thought at first that it was an approaching storm, but then realized that the sound was not broken, but continuous. He remembered it from Russia: aircraft, in a big formation. He got up and started for the window, to look out.

The telephone rang.

Cole heard the bell, very faintly, over the rumble of the approaching planes.

A second ring, while the engine noise grew.

A glow burned in the sky behind him. Peiper's flare. Seconds now. Five, six—

The lights went out.

Go.

He leapt to his feet, racing for the hut. Out of the corner of his eye he glimpsed the terrorist at its right end crumpling, thrown against the hut's foundations. Dalia and Avi were running shadows on his right.

They were there. Dalia already had the G3 up, the muzzle flash sudden and startling, the window glass suddenly dissolved, the grenades armed, through the window with them.

Crack. Light flared inside the hut. Avi's G3 was clattering, the door flying open in front of him, Cole on his heels. There was a stink of explosive fumes in the hut, a shadow moving, two shadows. *Christ one of the guards is inside.* It was too late to swing the

G3; another muzzle flash, Avi thrown back against the wall.

There. Fire half the clip, the terrorist down, the interior lights suddenly coming on as Dalia hit the switch.

Where's Foerster?

He was standing at the desk, stunned but coming out of it, recognition sudden in his eyes. The bomb. Cole raced around the end of the counter. It was there in its crate, Foerster reaching for it, coming under the muzzle of the G3. He was going to make it—

Cole brought his boot up and slammed it into the German's jaw, knocking the man sideways, away from the bomb, between two desks. Even then Foerster tried to scrabble toward the weapon, crab-like, until Cole kicked him again, this time in the stomach. Foerster shrieked and clutched at his belly.

"The other one?" Cole asked Dalia, his voice cracking.

"He's dead." The man was slumped on the floor, his face gone. "He wasn't supposed to be here. Avi's been hit."

"The bomb," Cole said. "We have to get him away from it." He had the G3 trained on Foerster but was still terrified the man might somehow manage to reach the weapon, invulnerable somehow to a sleet of bullets. He had come so far, so close, against such odds. Could they make him tell them, in time, exactly where the bomb in Israel was?

Foerster was uncurling. "Don't get up," Cole said. "Slide away from the bomb. Over there, in the clear space."

Mordechai and Webster entered the hut; Webster hustled Langstrom out. Mordechai bent over Avi. "I couldn't warn you," he said. "The other one

423

must have come in just moments before we got here."

"Has he got a weapon?" Cole said, gesturing at Foerster with the muzzle of the G3.

Dalia kept her gun at Foerster's throat while she ran one hand over him. He stared up at her with ferocious eyes. She found the Makarov in his pocket.

"Up, now," she said, standing, drawing back a meter. Someone else came into the hut. Cole glanced around for a split second. "Alexander, what in hell are you doing here?"

Markelov was carrying a submachine gun, the other terrorist's. "I had to be here at the end," he said quietly.

"My cane," Foerster said. "You've done something to my stomach. Give me my cane."

It was almost underfoot. Dalia kicked it to him, then moved away a little more, flanking Cole and a little in front of him. Foerster struggled to his knees, holding onto the black shaft, obviously in great pain. Finally he was on his feet, crouched almost double. His hand went over the cane's butt, the other still halfway down the shaft.

He moved, blindingly fast; Cole would not have believed it possible. The blade shot out in a bright flicker, its tip sweeping wide towards Dalia as Foerster came up, her left arm instinctively swinging out to protect herself, the G3 forgotten, the end of the blade biting into her stomach as she twisted sideways, falling into Cole and making him stagger, his aim blocked, the gun useless. Foerster dropped the cane in one last ferocious lunge toward the bomb, arms outstretched, fingers like talons clawing for the triggers—

Markelov fired. The bullet stream took Foerster in the neck and shoulder and smashed him against

424

the bomb crate, right arm over its edge and his fingers not ten centimeters from the nearest button. Markelov fired again and the arm slipped down onto the bloody shattered heap on the floor.

Dalia had already collapsed onto the floor, with Cole cradling her. The bleeding was very bad; the tip of the blade had slashed her deeply, up under the rib cage and into the lungs. Arterial blood pumped brightly. She didn't speak; she was rapidly going into shock.

Mordechai was suddenly above him, swearing in Hebrew. "Get the medical team here," Cole shouted, over the deafening thunder of the aircraft. "Quickly."

He could hear Mordechai yelling on the telephone, but not the words. He pulled off his sweater and got pressure on the wound, slowing the bleeding. Dalia's eyes turned to him, glazed, shocked. Her lips moved. He put his ear close to her mouth. "Sam," she said. "I was careless. I'm sorry."

He could barely hear her. "Help's coming," he said. "You'll be fine."

She did not hear him. She had already slipped into unconsciousness.

"Alexander," said Cole. "Is he dead?" Even now he was afraid that Foerster might, somehow, get up again.

"He'd dead," Markelov said. His voice was distant. "He nearly did it. I stopped him." He put the submachine gun on a desk.

"If it hadn't been for you—" Cole began. He couldn't finish.

"Yes," said Markelov. "I know. Samuel, I have to go now. I have to get back to my people. I know what those planes are carrying."

"Good luck, Alexander."

425

"Good luck, Samuel. *Shalom.*"

Cole heard him leave. He kept the sweater pressed hard against Dalia's wound. The drum of the aircraft was lessening, receding away to the east.

Mordechai crouched beside him. "The medical team's on the way."

"Avi?"

"He's dead." Mordechai's face convulsed for a moment. Then he said, "How is she?"

"I think he hit her in the lung."

The telephone jangled. Mordechai kept the sweater pressed against Dalia, as Cole reached for it. "Cole. What?"

"Webster. The medics are coming. Sam, you've got to do something. The Russians have dropped paratroops, a lot of them, a kilometer east of us. Tobur's going to try to hold them off with his guard troops but they're going to have to fall back, he doesn't have enough men. We have to get that bomb out of the camp before the Russians get here. It's the evidence the Russian Jews are safe. I'm sending a truck in to move it."

"*Jesus,* Davis!" Cole realized that he was shouting into the receiver, and with an effort controlled himself. "The goddamn thing's still armed. I can see the firing circuit from here. Where in hell is that arms expert?"

"We can't wait for him. We've got to move that bomb, Sam."

"We can't move it with the firing circuit in place. You *know* that."

"Can you safety it?"

From the east, Cole heard a sudden spatter of small-arms fire. "You're kidding. This is a nuclear bomb."

426

Webster's voice was patient. "I know, Sam. But it's important. Really important."

"Let the Russians have it. They're not going to push the buttons."

"Sam, okay, I better tell you now. The camp wasn't the only target. The Russians have dropped troops on both sides of the straits, just north of the Bosphorus bridge. They're using the bomb in the camp as an excuse, to grab the upper part of the Bosphorus and let the *Admiral Gorshkov* start for the Mediterranean. You know what that could mean. But if we've got the bomb, they *haven't* any excuse. Do you understand me?"

A silence, broken by more gunfire. Cole looked at Dalia, and then at the bomb, with its two buttons. A great tide of fatigue washed through him.

"Okay," he said. "I'll try."

He put the receiver down on the desk, not hanging it up, and went to kneel beside the bomb in its crate.

There was a battery, a voltage meter, red and black wires. The bomb appeared to be no more than a silvery metal canister, featureless except for the two buttons set in plastic resin on its upper surface. The wires from the buttons led underneath the canister, out of sight.

If I can cut the electricity, Cole thought, it'll probably be safe for the moment. As long as I don't start the fuse timer running when I do it. He reached out for the knurled nut on the red battery terminal.

The hut door flew open with a bang. Cole jerked his hand back from the terminal. "What the *fuck*—"

It was the Turkish medical team. They stared at him, paralyzed by the expression on his face. Cole slumped back from the crate. "Sorry," he said, gesturing. "Go on."

427

He didn't dare look around, in case they found that she was dead. Somebody took Foerster away, and the *Jund Allah* man. Then there were mutters and clinks around Dalia while he stared unseeing at the bomb. After a minute or two they took Avi out on a stretcher, then Dalia. Mordechai came and knelt beside him, next to the bomb. His hands, like Cole's, were rusty with Dalia's blood. "We'll do it together," Mordechai said.

"You don't have to stay," Cole said. He felt dull, numb.

"I know. But I will." The Israeli grimaced. "I might as well be here as a hundred meters away."

"What do you think?" Cole asked, looking at the bomb.

"I'm not an expert, but it might be simple. Perhaps we should begin by disconnecting the battery."

Cole nodded. He reached out again to the battery's brass terminal posts, selecting the one with the black wire. The knurled screw was on tight. He stressed it slowly, feeling it at last beginning to turn.

"Hold the wire," he told Mordechai. "We don't want to short it."

The Israeli's fingers slipped under his, grasping the black lead. The gunfire was coming closer.

Cole loosened the nut further. "Okay," he said.

Mordechai pulled the wire delicately away from the terminal post, insulating its bare tip with his fingers.

"Now the red."

This nut was looser. Cole backed it off, Mordechai securing the red lead with his other hand. Now the Israeli held the end of each wire, the battery disconnected. Not safe enough yet.

"Hang on. I'm going to take the battery out."

It was secured to the side of the crate with a metal

428

strap and a turnbuckle. Cole backed the turnbuckle off, waiting. Nothing happened. The rough metal hurt his fingers. The battery slid free.

"Battery out. We need to insulate those leads."

Mordechai said, "The medics left some tape. It's by the desk."

Cole got up, stiff-kneed, and went to the desk. The rough wooden floor was stained with Dalia's blood, and some of Foerster's. He found a half-roll of adhesive tape and brought it back to the bomb. Together he and Mordechai taped the exposed wires and then retaped them to opposite sides of the bomb container. Mordechai stood up.

"We did it," he said.

"Yes," said Cole. "But it's still an atomic bomb." He went over to the desk and picked up the phone. "Davis?"

"I'm here, Sam."

"The firing circuit's out. I don't know how secure the fuse is."

"We'll have to risk it." A pause. "I heard it all, on the line. Thanks, Sam."

"Just get the son of a bitch out of here," Cole said.

"A truck's coming."

"Is Dalia all right?"

A pause. Then, "I'm sorry, Sam. She was in shock. Blood loss. They couldn't stabilize her."

"Oh, no," Cole said. "No. She can't be."

"I'm sorry, Sam."

He put the phone down, fumbling for the cradle. Mordechai was looking at him. "She didn't make it," said Cole. His lips felt numb.

Mordechai covered his face with his hands for a moment. Then he said, "We'd better go."

The floodlights outside the hut were back on. At

the edge of the pool of light, a silent crowd had gathered: the Jews of Kilincli. Saved, for now. Perhaps it was only a respite, and a brief one, before the second Holocaust. This one would be less selective than the last.

Cole and Mordechai went down the hut steps to wait for the truck. Cole could hear its rumble from the direction of the main gate. The gunfire to the east was much closer now; the Russians were on their way.

Istanbul
April 28

THEY LEFT THE CAMP by the coast road, the Milstar communications vehicle leading with Cole behind the wheel, followed by Tobur in a Turkish armored car. The bomb had been squeezed into the Milstar van, under one of the consoles. They were trying to cross the Bosphorus Bridge and get to Turkish First Army headquarters in central Istanbul before the Russian paratroops seized the bridge approaches.

The communications vehicle's lights bored into the night, illuminating the rough pavement ahead. What had become of its regular crew, Cole didn't know; there hadn't been time to locate them before the convoy fled the camp, only minutes before the first Russian paratroops arrived. Even as they were shutting down the generator trailer, Cole had glimpsed Turkish infantrymen falling back along the highway leading east. But they'd held the Russians off long enough to get the bomb out of the camp.

"You think we're clear for the moment?" Cole asked Webster. The CIA man was in the passenger seat, bracing himself against the sway of the big vehicle. Cole was driving as fast as he dared on the poor road, longing for the power and nimbleness of the Maserati.

"As long as they didn't stop west of the camp," Webster said. "We'd have run into them by now if they had. But we'd better turn inland. If we keep to the coast road we'll be blocked by the paratroops near the bridge."

"Okay. Where did they drop, do you think?"

"The closest good landing zone would be north of Emirgan, and they'll have to organize. If the Turks have got some troops they can throw in their way in a hurry, that'll slow them down some more. We may just have enough time to reach the bridge."

"I have to report in," Cole said. "They'll be going crazy back home. It means we'll have to stop. The dish won't track the satellite signal while we're moving. But we've got to let them know what's happening."

"Okay. We'd better chance it."

The vehicle slowed, grinding to a halt. The two men scrambled back into the radio compartment, and Webster fed the transmission frequency and Milstar coordinates into the console. Overhead, the motor aiming the satellite dish hummed. The console clock showed 2:45 A.M.

Someone knocked on the compartment door. General Tobur.

"Why have we stopped?"

"I need to contact Washington," Cole said.

"Be quick. We must get across the bridge."

"I'll be quick."

Tobur closed the door. "High Tower," Cole said into the microphone. "Baseplate. Over."

Richland answered instantly. "Baseplate, High Tower. Are we glad to hear from you. What is your situation? Over."

"High Tower. We have the bomb, and we're out of the camp. The Russians've overrun it by now. We're heading into Istanbul, toward Turkish headquarters. If we can get across the bridge. Over."

"Baseplate, we have additional information for you. One. Defense Intelligence estimates that the Russians are preparing a second paratroop lift. There's no point in their holding the upper straits if they don't have the lower as well. Estimate that the second lift could be over the Dardanelles by dawn. This time there would be air cover from air bases in the Crimea, and from *Admiral Gorshkov*. Item two. We've been monitoring radio traffic out of the Soviet consulate in Istanbul. It has doubled in the last hour, and it's all in codes we haven't seen before. There's somebody senior there, probably entered the country under diplomatic cover in the last few days. Over."

"High Tower. He's at the consulate? Over."

"Baseplate, yes. Wait one. Somebody here wants to talk to you."

A different voice. Even with the scrambling, Cole thought he recognized it. "Dr. Cole. Sam. This is Green Key. Can you hear me?"

Jesus, Cole thought. The president. "Yes. Over."

"Sam, I want you to do something for me. I know you speak fluent Russian, and I need that. I'll tell you why in a minute. The Soviet ambassador here won't respond to my calls, and their embassy staff started burning their papers an hour ago. I don't need to tell you what that means."

"I understand," said Cole. He thought: That's it. The Russians are going to go. "But, sir, the hotline—. Over."

"I can't reach Kulagin on the hotline. But we think the Soviet consulate there is likely in direct

433

touch with him. You're the only link we've got at the moment, Sam, and we may not have time to find a more official one. We haven't much time at all. I may not be here in a little while. Do you understand me?''

Cole thought: It's bad. He's thinking about going to the airborne command plane. Soon after that, the missiles. . . . "Yes. Over.''

"We must persuade the Russians to back off. But we have to give them a way to do it without looking like they're doing it. If that second paratroop lift hits, or the fleet enters the straits, they may not feel able to climb down. And the Israelis haven't found the bomb yet. It they don't and that carrier enters the Mediterranean . . . I'm putting a great load on you, Sam, but your superiors here think you can carry it. Will you help us all?''

The responsibility was crushing. "Yes. Over.''

"Okay, Sam. This is what I want you to do.''

The communications vehicle pulled up at the ramp leading to the Bosphorus Bridge. Ahead, the great light-speckled span, more than a thousand meters long and nearly seventy meters above the water, soared toward the European shore. There was little traffic on it. It was 3:10 in the morning.

Cole studied the long slope ahead. "Looks safe enough,'' he said to Webster. From not far away he heard a sudden spatter of automatic weapons fire. "Shit. Not for long, though.''

Tobur's armored car pulled up beside them. The general was leaning out of the hatch. "I've been in touch with HQ. The Russians are two hundred meters from the approaches at the far end, nearly that here. Our headquarters troops are holding them, but

434

the battalion from the Taksim Barracks isn't in position yet. I'll go ahead. Follow close."

Cole put up a hand in acknowledgement. He gunned the engine and the communications vehicle started up the great span of the bridge, following Tobur's armored car. We must be crazy, he thought, bringing a fused atomic bomb into one of the biggest cities on earth. Probably it's safe. I hope.

They reached the crest of the span and started down the other side. Cole watched the approach ramp draw nearer. Figures were running across the pavement, turning with weapons, kneeling, getting up and running again. One of them fell down and didn't get up.

"Oh, Christ," Webster said. "The Russians are just about here."

Ahead, Tobur's armored car speeded up. Cole jammed the communications vehicle's accelerator down and the big machine bucked and rumbled.

Nearly on the exit ramp. Something hit Cole's door with a clang. Spent bullet. He wondered what would happen if a bullet hit the bomb.

Almost down to ground level, swinging off the ramp, through a red light, the communications vehicle's engine roaring, the armored car almost in a skid in front of them. I should invite Tobur to come and drive at the Glen, Cole thought fleetingly. A white signal flare bloomed in the sky to the north, the Russians or the Turks signaling.

"We're through," Webster said. "Jesus. Where did you learn to drive?"

"Around. Four kilometers to the Russian consulate. We should be okay."

They roared through the streets. Cole was getting used to handling the big machine. Past the Maritime Museum, then a column of Turkish armored cars

435

and trucks full of soldiers going the other way. Not far to the consulate. Cole tried to banish his apprehension.

Seven hundred kilometers to the northeast, the Antonovs and Ilyushins had landed at the staging bases and were refueling. Columns of paratroops filed into the huge dim cargo bays. Some of the planes had already restarted their engines.

Tobur's armored car pulled up in front of the consulate, the communications vehicle almost nudging its rear. The consulate entryway, as with most diplomatic offices now, was fortified with a concrete blast wall. Turkish military police were guarding it. They looked angry and nervous, as though they would prefer to be attacking the place rather than protecting it.

Nearly half past three. Cole got stiffly out of the communications vehicle. Tobur was already on the ground, walking toward the guards. Cole offered silent thanks for the presence of a senior officer; he'd never have got past the guards otherwise. Tobur hadn't demurred when Cole asked him to provide an escort to the consulate; perhaps he also realized that the time for desperate and unconventional measures had come.

The guards let Cole through the blast wall on Tobur's orders; the Turk stayed outside. A large Russian guard was standing at the main doors to the consulate. "Your business?" he asked in execrable Turkish.

"I want to see your consul," Cole said in Russian.

"The consul is occupied."

"Tell him," Cole said, "that I am from the Kilincli camp. Tell him I have brought an atomic bomb with me."

The Russian's eyes widened. "What?"

"Tell him, or it will go hard with you."

The guard frowned and went inside. A couple of minutes later he returned, holding the door open. "Enter."

Cole accompanied the Russian into the building. There was no one in the lobby except for another large Russian behind the reception desk.

"Wait," the first Russian said. A minute passed. A door off the lobby opened and a small slender man came through it. He had silver hair combed straight back and delicate features, for a Russian. "I am Consul Dmitriev," he said in Russian. "What do you want?"

"I've come from the Kilincli refugee camp," Cole said in the same language. "I'm happy to tell you that your citizens are safe. I'm an American. My name is Samuel Cole. I need to talk to whoever is in military command here."

Dmitriev stepped back as though Cole had struck him. "This is a consulate," he answered. "There are no military personnel here."

"Consul," said Cole, "we know there are. Your signal traffic betrays it. Listen to me. I am bearing a proposal from the president of the United States, suggesting a way to get out of the danger we are all in. But I need to have contact with your commander here."

"I cannot do it."

Cole sighed. "Consul, there is no reason now for your troops to be on Turkish soil."

"They are here to rescue our citizens."

437

"Your citizens have been rescued, I told you. The terrorists are dead. The bomb is disarmed."

"Where is the bomb?"

"Outside, in a truck," Cole said nonchalantly. "I brought it to prove to you that your citizens are safe."

Dmitriev turned greenish-white. "Outside?"

"Yes. Would you like to invite the military commander here to verify it?"

"Wait," Dmitriev said. He disappeared through the door by which he had entered. The minutes began to pass.

On the hardstands of the northern Israeli air base of Mahanayim, the armorers were finishing their work. The big nuclear attack missiles had been clamped under the bellies of the F20s, and the escort fighters had been armed with Shafrir and Sidewinder air-to-air missiles. There had been no word yet as to whether the target was to be Syria, the combat ships of the Soviet Union, or Russia itself.

Dmitriev came back into the lobby, followed by a large scowling Russian in his fifties. He didn't have the bearing of a military man. He saw Cole and looked startled, then covered it quickly. "I am Pavel Osipov," he said. "Who are you?"

"I speak for the president of the United States," Cole said. "This is outside all protocol, but the president knows that time is short. My name is Samuel Cole."

"What's this about an atomic bomb?"

"It's the one from the Kilincli camp. It's outside

in a truck. I came to tell you that the need for you to rescue your Jewish citizens has disappeared.''

"Let me see it," said Osipov.

Cole and the Russian went outside. Osipov got into the back of the Milstar van. He looked down at the bomb. "It's a fake," he said.

"It's not a fake," said Cole, "and you know it. Look. You know how everything is escalating. But your excuse for action is gone. If you keep on, if the *Admiral Gorshkov* enters the straits, for example, or if your second paratroop wave lands at the Dardanelles, it will be overt war. Surely your General Staff and the Politburo understand that.''

Osipov stared at him. "How do you know about the second wave?''

Cole shrugged. "I told you I was legitimate."

"Come back inside," Osipov said.

Cole followed him back into the consulate. Instead of leaving him in the lobby, the Russian took him down a corridor and into a small office. Dmitriev was sitting behind the desk. There were no other chairs. Osipov closed the door.

"What?" Dmitriev asked. He looked frightened, but not of the bomb; of Osipov.

"They've recovered the bomb," Osipov said. He looked at Cole. "What do you want to talk about?''

Here we go, Cole thought. "First," he said, "you have no more excuse to keep your men on Turkish soil. Second, the president has instructed me to tell you that despite Ankara's declaration of neutrality, we will consider a further paratroop drop on the Dardanelles to be an act of war against a friendly nation. Third, it is very likely that if the bomb the terrorists placed in Israel goes off, they will attack Syria with nuclear weapons. They might also be tempted to strike at the *Admiral Gorshkov,* the ships of

439

your Fifth Flotilla, or even the Soviet Union. You know what that may lead to."

"Yes," said Osipov. "I will relay any solutions your people might have."

Who is this man? Cole thought. The consul's scared stiff of him. Not military, then.

KGB. Why?

"Order your commander here to negotiate a cease-fire with the Turks immediately, and then send ships or aircraft to withdraw his troops. We will announce that your rescue was successful, and turn the bomb over to you so that you can prove it. In the meantime, if the bomb does go off in Israel, we will try to restrain the Israelis from using nuclear weapons against your ships or your country."

"If you *can* restrain the Israelis."

"This is what the president wants you to tell Secretary Kulagin."

"I see."

"There is one thing."

"What?"

"Tell the general secretary that if he will accept this offer, withdraw his troops, and then negotiate regarding the treatment of Soviet Jews, we will not release certain information publicly. Tell him the words 'Winter Palace.' He will know what they mean."

Something flickered in Osipov's eyes and then was gone. "Wait," he said. "Dmitriev, come with me."

Ten minutes passed. Osipov returned, alone. "I have been in touch with Moscow," he said. "Your offer has been directed appropriately."

"That's all?" Cole said. He had not really expected anything else, but he felt a bitter disappointment. The Russians aren't going to back down, he thought. Kulagin will never let them.

440

"Yes," Osipov said. "That's all at this time. Contact your people and tell them this. Then we will wait. All of us."

It was two minutes to four in the morning.

Khodinka Central Command Post, Moscow
April 28

FROLOV, in the private annex to the main communications center, put the telephone down and stared at it. This was Osipov's second call; the first one, reporting that Cole and the Americans had recovered the Kilincli bomb and defused it, had come in an hour and a half ago. Now Osipov had told Frolov that there had been no further information from Cole, which meant that the Israelis were still searching for the other weapon. And they had less than forty minutes left.

It was a good thing he'd sent Osipov to Istanbul when he had; he was able to know before Kulagin what was happening in Turkey. But he'd expected the Israelis to have found the bomb by now. If they didn't, and it exploded. . . . Lesiovsky and the General Staff wouldn't pull back the Black Sea fleet until they knew the weapon wasn't going to go off. As soon as Kulagin was disposed of, he'd have to make some very urgent arrangements to verify that it hadn't, and make sure it didn't. He'd use the KGB section of the East German embassy in Tel Aviv, that was it. He picked the telephone up again and called Dzerzhinsky Square to get that under way.

The call took less than a minute. At the end of it, Frolov looked at the wall clock. Twenty-seven minutes past five. He could *not* be late, not for this meeting, even if Kulagin had found out about Frolov's plot and laid an even more devious one of his own. One of them was going to come out of the meeting in a bad way, that was for certain.

He hurried out of the annex and down the concrete tunnel into the Military Council conference bunker. On the wall screens lights flickered; one of the screens showed the Black Sea and the real-time location of the *Admiral Gorshkov* task force. It wasn't very far from the Turkish coast.

He sat down. The pistol bumped against his thigh. If Kulagin turned the tables somehow, he'd try to kill him before being overpowered himself. The general secretary was at the head of the table, looking up at the lights that traced the task force's course. He still looked feverish and was smoking, as usual.

They were all present except Defense Minister Lesiovsky. Frolov felt a chill of apprehension. If Lesiovsky didn't turn up at all, either he'd betrayed Frolov or had been arrested himself.

A few moments later, the door opened and Lesiovsky entered. He was in full uniform and wearing a sidearm. That would have been impossible anywhere but here. Even Kulagin had to bow to that; the military wasn't about to let go one of its badges of rank in its own central command post.

A bad mistake of his, to meet here, Frolov thought as the defense minister sat down. Beria's ghost must be pleased. The tables turned, after so many years.

443

"We shall begin," Kulagin said decisively, "with the military—"

He stopped. Frolov was holding up a palm. "What is it, Comrade KGB Chairman? We don't have any time to waste."

"That's right," Frolov said. "We don't. Comrades, I wish to submit that in the last six months, beginning with the Winter Palace scheme which has led to this madness of military intervention in Turkey, General Secretary Kulagin has proven himself incompetent, and worse than that, to be dangerously irresponsible. We now face thermonuclear war with the Americans, our forces in Europe are unprepared for invasion, and we may be hit by preemptive nuclear strikes from the Israelis within a couple of hours, all because Valentin Vasileyevich Kulagin insisted on this scheme, without regard for socialist legality or even common sense. I submit that this is a monstrous criminal action and that he should be removed from his post forthwith."

Kulagin was staring in disbelief at Frolov. Finally, the KGB chairman thought, I've put something other than self-satisfaction on that face of yours.

"Arrest him," Kulagin said, holding out an arm and pointing at Frolov. "This is treason. Lesiovsky. Arrest him."

No one spoke. Only the minister for armaments, who had not been part of the coup, sat with mouth open.

Lesiovsky stood up. Frolov slipped his hand into his pocket, feeling for the pistol. If Lesiovsky were really working for Kulagin—

The defense minister drew his pistol and pointed it at Kulagin. "You're under arrest," he said.

Kulagin snarled and leaped to his feet. There was a gun in his hand. Tyurin, the chief of staff, grabbed

444

at Kulagin's arm but didn't get a firm hold. Kulagin threw himself behind Tyurin as Lesiovsky fired and missed, the bullet ricocheting viciously off the concrete wall and slamming into the false ceiling. Tyurin wrenched around, trying to grab the General Secretary's gun hand, but too late. Kulagin shot him in the jaw and Tyurin fell backward over the conference table, his face bloody and ruined.

Frolov had his pistol out now, aiming, a clear shot now that Tyurin was down. He fired an instant before Lesiovsky did. Both bullets hit Kulagin, the first in the shoulder and the second in the pit of the stomach. Kulagin managed one more shot, hitting the terrified armaments minister in the throat, and then collapsed sideways into his chair. His eyes were open and he was still conscious. The room stank of explosives and fresh blood. Frolov's ears rang.

Lesiovsky was standing over Kulagin. "Well?" he said.

"Kill him," said Frolov. "Truschenko?"

"Yes. Kill him."

Kulagin's face contorted with pain. "You're all with Frolov?" he rasped. "How long do you think you'll last with him? You're slitting your own throats—"

Lesiovsky fired again. Kulagin jerked, once, then twice. His body slid onto the floor. A faint odor of excrement seeped into the room.

"Now what?" Lesiovsky said.

"The Israelis still haven't found the bomb," said Frolov. "They've only got twenty-three minutes. We have to protect ourselves."

Lesiovsky holstered the pistol. "The *Admiral Gorshkov*," he said. "She has to get her planes up. If that bomb goes off, the Americans or the Israelis will

445

strike at her without warning. We may have to preempt them.''

"Full alert of our missile and naval forces," Frolov said. *"Admiral Gorshkov* to prepare for attack. Declare it. *Now.''*

Far to the south, almost at the same time the *Admiral Gorshkov* began catapulting her Mig attack planes into the night sky, the first waves of Israeli combat aircraft howled away from their runways. They could not risk being caught on the ground anywhere near a nuclear burst; the radiation would destroy their electronics systems and render them blind and defenseless. If the bomb exploded in Israel, one squadron would retaliate against Syria, and the country would cease to exist. Assuming that the Russians would take revenge for their Arab ally, the General Staff in Jerusalem had assigned their remaining planes to strike at the ships of the Soviet Fifth *Eskadra* in the Mediterranean, against the *Admiral Gorshkov* herself, and against key targets in the Soviet Union.

The Israeli surge was noted by both American and Soviet reconnaissance aircraft. Backfire medium-range bombers armed with nuclear antiship missiles were scrambled from airfields in the Odessa Military District, and out in the Mediterranean the huge American carriers turned into the wind to launch their planes.

Haifa—Istanbul
April 28

ABOVE THE QUAYS the arc lights blazed in the night. The great floodlit bulk of the Dagon grain silo loomed in the northwest like an iceberg driven ashore by some monstrous storm. The harbor was empty of shipping, cleared for the search.

Likely, David Eliav thought, it has never been so deserted since we built it. If that thing explodes, there may never be a harbor here again. There may never be an Israel again.

Out on the water, the little Zodiac search boats were plying back and forth, the hum of their engines clearly audible. Normally the night air would have carried the traffic rumble of a great port city, but tonight, except for the searchers, Haifa was almost deserted. The search teams would stay until the end, however it came.

At least we got the civilians out, Eliav thought. He looked at his watch; twenty to six, and nearly dawn. Maybe his last one. Eliav was in charge of the Haifa harbor search. He was trying to keep up a facade of confidence for his men, but privately was beginning to lose hope. They'd been over every

447

square centimeter of the harbor floor, and well outside it until the water got too deep for even helium-equipped divers. The bomb might still be out there, of course, beyond the breakwater, but with the men and equipment available, there was no chance of locating it in twenty minutes.

Maybe it isn't here at all, Eliav thought. Please let it be a bluff. But we have to search, and search again, until we find it or it kills us all. Even if it isn't a bluff, God knows it's hurting us. Mobilization, all the dislocations of evacuation. . . . Maybe the Americans would foot the bill, if anyone survived to present it. After all it was one of their bombs, damn them for being so careless.

He was about to turn to go back inside the Customs House, where the search team headquarters had been set up, when someone hailed him from the doorway. ''David? You there?''

It was Arnon Haberman, his second-in-command. ''What?'' he called back.

''They may have found something.''

Not a bluff, then, Eliav thought. How much time do we have? It isn't over yet. We have found it, perhaps, but can the team the Americans sent disarm it in time? ''How sure?''

''Best contact yet. There's radioactivity, but it's very weak. They were within a meter of it before it registered.''

''What's it look like?''

''Visibility down there is half a meter, and the object is silted over, so we don't know. The divers are working by touch.''

Eliav looked out at the harbor. The launch tender was churning toward one of the yellow Zodiacs carrying the search teams. A second Zodiac raced for the same spot, the white foam of its wake luminous against the dark harbor water. He fumbled his binoculars out of their case and trained them on the tender. She was coming to a halt, white water boiling under her stern as the propellers reversed. She already had a line and a cargo sling over the side. Quick work, Eliav thought. I hope quick enough.

He heard footsteps behind him and lowered the binoculars. It was Dr. Shapiro, leader of the American weapons team. "What've they found?" Shapiro asked.

Eliav started thinking in English instead of Hebrew. "Don't know, yet. But they've put a line out."

He put the binoculars back to his eyes. He could see the pale scratch of the lifting cable stretching from the tender's cargo derrick down to sea level. It hung slackly. As he watched it, it tightened.

"They're bringing it up," he said.

"Christ," Shapiro said. "We haven't got much time now."

"I know."

The object, whatever it was, broke surface, dripping harbor silt and runnels of water. As far as Eliav could tell, it was about a meter long, a wooden crate.

The launch tender was swinging her bows toward the Customs House, gaining speed. "Here we go," Eliav said. "We've got fifteen minutes. Maybe. Is your team ready?"

"We're ready."

Eliav watched as the tender reached the quay. Sailors threw lines, snubbing the vessel in. Shapiro returned with the other three Americans and a pair of Israeli soldiers who were pulling a wheeled cradle. The weapons expert looked down at the tender's deck, where the crate was being pried open.

449

"That's a W33 storage container," Shapiro said, when the lid was off. "We've got it."

"Are you certain?"

"Yes."

The tender's winch clanked. The crate rose, the crane's boom swinging it over the quayside. It paused for a moment in midair and then settled gently into the cradle, guided by the Americans and the soldiers.

"Inside, quick," Shapiro said.

Eliav followed the others as they raced the cradle into the Customs House and the impoundment room. As soon as the Americans were absolutely sure, he would call Jerusalem, tell them that they'd found the thing, at least.

They got the cradle under the worklights, among the ranked instruments. Shapiro scrubbed drying mud and silt off the exposed canister, using his coatsleeve. "That's it," he said. "That's one of the serial numbers."

Haberman had come into the room. Technically, Eliav knew he should call Jerusalem himself, but he didn't want to leave at this point. If it was going to kill him, he might as well be close to it. "Arnon," he said. "Contact Jerusalem and tell them we've found it. I'm staying here to watch the disarming."

Haberman left, with an expression of faint relief. Lot of good it will do him, being on the other side of a wall, Eliav thought, if this thing goes off.

The Americans were dismantling the crate from around the weapon container. Eliav withdrew into a safe place in his mind, the one he had found when his tank platoon was surrounded one night by the Syrians, up in the Golan. He listened to the words without thinking about what they meant, and watched the far wall. It needed paint.

"We've got nine minutes. Alan, do we go right into the canister?" Shapiro's voice.

"I think we'd better. We have to believe they were in too much of a hurry to be sophisticated. Audio on."

Scratchings and clinks, metal on metal.

"I'm withdrawing the end cover."

Another American voice. "Have a look."

"They got through the container interlocks."

"This is an old one. Anybody could." Shapiro. "Any fuse sounds?"

"None."

"They've bypassed the mechanicals. Do we extract the shell?"

"In the dry runs, we got the baseplate off with the shell in the container. I'm for trying that."

"Okay. Put the field detector on it."

More scratchings.

"There's electronics in there," the voice named Alan said. "It's not ours."

"Shit. Anti-handling?"

"Can't tell. It's just a field. But from the signature, I'd say an electronic timer. It's pulsed."

"Seven minutes," Shapiro said. "We'll have to go for broke. Scramble the timer. If that doesn't work we'll take the baseplate out with the thing running. We'll have to."

"Suppose we scramble it, and it reverts to zero?"

"We have to chance it. If the timer isn't hardened, it should freeze. It won't tell the fusing links anything."

"Okay."

They sounded, Eliav thought, like a team of surgeons carrying out a delicate brain operation. However, with a brain operation, the patient might die,

451

but the doctors could leave the operating room afterward, leaving someone else to clean up the mess.

"Okay. Zap it."

A deep hum, then silence.

"Jesus, it's still running. The timer's hardened. If it is a timer."

A very brief silence. Then Shapiro's voice said, "I don't know what we're waiting for. If it had hit zero, we'd all be dead."

"Pull the baseplate?"

"Yes."

Eliav was trying to make images form in the peeling paint of the wall he was studying. For a second, he thought he saw his wife's face in it.

"Baseplate off."

"*There* it is," Shapiro's voice said. "No anti-handling stuff—*Christ! The display. The goddamned thing's running fast!*"

"Jesus," Alan said. "Clip it?"

"We've got to trace the electrical circuits. Give me the probes."

Another silence, then Alan's voice. "Nineteen seconds on the display."

"There it is. Fast, now. Wire cutters."

Snip.

"Twelve."

Snip.

"Now the battery."

"Got it."

"Timer stopped."

"Christ. That was too close. Detonator now."

"Removal tool coming up." There was great relief in the voice.

Noises, metal on metal.

"Detonator is out."

"Go throw it in the harbor, for fuck's sake."

"You must be kidding. We have to take everything back."

"Okay, I'm kidding. Just keep it away from the goddamned bomb."

Eliav turned to look at the Americans. "It won't go off?" he asked.

"No," Shapiro said. He was still holding the detonator, studying it seriously. "We were lucky."

"What happened? Almost happened?"

"They set the timer wrong. It was four minutes fast."

"Arabs," Eliav said. His knees were weak and he wanted to burst into wild laughter. "No sense of time. How much did we have left?"

"Seven seconds. For God's sake, call Jerusalem."

Cole stared dully at the communications console, barely seeing it. Outside the van, the light was increasing. The digital clock showed one minute past six. Still nothing from Israel or Washington. He wondered whether Parnell would go ahead and order a first strike if the bomb had gone off in Israel, or whether the Russians would, or whether both sides would wait to see what the Israelis would do. The Russians must know that whatever Washington promised, if the Israelis were determined to bomb Syria flat, there would be little the Americans could really do about it.

There'd been a little progress. General Tobur had said the Russian paratroops were withdrawing from Istanbul toward the north, and in the last communication from Washington Richland had said that the Black Sea fleet had slowed down a bit. Apparently the second wave of paratroops hadn't yet taken off from their bases in southern Russia. Parnell still

453

hadn't been able to talk to Kulagin, though, and the hot line was still dead.

It's gone off, he thought. We'd have heard by now if they'd found it. I suppose I could call Megan from here and tell her to try to get to a safe place. But where is safe?

"Family in the States?" he asked Webster. The other man hadn't spoken since the clock passed the hour.

"Parents," Webster said. "My wife's in Ankara. I hope she got out in time."

The radio squawked. "Baseplate. High Tower. Come in, please."

Cole grabbed up the microphone. "Baseplate. Go ahead."

"They've found it." Even with the scrambling, Cole could hear the relief in Richland's voice.

"Disarmed?"

"Yes. A few minutes ago. The Israelis are recalling their planes. The president wants you to tell the Russians to do the same, right now. And to get Kulagin on the hot line. He wants to settle the matter of Winter Palace."

"I'll tell them," Cole said. "Over."

"We'll keep the line open," Richland said. "Over."

A rap on the back door of the van. Cole got up, almost staggering with fatigue, and opened it. It was the Soviet consul.

"Come inside, please. There is news."

"You bet there is," Cole said, and followed.

Inside, they went up to the third floor. A steel door was set into a concrete wall: the entrance to the *rezidentura*, the control center of the KGB station. Dmitriev pressed a button set into the wall.

"Yes?" from a loudspeaker.

454

"The American is here."

Clicks from the door latches. "Send him in."

Cole was startled. To the KGB, an embassy or consulate *rezidentura* was holy ground; not even a Soviet ambassador was allowed in. Cole stepped through the door, which automatically closed and locked behind him. He was in a short green-painted hallway. Osipov was waiting.

"Follow me."

Cole could hear the clatter of teletypes and computer printers from the offices beyond the hall. Osipov turned right, along another hall with closed doors on each side; he opened one of the doors. Inside was a windowless room with a single overhead light, a table with a telephone on it, and two chairs. Osipov sat down in one of the chairs and motioned Cole to the other.

"What now?" Cole asked.

"Wait."

Cole regarded the Russian, who regarded him right back. The man seemed to be faintly amused at something.

The telephone rang. Osipov picked it up. "Osipov. Yes, he's here." He handed Cole the receiver. "The direct line to Moscow."

"Hello?" Cole said.

"I am told you speak Russian, Dr. Cole," the voice at the other end said.

"Yes."

"Good. Please tell your president that we are withdrawing our troops from Turkish soil as soon as possible, now that the Israelis have found the bomb you Americans so foolishly lost track of, and that we are also ordering our Black Sea fleet to return to port. Our planes are being recalled. We would be obliged if you also would lower your alert levels."

How did they find out so fast? Cole thought. Somebody in Israel, East German maybe, watching for the flash. When there wasn't one. . . .

"I'll tell him. Secretary Kulagin, why don't you use the Kremlin hot line? It would be better than going through an intermediary—"

"I am not near a hot-line terminal. And I am not Secretary Kulagin," the voice said.

Oh, no, Cole thought. Now what? "Can you speak for him?"

"No. I cannot, because Valentin Kulagin is no longer general secretary. The post is empty at the moment. I am speaking for the collective leadership which is trying to resolve the crisis that Kulagin inflicted on us all."

Cole found his voice. "May I ask who you are?"

A dry chuckle. "Yes. I am Viktor Frolov. You've heard of me, Dr. Cole, I think."

"Chairman of the KGB."

"Exactly. Tell your president that there is no need for this crisis to be aggravated further. The person who caused it is no longer in a position to harm anyone."

"Yes." Pause. "President Parnell wishes to speak to you regarding Winter Palace. Were you aware that we knew about it, in considerable detail?"

"Oh, yes. It was a violation of socialist legality for which the former Secretary Kulagin was largely responsible. We can no doubt work out an agreeable solution to the problem of the Russian Jews. Provided that your original offer, to keep certain items of knowledge to yourselves, is still in effect."

"I'll tell him. Chairman Frolov, why not tell him yourself?"

"Certain things are best done informally at the

456

moment. Please pass this on immediately. Goodbye."

The line went dead. Cole's forehead was prickly with sweat.

"You're satisfied?" Osipov asked.

"Yes." Cole hung up the telephone. "Kulagin . . . gone? How?"

Osipov shrugged. "I can only guess at *how*. I was not there. But I know part of *why*. It has to do with you, Dr. Cole."

"*You,*" Cole said. "You're why I got out of Russia. Why Markelov wasn't arrested. It was Frolov who wanted Winter Palace to reach the West. Without Kulagin knowing. Wasn't it?"

"Speculation, Dr. Cole. But you are right that you are here because you were helped in Odessa. Now go and tell your president what the chairman has said, before someone blows us all up."

Maryland
May 3

THE MASERATI was running sweetly. Cole shifted down for the turn into the lane; the scent of lilacs from the bushes at the lane entrance drifted in through the car's open window. Megan had been with him the last time they had been in bloom.

He wondered whether to try calling her again when he got back to the house, but there didn't seem much point in it. He'd been back for a day and a half, but she hadn't been at home, or at least she hadn't been answering her telephone or doorbell. And she'd hung up on him anyway, the second time he'd called her from Ankara. The gallery said she'd gone on vacation, but they didn't know where. Perhaps she'd gone back to Wales. It might not do any good even if he could talk to her. She might not have made the connection between his absence and the cataclysm that Foerster and Kulagin had almost inflicted upon the world.

The bag of groceries shifted in the passenger seat and he steaded them with one hand. So very ordinary, the groceries: milk and bread and eggs, purchased less than an hour after his private meeting

458

with the president in the Oval Office of the White House.

He winced, thinking of how angry he'd probably appeared when he went in. It was understandable; nobody had told him anything. The anger had been only partly mollified by the charm and grace of the president, and by his thanks for what Cole had done in Russia, Turkey and Syria.

It was not enough.

"Mr. President," Cole said, "I would like to know what we are going to do about the Soviet Jews. They're still in the camps, inside and outside Russia. They're still dying."

Parnell smiled. "We haven't forgotten, Dr. Cole. And what you've done has put us in a far better position to help them. Viktor Frolov appears to be well on his way to becoming general secretary, and he wants no trouble with us while he consolidates his power. We could cause him a great deal of trouble, Dr. Cole. He let you out of Russia, knowing that you were taking the news of Winter Palace to the West. No matter why he did it, it could be construed as treason. And he'll have enemies in the Central Committee and the Politburo, men who were followers of Kulagin. They'll know we found out about Winter Palace, but not how. If they discover that Viktor Frolov arranged it, they'll use the knowledge to bring him down. We've got him over a barrel, and he knows it."

Blackmail, Cole thought. Although Parnell would never use the word. For us to have that hold over a Russian leader. . . .

"Anyway," Parnell continued, "I spoke with him very early this morning. He has undertaken the following: all Jews in detention in the Soviet Union are to be released immediately and to have their homes

459

and jobs restored. If they still wish to emigrate, they will be allowed to do so, under civilized conditions, as soon as those who are already out are settled or repatriated, whichever they wish. The Russians have already begun to send equipment and supplies to relieve the sufferings of the Jews who have already been expelled, especially those in Turkey.''

"And those who *do* want to leave?" Cole asked. "Will anyone let them in?"

"Yes," said Parnell. "Emphatically, yes. It may be that the world came so close to its own Holocaust that explains these changes of heart, but no government I've consulted in the last few days will turn any Russian Jew away."

"Even," Cole said, "at the risk of KGB penetration? Those people won't go home, if Viktor Frolov can arrange it."

The smile passed from Parnell's face. "That was the other thing I discussed with him this morning. I told him that we knew what we knew, and that we would deal with the problem in two ways. First, every time we identify one of his agents, we give the fact a great deal of publicity, to demonstrate to the world that Moscow is still using the Jews to attack the West. Second, internal commissions will be set up in the refugee camps, run by Russian Jews, to identify the agents in their midst. Your friend Alexander Markelov is to be in charge of the commission at Kilincli. We can be sure that he, more than anyone, is not one of Frolov's creatures. I for one wouldn't care to be a KGB man or woman identified as such, in those conditions. Most of them will go home as quickly as they can manage it."

"What did Frolov say?"

"He would not, of course, admit to anything. But he did say that we should have no cause to raise the

460

issue publicly. Remember, he has his hands full at home. He can't afford any disasters in foreign affairs."

"I see," said Cole.

"We have a chance for a new beginning, I think," Parnell said.

The lane was swinging toward the house. He slowed a little and watched as the gray shingles and white siding came into view among the beeches and oaks. It was a healing place; he would need it for a while. He dropped the Maserati into second gear as the lane opened into the curving gravel drive. New beginnings, Parnell had said. Perhaps; except that Megan was gone. Perhaps she was already on her way back to Wales, perhaps for good.

"God damn," he said aloud.

There was a blue station wagon parked in front of the garage, which he didn't recognize. The last thing he wanted at the moment was company.

He stopped the Maserati in front of the house and got out. No sign of anyone. He skirted the end of the veranda past the side of the house to check the rear. The river was calm and blue-green, marred only by the absence of *Whiskeyjack*. That was something he was going to have to take up with Jackman. He stepped around the corner onto the terrace, and stopped.

She was sitting on the back steps, beside Griffin, wearing a green dress and a white sweater. Her hair was the color of a bronze swordblade in firelight.

His breath caught in his throat. "Megan?"

"Hello, Sam," she said. "I heard you were back."

461

PINNACLE'S FINEST IN SUSPENSE AND ESPIONAGE

OPIUM (17-077, $4.50)
by Tony Cohan
Opium! The most alluring and dangerous substance known to man. The ultimate addiction, ensnaring all in its lethal web. A nerve-shattering odyssey into the perilous heart of the international narcotics trade, racing from the beaches of Miami to the treacherous twisting alleyways of the Casbah, from the slums of Paris to the teeming Hong Kong streets to the war-torn jungles of Vietnam.

TRUK LAGOON (17-121, $3.95)
by Mitchell Sam Rossi
Two bizarre destinies inseparably linked over forty years unlease a savage storm of violence, treachery, and greed on a tropic island paradise. The most incredible covert operation in military history is about to be uncovered — a lethal mystery hidden for decades amid the wreckage of war far beneath the Truk Lagoon.

LAST JUDGMENT (17-114, $4.50)
by Richard Hugo
Seeking vengeance for the senseless murders of his brother, sister-in-law, and their three children, former S.A.S. agent James Ross plunges into the perilous world of fanatical terrorism to prevent a centuries-old vision of the Apocalypse from becoming reality, as the approaching New Year threatens to usher in mankind's dreaded Last Judgment.

THE JASMINE SLOOP (17-113, $3.95)
by Frank J. Kenmore
A man of rare and lethal talents, Colin Smallpiece has crammed ten lifetimes into his twenty-seven years. Now, drawn from his peaceful academic life into a perilous web of intrigue and assassination, the ex-intelligence operative has set off to locate a U.S. senator who has vanished mysteriously from the face of the Earth.

Available wherever paperbacks are sold, or order direct from the Publisher. Send cover price plus 50¢ per copy for mailing and handling to Pinnacle Books, Dept.17-278, 475 Park Avenue South, New York, N.Y. 10016. Residents of New York, New Jersey and Pennsylvania must include sales tax. DO NOT SEND CASH.